A Black Horse

Also by Michelle A. Sullivan

The ARC Series
A Pale Horse

A BLACK HORSE

VOLUME 2 IN THE ARC SERIES

MICHELLE A. SULLIVAN

WordCrafts Press

To my mother and father, the two people who always believed in me and encouraged me to work hard for what I want in life, and to my grandmother June who taught me that it's okay to be a little sassy now and again. All my love...

Chapter 1

When the Lamb opened the third seal, I heard the third living creature say, "Come!" I looked, and there before me was a black horse! Its rider was holding a pair of scales in his hand. Then I heard what sounded like a voice among the four living creatures, saying, "Two pounds of wheat for a day's wages, and six pounds of barley for a day's wages, and do not damage the oil and the wine!"

Revelations 6:5-6 NIV

Lev Avatov was an important man. He was a man to be reckoned with—the kind that you admired and feared in equal measure. In his opinion, he had made smart, strategic decisions. He had cultivated advantageous alliances and bedded the right women. He had used his gifts to rise from nothing, and he had built an empire in Russia—*his* empire—that was respected the world over; an entity that either moved or stopped cold at his whim. He had a son who was everything he made him to be. He had his work, his employees, his possessions and collections, and his money, which made him obscenely wealthy. Lev angrily twitched and flared his nostrils, the height of any show of perturbation for the stoic man.

And now… gone! All of it, he shouted in his head, *Gone! Gone, by way of betrayal and my son's lust for his treacherous, American whore. No, not my son,* he reminded himself. *Margueritte's son… she and that weakling Rene.* He fastidiously plucked a bit of lint from his cuff as he recalled the events that had recently brought him to near-ruin. *Assets? Frozen by the Russian government. My estate and furnishings? Confiscated to the "needs of the state." There is probably some government lackey mishandling my Mondrian and tapestries right now.* It made his stomach wretch thinking of all of the priceless artifacts he had acquired over the years disappearing into the bureaucratic ether. Everything had escaped him. His wife, whom he had painstakingly locked away from the world, had escaped with his son, with the help of the Preston girl; there would be no more experiments using Margueritte. He found it all to be very annoying and tedious.

A lesser man would crumble and wither. Luckily, I have options and friends in high places. The thought cheered him slightly, as did the thing that he thought next. *I will hurt them when the opportunity presents itself.* He was adept in the torturous arts, and he wielded the instruments of pain much as a sculptor used a chisel or a painter, a brush. *Then I will kill them all… for my trouble.*

Lev paced away from the dreary window in the long corridor which had been his vantage point for the past few minutes. He never saw anything outside of the window, lost in his own thoughts, but momentarily his attention once again focused on his surroundings. He marveled at the workmanship that went into the walls of the hall, and he stepped back into the room that his back had been facing just moments before. The room itself was more like a long hallway with doors than an actual room. The walls were made of obsidian, marble, chalcedony, and onyx, and constructed so as to be seamless. Lev was awed by the presentation—they seemed to all be hewn from one piece, as if he was standing in a hollowed-out, rectangular prism of black. At eleven-foot intervals, a dragon of the same material protruded from the darkness, itself only becoming visible by the jade inset eyes that glowed a faint green. That and the silver that glinted from the dragons' scales were the only things that reflected the scant light. Everything else was the deepest black.

Black is such a comforting color, he thought. *Hard and absolute. Sharp… so becoming and clean.* Lev wore mostly black, and there was very little in the world that he appreciated more than his Aved Androkovich suits, each measured and tailored every twenty-eight days, and each costing him exactly one hundred and eleven thousand dollars. Lev walked slowly down the expanse of midnight wall, watching the dragons appear and disappear, admiring the precise craftsmanship as he went. He stopped in front of a sculpture, mesmerized. The detail was incredible, and, looking at it, he was slightly furious. As a man who collected the best works of art, whether they were known to the world or not, or even available or not, he stood in front of a prize that should be his—should have *been* his long before today—and he lusted for the powerful, sinewy, perfectly—carved beast. He reached out a hand, annoyed to find that it was trembling slightly, to touch the massive head, when he was interrupted.

"Come." The man was wearing a severely sharp black Armani suit with a black shirt and a silver tie. He watched Lev with hooded eyes and no real expression on his face.

Lev was not easily frightened, but this man, with his cold, calculating stare made him feel as if there really were a dragon in the next room awaiting him. Lev had met this man before; he kept order as an enforcer for the organization. He didn't have a name. He only knew him by a number—*426.* He thought, bemused, *The Triads have at least 425 more just like this one… not a group to cross.*

Lev stowed away that mental note as 426 took him through the door and down another long dark hallway, this one broken up by scenes on what appeared to be prehistoric tapestries of dragons flying over mountains. Lev was awestruck. Over the years, he had cultivated a masterful appreciation for pieces like these, and as a connoisseur, these priceless subjects spoke to him, loudly. He was consumed with envy. To his right, a phoenix enveloped a crowned dragon and multi-headed serpent, all made out of ivory. He didn't have time to admire the intricacies of the works before he was led to an expansive set of double doors, easily as wide as four men standing side-by-side. They were being guarded on either side by a large silver *shi.* Most plebeians thought of them as Chinese foo dogs, but Lev had been in antiquities a long time and knew better. He admired the ancient pair of lions.

The stark black doors opened silently and Lev entered a massive room. Six sets of pillars ran the length of the room and each one held a dragon carved out of teak that wound around the pillar following the travels of the person seeking an audience. To Lev's eye, the pillar and dragon seemed to be one large carving, not separate, which stunned him.

Lev knew teak—in spite of its hardness, teak rips and crosscuts more easily than oak. You must always use carbide blades when working with teak, as the silica in the wood can dull tools quickly, and Lev was amazed that the piece could even exist. Lev took a deep breath and moved forward into the room. Like the others, this one was also largely unlit, the only color coming from a few ivory and silver pieces placed artistically around the room, and the red eyes of the dragons that wound from and around the pillars.

Lev was stopped before a large desk. An imposing, high-backed chair faced away from Lev, the height of it so tall as to block the view of its occupant. Lev waited. He wanted to scream at the man to turn around, but one look from 426 was all it took to keep him quiet.

Finally, the chair revolved to reveal him. Lev had never met the Dragon Master before, so he was not prepared for the sheer size of him. He almost took a reactionary step backward, but steeled himself and blanked his face. If Lev had thought that 426 was fearsome, the Dragon Master was ten times worse. The man was bald and blubbery from the neck up, the face pudgy and smooshed, with rolls all over, like a pug had gotten hold of a shar pei. He was robed and seated, voluminous folds of cyan silk exploding everywhere around him, vast as the ocean. Lev could just make out the fanged mouth of a dragon tattoo poised at the left side of the giant's throat. He assumed from the size and position that the ink was extensive and started at the man's feet.

Then the Dragon Master stood, and Lev was once again astounded by his size. He understood now why the rooms were so big. The man was at least nine feet tall and, while Lev couldn't see every inch of him, he could tell that he housed quite a bit of muscle as well as pudge.

Lev cleared his throat and was going to speak when he saw 426 take a step forward. It was enough that Lev stopped instantly. He loathed appearing weak in front of anyone, but he needed this man's help and was willing to wait. He was not long in waiting.

"Mr. Avatov," came the surprisingly soft voice. The mountain of a man sounded almost childlike. It was most disconcerting. "I have heard of the catastrophe that has befallen your organization." Lev acknowledged the words with a slight nod. "How can we help you?" At an almost imperceptible ascent from 426, Lev cleared his throat and spoke.

"I have made tangible progress for the Association that—"

"I have heard of your recent trials and also of your advances for the Association. I am also aware of the attention you have drawn, not only to yourself and Velik Bratva, but to groups like ours and the Association. Your hubris has made you careless, and you have made many enemies needlessly... you seem to collect those as adeptly as you collect antiquities." The Dragon Master cut him off softly. "That does not tell me what you want from us."

"There have been some ... unfortunate misunderstandings in recent months, but that is not why I have come to you. I was betrayed—"

"Ah, yes—most unfortunate. To lose a family member is hard, but to lose a son... and his loyalty, is harder still. I, too, have lost a son, but I am lucky that I have three others to carry on my lineage. Maxim was your only child?" the big man asked gently.

Any thought that Lev had entertained of keeping his business private had evaporated, and he knew that the giant had done his homework. *Good—I hate pretense.* "No, I have a daughter who is off at school. She is not in contact with me at the moment" Lev told him, "but she is not the reason I am here." Lev paused a moment and the big man gestured for him to continue. "I need a place to continue my work. Someplace secluded. I no longer have the option of traversing my country at will, and even if I could, it would take too long to find a suitable location to spin my operation back up. The time lost would be catastrophic to our progress. I would be willing to work in China temporarily. Underground. Do you have access to such a place?" Lev had also done his homework, and knew full well that the Triads did indeed have the location he desired. A large facility perched on and inside a dormant volcano, mostly used for storage and the occasional pharmaceutical-grade development and distribution. The mountain was situated on the northern end of the island of Hainan and the South China Sea, which made the approach by land almost impossible. *Boat in, boat out. Quiet, no disturbances, high ground, excellent vantage point, built in thermal power... ideal.*

The Dragon Master looked thoughtful for a moment and then said, "I may know of such a place, but I will need to know exactly what is being brought there. I will not have my other operations interrupted or…" he paused and sat, looking Lev in the eye, "jeopardized. ARC found you once—it stands to reason that they could easily find you again, and I should be most put out with you if that occurs. Once again, I will need your reassurance that what you will bring into my facility will appease my standards and abide by my wishes." The giant man placed a massive hand under his chin, pensive. "You are tipping the scale too much for me as a liability, so to ensure your cooperation and discretion, I will be sending someone to work with you. I believe that you have already been introduced." The big man turned and gestured to a darkened corner. From the shadows stepped Narcisse Olivier, his eyes radiating hatred in Lev's direction. "Mr. Olivier seems to think that he is owed some recompense—"

"Avatov! Your bastard shut down my entire operation on the river and cost me many good people."

Lev turned to assess the rapidly approaching Olivier, and he spoke to him with his trademark suaveness, belying the ire and disdain he felt. "I owe you nothing, vampire—and you didn't have any good people. You didn't have people at all." Olivier hissed and bared his teeth, lunging for the well-dressed Russian. The Dragon Master stood abruptly and fluidly. Lev squared up, ready to deal his own blow when he suddenly howled in pain, jolting back, while at the same time, his target let out a gurgling scream, grabbing at his chest.

"Please, stop gentlemen." The diminutive voice belied the power emanating from the raised hands high above them, obviously dispensing the punishment with which they were currently afflicted. The two men settled as the massive arms and hands of the giant came down. Lev took a deep breath and straightened his tie. "Better, are we? As I was saying, Mr. Olivier feels that you owe him for the damage he has suffered at the hands of your son, Mr. Avatov. He lost everything when his warehouse was destroyed, including some rare Qianlong urns that I had him procure for me at great expense. Your onus to him is an onus to me. You do not want to be in my debt any more than you already are." The Dragon Master walked back around his desk and sat himself in the throne-like chair. "Since my money and resources have been affected by your family dealings, I will now have part of the stake in your research... and, Mr Olivier will be watching you."

Lev was furious. He was not in a position to refuse this offer, but he did not have to like it. He looked from the giant to the vampire and back again.

"I assure you, Dragon Master, I have no intention of deceiving you or hurting either your people or property. I just want my research to continue to completion. I must get it to the Association. I spoke with the Chairman this morning and he assured me that the Triads would welcome this opportunity. When I made him aware of an exceedingly generous offer from the Yakuza, I was told by the Chairman that the Triads have honor in tradition. He said you had established a mountain facility in which you made and shipped product and that you would be willing to part with a piece of that facility to accommodate my small operation. You have always honored your pacts and would welcome a chance to help the Association. We have ever aided you. Such loyalty deserves reciprocation, yes?"

Lev was gambling and he knew it, but he needed the Triad giant to allow him access to the mountains they used to make their drugs. He watched the face of the large man. He had already demonstrated that he could destroy him utterly, combust his chest and erase him from existence. He also knew that enfolded inside 426's clothes were random pockets in which lay an arsenal of weapons. The big man didn't even bat an eye. Lev wanted that kind of control.

Maxim had had that ability. He could have been great, but then he met that reporter...

Lev had every intention of dealing with her later. He noticed that the towering man had been watching him and gave himself a mental slap.

"Mr. Avatov, I will be honest, I was going to deny your request but I, too, have spoken with the Association. They have taken great pains to relay to me the importance of your work. I will allow the use of our facility and you will be able to continue your research, but I have asked the Association to allow Mr. Olivier to..." he paused, searching for a palatable way to put their arrangement, "be of use to you and, in return, me. They have agreed, as they know that you are in short supply of help these days."

At the jab, Lev mentally winced. He lost Maxim, and Boris had been detained by U.S. officials trying to get back to Russia. He was currently being hosted by the United States Department of Homeland Security.

Another thing to thank Magdalene for when I catch up with her.

"Thank you for your consideration. Of course, Mr. Olivier will be welcome. Once we get set up again, I will be able to show you what it is we are trying to do. The Association is most excited about the prospects and want to get started as soon as possible."

Lev was anxious to continue his work. He would, of course, be relocating the underdwelling creatures from his catacombs. They would like the thought of a new cave system to explore. The Naga were loyal, and they were exceptionally smart. All they lacked was leadership, and he made sure that he fit that role. There were the occasional snakes that knew too much and were a little too smart, but they were dealt with swiftly and in view of all the others so that they would all see the consequences of getting above themselves.

"When can your team arrive, Mr. Avatov, so that we may arrange for your escort?" the Dragon Master asked him.

"They will come in two days' time. By night." Lev was beginning to feel like himself again. He smoothed his hair and plucked an imaginary piece of lint from his tie. He would soon be back in his element with a passel of scientists and researchers at his control. He would continue. He would finish the Solution and hand it over to the Association, punching his ticket and earning their permanent favor. As for the vampire, well, he would deal with that unpleasant complication when the opportunity presented itself. "I will, of course, send for my scientists today, if that is acceptable? The sooner we begin, the better, I think you would agree."

"Why not during the daylight hours? Why at night?" Olivier asked in his oily voice, referring to the Naga.

Lev noticed Olivier wince when he moved his right arm. He saw him flex his fingers and noticed the end of a jagged scar poking out from beneath the end of his coat. Olivier caught him watching and put his hand in his pocket.

"They are exceptionally susceptible to light, particularly when humans see them and scream. You see, the Naga are very timid but exceptionally bright creatures. They will be a great asset to the team, but we have to get them situated first. We will bring them only at night." He smiled at the surprise on not only Olivier's face, but that of the Dragon Master as well. The giant smiled. It was the first sign of emotion that he had shown since Lev entered the room.

"You surprise me yet again, Mr. Avatov. Alright, we will send for your human team immediately, and we will expect you in two days time with your… other associates. Plan to leave at midnight. That should give your friends enough darkness to hide in."

The Dragon Master rose gracefully for a man of his bulk and made his way down the long corridor. At every dragon sculpture, he stopped and caressed the heads of the dragons that nestled around the posts. Lev swore he saw one of the dragons lean into the caress like a housecat, but before he could be sure, it stilled. Lev started a bit when he noticed that Olivier had come silently up beside him.

"Not the boss... not in charge… not even free to be unsupervised. My, how the mighty have fallen." The vampire clucked his tongue to the roof of his mouth in mock pity. "My assertion is that you should not be allowed to oversee anything, and I will make certain that the Association knows my feelings." Lev whirled on the vampire, who had disappeared into the pitch black recesses of the rafters. The vampire continued to hurl spit and rage at the floor-bound man. "I lost my business and my whole family in one day!"

Lev calculated quickly, and decided that Olivier as an ally would be more advantageous to him than Olivier as a wall hanging.

"Vampire—come down. I would talk to you." Lev coaxed him from his perch and the two stood facing each other. "It is certain that we have both lost much—thriving businesses, families, and standing. I still have my connections, though, and it seems that you do as well. We do not need to be at each other's throats… so to speak," he added as he saw the vampire's teeth flash and the eyes redden. "That, and our cooperation will help us in the long run. Do you have thoughts on the matter?"

The vampire considered the figurative olive branch being proffered, and relented, smoothing his coat, and brushing his hair back. "There are a couple of scores I need to settle. One with that woman that helped your son and the other with ARC. They have been a thorn in my side for years. We must strike a blow at them as well… my cabal demands it."

Olivier had pressed close to Lev and was looking him in the eye. Lev could see that the more he talked, the redder his eyes seemed to turn, until it looked like he was looking into the fires of hell.

He really is a loathsome, wild animal, thought Lev.

He took a step back, offering "I will help you with your revenge as it was never my intention of hurting your business or your family. I, too, wish to cause a great amount of pain to the harlot who stole my son from me. I, too, wish for ARC to suffer and disappear. They have caused me embarrassment and inconvenience for too long. I need my Naga here to begin. Once that is finished, then we can plan. This association may not be as painful as we both originally thought, Narcisse." Lev made to clap Olivier on the back but, with other-worldly speed, Lev found Olivier on the other side of the room, leaving through the big double doors.

"I will find you after I've talked to my cabal" he called over his shoulder.

Lev shrugged at 426 and followed the course of the other two out the double doors and past the foo dogs, with 426 bringing up the rear.

Chapter 2

The hush was astounding and palpable as Uriel walked quietly ahead of Paul. The man could hear no sound, not from the angel's massive feet, not from the surrounding wildlife, not from the leaves rustling in what seemed a perpetual breeze. Paul had been in Eden for an indeterminate time, but, being human he was still adjusting. The sensory overload, even after days and days among it all, was still too much for the young man and, as a defense, his body, his human senses, shut most of it out. He could not hear or see or smell adequately unless he was in the presence of Uriel, his champion angel. The young man rubbed at his temples and blinked rapidly, calling to the angel with a wince.

"It's happening again. Can you—"

The angel turned back to face him and immediately the colors muted, the sound returned and he was able to hear the angel speak again.

"You've got to get over that, Paul. You're going to be here quite a bit, and I can't have you tuning me out." The large angel, dark-haired and quite a bit taller than the impressively tall Paul, laughed good-naturedly and slapped a gentle hand on his friend's shoulder. "Okay, where were we?"

Over the last couple of days, Uriel had taught Paul much about the war between the nephilim and angels. He knew some of it already, like how many of the Watchers had chosen to disobey the Master's orders, consumed by lust, and had taken humans to mate with, creating the abominations known as Nephilim. The Nephilim, with the help of the Fallen, had decided to make a play for Earth's domination, and the Master had sent the flood to wipe them out. The Nephilim ceased to exist bodily, but their spirits lived on, necessitating the need for bodies that could withstand the corruption within them. How ARC had been created to oppose these Nephilim and the Fallen and to further the Master's plan, with angelic beings and humans joining forces. It was all familiar to Paul, but he was surprised when Uriel expounded on Paul's new guardianship and what it entailed. He was also apprised of the fate of the Avatovs since the events in New Orleans. Paul, in his former life, was the scion of that family and the heir apparent to his father's concerns. Now, he was getting used to the changes that had occurred, like the fact that his new name was Paul and that his monster of a father had gone to ground and no one knew where he was.

Max Avatov, the only son to Lev Avatov, famed Russian mafia boss, such as he was, was dead. As they walked, the thought came to him again in a wave as it had done many times since his death at the vampire's lair. *No more fights, no more compromises, no more death. No more doing what galls me or grieves me. No more loyalty to the family.* That was sobering, yet liberating. He no longer had to maintain loyalty to Lev, or Boris, or indeed anyone but Uriel and ARC. ARC was where his heart was now, anyway. Every friend he had, all of his remaining family except Ilyana, even his love, were there. *Maggie... would she know him? Would she still be with him if she knew the truth?*

Uriel looked sideways at Max/Paul, and noticed that he seemed to be in deep introspection. Uriel thought that Paul had always been quiet, and he knew that often in his other life his safety would have depended on him keeping his mouth shut. Although Uriel could have looked into Paul's mind and found out what it was that was troubling him, he knew that, given enough time and space, Paul would ask his questions and the truth would be known. He didn't have to wait much longer before Paul spoke up.

"Uriel, what exactly will I need to accomplish as your guardian? I mean, I have a rough idea from being with Peter and Michael, but I am afraid that I only see part of the big picture?" Paul asked him, looking off into the near distance at what he saw as the facade of the Palais Garnier.

For Uriel, Eden was what it always was—a garden paradise city with every conceivable plant and animal abounding. Every incredible terrain feature that the Master had ever created was here; rolling hills, azure seas and lakes, endless fields, meadows, orchards, and plains. It was quite breathtaking and the walls that skirted the perimeter belied the expanse of what lay within. After the fall of Adam and Eve, whenever a human entered Eden they only saw what they have seen in memories. For Abe, it was the forest around his home in Gardendale, where he was happiest in his youth. For June, a busy office filled with desks and people working. She was most efficient in an office environment and genuinely seemed to enjoy helping others. For Paul, he saw the theaters and opera houses that Margueritte had exposed him to in his youth, before he was taken and trained by Lev in barbarism and brutality.

Uriel smiled sadly, "I'm afraid that I cannot reveal all of it to you, Paul, only the part you will play in it. You're a guardian, but you're also a human and, as such, have free will. You must be allowed to form your own conclusions and opinions. Otherwise, we wouldn't be any different than the Fallen."

Paul nodded, but Uriel could tell that he was not at all happy with the answers. Uriel moved on to another question. While they walked and talked, Paul pulled an object from his pocket and considered it, glancing from it to Uriel. The angel had silently given it to him earlier that morning, and he had been curious ever since. He stopped and turned to the angel.

"What am I supposed to do with it?" Uriel took the object from Paul's open palm and looked at the etching on it. Uriel's sigil was prominent on the front of the smooth oval disc. The angel traced it, starting as a circle, it hooked at the top on the left side then curved and dropped to a V, then continued up the other side like an unfinished heart before dropping straight down like a number one with a cap on the end. He handed the sigil back to Paul. When Paul reached out to take the object from Uriel, a matching sigil was seen on the palm of Paul's hand, and Uriel reached out and gripped Paul's wrist. The massive angel looked deep into the younger, shorter man's eyes.

"I hope you realize the significance of this, Paul. I haven't had a guardian assigned to me in… many centuries." The angel dropped his hand and stepped away, shaking his head wistfully. "You know, I sort of have a reputation as a loner among the host," he said with a wink. "I don't take on charity cases or projects because my missions don't allow for on the job training… do you understand? No, how could you?" he answered himself, then reset, trying to convey his meaning. "When you grasped that sword, bearing the excruciating pain that it brought with it, just to protect your friends—I…" he stumbled over his words, searching and bewildered "I've honestly never seen your like, in all these millennia. What I mean is, thank you, Paul, for your selflessness. You are going to be a great partner."

Paul, for his part, stood shocked at the angel's gushing, and felt truly humbled. Uriel had chosen Max when he had seen him holding the angelic weapon, knowing the pain and determination that were involved for a mortal to wield one.

The angel cleared his throat and continued. "This", Uriel pointed to the disc, "is your badge of office. In times of need, it will become what you require. When you call my name while holding this, the ideal weapon will manifest."

Paul let the enormity of everything he had been through recently fall from his face to his legs, and he wobbled a bit. Uriel reached out to steady him.

New. Everything is new, nothing familiar. New life, new name, new mission. No mother. No Maggie. Max had wanted to keep his old name, but since he was not himself any longer, this was an impossibility. He had chosen the name Paul to symbolize his transformation. He felt a similar transformation, having himself once been blinded, but now awakened to leaving his life of crime and giving himself over to ARC's cause and Uriel's righteous service, alone. As much as he ached for it, his relationship with Maggie was, like the person he used to be, dead. Briefly, he allowed himself to stand, once again, in the Winter Garden, her hand in his, her head on his chest, feeling the chill in the Russian air, tempered with the warmth of pure love. He came back to himself and his present circumstance, only feeling an emptiness where a moment ago her head had rested. He would have to bear up under the emotional pain of losing her and focus on his mission. He shook his head briefly and vigorously to clear his mind.

"You said it would become what I need when I need it, right? Will it be *anything* I want?" Paul asked him.

Uriel smiled broadly. "You would have figured it out after a time, but yes, it will change into what you need it to be, but will usually manifest itself as the protection or weapon you are most comfortable with. Try it," the angel said with an eager-looking grin. Paul gripped the metal oval in his hand, and he looked over at Uriel, who nodded...

Uriel. It came out as a whisper, and as he said it, the sigil in his hand started to glow and the disc expanded. It opened up to a surprised Paul, but Uriel only smiled wider. Paul's hand was now holding on to a magnificent amber shield. It was perfectly round and covered Paul from neck to waist. He raised and lowered it a couple of times, testing the weight and seemed pleased. "Wow! It feels perfect!" He gave it a couple of swings, brandishing it and committing to memory the way it felt. He turned to Uriel. "Now what?"

"Keep going!" Uriel urged him to explore, and he obliged. This time, the disk was replaced by a set of finely hewn throwing knives with keen amber blades. Uriel stood off to the side, observing and smiling as his guardian continued to discover. He watched as Paul plucked one and flipped it expertly, catching it comfortably in his hand. He nodded before putting it back inside the case. Once again he called Uriel's name and the sigil started to glow and lengthen into a full length spear of polished amber with a wicked point at the tip.

Paul, after twirling the spear a few times, stopped and looked back at Uriel. "How do I… that is to say, um… put it away?" Paul asked him.

Uriel laughed and said, "Just put your hand in your pocket."

Paul looked skeptically at the spear in his hand and moved it and his hand like he was going to stick both in his pocket. Just as his hand made to enter his pocket the glowing spear shrunk until it was the smooth oval sigil once again. Paul laughed, and like a little boy with a new toy, took the sigil from his pocket, called on Uriel and once a weapon had manifested placed the sigil back in his pocket. Uriel watched the process replay a couple of times before clearing his throat. Paul looked at him and smiled. "Extraordinary."

Uriel slapped him on the shoulder and said, "We need to find Abe and get you acquainted with your new self. You must go back soon so that you can meet your new charge."

"Excuse me? My new what?" Paul looked confusedly at the angel, cocking an eyebrow. "Am I not your guardian? Why am I to be guarding anyone but you?"

Uriel took a moment to consider and assemble his words. "Of course you are my guardian, but there will be times that you are assigned to others, as your services are required for the mission. Most of the time, you will be with me, but for this first one, you are assigned to help Raguel. I am afraid he can be a bit single- minded in his purpose, and it usually ends up with him in trouble."

"What am I supposed to do for him, then?" Paul asked curiously.

"Give him another focus, one that will help our cause. He knows exactly who he is and what he must do, but he has seen so many injustices in the human world that he gets a little distracted."

"So you want me to help him by keeping him pointed in the right direction?" Paul asked him.

Uriel thought for a moment. "Partly. You also must keep him safe."

He started walking, and Paul fell into step beside him. Uriel knew he was seeing a long hallway with a twenty-foot ceiling and an open second floor. Curtained archways along the hallway would take one, in Paul's mind, to the opera boxes behind them. To Uriel, it was a lush garden with many animals and trees of different varieties, some of which had never been seen on Earth. Uriel was Eden's protector, and as such, whenever a human was brought here, he made sure they saw only places of their happiest memories. Paul looked sidelong and said, "I know and have seen enough, Uriel. Angels require little in the way of physical protection. They are quite formidable, even in a muted form."

He looked back at Paul and said, clarifying, "You will need to keep him out of trouble. He will need to get on with his assignment, but he's going to have difficulty. He needs a guardian to look after him when he gets distracted. Keep him focused and moving forward. We can be distracted from our purpose like humans. Raguel is more susceptible than most, because he is the angel of justice. He is dealing with some of the fallout from Lev's crimes, and it has him bothered."

Paul looked sad for a moment. "I feel for him. Lev Avatov is not an easy person to be around and seems to thrive on causing pain and treating people harshly."

Uriel stopped for a moment and laid a hand on Paul's shoulder. "I know that you suffered at Lev's hands, and so did your mother and father. Lev was not your real father." He raised a hand at the questions he knew were coming and said instead, "Lev Avatov is a monster. He takes what he wants, and when he is done using it, discards it like trash. He was not your father, and he is what we need Raguel to help with. Unfortunately, he has been distracted by the Association with one of their many immoral pursuits."

They had reached the end of Paul's hallway. In front of them was a door which opened into a large office. The walls were lined with bookshelves and maps of various colors and sizes. Paul looked around, and Uriel gave him a little shove through the open door. They walked along the Persian carpet, that was easily as large as the room itself, to a huge table in the middle. There, stooped over a map of China, stood Abe. Paul still wasn't used to the young man, strong and wiry, that stood in the place of the wizened and grisled vet he had known. Paul smiled and shook Abe's hand. "It is good to see you again, tovarisch," he said warmly.

"You too, Max," said Abe. "Sorry—*Paul*," Abe corrected himself quickly.

"Right, down to business," said Abe, "you're a guardian and get to go back. Uriel," he turned to the angel, "will Max—I mean Paul—be working with Peter and Sam and the rest?" Abe looked to Uriel and back at Paul.

"Yes, Abe, he will. After all, he will need a good pilot to take him on his quest," Uriel said. "How about we fill Paul in on where Avatov is currently and where he will find Raguel."

Abe smiled and rubbed his hands together in anticipation. "Okay," he said, "Avatov has gone into hiding. Things have really heated up for him on Earth." Abe chuckled a little and went on, "Maggie sure did a number on his businesses and holdings. Avatov doesn't have a pot to piss in at the moment. He's gone underground, and," he said with raised eyebrows directed at Uriel, "we have it on good authority that he's gone to another criminal for help. Lev is currently under the protection of the Triads. They have him set up in one of their mountain drug labs. The Triads brought in a ton of lab equipment recently. It's also reasonable to believe he has brought at least some of the Naga with him."

Paul remembered meeting and talking to the creatures below his home and how they had assisted with their escape. "I must admit, the Naga are a mystery to me. I could not understand what allows Lev to lord over them. They seem intelligent, powerful, and capable of existing apart from him."

"Agreed, and I may have something for you on that score. I have it on good authority that he has to give them something in return for their help. Only problem is, we don't know what it is they want, but it is supposedly something only Lev has or can get."

"Interesting. So, he went to the Dragon Master for help?" Paul asked. "It would have had to have been at the request of the Chairman. Lev would not have had the courage to go there otherwise." Abe stretched his youthful, sinewy arms over his head, clasped his hands invertedly, and cracked his knuckles, rocking his head from side to side like a boxer. Paul was happy to see the once-graying and aged soldier returned to his vigorous youth. Abe continued, "The Triads have their own traditions but even they are afraid of the Association. The Chairman is swift in his reprimands and can replace heads of organizations with the snap of a finger. I wonder what it is that Lev promised them in return for their help?"

"Yes, the Chairman is particularly nasty. As the most long-lived of the Nephilim, he is directly responsible for the experiments that are being performed by Lev. If he has chosen to continue those experiments, then it must be because he believes Lev is close to a breakthrough of some sort. If the Triads have been chosen to help, the Association would reward them with a boon. We need to find out what this could be." Uriel started to pace and the two men watched him while he thought. He turned back to them and said, "There is no more time, Abe. We must get Paul back to Earth to join Sam and Peter. Raguel's waiting… he just doesn't know it. There's a lot to be done… just fill Paul in on who he is now and where he needs to go. I must talk with Michael and Sam." Uriel clapped Paul on the shoulder, "You ready for a new adventure? Don't worry—I will be with you when you need me, although maybe not always in the way you will expect."

"I am. Thanks for trusting me with this mission—I will not let you down, Uriel."

"Of course you won't, my friend. The Master doesn't choose guardians poorly. June will come and collect you in a bit to take you for transport back to Earth. Good luck, my friend." The two shook hands and, in a blink, Uriel was gone.

Paul looked at Abe and the two men shrugged.

"Okay," Abe said, returning to the business at hand. "Here," he said, pulling a sheet of paper out from a folder, "are the basics about you as Paul. It is so weird to try and think of you as a different person. You are Paul Maxwell," he chuckled a little at the last name, "I tried to leave you with a little piece of yourself."

Max/Paul smiled at his friend. "Thanks," he said sincerely.

Abe nodded and continued, "You are an archaeologist." This announcement surprised Paul.

"Why an archaeologist?" Paul interrupted him.

"Well, we went over your background from school and took into consideration the work that you did for Avatov. This led us to believe that you would not only enjoy working with antiquities, but also be able to know the difference between a knock-off and the real deal. You can speak several languages and have knowledge of the black market," Abe told him. Paul nodded and Abe continued with his new background. "You will be a relative of the philanthropist Maxwells of New Mexico working for the *Maxwell Museum of Anthropology.*" Abe flipped quickly to another page and then back again, skimming notes. "Um… conservationists of human culture, blah, blah, blah… oh, here." He pointed to an entry. "They collect and maintain information on different civilizations and research human behavior, which will open doors for you to gather information on the Triads. And, you'll love this." Abe smirked, looking at his friend.

"What?" Paul was curious now.

"They will take the information you provide to them on the Russian and Chinese mafias and use it to create an exhibit in their institution on the organized crime families and their internal structures and traditions." Abe perused a couple of more entries, then looked up. "Welp, that's the gist. Is this something you can work with?"

Paul blinked. The knowledge of many years of schooling in antiques and anthropology, along with the many years of servitude to Lev Avatov came flooding through his mind and he knew that, with this knowledge and his new persona, he could help ARC and the angels. He could be a guardian and make a difference in the world. That's all he ever really wanted, anyway. He wanted a chance to make right all the wrongs that were forced on him by Lev Avatov and the Association. "It is, Abe," he said smiling at his friend. "I will be fine, I only hope that I can keep this secret. There are so many friends I have left behind and I am afraid that I will make a mistake." His fear was very real and caused his stomach to flip-flop.

Abe considered the man before him, comparing him mentally to the man he knew as Max Avatov. Gone was the dark hair and chiseled jaw. Gone was the girth, as well as the almond eyes of blue. Before him stood a thin, fit man with shoulder length hair in a topknot. The rounded chin was bearded and the eyes were brown and round. Slightly shorter, but definitely narrower... *no one would know it's you, buddy. Margueritte wouldn't even recognize you.* "Well, you sure don't look like you... I mean, you look like Paul, not Max. Physically," Abe said, "you're not giving anything away. Also, you won't be alone, friend. You will have Uriel and all the angels of heaven to help you. You only have to call... you know how it works." He chuckled again. "Friends in high places and all that. Oh, and Paul, there is something that Lev has on the back-burner, something that he has promised the Triads, I don't know what it is but... keep your ear to the ground. If we can get a bead on that, we may have an advantage in dealing with them all."

"Right." Paul looked around briefly at the intel on the walls and the stuff in Abe's hands. "Are we good, then?" He was anxious to get back to Earth.

"Yeah, man. We're good—be careful, my brother." Abe reached out and clasped the man's forearm, a gesture that Paul returned.

"Okay, Abe... where do I need to go?"

Chapter 3

Ask any New Orleanian, and they would quickly tell you that there is very little difference between spring and summer there. The swelter is pervasive, constant, and ever-present, but most would also say that one gets used to it.

Peter sat at his desk, window open to the street below, enjoying what little breeze there was to be found for an April day, and sipped an iced tea, working casually at his Wacom. He had Keane playing in the background. He sat forward a touch in his chair to allow the thin tee that he was wearing to become unstuck from his back. He loved the feel and durability of the leather, but he much preferred it in the fall and winter, not so much now.

He was putting the finishing touches on his newest creation, an avatar concept of an angel in black armor—armor that he hoped to parlay into a contract to outfit a three-film series shooting in November. The angel looked quite a bit like Sam in his Death guise, though not as tall or nearly as frightening. The figure had six wings that were larger than it, and they were stretched out in all their glory. This incarnation would be finished off with a black blade, matching the armor.

Ever since the revelation of ARC and being a full-fledged card carrying member, he had really been set free by Michael to explore his affinity for weaponry and armor. He had long ago mastered working with worbla and all manner of plastics, and with the advent of 3D printing, he had started to pioneer bringing his creations to life printing in Kevlar and carbon fiber shortly before their adventures started. Now he was becoming an unofficial armorer of sorts, and Michael had asked him to lend his expertise for the human side of outfitting their operatives. The prospect made him positively giddy. Michael had teased after their last adventure a series of meetings with Torniel, who was basically the resident angel blacksmith. The prospect of working with metals intrigued him, and he wondered at the notion. Michael had driven home to him that his usefulness and brilliance would be required, and he was just so happy to be of use to his new allies that he relished every inventive minute to contribute to their cause. He hadn't been able to find his purpose himself, but he was just as happy that someone had pointed it out and presented it to him.

He continued to think and create the figure, tweaking little things here and there, until his avatar had morphed into something a bit more fearful than what he had intended. *It's not far off, though, is it?* he asked himself. *You saw what Sam became in Russia. You're still a bit freaked out by it, if you're honest.* He shook his head and blasted himself with the other side of his internal dialogue. *But, it's SAM! Death is Sam, but Sam isn't always Death.* Weird, but true. Sam was his friend, and his ally. He need not fear him, and he had told him as much, hadn't he? Sam was Sam until he put on his uniform and went to work, just as if Sam were a policeman or a sewer worker.

But it's a foolish man who doesn't fear Death.

"If that's supposed to be me, homes, well, I just don't see it..." came the voice from beside his right ear.

"Gah!" Peter instinctively jumped up, knocking his desk chair and his glass over in the process. "You scared the hell out of me, Sam!" Peter cursed and bent down to scoop up the ice off the tile. He deposited the ice back in the glass and put it on the window sill, turning and running an exasperated hand through his hair. Righting his office chair, he sat back down. "Do you always sneak up on people or is it just me you delight in tormenting?"

"Of course, it's just you," Sam told him with a smile. He appeared much as he always did—boots, jeans, and aviators. His hair was the same shoulder-length black, he still appeared Hispanic, and the only deviation from "Standard Sam" was the colorful light green v-neck he sported. Peter gave him a quizzical eyebrow, and Sam muttered.

"It's spring. I dig pastels in spring. Oh, come on, Peter. You'd miss it if I didn't pop in on you unexpectedly."

"Yeah, speaking of… where have you been? Look, I'm glad you know you're an angel again and stuff, but do you have to do what Michael does? He's the king of apparating and scaring the piss out of me," Peter said.

"Did someone say my name?" came from Peter's left.

Peter jumped again at the addition of another voice, and another angelic being in his apartment, this one however was dressed in baggy cargo shorts, flip-flops, and a black, tattered tee with the words "got angel?" in white.

"You're definitely trying to kill me." Peter mumbled, righting the chair he knocked over with Michael's arrival. Peter noticed Michael's shirt and said wryly, "Cute… who does your marketing?"

Michael laughed good-naturedly and glanced toward the ceiling. "We have people for that stuff, you know? I don't know, brother, I just came up with it. Catchy, huh?" Michael flashed a toothy grin and added, "I think it could really take off."

"So, why *are* you two trying to kill me? Have you ever seen someone under thirty have a heart attack?"

"I have," Sam raised his hand.

Michael glanced at him sidewise, conveying with a look his feelings on the direction of the current conversation. Sam knew that Michael didn't like him to joke about death, and it bothered him when he treated it lightly.

"Well, I *have*," he said, this time with a little less brightness.

Michael moved closer to Sam and was about to wag a scolding finger at him, but Sam stayed his rebuke. "I know, I know—we shouldn't joke about it." Sam turned to Peter, "Sorry, Peter. We aren't trying to kill you… it's just how we get around. We take your health and survival very seriously and are the last guys that would hurt you. You are going to have to get used to the odd unexpected thing—and the odd unexpected angel—showing up unannounced."

"It's fine. So what have you two been up to lately? I haven't seen you in a while." His tone was a bit accusatory, and Michael noticed.

"Pete, we are friends… you know that. That doesn't preclude us from having the Master's business to deal with, whenever and wherever, and however long, it is.

"You know how we are only allowed to tell you certain things, on an *as-needed* basis? Turns out that we have an *as needed* situation," Sam said, making air quotes.

Michael rolled his eyes at Sam and turned back to Peter. "Sam will be flying to China soon," Michael told him, hitching his thumb in Sam's direction. Sam arched one eyebrow and let the slightest bit of his wings materialize just for fun. "On a *plane*," Michael added quickly, and the wing tips disappeared.

"Am I going?"

"That's the plan."

Peter stepped past the two of them to his desktop and started typing. "This… this is weird. Look." He directed the two angels to the display on his monitor, which was an email from an entity called Galaxy Xinxang, explaining to Peter that he had won an award. He took his finger and directed them to the last paragraph of the email:

Mr. Devereaux—please know that it will be our honor to host you in downtown Hong Kong prior to your reception banquet and awards ceremony on 2 May. Please reply graciously with how many of your employees or retinue will be in attendance. Again, please accept our most heartfelt congratulations on this prestigious occasion.

"It's in four days. I'm beginning to think that you guys know more than you tell me…"

"That's… um… serendipitous," Sam said, bewildered.

"We were hoping that you would want to go," Michael told him, stone-faced.

"We need a team this time, actually." Sam agreed with Michael with a nod of his head.

"We need to get Naomi on board as well. We'll leave that to you," Sam told him, grinning knowingly at his friend.

"Naomi, huh?" Peter was surprised, but he was not at all disappointed. He and Naomi had been spending a lot of time together since the passing of her uncle Abe, and he had never kept his feelings for her to himself, although he wasn't exactly sure where she was with their relationship. Peter had found that he had no problems talking to her, even as beautiful as she was. He also found that developing the words to tell her he was in love with her just… *just didn't happen. I can't be blamed, though*, he told himself. *I've never been in love. With anyone.* So, in the meantime, Peter was happy to help sort out all the legalities and emotional upheaval losing a loved one leaves you with. He had received the same type of support from Momma Rose after his own parents died, and he could do no less for the woman he cared for so deeply.

Naomi had recently become quite attached to Momma Rose and Margueritte, in fact, as the older women were helping the younger harness and control her abilities as a receiver.

"What will Naomi be doing?" Peter asked out of genuine concern.

"Relax. She'll help me fly the big plane with you and a couple of other people. It's a long flight, and Chinese officials have already received information from our other passenger, so there will be four coming in on our flight. She'll be safe," Sam told him.

"Other passenger?" asked Peter.

Michael perked up. "Yep. New guardian. He will be helping us with some of our dealings in China, as well as helping us to follow up on some leads concerning Lev Avatov," Michael told him. "Apparently, he's thrown in his lot with the Triads."

"Lev's in China, huh? Well, I can't say I'm surprised. There were a lot of different ways I thought he might go. Maggie and I have discussed it a little. She thought he might go to Japan and the Yakuza, I thought maybe he would go to England or France, just to lay low for a while, but I'll admit that the Triads would be a great option for him. You guys want some tea?" Peter licked his dry lips and considered the warm breeze entering his window. Not waiting for a reply from either angel, he turned and padded to his kitchen. He returned a few seconds later with another glass of iced tea. "You guys are lucky you don't feel this crappy heat, I'll tell you. Anyway, the Triads... super-steeped in tradition, not at all against using Lev's methods of accumulating wealth and supplies, and they are notorious for human trafficking. They deal in a lot of the same things that Lev did over in Russia. Good fit," Peter said, taking a gulp of the cold beverage.

Sam and Michael looked at each other and then back at Peter, "Gold star for the prized pupil. Someone's been learning," Sam said, clapping Peter on the shoulder.

"Well, I wasn't really doing much of anything, and after all the excitement of the last few months, I felt that I needed to be doing more. Maggie has been checking on things, too. Lev did a really good job of covering his tracks. She figures that he had money squirreled away somewhere it can't be traced for just such an emergency. He would have had to have gone to an outfit that could set him up with the latest equipment for a new lab. She also said that one of Max's friends from Russia said that the Naga have not been found and the tunnels have all been sealed off, so where did they go?" Peter looked at Michael for the answer, and when one wasn't forthcoming said, "I think he moved them."

"Well, that could be the case, Peter. Only one way to know for sure, though. We'll have to get to China and see what we can find out. In the meantime, why don't you call Naomi and get her ready?" There was really nothing Peter wanted more than to have an excuse to call Naomi today, so he eagerly agreed.

"Okay. I'll also call Tammy in the morning and let her know to make the arrangements for Hong Kong." He started to make a note on the pad by his computer, but stopped, remembering what Michael had said. "Who is the other passenger?"

"His name is Paul Maxwell. He is an archaeologist working for the Maxwell Museum of Anthropology. He will be doing a Chinese cultural study and will be looking into a loan of some Chinese artifacts to take back to New Mexico for display," Sam told him.

"You said he was a new guardian?" Peter asked, "What will he be guarding, exactly?"

"You know those *are* great questions, Peter. Need to know, my man... *need to know.*" Michael slapped Peter on the shoulder.

"Okay, well can you at least tell me how long we will be gone this time? I need to make sure that Momma and Margueritte are taken care of while I'm gone." Peter told them, feeling a little cross at being left out.

"It shouldn't be longer than a couple of weeks." Michael told him, looking to Sam for confirmation.

"Yeah, I would say two weeks should do it."

"Okay, so two weeks with Naomi, Sam, and this Paul guy. We'll be in China, being wined and dined by Xinxang Galaxy, sightseeing and attending museums, all while plotting to bring down not only the most dangerous and elusive modern crime boss, but also one of the most well-hidden, well-supplied, not to mention ancient evil organizations ever... all of this with eternal consequences. Did I get all that?"

"Yeah, that pretty much covers it, bro." Sam said.

"Sounds like fun. I'll give Naomi a buzz. She just might be ready to get away right about now. After Abe's death, she has had to get through a lot of paperwork. He left her everything he had, of course, but it's still a trying time." Peter thought for a moment and asked them, "What about Maggie? Can I tell her where you found Lev?" Peter asked them. "I know that she is not going with us, but that doesn't mean that she can't try and gather some intel for us."

"I think it might be better for now if we kept Maggie out of the loop. She is still in a tough place mentally and may do something that could get her hurt." Michael told him. "Please do not share this information with her yet. We are sending someone to help her out."

"You mean Dr. Jo, don't you? Jophiel," Peter corrected, and watched Michael who was grinning and shaking his head at Peter.

"Need to know, Pete. *Need to know.*"

Peter growled a little and said, "Fine, but you will let me know how she is, right? Or if there is anything I can do for her?" Peter asked him. Michael's face softened at the worry in Peter's voice.

"Yes, Peter, I will let you know when the time is right."

"Okay, when do we leave, then?" Peter asked, turning to Sam.

"Two days."

"Not much time, but I can work with that. Okay, you two, there is a lot to do and not much time to do it in. How about you guys get out of here, and I'll get to it?" Peter told them.

Michael laughed and punched Sam in the arm. "I think you're a bad influence on him. Alright Peter, meet Sam at the hangar Wednesday morning at 4." Michael told him.

Sam, who was rubbing his arm, smiled and said to Michael as they were leaving, "You still punch like a girl…" Peter smiled at their bantering after they had popped to wherever it was they go. He assumed it was heaven, but it could just as easily be Hoboken.

Heaven. He had never been, but these days he did think about it more than he did in his early life. He couldn't say for sure, but he sure hoped that he had gained a better understanding of his place in eternity, and he knew somehow that what he was doing and would do would make a difference to many people. *Michael would probably be eager to talk about it… I should ask him sometime. Forever. That's, well… forever. I can't really wrap my head around it.* Would he have someone to spend forever with? He thought about Naomi again and about how he felt when he thought of her… the meta made him dizzy and he had to sit. *If I could spend every day with someone like Naomi… No,* he corrected himself, *not someone* like *her… it had to* be *her.* He knew it in his heart just as he knew his own name. They were meant for each other, and he had to find a way to make that happen. *Or not. Maybe I'm wrong.* But he sure didn't feel like he was. *I have to talk to her, right now.* He smiled, a sort of dopey smile, but then sobered quickly, remembering. *Wait—I do* have to talk to her right now. He picked up the desk phone and, taking a deep breath, dialed Naomi's cell. She picked up after two rings, and Peter's heart ached at hearing her exhaustion.

"Hi."

"Hey—how are you?" Peter asked her. More than anything, the tone of her voice and her sigh just made him want to scoop her up and hold her until she could speak in that bright, happy way that he loved so much.

"I'm alright. I've just come from signing the last of the papers for the insurance company," Naomi told him. "I never knew there was so much red tape when you die."

He could tell that she was having a rough time and that she was relieved that it was finally over. He was too, truth be told. Abe had been her uncle and a surrogate father to her after her mom had died. He was her only family and she had inherited everything from him, including his aircraft and the business. She was a pilot herself and had accompanied Abe on many flights. She was also exceedingly intelligent and possessed her uncle's acumen—she would be able to take over Simms Cargo, no problem.

"I'm just glad he had everything so squared away for… you know. After." She sounded as if she may break down, and Peter tried to head it off by changing the subject abruptly.

"Are you ready for a break? Don't answer that—I know you must be, so I have a proposition for you." Realizing what he had just said, he got a little flustered and corrected quickly, "Well, not a *proposition*, proposition, obviously." Peter heard giggling on the other end of the phone, and his face turned a slightly darker shade of red, but it did his heart good to hear her laugh again.

"Yeah, I could use a break. What did you have in mind? I've had a spectacular time on our adventures so far… other than creepy, crazy Grandpa Vampire trying to kill me." He heard Naomi giggle again and smiled. Hearing her laugh was worth the humiliation.

"I have to fly to China—"

"China? Hon, I've got a business to run and—"

"I know, but hear me out." Peter could feel things going south, and he had to figure out how to rescue the situation. *Think!* He willed himself to continue. "It's not for that long, and Sam really needs you. He can't manage the trip alone." Peter and Naomi had been spending a lot of time together, and he had felt his feelings for her grow steadily. She had broken it off with her boyfriend before their adventures underneath Olivier's dockside lair, and they had been out as friends, but the tension was palpable, with both of them, whenever they saw each other. They were both dancing around the edges of getting more serious, and their conversations reflected that. He was desperate at this point to know whether she felt the same, but he would die before he would push the issue. He knew one thing, though. His first impression of her was right on the money.

"You and Sam, huh? Well, I don't know Peter—there is a lot to do around here—" she started to protest again but he cut her off.

"I know there is a lot to do, but Naomi, you have to take a little time for yourself. Step back and let yourself relax. You have been doing things non-stop since Abe passed. Give yourself a little time to breathe!" Peter sucked in a breath and continued, "I promise, it will be fun. Xinxang Galaxy in Hong Kong will be giving us the full five-star, and they really know how to treat you. We'll have to go to this awards reception, but we can check out some of the museums, caves, and temples when I'm not dealing with that."

"How long will this be for, Peter? Wait—you're getting an award? Hon, that's awesome. What for?" Naomi sounded genuinely proud, and he felt his tongue fall into his shoes—to have her be proud of him was almost too much for him to take.

"Ah, yeah. I am—it's for advancements in science fiction tech in movies and TV. Two weeks." Peter told her, still stunned that she was so enthusiastic about his achievement.

"Two weeks? That's a long time to be away…" Naomi hesitated and said, "I don't think I'll be able to go. That is such a long time, and there is so much to do around here."

Peter was desperate and a little annoyed, "Do you have any charters or runs scheduled?"

"No, not until May."

"Then, come on. Stop making excuses, Naomi, I know you cleared the flight schedule until next month, and now that the final papers are all signed and sealed, there wouldn't be anything to stop you. Sam needs you to help him fly, and I need you to come and relax, take a moment for yourself. And on a purely selfish note, I want to spend some time with you. Do this for... do this *with* me," Peter said in a much smaller voice. He had come a long way with women, but some of his old insecurities popped up now and again.

He heard Naomi shuffle the phone around for a moment then, "Fine." Peter's heart skipped a bit, knowing that he would have two whole weeks to spend with her. "You talked me into it with all of the caves and temples. When do we leave, and are you paying for this?" Naomi asked with a chuckle. "Girl's gotta eat!"

Peter smiled and let out the breath he had been holding. "All of it. I'm loaded, remember?"

"You know I don't want you for your money, right? Let me go—I have a crap ton of stuff to do before we go."

The fact that she had said it so nonchalantly and naturally almost made him cry. No woman had ever wanted him—for his money or otherwise—and he had never loved one the way he loved her. He came back to himself, deciding not to inquire or push for an explanation.

"Okay," said Peter. *Maybe I will push, just a little.* "Hey—wanna come over to Momma Rose's for dinner tonight?" Peter asked her on a lark.

"Stop! You just told me that I have two days to pack for a two week trip." Peter was a little sad that he wouldn't see her tonight, but he understood. Then she said, almost coyly, "But I wouldn't mind if you brought me a little something, and we could eat here? That way I can continue to prepare and not feel guilty. You down?"

There was still a lot for him to do as well, but he was overjoyed at the prospect of being able to see her that night and not having to wait until Wednesday.

"Momma's making gumbo… it and I will be around your place at 5:30."

"See ya then, then." He could hear the smile in her voice, and the earlier sadness washed away. He pressed the red icon on his screen, slapped his hands together, and bent his head to read the pad next to the computer.

One down, thought Peter as he crossed off the first thing on the list he had made as he was on the phone with Naomi. *Only twenty more… not much time.* The fact that he would see her in a couple of hours cheered him greatly, as did the words that kept ricocheting around his brain.

"I don't want you for your money, you know."

But, she did want him.

Chapter 4

Peter, in higher spirits, meandered slowly downstairs to Momma Rose's little cafe. The sun had traversed its way to the spot where it shone lower in the afternoon sky and, consequently, directly through the little rosette window that cast pretty-colored light directly onto the inside staircase from his apartment. He had his phone in one hand and was looking at the piece of paper that contained his to do list in the other. He wasn't really paying attention to where he was going since he had traveled this way hundreds of times. What ultimately garnered his attention was the laughter and talking coming through the little door that led into the cafe.

Peter hadn't heard much laughter coming from the cafe in the last month. After Max died, laughter was in rather short supply around La Cuisine Ouverte. It turned out that Max had been Momma Rose's nephew, and he had brought her sister Margueritte back to her. With the untimely death of Max in that warehouse/vampire's lair last month and Abe's death shortly after that, what joy was given by the reunion of the family was swiftly replaced with devastation, although it had allowed the sisters to mourn together rather than on opposite sides of the world.

Momma and Margueritte would be an absolute force together, if they weren't both so broken-hearted right now, he thought. *It's not Margueritte that's laughing with her, though… the voice sounds too young to be her. So, who is it?* he pondered as he took the last two stairs and turned to the doorway. Peter smiled as he heard the laughter once again fill the small kitchen. He pulled open the door and stopped in his tracks. There, sitting at the table with Momma Rose, was a strikingly beautiful woman. She had beautiful, long, red hair that fell in waves down her back. Peter smiled when he saw the teal blue tips. *Beautiful and edgy*, thought Peter. *Like my Naomi.*

Not yours yet, but maybe someday. Let things unfold as they will. The thought was not his, and it invaded his mind, albeit gently-spoken and with some reassurance. He looked up to the girl sitting with Momma Rose, and he knew that the thought came from her.

Another angel? he thought to himself. *Or a transmitter?*

"I can see that you trained him well." The younger woman turned to the older and winked. "Right twice, Peter," She said, extending her hand with a flourish as if she were a magician and just completed some incredible feat of prestidigitation. Momma Rose smiled and got up to give Peter a big hug and pull his stunned body into the room at large.

"*Mon chou*, I would like to introduce you to Ariel, one of the Seven." Peter recovered from his initial shock and swallowed hard.

"Hi," he squeaked and covered it quickly with a cough.

Momma Rose *tsked* in response to Peter's less than ideal introduction. She cocked a half-smile and quietly handed Peter a cup of coffee, pushing a plate of her beignets towards him. He silently picked up a pastry and took a bite, chewed for a moment and swallowed it down with a bit of the black coffee. He looked up at Ariel and said, "I apologize for my rudeness. It is very nice to meet you. I should be accustomed to meeting the host by now, but—oddly, it doesn't get easier the more you do it. Your brethren speak highly of you." Peter smiled and received silent approval from Momma Rose in the form of a pat on the hand.

Ariel beamed at him. "Me? You should hear how they talk you up, Peter. We all owe you a great deal for your help with Sam. It's an honor." She cordially extended a small hand, and he took it, awkwardly. She went on, pulling her hand back "I was just reminiscing with Momma Rose about the old days and how wild she was. When she moved here she settled down some. She raised you and Jeanne, but she has never lost her sass."

Peter heard Momma Rose *harumph* in the chair next to him, and he smiled. With sarcasm in his tone, he feigned surprise. "Momma Rose has sass?" As he turned he caught the end of the towel she had thrown at him and laughed uproariously.

Rose giggled along and said to Peter in her best Momma Rose voice, "Take care mon petit, or you will find that Momma Rose's kitchen will be closed to you."

Peter lost the smile right away.

Ariel said, "Rose, don't tease the boy so." She turned to Peter, saying, "I'm glad that you will be working with Samael again."

Momma Rose's eyes widened at this news and she turned to Peter. "What is this? What about working with Samael again?" She started to wring the towel that Peter had reluctantly given back to her. He placed his hand gently over hers to stop her fussing.

"I was just coming downstairs to tell you when I heard your laughter. I received a visit from Michael and Sam this morning, they kinda just popped in. They came to tell me of another person that needs our help." Momma Rose waved her hand at him in an attempt to get him to move along with his explanation. "Well, he wants me to meet up with a man named Paul and fly to China."

"China!" exclaimed Momma Rose. "What is in China?"

Ariel reached across the table this time and gently placed her hand on top of Rose's and Peter's joined hands. Peter could feel the peace flow through them and was truly thankful for his new friends. Ariel looked up at him and smiled. Each time she did that Peter found it hard to breathe. She was so beautiful. Ariel laughed out loud and tossed her long hair over her shoulder showing a little more of the teal blue underneath the red. Peter turned a nice shade of scarlet.

Now it was Momma Rose who gently scolded her friend, "Ariel, don't tease Peter like that. Pretty girls scare him. Peter, what do they want you to do in China?"

Ariel stopped Peter from telling too much by saying, "Rose, you know that if Michael had wanted you to know everything he would have told you. Suffice it to say, Peter will be helping with Paul's quest. He will not be alone, he will have Sam and—oh, yes; Naomi?"

Peter blushed again and heard momma Rose say, "*Ariel,*" in a warning, mama bear sort of way.

"I really wish that people would quit reading my mind." He softened his admonishment with a smile.

"Sorry Peter, but you blush spectacularly. We don't do that. The Master created humans to be able to do wondrous things, like using their imaginations to build cities, cure diseases, and go to the stars. They also blush, which is really cool in its own right. Angels were designed for a specific purpose, and some things, like blushing, are foreign to us," Ariel told him by way of an apology.

Peter had never really thought about it before, but now that he did, it seemed kind of sad that angels could not experience all aspects of a human existence. He knew that, according to the Bible, angels had varying jobs in heaven. Some announced the coming of special events, some were guardians, and some were soldiers—but he had not thought they were different from anyone else.

"No need to feel sad for us, Peter. I am hand-chosen for specific tasks, and I am grateful to be able to carry them out at the Master's pleasure. When angels try to separate themselves or be something that we are not, that is when we get into trouble. That is how our war began. We do enjoy watching humans, though, and it is special circumstances that allow us to interact with you now," she told him.

Momma Rose patted Peter on the hand once again to gain his attention, and then asked, "When will you be leaving, Peter?"

Peter looked over at her worried expression and laying his hand atop hers said, "In a couple of days. I'm not taking any inventory this time—just getting an award. I would appreciate it if you could throw my mail in the office and water the plants while I am gone."

"Of course, just drop the keys off to me before you leave," she told him. "And, Peter? Please be careful. I have a feeling that you will be going after Lev Avatov, and I don't like it," she hesitated briefly, "but I know you will be in great hands."

Peter heard the gasp before he saw her. *Oh no,* he thought, *not now.*

"You are going after Lev?" The question came from the little woman that Peter had only met a few months before. Margueritte did not look how Peter remembered her when she came to them. She had gone through a metamorphosis recently. Gone was the frail, pitiful woman that needed the support of her son and Maggie to get around. In her place stood a fit woman of fifty-three years, spartanly dressed in tennis shoes, jeans, a sweater, and a cap. From beneath the hat, a shock of gray hair poked out. She had her long hair pulled into a French braid in the back, changing the color to a silver ice to match her new countenance, and her eyes were set with a glint of hard steel. Peter recognized that look—it was the same one he had seen only months ago as Max had shouted at them to get out of the warehouse.

Right before it blew up. Blasted Olivier and his vampires! Peter was really missing his friend, and his death has caused ARC so many problems that he couldn't wait to have the opportunity to repay Narcisse Olivier for what he had done. Margueritte had thrown herself completely into getting better and healthier, but Peter wondered about her motives. She wore her determination like a Purple Heart, the wounds on display, front and center, no longer hidden from view. Peter knew that the loss of the son that she had only just found again, had broken something in her. She wanted vengeance against the man who had held her against her will for so long, who had stolen her son from her, her life from her, and had killed the only man she had ever truly loved. Peter felt fairly sure, looking at her now, that she could have it.

"I will go with you," she told him.

Peter shook his head, but didn't know how to answer her. He looked to Ariel and Momma Rose for help, pleading with his eyes for one of them to address the situation. Rose came to his rescue first, addressing her sister.

"Absolutely not, *petite fille*. I will not have you hurt or captured again. You know as well as I that revenge is not yours to take." Rose was adamant, but gentle with her little sister. Their relationship had prospered much since their reunion months before, and Rose knew better than anyone what sort of anguish Margueritte was still experiencing. *Anguish makes us foolish, mon petite. I hurt more for you than anyone else, but I won't play into that monster's hands—he cannot have you. He already cost us Maxim.* The words she would not speak bounced around in her mind. Margueritte took a deep breath intending to tell her big sister exactly why she *was* going when Ariel, who had been watching the interchange between them forestalled her tirade.

"No, Margueritte, listen to your sister. You will not be going with the others. There is a different path waiting for you, and you must come with me to ARC in order to be ready for it."

Margueritte looked for a moment like she was going to argue with the angel, but bowed her head and took a deep breath. She said nothing, and she looked beaten and dejected.

"Peter." The voice came from a place deep within the small woman, a shadowed and shattered place. "If it is at all possible, make sure he knows how I feel. Deliver my message with pain."

Peter swallowed hard and looked into her eyes. "I cannot promise anything Margueritte, but I will try my best."

Margueritte nodded as if in acceptance, turned and walked out the door saying as she went, "I will go get my things."

Peter looked from Ariel to Momma Rose. "Will she be alright?"

Ariel spoke as Momma Rose nodded. "She'll be fine. ARC is a safe place that will help her learn her talents and teach her how to use them to help us in our cause. I see Margueritte going on to do great things. I have a friend who would like her spunk." She smiled her brilliant smile and clapped Peter on the back. "Speaking of friends, ARC has agents in China right now. One of them is a man that I think could help you. His name is Jonah, he runs a small orphanage just outside of Zhiangjiajie. He is a very resourceful person and handy to know in a pinch."

Peter frowned, "Forgive my ignorance but what kind of help will a person who rescues orphans be? Won't he have other duties to keep him occupied?"

Ariel *tsked* and spoke with authority, "I keep trying to tell you that we cannot reveal things to you, but you just don't, or won't, listen. Humans and their free will—it gets them into so much trouble." Peter watched in wonder as the teal blue streaks in Ariel's hair turned from teal to a purple color and back again, repeating the process like a slow strobe. He wondered if it did that because she was irritated with him.

He quickly apologized. "I know that you and the others can only tell us certain things. I get it, and I'm grateful. You have to look at it from my point of view, Ariel. Without asking the question, how will I know if it is one of the things you can tell me or not?" Ariel's hair went back to the true teal blue hue as she looked at Peter. All of a sudden she let out a tremendous laugh and clapped her hands in front of her.

"Oh, Peter, now I know why Michael chose you. You are very bright and inquisitive, and of course, correct. You would not know what was allowed without asking the question. I will bear that in mind the next time I speak with you, but for now I must go. Please tell Margueritte that I will return for her shortly. There are many things to do, and I believe I will stop by the orphanage and let Jonah know he will have visitors soon."

Peter blinked, and Ariel was gone. He really wished he could perform that little trick. She could blink herself instantaneously to anywhere. She had said as much, stating that she would drop in on Jonah *in China* this afternoon before returning for Margueritte. Shaking his head to clear his thoughts, he looked over at Momma Rose as she twisted her cleaning towel in her hands. He very gently reached over and pulled it from her grasp.

She looked at him with unshed tears in her eyes. "I don't want you to go, Peter. My heart is sick over the thought of possibly losing you like we did Max."

Peter grabbed her hand in his and told her fiercely, "Momma, that's nonsense. You know that the host will be with me, and I am working for ARC. If Michael and Sam can't protect me, then who can?"

"That's just it, *mon chou*—the host was there in the warehouse and my nephew still—he still..."

"We have to trust the Master's plan, Momma. You know that better than anyone. Besides," Peter said, enveloping her in a hug, "you have given me the gift of beignets. Do you think I would forsake those?" He squeezed her again and whispered in her ear. "I'll be fine. *Je t'aime.*"

Peter grinned as Momma Rose shook her head, "I know that you will be alright in my heart Peter, but my head, she has a mind of her own." She gave a small laugh at her own silliness. "Just please try to be careful. You call and check in every night so I know you are alright. Oui!?"

"Every night?" Peter asked her with a grin.

"Well, maybe not every night. I know that you promised a certain young lady you would show her the sights." Momma Rose stood and gathered the teacups and dishes from the table. She held out her hand and Peter laid the towel he had removed from her clutches earlier, back into the small and work-toughened hand. His face had once again taken on a lovely pink hue. Momma Rose giggled, "She is right, you know?" At Peter's blank look she continued, "Your face does change spectacularly." Peter's pink cheeks changed to scarlet in a blink, and Momma Rose laughed again before taking her towel and the dirty dishes back into the kitchen.

When the door to the kitchen closed behind her, Peter felt his face return to normal. He smiled and thought of how long it had been since he had seen her laugh at all. If it meant a little teasing at his expense, he was more than willing to take the punishment. His thoughts turned to her visitor. The angels he had met were all so different. Just like his friends, they each possessed a different style, wit, appearance, and perspective on humans. He liked Ariel very much. *She is very much like Momma Rose and mom.*

Susan Devereaux had been a very beautiful and caring person, Peter remembered that she would save loose change only to walk down the street and distribute it to all the street performers. He smiled at the memory. His father would add his change to her change jar while she wasn't looking so it seemed the jar was always full. Those moments were some of Peter's best memories. He thought about how he was glad that he had his grandparents and Momma Rose after his mother and father had been killed. This thought led him back to what Ariel had told him about Jonah. He wondered what he would find when he met the man and how exactly he would be able to help. He continued to think on this as he climbed his stairs. He needed to make a phone call.

"*Xièxiè-wǒ hěn qídài.*" Peter hung up the phone with Xinxang Galaxy and rose from his desk chair.

5:00 almost on the nose. Time to go. Peter showered, dressed and galloped down the stairs to the kitchen door. He could hear Momma Rose working and singing softly to herself.

"Her name was Rosie, she was a showgirl… la la la la…"

Peter laughed to himself at the sound. Rose was a huge Manilow fan, and he thought it was adorable. He cleared his throat and spoke through the door, calling, "Can I get some of that gumbo to go, please? I'm taking it to a friends'—ow!" Peter was interrupted by the swinging door smacking his forehead, and Momma Rose bustling through the door with a medium-sized basket.

"*Pardon, mon chou*—please go take this to Naomi so she does not starve. Send her my love." She deposited the basket in his hands and swiftly pivoted back into her incredible-smelling kitchen.

"Thank you," he said, turning toward the front door. He took two or three steps and then called back over his shoulder, optimistically, "I may be late."

Rose popped her head out of the door. "You are a big boy, mon chou. You come and go, go and come. The light will be on." She smiled sweetly and said sincerely, "She is a lovely girl, and she has a gentle heart. I am very happy for you. Have a good time together."

Chapter 5

Zhiangjiajie's fabled forests provided the perfect background for Jonah as he labored, and he marveled at his fortune to be able to live in such a beautiful country. He was tending a small garden in the back of the orphanage that butted up against the protected area, just as he did every other day. Just as every other day he was treated to laughter and cries of joy from the children that played on the grounds a short distance away. Jonah and his mother had been running the facility for six years, and they had their hands very full just with the abandoned children in their immediate province. The orphans came to them constantly, as they were one of the few facilities that offered complete amnesty for parents needing to divest themselves.

He worked so diligently with his onions, that he didn't notice the truck approaching. Jonah turned to see the lumbering Tianye BQ123 had made its way up the small, winding, country road. He leaned on the handle of the hoe he had been using and wiped his forehead with a handkerchief he had taken from his back pocket. The truck pulled right up to the garden and stopped in a cloud of dust and rock. A very large fellow with jet black hair that hung low on his back emerged from the cab of the truck. Jonah could tell that something was eating at the big man, but he just wasn't sure what it was this time.

"What's up, Rags?" Jonah asked him.

The big man held up both hands and in an exasperated tone said, "They are at it again, Jonah."

Jonah tilted his head to the side a little and asked, "Who is up to what?"

"The farmers—they're back to dealing with the stall merchants again. I can't keep the people from the village from selling baby turtles, fish, and salamanders to them. You know those animals end up in keychains for tourists to buy, right? Most of them die before they ever make it out of the market. They have no air, Jonah."

Jonah wiped his hands and set down the tool, turning to look at the angel. "Calm down, friend."

"They suffocate and die in those little tiny plastic bubbles." Rags leaned up against the bumper of his truck and ran his hands through his long hair.

Jonah sighed and handed the man the hoe he had been leaning on. "Here—you need to work off some of your frustration before the kids see you. That patch right there is ready to come in. The potatoes are just right for harvesting. Make sure you leave the plant, though," Jonah instructed.

Rags looked from the hoe to Jonah and back again. "I do know potatoes. I was there when they were first planted." He heaved a great sigh and moved to the spot that Jonah had indicated.

Jonah smiled and said, "I don't like it any more than you that they do what they do. You know as well as I do that they can't feed their families under normal circumstances."

"I know that." Rags punctuated his frustration by stabbing the ground with the hoe. "It's unfortunate for the poor animals that suffer and die if left in those plastic bubbles."

The two worked silently for a minute or two. Jonah spoke after considering. As a native Chinaman, he loved his country and prayed for its prosperity. He also ached for freedom, as did many of his countrymen. The CCP had started out by promising everything, but delivering little. They eventually progressed to promising less and delivering nothing. Now, they didn't even bother to promise. It made him sad to think of what the Motherland could be. He had held Ephesians 6:5 close to his heart since his boyhood: *Slaves, obey your earthly masters with respect and fear, and with sincerity of heart, just as you would obey Christ.*

He understood it to mean that if one found themselves enslaved in a foreign land, that it was good to hope for the prosperity of that land, because if the land and master prospered, so would the servant.

It's a wretched man, indeed, he thought, *that finds himself a slave in his own country.* "I can sympathize. It's just as unfortunate for the families that need the money. They make so little on the things that they grow that they have to turn to selling these animals and more just to survive." Jonah shuddered at the thought of the *more* part of his statement. *It isn't only animals that they sell to survive, sometimes it's their children.* He turned his head to see a group of girls giggling together as they sewed new dresses for the ragdolls they had made. He smiled as one of them held up the little dress made from scraps that were left over after hemming and mending clothes for the other little ones. Jonah made sure that nothing was ever wasted around the orphanage. He turned back and found Rags watching him.

"It's odd to me, but you are a good man, Jonah. That is one of the reasons I like to be around here. You have such love for people, especially children. I only wish that we could save them all."

"I agree with you there, brother. None should perish." Raguel smiled at the reference to John and kept working, bringing out the potatoes from the little plot and depositing them in a basket. After a time, Raguel spoke again.

"There—that's done, then."

"Solid job for an angel, I must say." Jonah smiled and surveyed the basket, now full of the tubers, and wiped his own hands and brow, glistening from his own toil. "Not a moment too soon, either, my friend. I need you to go check the Pit."

The Pit was a local landfill that served the village to the west of their orphanage. It was accessible by only a service road, and the most traffic that it saw was as a baby dumping ground. The villagers as well as outlying farmers had originally used the Pit as a burial ground for unwanted or stillborn children—mostly girls—refusing to give them even an opportunity to survive. Jonah and his mother,

Rachel, had gone to the village to plead with the families there to not dump their newborns, but to instead bring them to the orphanage where they would be cared for and possibly adopted. Since their intervention, lots of folks had availed themselves of the orphanage's service, but many still chose the Pit out of shame or fear of being exposed to the CCP, so Jonah, Rachel, and Raguel checked it often, especially when they got wind of an imminent birth in the village.

"The women in the village say that there is a young mother that gave birth just yesterday. Mai said that she saw her near the pit with her husband. They did not have the baby with them, but they definitely appeared to be checking the area for observers." Jonah looked sick. "I just want to make sure that the baby is safe when they do—what they are going to do."

Rags chucked the hoe down, a fierce frown on his face and said, "Why didn't you say so earlier?"

"I know that they would not have dropped the baby with anyone watching, and they saw Mai. She made sure of it. Better to let them get done with it and then rescue the baby."

Rags jumped into the truck and threw it into reverse. "I'll be back shortly," he yelled as he peeled out of the yard leaving Jonah in a cloud of dust. Jonah held up his hand in farewell and then waved it around in a hopeless attempt at staving off the dust that surrounded him.

He picked up the discarded hoe and returned to attacking the weeds that seemed to pop up overnight. He hummed as he worked. He found that he enjoyed working in the garden. Turning the soil over, planting the seeds, and watching his garden prosper. Just like the children in his orphanage. He got them as seedlings, nurtured them as they grew, and watched them reach maturity, hopefully able to move on and have full lives. The orphanage gave them a place to live, meals, and a teacher to school them in what they needed to know to survive. Jonah had also made sure that, even if it didn't stay with them when they left him, they had at least heard of the Creator. He taught the children gratitude, humility, hope, perseverance, and love for each other and the world at large. *Instruct a child in the way they should go and when they are old they will not depart from it.* He believed that—he had to. Most of these kids would never hear it from anyone else, so it had to be him.

Jonah had just quietly celebrated his thirty-third year of life. He was an orphan himself and knew that in some countries orphans did not make it as long as he had. He was one of the fortunate few. His adoptive mother and father were missionaries who still worked in orphanages, teaching and nurturing the orphaned, or oftentimes, unwanted children. They were fighters; the staunchest advocates for children that he had ever seen. Jonah did not like to remember how he came to live with them, but he was eternally grateful that he was chosen.

Finished with his weeding, he grabbed the hoe and spade that he had been using and walked to the small bucket that he kept near the gate, full of water and a bit of soap, and set about cleaning the implements. Jonah had come from a wealthy family as a young boy, but had lost, literally, everything, so he never took what was provided to him for granted. He fervently washed the garden tools, dried them with a rag, and replaced them in their spots, standing alongside the east wall of the orphanage. He turned once again to survey his little garden as he remembered past events. He was only eleven when China had established martial law in 1997. After regaining Hong Kong from the British, there was unrest as the once free and capitalist city was reverting to communist control.

The CCP military presence was overwhelming, and he recognized even at his tender age, that there was much to fear in his city. His father had been vital to the British Foreign Secretary, Sir Malcolm Rifkind, as a transportation liaison that specialized in underground conveyances, specifically the MTR. Once the hand-over happened, he became *persona non grata* , and the family's future became uncertain. It was his father's contention that laying low and quietly finding a new line of work would be best, so he became a grocer, going to work with his cousin. He had only been involved at the store in Aberdeen a couple of days when he realized that laying low was not really going to make a difference.

Revolution was what people wanted, and the fighting was becoming more common, and more deadly. He remembered that his family had been walking briskly toward home on the Heung Yip Path. It was close to mid-afternoon, and they were returning from an event at his sister's school. Jonah remembered that his father had looked apprehensive about being on the streets and was urging them to go faster as the big tanks rolled down the street. He remembered the soldiers lining up behind the tanks spanning the breadth of the street, and around the corner came protesters, students out at mid-day armed with rocks, bottles, some with guns. Hundreds of them, all protesting the CCP.

Jonah's father had had a rough conversation with him just that morning. His father had warned him sternly about traveling anywhere alone, and informed him that there were no circumstances that would arise in his young life that would require him to be anywhere other than his house immediately following his school day from now on. It was too dangerous to play in the park, and, regardless of what he heard or what his friends did, that was the way it was going to be from now on.

He was lagging behind shuffling his feet and feeling sorry for himself when he heard his mother scream. He looked up to see soldiers advancing toward them with guns drawn. His father had just pushed his mother and sister behind him when the shot rang out from the line of soldiers. It was then that all hell broke loose. The group of student protesters started throwing bottles and stones at the soldiers, and Jonah watched as one of the protesters went down and a red stain spread over his crisp white shirt. He saw his father turn and start ushering his mother and sister back the way they had come, trying to escape the onslaught of violence.

As if in slow motion, he saw his father take a bullet to the back and, as his mother turned to go back to his father's side, he saw her get shot in the chest. Lastly, he remembered his sister standing and crying. Jonah lunged forward to try to get to his sister before she was shot as well. He grabbed her by the hand and pushed her behind him and up against the wall. He spoke to her and told her to crouch down into a little ball, to make herself a smaller target.

That's when he felt the sting in his side. The pain was more than his young body could handle. His last thought was to protect his sister, managing to fall on top of her and hide her from the soldiers. When he woke up he was in the hospital, and his sister was nowhere to be seen. He asked about her and was told that she had been killed. The bullet he had taken in the side had gone right through him and, as she was crouching, went through her neck.

Jonah had spent a few days in the hospital and was then released to a local orphanage. He remembered clearly the day he had his first visit from Ariel. She was the most beautiful person he had ever seen. She had come as a social worker to check on the kids in the orphanage, or at least that was the story that was told. She had actually come to see Jonah's adopted mother and father. He learned later that they were part of a group called ARC, and they protected the Earth from both the natural and unnatural forces.

His visit with Ariel was scary and exciting all at the same time. He was hurting over the deaths of his parents and sister and had chosen not to speak to anyone. Ariel had come upon him in the garden a few months after he had come to the orphanage. He had found a rabbit that had been hurt by one of the village dogs. He sat nursing the poor animal on the back stairs of the orphanage. None of the other children would play with him because he would not engage with them. They had tried the first couple of weeks but swiftly gave up when he wouldn't talk to anyone. Ariel had walked up to him as he sat calmly petting the rabbit as it labored for breath.

"How's he doing?" she had asked him. He looked up at her with tears rolling down his cheeks, but as usual didn't answer her. She reached down and stroked the rabbit from its head to its little fluffy tail. When she was done, the little rabbit, who had been fighting for its life only moments before, jumped off of Jonah's lap and, after one brief look back, scampered off into the nearest bushes.

Jonah had been amazed at the little miracle he had just witnessed. He looked up into eyes so blue that they could put the sky to shame and, for the first time since his family's murder, smiled. They had become fast friends after that. It was she who had renamed him Jonah since he refused to take his old name of Liang back. Ariel had told him that, when he asked her its significance, that he would not always want to help their cause but in the end he would.

It took him a long time to figure out what that meant, but after the Rossis adopted him and gave him a new home and job at the orphanage, he figured out what she meant with her cryptic words. She told him of ARC, and he knew his adoptive parents were a part of it, but he didn't understand much. They kept from him a lot of the unnatural aspects of ARC, choosing instead to protect him by leaving him behind to care for the orphans. He went through a period of rebellion in his teenage years and was not as helpful as he should have been. That was when he received another visit from Ariel. This one was not pleasant and to this day gave Jonah the shivers.

He was sent to America to college, and being attentive to his studies made him the top of his class. He graduated with a Bachelors in education and applied for an international teaching position. He spent a couple of years teaching in Thailand and, upon receiving word that his adoptive mother was ill, flew back to China to take over the orphanage from them. She recovered, and they stayed with him to help him care for the orphans. He had been here for the past six years. Ariel visited him a couple of times a month, and Rags came to help about a year ago at a request from Ariel. She had a soft spot for children and animals alike.

Jonah's orphanage was on the outskirts of a territory worked by one of the largest smuggling rings in China. She enlisted Raguel, or Rags, as Jonah liked to call him, into helping to end the smuggling and mistreatment of both animals and children in the area.

His thoughts were interrupted by the sound of tires on gravel—he knew that Rags was on his way back. He put down the hoe once again and went to meet the truck. He saw the black-haired angel get out of the truck holding a small bundle. His heart sank. He knew that the young couple had dumped the baby in the trash heap. He hoped she was okay.

"How is she?" he asked Rags.

"*He* will be fine." The angel smirked slightly at Jonah's expression.

"He?!" Jonah reached for the newborn baby that was making little mewling sounds. He uncovered the child and saw immediately why the baby was dumped—where the right hand should be, there was a deformed stump. The child had a birth defect and was unacceptable to his parents. He was silently grateful that the baby lived at all. Usually, the deformed babies ended up drowned in the river.

"Let's get him inside and fed," Jonah said.

He called out to Mai, one of the older girls who often checked the Pit along with the angel, Jonah, and Rachel. A bright, energetic young lady of fifteen, she was a great help and the oldest child in the orphanage.

"Oh my gosh! He's adorable!" She cooed over the baby as she rushed up to Jonah. "Should I take him inside to Mrs. Rachel?" She reached for the boy before Jonah had even answered.

"Please, and let her know that Rags is here."

"No need, Jonah—I'll head inside to talk to her. After you, Mai."

The angel gestured in a gentlemanly fashion for the girl to precede him into the orphanage's kitchen door. "Rachel—look at this." Raguel offered the baby to a plump woman seated at the kitchen table, who immediately took him in her arms.

"Give her here, Rags. Is she hurt?"

"It's a boy, Rachel." The angel saw the same expression cross the woman's face that had only minutes before crossed the face of her son—utter disbelief.

"No. Really, a boy? There hasn't been a boy left at the Pit that we know of for these many years." She loosened the dirty blanket from the newborn, and she could immediately see why. A tear escaped down her cheek, and she held the little boy tightly to her bosom. "You poor, poor thing. How could they?"

Rachel had been doing this long enough, so she knew very well how they could. Children in China were a commodity and, as such, had to be the right gender, had to be planned for and expected, and had to be whole. The ones that weren't… *Well, we give them what their parents cannot or will not, and that's all that matters. Thank the Maker that we even get the opportunity.* The thought was always sobering and humbling, and as Rachel Rossi was an exceedingly humble woman to begin with, thoughts such as these occurred to her often.

Jonah dug through the widely used box of baby clothes to find the child something suitable to wear. He selected a onesie from the box, along with a clean blanket and socks, and laid them on the table. Mai was busily making a bottle for the hungry baby as Rachel proceeded to shoo Rags and Jonah from the kitchen, all the while reassuring them that the baby, who was now eating hungrily, would be fine. The door to the kitchen shut firmly in their faces, the duo turned and grinned at each other.

Rags slapped Jonah on the back and said, "You have a great family, Jonah. I am glad I came here to help."

Jonah smiled. "Yeah, they are something. Not just mom and dad, but Mai and the rest of the kids—great. I only wish that I had more to offer." The young man looked concerned as he spoke.

Rags looked sideways at Jonah. "What do you mean? They have everything they need. You give them love, an education, a place to live, faith, food in their bellies—I think they have been blessed to be with you and not eaten by rats at the Pit."

Jonah winced at the picture that formed in his head. The angel had a tendency to be indelicate, but he was right. It was always a very real possibility that the little boy Rags had retrieved out of the garbage field would have ended up starving or worse. Jonah was always thankful for the children he could save. There was a darker side of humanity that he tried desperately to keep his kids away from. He knew that there existed a robust child trafficking market, and he knew, thanks to his association with ARC, that there was also far worse. He suspected that's why many of the orphanages in the cities were adopting out their children at an incredible rate. Jonah didn't want to think about it, but he knew the only reason anyone would want to abduct infants was for organ harvesting— or to be sold to the highest bidder. They would have to be raised before they could be of marketable age, and that would require many years of care, so he was thinking it would have to be organ harvesting. The thought made him sick to his stomach.

He looked over at Rags. "Do you know why anyone would want to abduct infants?"

"Just what has been going through your head in the last few minutes." The big angel sighed heavily, and Jonah could see that it weighed on his friend, too. "Yes, and so do you. You can't save them all, my friend. Make the difference, one child at a time."

"Why would the Maker give me this passion and calling if I couldn't do more?" The young man kicked at the ground angrily, thinking of the millions of children left to crueler fates than his kids every day.

"I don't know, Jonah. I've never been a human, and I don't know what it's like to have to deal with limitations. In this respect, I feel that my life on this Earth is easier than what you have to endure. We are made for a specific purpose; that purpose is all consuming and is all we can think about. I was tasked long ago with a monumental job, and it is the kind of thing that is not always pleasant or easy, but needs to be done. This is why we exist—to uphold those things that the Master has set into motion. I have watched humans over the years, and they use the free will granted to them to satisfy every urge and want. When given a choice between what is right and what is wanted to satisfy an urge, the want is usually what is chosen. This is the reason that there are so many unwanted and aborted children in the world. Humans give into want, and then, when faced with the consequences, choose the easiest option, whether that is to get rid of the unwanted child, or to have it and leave it in the care of someone else. Never do they think that they would be forced to make that decision, yet they engage in the very act that would cause such a situation without regard for the outcome. Sometimes that leads them to the seedier characters of life and what they offer in exchange for innocence."

Rags sighed again and slapped Jonah on the back. He started to walk toward the old farm truck but stopped about halfway there, "Nope, I would not want to be human; too difficult. I like my existence as it is, but my friend, I will help you as much as I am able. I will ask around and see what I can find out about your missing babies, although I am afraid you will not like the answers much."

Without another word or glance he got into his truck and in a cloud of dust drove off down the long drive.

Chapter 6

Jonah watched as Rags drove away from the orphanage. He was thinking about what he had said earlier and could not find fault with his words. There were parts of humanity that he did not entirely like but, on the whole, he wasn't sure that he would like being an angel, either. One job for all of eternity didn't sound very appealing.

"It is what you make of it." He spun around to find a grinning Ariel standing there watching him.

Clothed in holey jeans and a charmingly oversized t-shirt emblazoned with the slogan, "*If You Can't Clean Your Surroundings, Don't Make Them Dirty,*" with wild teal blue streaks in her shining red hair, grinning, she was the picture of every normal teenage girl. Jonah knew her as one of the Seven, specifically the Angel of Nature, patron of every living non-human thing in existence.

"You know, it's fortunate that I don't startle easily. And," Jonah looked at her glumly, "I suppose you're right. How *do* you feel having only one job for, well, forever?"

Ariel laughed and said, "You sound like Peter."

"Peter?" Jonah looked perplexed.

"Oh, yeah" she said, remembering why she had come. "You will have visitors soon, Peter, Paul, and—"

"If you say Mary it will make my year." Jonah's parents were pretty big into folk music when he was a teenager.

"No silly—Sam."

"Peter, Paul, and Sam? Who are they? Are you bringing me investors for the orphanage?" Jonah asked hopefully.

Ariel's smile slipped briefly but was put right back into place as she said, "They are friends of ARC. They will need a guide while they are here and I volunteered you for the job. Isn't that fun," she exclaimed and clapped her hands together.

Jonah was shaking his head vigorously as she completed her statement and said, "I don't have the time or the resources to go off into the wilderness with members of ARC right now. Rags just brought in another infant this morning, and I have to come up with a way to feed and clothe 230—make that 231—orphans. I need money and supplies to run this place, and all I seem to get is more kids." Jonah was on a roll. "Not to mention most of the children have a disability of some sort and require specialized help. Mom, dad, and I do the best we can and have organized some of the older children to help the younger ones, but what we *really* need is a doctor that would be willing to work for little to nothing except what we can scrape together and our undying gratitude." Jonah was filled with righteous indignation. He had a lot of people depending on him to steward them well, and now he was expected to take three tourists on some sightseeing tour of China?

Ariel sighed deeply, hair flashing murky purple to black and back, and exclaimed, "You know, you are very like your namesake. He, too, thought he knew better and had an excuse for why he couldn't do as he was asked. Let me ask you a question, my friend. How many times have you fallen short on the things you need? Doesn't it seem that you always have just enough when you need it?" She arched a delicate eyebrow at him waiting for his response.

Jonah thought about it for a moment. In all the years he had run the orphanage, he could not ever remember falling short. Not once. The money for the new roof on one of the dormitories came in the mail to him last fall. The children always had clothes and shoes when they grew out of the old. Books and supplies always found a way to their doorstep when they needed them. He even had a doctor that would visit. Now that he was really thinking about it, he always came when he was needed the most and always had exactly what was needed at the time. Jonah looked back at Ariel.

"See Jonah, you are not as bad off as you let yourself think you are. You have always been looked after. By me, by Raguel, by ARC, even by the Master. Those supplies are sent to you by them, but they are in need of you now. You are the man that will help them with this, because you know the surrounding areas, you are familiar with the language, and you know the people who can help them." She seemed very certain of his utility to these visitors.

"What exactly is their *task?*" Jonah asked, making air quotes when he said task. Ariel rolled her eyes, something she picked up from humans in her very long association with them.

"I can't tell you." Again, certainty—she wasn't budging.

"Why not? You expect help from me, but won't tell me how my help will affect their unnamed mission?"

"You know as well as I that we cannot tell you all the details. Humans are allowed free will and a choice in whatever they decide."

"So then, I am free to tell you that I do not want to participate?" Jonah asked her, smiling wryly.

Ariel looked thoughtful; her eyes flashed for a moment before she nodded and looked back at Jonah, pointing a finger in his chest. "I *am* allowed to tell you that if you decide not to help there will be a bunch of children that are hurt because of it."

Jonah frowned at her. "Wow—you fight dirty, Ariel."

"Hey, do you think we randomly choose humans for certain tasks, buddy? We choose the humans that we do because they show the most promise, the most compassion, and, along with a certain bloodline, they always choose the side of right. They may be a little slow to the punch," she winked at Jonah, "but they always choose a fair and moral path. I just thought you would like to know the stakes before making a decision."

Jonah frowned again, "It isn't much of a choice when children are involved. I don't suppose you can tell me how they are involved?"

Ariel frowned. "Nope, nope, nope. I cannot reveal anything further, but you will be allowed to take Raguel with you. You won't be alone, Jonah—who better to be at your side than the Angel of Justice? Not to mention the angel of Death?" she told him nonchalantly.

"The angel of *what*!?"

"Death," she told him succinctly. "Sam—Samael—is the angel of Death. You will meet him when you meet the others. Just don't make him mad." She giggled as she watched the color drain from his face. "Humans really are so much fun. Sam is just like the rest of us, Jonah. He has a job to do, and he is very serious about it. He and Raguel go way back so you will be in good hands. So, are you ready for a new adventure?"

Jonah looked around the orphanage complex. He watched the boys playing ball outside. They looked so happy, even though most of them had a disability. Most managed very well, and those that did helped those who couldn't manage. The girls played with their dolls or tended to toddlers as they played. Happiness was everywhere, and simple joys commanded the kids' lives. Jonah knew that his family played a part in that, and he was humbled. One of the children, a quiet girl named Rou, walked over to them carrying a piece of paper.

She handed the paper to Jonah and smiled. "I have been practicing my letters today, Mr. Jonah." She ran off and left him holding the note. He opened it up to see a few roughly drawn flowers and in the middle scrawled in a childish print was the words, *Thank you for teaching me*. The words of the child humbled him again, and the laughter and childish noise was music to his heart.

He sighed and looked back at Ariel. "I guess it won't take a whale for me—just a group of children. I don't know what good I will be to the angel of Death or the Angel of Justice, but let's find out. Sign me up."

Ariel beamed at him and said, "I knew you would make the right choice. I feel there are great things in store for you, Jonah. Like your namesake, you will go, and you will do great things," she proclaimed.

In that moment Jonah felt like he actually could be what she proclaimed. He was eager to get started but did not know when or how.

"When do we start?" He asked her, smiling.

"Be ready in three days' time." With that pronouncement she was gone, leaving Jonah alone.

He sighed again and laughed to himself. "Isn't that just like an angel? It's all, *you are important and will do great things,* and then they leave you hanging." He laughed again and, after re-reading the note Rou had given him, he carefully folded the letter and placed it in his back pocket. He picked up his discarded hoe and whistled an old hymn as he went back to work.

Chapter 7

Paul rounded the corner onto Governor Nicholls and stopped. He could see his aunt's restaurant down the block, and he suddenly felt sick. *Maggie. My Maggie. I am not okay with this.* When he had been with Uriel and Abe in Eden, discussing and planning, the reality of where he was going and who he would be working with wasn't registering. But now the truckload of sorrow and regret hit him right there in the New Orleans springtime. *God, I cannot do this. My mother… Maggie… my friends. I still miss them all so much. I miss them as Max, and I can never go back. Please, do not make me.* He stood planted on the spot, immobile and desperate. A slight shift in the wind and the scent of oiled teak greeted him from the alley to his right. He turned and saw the figure of Uriel beckoning, and he approached him.

"You okay, guardian?" Uriel grasped Paul's shoulder to steady him as he swayed, overwhelmed with what lay before him. "Paul, I'm here—let's work this out and get you mission-ready. What's going on?"

"I thought I could do it. I cannot. I cannot be with them as Paul when my life before was full. I had my mother, I had my friends, my love. I have nothing now." Paul was shocked by a great shake, and he suddenly found himself lifted completely off the ground, being held by his shirt and trousers by two great hands and a miffed angel.

"Do not throw this great gift back at the Master, Paul. You have all which you have stated you lost, you are just blind to it. You have been given a second chance to complete a great commission, and you will do it with those that you love. So what if it is as Paul

Maxwell and not Max Avatov! Are you not you? What do you care what your wrapper looks like? Do you understand, I mean *really* understand, what we are about here, Paul? This mission, this charge, is *eternal.*" The angel emphasized the word as he settled the man back to Earth and smoothed his shirt. "Humans don't really get eternity and its nuances, and I understand that, but if you could step back away from your grief for just a moment, you would rejoice knowing that eternity is there for you, for Maggie, Margueritte, and all of the rest of the people you care about. Consider this a training ground for you all to work and earn a bit of what is coming. You can do this—be yourself. Physically they won't ever be able to detect you. I'll leave your comportment to you, but there will be grave consequences if you are not discreet. They must not know of your rebirth and who you really are. You can do that, or you wouldn't be my guardian." He once again clasped his shoulder and looked into his guardian's eyes, smiling. "Now, Paul Maxwell. Go do what a guardian does."

Paul walked into La Cuisine Ouverte. The familiar smells came wafting to him on the opening of the door. He inhaled the heavenly scent as he walked inside. Momma Rose came bustling out of the kitchen and called out, "Just sit anywhere, chere. I'll be with you in a moment." She placed the cup of steaming coffee and a beignet in front of her customer and, wiping her hands on her apron, came over to the table Paul had just seated himself at. Paul studied her as she walked over to him. This was the test that Uriel had told him was necessary. "What can I get for you today, chere? You want one of Momma Rose's famous beignets, oui?" she asked him with a smile.

"Yes, and a cup of tea, please," he told her. *She does not know it is me. Let me make sure she gets a good look.* Before she could leave, he reached out and grabbed her hand, stopping her. Her smile faltered briefly before she put it back in place.

"Was there something else you needed?" she asked him. He regarded her only a moment, trying to see if there was any recognition there.

"Yes, ma'am. I am here to see Peter and Sam. I was told to ask you where I can find them," Paul told her, smiling sadly when he did not see even a spark of recognition in his aunt's eyes. He had thought that if anyone would have recognized him, it would be Rose.

Momma Rose smiled and said, "It's funny, but I feel as if we have met before. Have you been here before?"

"Not for a while, and then it was only briefly, on business."

Momma Rose nodded. "I have never forgotten a face; maybe it will come to me later. I will go and let Peter know you are here, and while you are waiting, I think a little treat is in order. Momma Rose is going to fix you up, chere."

She bustled away into the back of the cafe and, as he watched her go, Paul decided that he loved her just as much as Paul as he had as Max. She reappeared a moment later carrying a tray of beignets and a steaming cup of tea. She placed the tea and treats in front of Paul and said, "Peter will be down in a moment. You best eat those before he gets here, chere, or they will disappear before you can," she told him with a girlish giggle.

Paul smiled at her carefree laugh and was about to make a pithy reply, when the bell at the front of the cafe jingled to make them aware of a new visitor. When he looked up, the smile froze on his face and the cup of tea he was holding made its way slowly back to the table.

"*Magdalene.*" He spoke in a whisper, but saw Momma Rose turn her head and look at him oddly. She shook her head and bustled forward to embrace Maggie at the door.

"Maggie! It is so good to see you," she exclaimed. "I was wondering if we were ever going to see you again," she finished and gave Maggie another hug.

"Maggie!" came a shout from the kitchen door and, as Paul watched, Peter flew past him to scoop Maggie up and twirl her around. "I have been so worried about you," Peter admonished her. "You didn't call back last night, but I guess I forgive you since you're here." Peter laughed and enveloped her in another hug.

"Hi. It's good to see you, too," Maggie said, laughing. "And Momma Rose, thank you for all of your letters. It took me a while to get everything settled with the Avatov piece, but I finally put it to bed. I'm sorry that I haven't been in touch more, but I had so much to deal with—" She trailed off, sadly. Just as quickly, she recovered and smiled wanly. "You two, however, are very persistent and would not let me forget you, so instead, I made the decision to work here to try to make sense of it all instead of Baltimore. Plus," Peter led her over to a table in the corner and sat down with her, "I took your advice, Peter, and called Dr. Jo. She's great and I think she'll be able to help me the way she helped you. Fingers crossed."

Paul was close enough that he was able to pick up everything she was telling Peter. He was glad that she was okay. He had worried about her after he found himself in Eden. Uriel had assured him that she was coping and that she had a support system, but it was nice to see her for himself. It was also very painful. His heart was so full of love for her, but he could not do anything about it. He was not Max Avatov anymore. He was Paul Maxwell now; he looked and sounded totally different.

"Is there something wrong with your tea, chere?" came Momma Rose's voice from beside him, making him jump slightly.

"Huh?" he said stupidly.

"Your tea, chere. You haven't touched it, I was concerned that there was something wrong with it?"

Paul glanced from Momma Rose to the table where Maggie and Peter sat, then back to Momma Rose. "Oh, no there is nothing wrong with the tea," he said quickly, then followed it just as quickly with, "Is that Maggie Preston? The reporter that broke that big human trafficking story a couple of months ago?"

Momma Rose smiled like a proud parent and said, "Yes, that's her, indeed. She is something special." Her eyes turned sad for a moment, and then she said, "That is Peter with her. Let me remind him that you are here. Drink your tea before it cools, and if you want even one of those beignets, I would eat it before Peter comes over." She smiled at him and made her way over to Peter and Maggie's table. "Peter, don't forget that you have someone waiting for you. I will take Maggie back to see Margueritte. She will want to see you, chere. She has been asking about you for a while now. Please, come put her mind at ease."

Paul heard these words, and his heart did another flip. His mom was here as well as his Maggie. He had almost forgotten. The two women who meant the most to him in life, in the same establishment. He longed to see his mother again.

Maybe, he thought, *I could catch a glimpse of her before their business was concluded.*

Maggie rose from the table and followed Momma Rose through the kitchen door in the back of the cafe. Before she went through the door, she looked back out at the cafe, and her eyes locked for a moment with Paul's. Giving her head a little shake, she slipped through the door. Paul followed them with his eyes until they disappeared from sight. When he turned back around, it was to find Peter sitting on the other side of the table, watching him. Peter smiled and ate one of the beignets that were on the plate before Paul.

"She is very beautiful, isn't she?" Peter asked, still staring at him.

Finding this a little disconcerting, Paul cleared his throat and said in his most proper voice, "She is also very talented. I followed all of her stories about the trafficking ring you helped her stop. I am sorry for your loss, by the way." It felt odd referencing his own demise with his friend. "Is it true Lev Avatov escaped? Has no one seen him?"

"Sad but true, yes. And, thanks." Peter answered, looking a bit down. It was obvious that Max's death still affected him; affected them all. The fact that Paul could just, very easily, look into Peter's eyes and tell him that he hadn't died at all, or that he could gather them all together, right now, and put their minds and hearts at rest with his return—it was very tempting. It was also extremely selfish.

I could no more do that than I could go back to Lev. That is not who I am, what I am. I am here to do a job and to ensure that more people are not hurt by my father. I am here to make sure that ARC succeeds. I am needed as a tool, a weapon, and a protector, and that is what I will be, my old life be damned.

"So, you followed our adventures, huh?" Paul needed the prod from Peter as he was lost in thought.

"Yes." Paul snapped back to the topic at hand. "That is why I am here, Peter. Uriel sent me to assist you to help bring Avatov down."

Peter, who had yet to break eye contact, was already on his second beignet when he finally said to Paul, "Ah, you're Paul, then. Michael said you would be coming by today." Peter looked over the newcomer's shoulder and gestured. "And, here is Sam, right on time."

Paul turned to see Sam walk through the door.

"Hey, Paul!" Sam said, coming over and shaking Paul's hand. He winked and turned to Peter and said, "Are you ready?" Sam looked so excited by this prospect he was literally bouncing up and down in anticipation.

Peter smiled warmly. "Getting there. My arrangements in Hong Kong are all good. Naomi will be traveling with us, so you will have another pilot. She's seen to it that the flight plans have been logged and approved. All we were missing was Paul here—oh and before I forget…"

Peter trailed off as a sudden, "Sam?" came from the doorway.

Sam whipped around to find Maggie standing in the doorway watching him.

"…Maggie's here." Peter finished lamely.

Sam smiled and turned back to Peter. "Man, this is perfect, Peter!"

Peter was confused. Michael had made it clear that he wasn't to tell Maggie anything about China, and he hadn't. The archangel had his reasons, and Peter had to assume they were good ones, so this development probably did not bode well.

"How do you figure?" Peter asked him hesitantly.

Paul, who was following along with the new conversation, was interested in his answer, too.

"Well, I figure that if Maggie is up for it, she can tag along with Naomi, and the two of them can catch up while we are looking for Jonah."

While this was just fine with Paul, Peter was neither happy with the news that Maggie was invited, nor that Naomi and Maggie would be spending time together. If Paul was taking bets, he would lay a wager that Peter had other things in mind for Naomi.

"But Michael was specific—no Maggie."

By this point Maggie was tapping her elegantly clad foot against the tile floor. Paul knew the gesture, just like he knew the look that she was currently wearing. She was getting ready to blow her top.

"Just what *is* it that you two have planned that *I* am not *allowed* to be a part of?" Maggie accused.

"Now, Red—hang on a sec," Sam started, but Maggie had moved away from the door and was on trajectory directly for him.

"Don't you 'Now, Red' me, *Samael*. I am really freaking tired of people trying to decide things for me." She fumed a bit, but brightened slightly, her pretty mouth turning up in a smirk. "At this point, if you don't allow me to go on this trip with you," she was now pointing her brightly-painted fingernail at Peter and Sam in turn, "I'll just book a flight and meet you there, anyway. I'll bet my Pulitzer this involves Lev in some way, since it's China." Maggie looked to Peter, and his assent told her she was correct. "And I'm not losing anyone else to that asshole. Period." As Paul, Rose, Sam, and Peter stood with their mouths agape, Maggie zeroed in on Peter. "I am disappointed in you. Why didn't you tell me?"

Peter, who had stood there mutely during her tirade, tried to defend himself. "Look, Mags—I was told not to tell you we were going. This is Michael's deal, but I'm guessing it was because he knew this would be the response. Michael wasn't sure you were up to another adventure this—" he struggled for the words and wrung his hands, "—this soon after Max."

Paul winced and saw Maggie wilt a little at the mention of him. The silence settled for only a moment before the fire was relit.

"Peter, you of all people should know how much this means to me, not to mention what lengths I would go to when it comes to him. I will be going, even if Michael doesn't think it's a good idea. I have a will of my own, and I have not given up on sticking it to Lev Avatov on a very personal level."

Paul was so proud of her at that moment. He loved the fire in her eyes, and he missed seeing her righteous indignation. Maggie was unstoppable when it came to her passions. "I think she should come." He spoke softly, but all eyes swung to him.

"Thank you for your support, Mr...?" She paused, and Paul spoke quickly, taking her outstretched hand.

"Maxwell. Paul Maxwell, Ms. Preston."

"Am I to assume, Mr. Maxwell, that you are attached to this excursion in some way?" she asked with one raised eyebrow.

Paul smirked at this. He remembered that this was how Maggie fished for information. It was a tell he wasn't sure she knew about. Maybe they would have that conversation some time. She pulled on her hand, and he remembered he had not released it yet.

He smoothly unclasped her hand and said, "I have some artifacts that I will be picking up from Hainan and delivering to their new home, for a limited engagement, at the Maxwell Museum of Anthropology."

Maggie looked unimpressed, and he could tell that she was now sizing him up as a spoiled rich kid. "Let me guess—your family owns the Maxwell Museum of Anthropology?"

I need to fix this—cannot have her thinking I have nothing to contribute, Paul thought.

"My family does not, although they have contributed countless artifacts and display pieces over the decades. I became an archaeologist because of my father, and we believe in sharing other cultures with the world. We have brought many forgotten cultures back to the forefront, so that their stories will be known." Paul realized that he was selling the Museum to the others and quickly shut his mouth. Maggie took his measure again, this time he thought she looked a bit more impressed.

"Your Museum was the one that created the exhibit on the Moche a few years back?" she asked him.

"I am surprised that you knew about that exhibit. That was not widely attended, and the Moche are not well-known people."

"I have traveled a lot, Mr. Maxwell. I'm sure you can surmise that. Sometimes, I need to find a quiet place to get my thoughts together. I find that museums are perfect for this. I remember your exhibit because it was engagingly informative and very well presented."

The praise made Paul happy, but at the same time it made him squirm. He had not been at the museum when that exhibit was there. *As far as I know, Paul Maxwell did not even exist then.* "Unfortunately, I cannot take credit for that exhibit. My father was the curator and put that exhibit together. After school, I went back to the museum to learn from him. He was an amazing teacher."

"Was?" Maggie asked.

"He died last year. I took over his duties as chief benefactor and curator," he said.

"I'm sorry." She said it softly and sincerely.

He nodded and continued. "This will be my first official exhibit, both in procurement and curation. It is based on Chinese mythology. I will be collecting pieces from a couple of smaller Chinese museums for loan to the Maxwell Museum, but I also hope to do a little digging myself. It is very touch and go, because I have to have the approval of the Chinese Government to take any cultural pieces from China, along with the permission of the prefecture."

"What happens if they won't let you have them?" She asked.

He blew out a large breath and said, "While that is a possibility, it is a remote one. I suppose if I have to, I will collect as many stories and pictures as possible and will put together an exhibit with replicas. I would not prefer that route."

"Okay, so now that you have his backstory," Sam broke in, "we have to get ready to go. If you are coming, Maggie, we are leaving tomorrow morning."

"Boy, you don't believe in giving a girl any notice. Good thing I always come prepared." Maggie smirked at him. "It doesn't hurt that Peter is a terrible liar." She walked lightly to the door, noticeably more chipper than when she arrived and offered back over her shoulder as she opened the door, "I'll be back here at two. I already talked to Naomi, so I know when the flight is leaving. Nice to meet you, Mr. Maxwell."

"You as well, and please, call me Paul. See you later."

"So long, Red." Sam waved her out the door.

Peter, whose mouth was hanging open, said in a pouty tone, "I can lie if I want to."

Sam clapped him on the back, "That is not something that you want, Pete. I would take it as a compliment."

"Well, Paul, I guess you heard that we will be meeting at two. If you want to meet us here, that's okay. Otherwise, just meet us at hangar four at Lakefront."

"I will meet you there if it is okay with you. I would like to have a few of these for the road," he said pointing at a plate, empty of beignets. "Mine seemed to have disappeared."

"Sorry." Peter said, "It's a sickness. You, too, shall be afflicted, as are the rest of us," Peter offered grandly, sweeping a hand around at the assembled group. Everyone nodded, and Momma just blushed.

"I will take your word for it, Peter." Paul laughed.

"Don't worry—I'll get us fixed up for tomorrow morning." Peter laughed, and he walked through the door to the kitchen.

Sam pulled Paul in closer, presumably to shake his hand, but surprisingly he whispered in his ear very quickly and quietly. *You're gonna be fine—I'm really glad you're riding with us again, my friend.* Just as quickly, he pushed back a bit, gave Paul's hand a solid shake and said loudly, "See you later, Paul." He winked and walked out the door.

Paul stood for a moment and thought. Sam knew who he really

was, but he was the only one. It gave him a bit of comfort to know that his friend knew his secret. Peter, however, was not privy to the knowledge, and he was not sure if he would ever be. This was going to be interesting. He would be surrounded by all the people he loved and knew, but unable to tell them he was Max. If it were not for Maggie, he would be completely calm and in the clear, ready to throw himself into being Paul Maxwell. He had been able to keep things from Lev his entire life. This would be no problem—if it were not for Maggie. Still, this meeting had been a success. No one suspected him to be anyone other than who he said, and he was able to interact with the group.

So far, so good, he thought.

As he was walking out the door into his new life, he caught a whiff of Maggie's perfume lingering on the wind. He inhaled the scent deeply.

I cannot deny this ache in my heart, though. I miss her so. This may be harder than I anticipated. God, give me strength.

He paused and waited until he could no longer smell her, and started to make his way down the street.

Chapter 8

Lev Avatov was used to working in secret. His accommodations were sometimes less than ideal, but he was finding that his new lab was astounding in its modern conveniences. *I suppose when you are in China, technology is a lot easier to come by. I should have availed myself of the Motherland long ago—it would have made things much easier.* Everything that he asked the Dragon Master for had been delivered and the *rooms* for his special friends had been established.

That was the easy part—this volcano was riddled with secret caves formed by centuries of lava flow. The volcano itself was dormant and was being used by the Triads for all sorts of purposes. He did not want to look too deeply into their business, so he stuck to his own tunnels. There wasn't much to see beyond them, anyway. The surrounding terrain that wasn't the South China Sea was hilly and scrubby, but mostly uninspired. He hated the water, so he wouldn't be doing any sightseeing.

The Triads themselves, the ones that came and went from the facility, were quiet and stern. He was not one for conversation at the best of times, and these were hardly the best of times. He was being monitored, watched by not only the Triads, but by Olivier and the Dragon Master, which, by extension, meant he was also being watched by the Association and the Chairman. If there was ever a time that failure would not be tolerated, he was living in it, moment by moment. The prospect made him edgy and laser-focused, so he was grateful that the Master had been so accommodating. He lacked for nothing he needed.

His newest experiment was lying in the bassinet in front of him, peacefully sleeping, unaware of anything. His assistants were moving around him like bees in a hive, attending to whatever assignment they were given.

The Naga—now that was a proud achievement. They are extremely intelligent and loyal to a fault. They know who brought them here and who it is that protects them from the outside world. They know their place in the world and in this organization, and they do not contest it.

They, in fact, thrived and prospered under him. Lev had no qualms about letting them venture afield when they were not tending him. They never stayed out long, and they always returned. *Always.* They worked in the caves during the day and only ventured out when the nights were darkest, when there was very little to no moonlight.

"Ssssir," one of the female Naga had come up behind him, and he jumped a little at the intrusion into his thoughts.

"Don't sneak up on me like that!" he yelled while his heart settled back into its normal rhythm.

The Naga bowed her head, retreated a couple of feet and said in a quiet voice, "Ssssorry, Ssssir." He could tell she was a newcomer, and fairly young. The human half of her was roughly a meter and a half tall with strands of scaly tendrils that supplanted hair for their kind. She was uncovered, a hallmark of those new to his employ. Naga did not normally wear any clothing, which left the women bare-breasted, but his tasks necessitated clothing for them under normal circumstances. She was also chalked and dotted; another custom of the Naga whereby the particular scale patterns of one would be outlined or filled in with a peculiar iridescent chalk, so they could be seen approaching or going in the low light.

Lev focused not on the lower, serpentine half of the creature before him, but on the heaving, human-like bosom. He shook his head, jarring himself. *I really need a woman,* he thought bitterly. *How long has it been? At least four or five months, and here you stand, being aroused by a damned snake-girl.* "Well, what is it?" he snapped, irritated at his reaction to the girl.

"There hassss been a new development and we thought you would like to be notified."

That got Lev's attention.

"What kind of development, and with which experiment?" Lev asked her sharply. He didn't give her an opportunity to answer. He launched himself off his stool, strode down the passage a few feet, and grabbed one of the other Naga. He bade him follow and gestured from the door to the bassinet and the baby within. "Take this one. Make sure he is observed throughout the night. The new serum I placed in him should start to take effect soon. I want reports emailed to me every ninety minutes. Do you understand?" he asked a bit impatiently.

"Yesssss, sssssir, I will watch thissss one." The Naga bowed and rolled the bassinet out of the room as Lev turned his attention to the young Naga waiting patiently in front of him.

"Take me." The order was curt, but the young Naga bowed and slithered silently in front of Lev.

He followed the female at a distance because of the snake body that trailed in its wake. If he could change one thing about the Naga it would be those tails. He had forever been stumbling over them until one afternoon when he had been in particularly nasty humor, he cut the tail off the offending Naga. Ever since that incident, they wrapped their tails around their bodies when Lev was near. Lev had noticed that the young female in front of him was taking great pains to keep her tail out of Lev's path. Lev smiled. *Yes, they are an intelligent species.*

They finally made their way through the twisting tunnels to a little cell at the end of a particularly long stretch. The girl positioned herself to the side and at the last minute pulled her tail in and wrapped it around herself.

"Ssssir, the sssspecimen issss sssshowing ressssisssstancccce to the new sssserum. Itssss temperature hassss riissssen to forty and is still climbing. At thissss rate, it will not live much longer, sssir."

The worry for the small infant on the other side of the glass partition was palpable. The young Naga had grown concerned for the infant, and Lev did not like that. Lev approached the infant as a biology student would a dissectable frog. The flexible thermometer that had been placed on the infant's forehead showed the temperature had risen to 40.85 degrees. Lev knew that the baby would not last much longer. At 40 degrees Celsius, brain function would start to suffer, and as a result the internal organs would shut down, and the baby would die. This subject was already in distress. Lev felt nothing for the child that lay on the other side of the glass and wanted to make sure that his Naga kept their distance as well. He didn't like attachments.

She needs to learn a lesson. "This subject is no longer viable. Terminate it and ready the chamber for another." Lev said without emotion.

"But ssssir, sssshouldn't we try to ssssave thiissss one before we terminate?" The Naga was genuinely concerned now.

Lev picked a clipboard off of the wall and leafed through it, briefly. "How long has this experiment been running?" he asked but waited for no reply. "No—this one is done. Do as you are told." The finality in his voice brooked no more argument. "Harvest the organs and throw the body down the lava tube." He gestured to the little offshoot in the wall and waved his hand like he was brushing away something annoying. The lab was designed on top of a dormant volcanic site. Although this particular volcano was not showing signs of pyroclastic activity, the back of Lev's mind always wondered about it's stability. He saw the young Naga deflate a little.

"Yessss ssssir," he finally heard her say.

Lev turned and, as he walked away, he said, "All of the paperwork on this will be on my desk by this evening. I am disappointed in this outcome."

Lev walked back along the hallway, his thoughts on the young Naga, but this time he was not thinking about her form. *I did not know that they could or would form attachments so quickly. This could be potentially problematic. A new trait? A complication of some kind?*

He would have to ask Simon about this unfortunate new characteristic. He found Simon hard at work in the lab. He was currently giving orders to some of the other Naga in their language. Lev had tried to make sense of the hissing language previously, but it had escaped his grasp, so he just required that all of them speak in his language the best that they could manage. He called out Simon's name as he approached to gain the snake's attention.

"Yessss, massssster Lev?" Simon said as he turned.

"The young Naga attached to experiment twelve has been told to terminate. The subject is no longer viable." Lev watched as a flicker of concern crossed the adult Naga's features. It was so fast that he was unsure he even saw it.

"A great lossssss, ssssir. Sssshall I give her a new tassssk?" Simon asked without emotion.

"Yes, but Simon, I do not want her forming attachments to the specimens. She is too soft and needs to toughen up. Put her on disposal duty for the rest of the month with Russell," Lev said.

"Kassssssall, ssssir." Simon offered. "Do you think that issss wissse sssir?" Simon asked. "I am not ssssure that she would be the ssssame after a month of disssssposssal duty."

"That is the point, Simon. Do this, otherwise she is of no use to me. You understand?" Lev could tell that his words had an effect on Simon. The scaly green skin along his jaw rippled and changed to a brighter hue.

"Yessss, sssir, but may I work with her alsssso?" Simon asked Lev. "She issss my sister's child, and I would hate to ssssee anything happen to her."

Lev looked at Simon in surprise, "So you do form familial attachments?" Lev asked him, now genuinely interested.

"Yessss, but not assss humansss do, ourssss are more bassssic. While we have young and care for them, teaching them becomessss the ressssponsssssibility of the community. Thissss young one losssst her mother in Russsssia. Sssshe never came out of the cavessss. She issss lacking in teaching."

"Fine, teach her. No attachments," Lev told him.

"Yessss ssssir, thank you massssster" Simon said bowing to Lev.

Lev turned and walked out of the lab. He didn't see the look of hatred that passed over Simon's face. Lev walked down the hall in search of his final target for the day. Olivier had been slacking.

I need more specimens, and I need them yesterday. What is that detestable vampire up to? Is he trying to foist failure on me? Revenge?

The suspicion churned in his brain as he walked. He only had one or two from the last ten children brought in that were worth anything to his research. He flew down the hallway thinking of nothing else but finding Olivier and taking him down a few pegs. He wasn't sure where the greasy little man had gotten to, but he knew that he liked spending his time in the darkest of the tunnels. He had turned the corner, trying to remember where he had seen Olivier creep into last. The tunnel was the deepest black that Lev had ever seen, no light at all could be seen in the darkness. It was as if the lights set in the hallway for guidance could not penetrate the inky space. It was almost as if someone had painted a black hole in the wall.

"Olivier," Lev yelled into the darkness. "Olivier, you bastard, come out here at once!" Lev waited a few moments before opening his mouth to yell again, but before he could make a sound he heard a voice come out of the darkness.

"Temper, temper. He hears you just fine. He is not a dog to be summoned." The sultry voice then giggled from the other side of the darkness.

He then heard another voice, an even more seductive voice say, *"My my, you are yummy, aren't you? How about you come in here, and my sisters and I will show you a fine time?"*

He heard a third voice, just as sensual, say, *"Ooh yes, come and play with us, little man. We will give you pleasure beyond your wildest dreams."*

Lev found himself walking towards the darkness and shaking his head.

"Come out into the light. After all, it is only proper to gain introductions first," Lev told the trio. He waited, and out of the gloom came the three most beautiful women Lev had ever seen.

Each one of them, different. Each of them breathtakingly exquisite. The first one to move was the blonde. She slinked past Lev on the right side, circled his back, all the while trailing one long bubble gum pink nail along his shoulder blades.

"You *are* a handsome devil, aren't you?"

Lev found he had no voice but his eyes followed her every move. Sultry, sinuous, and wholly mesmerizing, she undulated a bit as she spoke, and he could not stop watching her. As she reached the front of him again, the second of the two beauties, the redhead, moved. Although beautiful, Lev found that after the ordeal with the last redhead, he wasn't as turned on by them anymore. She gave him a quick once-over and shrugged her shoulders as if it was his loss and stepped back to make room for the last of the women.

Perfection, Lev thought, and he had never wanted anything more than he did at that moment.

Her hair was as dark and silky as a black scarf made of the night. Her painted lips were an elegant dark cherry wine, and her mouth offset her creamy white skin perfectly, skin that shone from her supple neck all the way down to her painted, peeped toes. Skin that revealed itself in treasured places that her black cutout dress did not hide. A glimpse of shoulder, of cleavage, of hip, and of thigh—this woman made him forget all others.

She will be mine. He knew it just as he knew his own heartbeat—a beat that was pounding so loudly in his ears that he thought for sure these women could hear it as well. They could, but he didn't know that, nor did he know what else they could, and would, do. As striking as her body and face were to him, her eyes were frosty and lethal—two icy azure darts aimed directly at his soul.

She trailed one finger down his chest, grazed the top of his belt buckle, and to Lev's shock and utter discombobulation, hooked a finger inside the top of the flap of his zipper, letting the back of a dark red nail glide down the teeth to where they stopped. The man's breathing became ragged, and a bead of sweat presented itself at his hairline. She spoke sweetly, looking him in the eyes and removing her finger, reluctantly.

"Who are you looking for, Mr. Avatov?" Lev's heart started to beat harder.

That voice—that heart stoppingly sexy voice.

"Olivier," he croaked, swallowing the non-existent spit in his mouth. Black Beauty walked slowly around him just as her sister had done, but Lev felt this time was somehow more important, that somehow he had to stand out to her.

"Hmmm, have we seen Mr. Olivier, girls?" she asked them in a mischievous tone.

"I don't remember seeing him. Have you seen him recently, Pharzy?" the redhead asked the blonde. She tapped a bubblegum pink nail on her perfectly applied pink lips. Lev thought the color distasteful and obnoxious. He turned again to the incredible brunette, entranced, half-listening to the woman speaking.

"You know, I *do* remember seeing him earlier. He was eating lunch, I think. It was hard to tell, the child was so small. Almost a snack, really." She giggled and the other two laughed at her joke. "He should be done by now, though. Should I send Tsoula to find him?" Pharzy asked the darker one. She smiled and Lev felt like his heart would pound out of his chest. He hadn't felt this way since Margueritte, and he loathed it.

Lev puffed up, not taking his eyes off of the preferred sister. "Whatever you have to do to get that bastard's attention is fine with me. I'm tired of him not doing what I need him to do. He doesn't want me to involve the Chairman in this." Lev was bluffing, he knew he didn't have any pull with the Chairman. The folly of the last few months had seen to that.

The dark haired beauty rounded on Lev, suddenly tempestuous and deadly. "You are in *no* position to threaten anyone, *little man*. You do not want to make an enemy today."

Her frozen blue eyes had taken on a dangerous glint, and Lev felt the once hot blood in his veins go cold. He swallowed but could only manage a nod in her direction.

The redhead giggled and said, "Now Lillith, don't make the nice man wet himself."

Lillith smiled and the hold was broken. "Call the little slut, then," Lillith told Pharzy.

Pharzy cooed into the darkness, "Tsoula, come on love. Come to mommy." Lev felt the air change before he saw them. Out of the murky black, two large red eyes stared menacingly. They were about level with his face, and a wave of rank breath came at him from the darkness. The foul odor turned Lev's stomach. It was the stench of something freshly eaten, yet long dead. "There's my baby—come here, love." She urged the thing into the light. It whined a little, and Pharzy comforted it. "I know you don't like the light, but it is only for a moment. I promise."

Terror flooded through Lev when he saw what emerged from the shadows. The beast was a behemoth, grotesque and distorted, as if drawn by a child or a lunatic. The thing was pitch black and stood easily as tall as a horse, but wide and powerful like a boar. The head, legs, and tail were decidedly lupine. Apparently, the creature was a large, powerful, wolf-like dog. It turned it's head in Lev's direction—like it had heard Lev's thoughts—and it growled low and shuddering deep in its throat.

Pharzy giggled and pulled the great beast's head around toward her. "It's alright love, he didn't mean anything by it." She stuck out her tongue and ran it along the creature's slobbering, misshapen jaw, almost seductively, never breaking eye contact with Lev. She got to the dog's chin and let a bit of spit dangle from the tip of her tongue, before sucking it up to her pink lips. "He has never seen anything as beautiful as you, right, Mr. Avatov?"

In his head he heard a female voice say, "*If you value your life, choose your words wisely. Hellhounds do not tolerate rudeness.*" He was unsure who was talking to him, but he heeded her words.

"Yes. Gorgeous. I was startled by her beauty, is all."

His words seemed to mollify the hellhound, because she gave a wag of her great tail in appreciation.

Pharzy nodded, turned to caress the giant head lovingly, and said to the beast, "I need you to go get Olivier and bring him here. Do not harm him, just bring him before me."

The dog looked disappointed at this last pronouncement, but turned and bounded back into the darkness.

Lev took a deep breath as Tsoula left. *What the hell is happening? Who are these women? I need answers.* Lev spoke. "Your creature obeys you. I am impressed with—whatever it is." He said, diplomatically. "What—exactly is it?" He was exceedingly careful to not cause offense.

The redhead spoke, "That was a slut, that's what that was. She smelled, Pharzy. Where has she been? A boneyard, or a *boning* yard? Typical for that whore."

Pharzy frowned. "Shut up Ono, at least she gets it regularly." She turned to Lev. "That, Mr. Avatov, is a hellhound. She is my familiar and my pet. She will do whatever I ask of her. Isn't she precious?" She clapped her hands with glee.

Lev looked at her in astonishment, possibilities running through his mind. The woman was obviously insane, as evidenced by the sensual display with the mutt and the way she spoke to and about it.

What would I be able to accomplish with it? he wondered. *I have never seen it's like, anywhere. It would be a fascinating discovery to be able to dive into its innards and explore.* Pharzy's grin turned scathing and murderous.

"I would not entertain that idea if I were you, Mr. Avatov. She does not suffer fools, and she has monstrous ways to kill you, both quickly and slowly. She is, what you might call, anti-social." As she told him this last, she smiled showing him a full set of teeth as she mocked biting him. "She is amazing!"

They all turned back toward a voice, currently swearing retribution if the speaker was not released immediately. Tsoula walked slowly into the light carrying a very pissed off Olivier.

"Pharzy, you will tell this beast to release me or so help me…" he trailed off as the hellhound gave a shake of her head. They all heard the rip as the clothing gave way under the great beast's sharp teeth. Considering how she was carrying him, Lev knew that he would have to change his pants before he could go anywhere. The thought pleased him, but not as much as the thought of those jaws tearing the pompous bloodsucker fully in half and letting his entrails decorate the dirt at his feet.

"Oh! What would you do to me, Olivier?" Pharzy asked, putting her face inches from his, displaying mock concern. She smiled evilly. "*Exactly?*"

Lev felt that these women were the only ones in the world that could ask a question like that in both a threatening and seductive way. She pulled his head up with her pink fingernail and licked her lips, looking him directly in the face.

"We all can see that you are in no position to make threats, Olivier. Besides, you wouldn't last two seconds against Tsoula, would he, my darling?" She finished by stroking and kissing the great head. The beast closed her eyes in obvious pleasure. "If you ask her nicely, she will let you go. Won't you, love?"

Lev could swear that the hellhound was seriously thinking of all the possibilities. He knew she was seriously tempted to just end the person currently trapped in her massive mouth, and he was quietly egging her on. She spat him out, grudgingly, and turned her great head in his direction, giving him a great canine smile.

I could have done it. The thought pricked Lev's mind, uninvited but amused, and Lev would swear she was laughing.

Olivier picked himself up off the floor inspecting the damage done to his pants by the hellhound's teeth. "This was a new pair of pants, Pharzy," he said in indignation.

"Now, now Narcisse—you know Tsoula was only playing with you, like a bone or a pair of dirty underwear." She looked at Lev as she said it, willing him to be mirthful at the vampire's humiliation. Olivier looked incensed. "If she had wanted to hurt you she would have." Pharzy said this so matter-of-factly that Lev almost laughed aloud. Tsoula, for her part, looked at him and gave him a toothy grin that was amusing and terrifying all at once.

Olivier gave Pharzy a cold look and said, "I bet Alaric would love to know what you bitches do in your spare time." He said it in a flat tone that held a wealth of meaning.

Tsoula whipped her head around and in the blink of an eye Olivier found himself underneath her, on the ground, her great paw at his throat. Pharzy's eyes turned red.

Lev thought he was seeing things so he blinked a few times to clear his vision. No, they were definitely red, and she looked homicidal and, if possible, even more unhinged than before.

"If I were you, worm, I would not threaten me with such things. Tsoula doesn't like you *at all*, and *I* have been the one to stop her from killing you."

Tsoula growled low and gave Olivier's neck a little more pressure for emphasis. He heard Olivier gurgle a response.

"That's enough, Pharzy. Tsoula, let him go. *Now*," Lillith said in an authoritative tone. "You have had your fun, but our friend here," she indicated Lev who was watching everything raptly, "needs to speak with you, Narcisse, and not everyone needs to hear family squabbles." She looked down at her immaculate dress and picked a non-existent piece of lint from the sleeve.

So amused by the banter, and in the lustful thrall of Lillith, he almost forgot why he was in their company.

He cleared his throat loudly, asserting, "Just so. You," he pointed with an index finger at the man who was getting up off of the dirty ground, brushing himself as he went, "were supposed to be bringing me a new batch of subjects. I find that the last batch was woefully inadequate and poorly chosen. You are slow-witted, but you are not foolish. I must assume that you know how dangerous it would be for you to keep specimens for yourself. Is this the case?" Lev sneered the last bit just for his own enjoyment.

Tsoula, who had dropped Olivier, chuffed a doggy laugh, and Olivier turned in her direction.

"You keep out of this, dog."

Tsoula growled low and Lev, intrigued by the hellhound, snapped at Olivier, "From what I have seen tonight, Tsoula knows how to do her job. *You* appear to need some more training."

Lilith, whose curiosity had been piqued at the revelation of Olivier's indiscretion, now took a step or two toward him, ready to mete out a suitable punishment.

Olivier growled in frustration, holding up his hands to the advancing sister. "Look, stealing children is not an easy task." He said this to both the man accusing him, and the woman ready to hurt him. "You kill them faster than I can replace them. The authorities are already suspicious. Orphaned or not, when a large group of children go missing, people will talk."

Olivier was correct. Lev needed more subjects, but he was going through them at an astonishing rate. Only a handful remained of the original batch, none from the second and none from the third. Lilith turned her attention to Lev, and she was looking for an explanation. Lev deflected, not wishing to have her advance on him. Well, not in that way, at least.

"Go further afield. Do I have to think for you? We cannot continue the experiments without more subjects," Lev demanded.

The three women had surrounded Lev, and Lillith, apparently satisfied with his solution, placed a lithe hand on his shoulder. She came to stand by him and spoke into his ear.

"Perhaps we can help?"

Lev looked over his shoulder at her and said, "No offense, Lilith, but what can you do to help with this?" He was genuinely interested in what the Sisters could do for him, but he was also uncomfortably aware of her proximity. He started to breathe a little more heavily, feeling her body against his back.

"Never mind," she purred. "We have resources at our disposal, just as you do. We will procure some new subjects for you." She had appeared in front of him so fast, he did not see her move. She looked at him squarely. "On one condition."

He raised an eyebrow at her and asked, "Oh?"

"I would love to see your work," she said.

"*Ahem.*"

Her pretty face frowned at the sound of her sister clearing her throat.

"*We*—would love to see your work."

She rolled her eyes when she heard a soft, "*That's better,*" come from behind her. Lev looked at the three of them in turn, each one of the women was intriguing in her own way.

"If you can do what you say, then I would love for you to see my research," he told them and smiled. He would get his new subjects with the added bonus of bedding this glorious woman.

"Fine," he heard Olivier say and turned to face the horrible little man once again.

"You will accompany these wonderful ladies and make sure they do not get hurt." He heard one of the women giggle and watched as Olivier's mouth fell open.

Then Olivier smiled that oily smile and said in a sneering tone, "You don't know who they are, do you?"

Lev looked at him for a moment, perplexed, before saying, "Yes, this is Lillith," he indicated the gorgeous brunette, "and these are her sisters, Pharzy and Ono. Do you?" he said, introducing his new friends. Olivier's smile grew wider and satisfaction entered his face.

"Yes, I know who they are. They are *family*, after all." He laughed derisively and said to Lev, "You just made a deal with… oh, I can't. It's too cliche." He laughed again and shook his head. "But you did." With that proclamation, he dissolved into a fit of laughter.

Lev heard Tsoula growl menacingly, and Olivier's head snapped up in reaction. "Dammit, Tsoula, *shut it!*" Tsoula continued to growl as Olivier looked back at the quartet. "Fine, we'll go tonight. Can I go now?" he asked with a nervous glance at Tsoula.

Pharzy spoke up, "Tsoula, let him go, love. You will have a chance to torment him more later." Then she giggled again in glee for the future encounter.

They watched as Olivier melted back into the nothingness of the tunnel. Lev turned to the ladies. "Thank you for your assistance, ladies. As to what our disgusting friend was referring to—who exactly are you?"

Lillith walked around to stand in front of him. "All in due time, Lev." He nodded, and she continued. "We will help you with your small problem and, in return, you will show us your research. And perhaps, we will tell you a little bit about ourselves. It is a very interesting story, isn't it, girls?"

The other two and Tsoula had come around Lev and stood just behind Lillith. They all nodded and gave him a smile as they retreated into the darkness.

Lillith held Lev's gaze. She reached a slender hand to caress him under his chin. She purred deep in her throat and pushed forward to slightly brush her lips against his. The shock to his system was electric. She backed away, letting her hand glide along his jaw line until she, too, sank into the black of the tunnel.

Her parting words sent a surge of longing through Lev as she said, "I'm looking forward to getting to know you much, much better, Lev Avatov."

Chapter 9

The night air whizzed by the open window of the Crown Victoria, and Paul watched the ancient yellow paint on the hood flake off in tiny bits and disappear forever behind the speeding car. The cab pulled up in front of the familiar, well-kept hangar. The metal doors were currently closed but, as he watched, with a creak and a loud groan, they slowly parted, giving Paul an unobstructed view of the plane waiting on the other side. Standing in front of the plane were two figures that, as Max, he could have walked right up to and joined their conversation. As Paul, he would have to hang back, not wanting to risk discovery.

Even though the encounter at La Cuisine Ouverte had been a success, Paul realized he may have a problem. He knew that his appearance was different, but a lot of his mannerisms were the same. He knew his friends were smart and would be able to piece it together if they had enough clues.

A door opened to the tiny loft apartment in the far corner of the hangar that had belonged to Naomi's uncle, Abe. Paul felt a pang at Abe's loss but remembered that he was now working for ARC and the hosts in Eden.

I literally just saw him earlier today. There is nothing to be upset about there. The thought cheered him as he disembarked from the cab's dingy backseat. He handed the driver a twenty and the cab sped away. Paul turned his attention to the right side of the hangar's interior. As he watched Maggie descend the stairs, he longed to run to her and confess who he was; to ask her to once again be his.

"Ah ah ahhh," came the chiding voice behind him. Paul whirled around to find Sam standing behind him. "No good can come from that, pal. Regardless of how tempting it would be." The smirk on his face told Paul all he needed to know.

It's not nice to sneak around in other people's minds, Paul thought and saw Sam smile in response.

"Well, when you think as loud as you do, it's hard not to hear, oso. Plus, you're being all emotional like a woman, which makes it impossible for me to ignore you," Sam told him matter of factly. "You humans leak emotion all the time. Negative emotion is what drives demons, they live off your misery, pain, and fear. You call them to you like ants to a picnic."

Paul looked like he wanted to refute the remarks but instead shrugged his shoulders and asked, "What do you think can be done when the world is bent on its own destruction? We allow murderers, pedophiles, rapists, drug dealers, and the worst of the worst to be out among the population. If and when they are caught, the punishments are little more than a slap on the wrist. Sometimes they will get life in prison and occasionally they will execute those who have committed incredibly heinous crimes." Paul found he was angry. He couldn't explain exactly why, only that he found himself seriously pissed off.

"Calm down, Max. You've been dealing with bad guys for years—"

"I do not understand why I am here, Sam. I know that ARC thinks I can help them, so Uriel gives me the opportunity to help bring down my… Lev. But really, what exactly do they hope I can do or teach them that you guys cannot?" Paul realized that he had started pacing in front of Sam and that he had balled his hands into fists. He bounced lightly on the balls of his feet and tilted his neck from side to side to release the stress that had settled there. It felt strange to have the mannerisms of his old, large self in a smaller, skinnier body. He thought he must look ridiculous.

Sam sighed and said, "Look, Max—I won't lie to you. There are serious problems on the horizon. I'm sure that you and Uriel talked about what you and Maggie found in Lev's underground lab, right?" When he nodded, Sam continued. "Well, among his other nefarious pursuits, our sources tell us that he is getting close to figuring *it* out."

Paul looked curiously at Sam. "Figuring *what* out?"

"Figuring out why ARC members can wield a holy weapon, and why the females sometimes have a special ability. In essence, what makes them valuable in the fight against evil. They have not had the opportunity in all these years to piece together that vital bit of information. They have always been interrupted and the information confiscated to the point that they have to start over again," Sam told him.

"I do not understand. Why would Lev need that information? When Uriel and I talked, it was about what we found, but he never told me why Lev was after the information in the first place. I can only assume that Lev was going to use it to sell to the highest bidder—drug companies, cartels, that sort of thing. The mafias would pay big money to be able to have, um, *powers*," he said, using air quotes. "But what does that have to do with the supernatural creatures that ARC is fighting?" He ran his hands through his hair in frustration. That was another thing Max was getting used to as Paul—he had never had so much hair.

"Look, there are certain things that I am not allowed to tell you, hermano, some of which includes why you each play a part in this adventure. Not why you are in ARC, but specifically why *you*," he pointed to his friend, "have been chosen. Suffice it to say, that you each have something special besides an Rh factor and a lineage that will allow you to complete the tasks that need to be done. I am not allowed to encourage you or dissuade you from your choices, but I can tell you that your choices, good or bad, have consequences. Remember that, oso—no matter what, your consequences are your own. That is the beauty of free will." He smiled like this was the answer to every question Paul ever asked.

Paul waited for a moment and then asked, "What is an Rh factor? And why would that determine who gets into ARC?"

Sam looked astonished.

"I thought you discussed this with Uriel?" Sam finally spit out.

"We discussed many things from the tunnels, the Naga, my mother, the information that Maggie smuggled out. None of that explains this Rh factor that you are referring to. So spill."

"There are some things that cannot be shared—"

"Nope. You brought this up," Paul said defiantly.

"All I can say is, look it up. You have the means, and I can't say anymore. I have already said too much." Sam took a defiant stance and crossed his arms in front of his chest.

"Sam!" They both turned at the sound of the new voice. Peter had finally noticed the two of them standing outside the hangar and was jogging happily towards them. He looked at both man and angel, and it felt to Peter like he had walked up on a quarrel. "Is there something wrong here?"

Sam turned to Peter with a big grin, "Nothing's wrong, bro. Paul and I were discussing genetics. It's a very deep subject, you know." Sam and Paul exchanged a quick, knowing look.

Peter eyed them both suspiciously and gave a tentative, "Uh huh." He reset his expression to a happier one. "Well, while you were discussing scientific diversity with each other, the girls and I have been loading cargo and getting us ready to take off. If you want to come this way, Paul, you can take a look at the cargo and where you will be sitting. It's not at all comfortable, but it will get you from point A to point B," Peter told them as they walked back towards the hangar.

"Oh, I remember." Paul winced inwardly and then corrected, "I have flown this way before."

Peter looked at him briefly before nodding. "Good, I didn't want you to be surprised by the in-flight accommodations."

Sam walked briskly and was soon outpacing the pair, racing to do preflight. The two men walked and talked.

"So, I hear that you work for a museum?" Peter said, by way of changing the subject.

"Yes, The Maxwell Museum of Anthropology."

"Anthropology—so civilizations—people groups and stuff?" Peter sounded intrigued.

"Specifically, ancient civilizations with oral culture progeneration…" Peter looked lost, so Paul offered a simplification. "Groups that pass on their lore mostly by stories and tale-telling. It's fascinating the number of myths that pass from culture to culture. Many of them are so close as to be identical," Paul said in his most teacher-like voice.

"Really, like which ones?" Peter asked in a curious tone.

Paul realized that Peter was actually intrigued by the notion, and it worried him for a moment. *How much will I have to come up with so he believes this?* He remembered a tale he had come across in Turkey, and went with it. "Well, have you ever heard of the roc?"

"Yeah," Peter replied,."The really big bird, right?"

Paul laughed, "Yes, an extremely large bird, big enough to carry off a full grown elephant."

Peter whistled, "That's crazy, but what does that have to do with identical myths?"

"That myth was out of Arabic writings in the Middle East, Turkey specifically. Here in America, we have a similarly sized bird and legend in Native American mythology called the Thunderbird. The Native American people believed that the Thunderbird would battle the water spirits by throwing bolts of lightning at them. This was usually only thought of during the yearly rains." Paul went on, gathering steam, remembering lore from his youth. "The Aztecs, for their part, have the myth of Quetzalcoatl, and the Chinese have a myth about P'eng and K'un. K'un is an extremely large fish and he phases into an equally large bird, P'eng, whose wings are said to be like the clouds in the sky. So you see, four different myths from four equally different cultures about relatively the same animal. I like to collect those types of myths and explore the possibilities," Paul told an enraptured Peter.

"Wow. *So* many ideas are running through my head right now.

Please excuse me while I write some of these down. We will definitely talk more later, though. You really know your stuff, professor. Thanks." Peter shook Paul's hand while pointing at him in promise of further talks before turning and sprinting for the notebook leaning against a rather disheveled backpack.

Paul watched as he scooped it up and started to scribble vigorously. He smiled and turned to see where Sam went and almost bumped into Maggie who had come up behind him.

"Oh, excuse me," he said.

She laughed. "Quite alright. I'm a ninja, you know." She winked at him and said, "Really, I'm sorry to come up on you unaware like that." Maggie looked over at Peter, scribbling intently. "Whatever it was that you just told him, it really made his day. I'm not sure how long he will be writing in that notebook, but I gather it will be for a minute." She shook her head while smiling in Peter's direction.

Paul felt a momentary pang of jealousy at the easy friendship between Peter and Maggie. He mentally gave himself a shake and told her, "I was telling him about the mythology of the roc in different cultures." At her blank look he said, "Extremely large bird capable of carrying off an elephant."

"Ah, I thought you were talking about music for a second."

He noticed that she was wearing a Queen t-shirt along with her leather jacket and jeans and boots. She looked amazing, and he momentarily forgot everything.

"How big of an elephant?" Then she laughed, and to Paul it was the most beautiful sound.

Maggie thrust her hand out to the man. "You know, I don't think we were properly introduced earlier, I am—"

"Maggie Preston."

She raised one eyebrow at him.

"Yes, I know who you are, Ms. Preston. I follow you." Realizing how that sounded when she raised both eyebrows, he quickly backpedaled. "Well, not *you*. I follow your work. Your piece on Lev

Avatov in LACE was revelatory, and it was very brave of you to come forward and tell what you learned." Paul meant this sincerely, as Max. *My brave, brave girl. You gave me the courage to do what I had to in that warehouse, and I am so sorry it cost us our future.* He gathered himself quickly and said, "I am not sure there is anyone in America that has not heard of you. Although, I will say that you are lovelier in person than on television."

Maggie blushed prettily at the compliment and said, "Thank you, Mr. Maxwell, but seeing as we will both be in this tin bird—"

"*Hey! Respect please!*" shouted Sam over his shoulder as he patted his plane on the side.

Maggie rolled her eyes in his direction, "—as we will be airborne for many hours together, please call me Maggie."

"Alright," said Paul, "as long as you return the favor."

Maggie smiled at him and nodded. "Have you met Naomi? She will be the other pilot on this flight."

Paul almost said yes before he corrected and said instead, "No, I do not believe I have had the pleasure."

Maggie looked at Peter briefly over Paul's shoulder, and then she leaned in to whisper to Paul.

She smells intoxicating, he thought. He closed his eyes to take in her scent. Thankfully, she couldn't see his face in her present position, poised at his ear.

"A word of advice," she offered. Paul nodded his approval and she continued, hushed. "Peter likes Naomi, and I believe they are at the start of a new relationship. I would try to stay as far away from that as you can."

He nodded his head in assent. He and Maggie walked slowly toward Sam and Naomi who were just finishing going over the plane. They turned as the pair arrived.

"Well, everything is ready. How about you two? Are you ready to fly the friendly skies?" Naomi asked with a grin, making a swooping motion with her hand. She noticed the newcomer and said, "Oh, by the way, I'm Naomi," she said, already shaking Paul's hand. He didn't remember much about Naomi, but he did remember that she was a firecracker, just like Maggie.

"Paul Maxwell. It's a pleasure, Naomi," he said with a grin, "And, to answer your question, yes, I am ready to go. Maggie?"

She grinned and said, "I was born ready."

"Great. If you will both excuse me a sec." Naomi walked over to where Peter was jotting and thinking. She walked up behind him and nudged his shoulder. "Hey, you. Whatcha doing?"

Peter closed his notebook with a loud clap and smiled, "Just finished. Paul had some fascinating information, and I was taking some notes. This is going to be great. Are you okay?" She put a hand on his shoulder and spoke softly.

"Seeing you last night did me a world of good, so you were right about that. Maybe you're right about this, too." She squeezed his shoulder and let go. "Thank you, for everything. You have been so amazing since, well, ever since the warehouse. I am very grateful for you. I just wanted you to know that." She backed up a pace, embarrassed. "So, you did say your awards thing is fancy, right? How do you like my ensemble?" She giggled and turned for him, mocking a lavish gown when really she was dressed in boots, cargo pants, a hoodie, and her uncle's old cap.

I'd take her, just like that, anywhere, Peter thought. *God, please don't let me screw this up.*

"Madame, you look divine," he said, standing and mimicking a low bow to her. "Seriously, don't worry. I will get us both something appropriate when we get to Hong Kong. You'll look perfect— well, perfecter." He joked, but she knew what he meant. Peter was smitten, she knew it, and they were on their way to something. That was enough for now.

She hugged him and said, "Come on, mister. You have a plane to catch."

He grabbed his stuff, and they slowly made their way aboard to the front of the plane. After a quick pre-flight check, Peter popped out three jump seats and took his place in the middle one. Maggie sat to his left and much to Paul's ire, he sat in the one on Peter's right. His grumpiness over the seating choices was short-lived when Peter produced a bag and handed it to Paul.

He could smell them without even opening the bag. He said, "Bless you, Peter."

Peter grinned and produced his own bag of beignets. "Like I said, this is going to be great." He let his eyes wander to the co-pilot's seat, and to Naomi.

Chapter 10

Tsoula was annoyed. Not that she didn't enjoy hunting with her mistress, but usually she was allowed to devour her prey indiscriminately. This time she had to *find* them.

"Find them only—don't eat them. Bring them to mommy." Pharzy had been very specific, and she would be very angry if her instructions were not followed to the letter.

She ran on silent paws and felt the humid night collect around her. She couldn't bother being too upset, though.

I am free. I love the hunt. I am the most dangerous creature on this plane.

Tsoula could sniff out her prey from miles away. She could devour an adult human in two bites, and had, many times. She could bound the length of a city block in four or five leaps. She was, indeed, dangerous. Pharzy was specific, though: no big cities, stick to the shadows and the small villages, and no noise. She was to collect a few without injuring them and return with them to Pharzy.

Then I will be rewarded.

The giant hellhound stopped and put her great muzzle in the air, sniffing long and deep. All humans were alike to her. She liked them best when they were afraid. Their fear made her strong. *And them, delicious*, she thought. The sweet stench enveloped their bodies and made them do reckless and foolish things. It was fun to play with them before they died. She especially enjoyed subtlety—pursuing them for a time, stopping, letting them think they were safe before pouncing on them again. She could usually do this a couple of times before they broke completely.

Then I have no choice but to eat them.

Her finest hunt to date lasted a solid week. The hikers knew there was something large stalking them, but Tsoula never quite showed herself to them. She was able to make them fear both the day and the night.

What other creature can do that? she questioned. *None. Only Tsoula. Tsoula the Great. Tsoula the Terrifying. Tsoula the Ripper, the Tearer, the Destroyer.*

She recalled the hikers again, pleased. The group stayed together until they got lax in their defense. They were exhausted from lack of sleep.

They feared what would happen if they fell asleep.

She was able to extract every last ounce of fear from the group before picking them off one by one.

It was a grand game and a bountiful hunt, she concluded. She gave a big doggy grin and a growl of pleasure at the thought.

Her growl changed to one of displeasure. She couldn't do that this time. This time she was supposed to collect the babies and give them to Pharzy. The only pleasure in this was knowing that Pharzy didn't get to play with them, either.

She had to give them to that human.

He was an interesting human. Pharzy thought he would be fun to play with but the great one, Lillith, has forbidden it. That was more interesting than what he was going to do with the babies, in her opinion. Lillith never forbade her sisters from having fun that Tsoula could recall. The three of them had been known to cause more havoc in one night that any one human could do in a decade. She gave a chuffing laugh, thinking about some of their more recent escapades.

Tsoula stopped suddenly as she came upon the small village. *This one,* she thought, changing her run to a low-slunk creep. She could see the fields and smell the cattle and chickens. Animals always presented a problem for her. They didn't like her smell and knew that to have her around meant trouble. She would have to be very careful in this village. She would stay to the outskirts of the village as much as possible. She could smell the oxen and the milk cow, as well as a few chickens and a lone pig. Luckily they were stabled together on the far side, away from her current position.

There is a dog. The thought displeased her and she wrinkled her nose. *Inferior things, not powerful or smart or terrifying or obedient. Not like Tsoula. No, not like she who rules the night with fear.*

She would have to turn the dog. Mind magic was tricky, though. She had to be close enough to see the subject, but not close enough that it could pick up her scent and let out a warning bark.

She crept around the outskirts of the village on silent paws; a figment, a shadow, a suggestion of a form.

Need to find that dog.

Every so often she would stop and sniff the air until she caught the scent she was looking for. She crept slowly forward until she reached the edge of the house. Easing onward ever so slightly, she beheld the tiny village in full. It was only about five ramshackle houses and a small barn. This was probably an entire family of aunts, uncles, and grandparents—at least a couple of generations—and across from where Tsoula was standing lay the dog, sound asleep.

It wasn't a large dog, but big enough that it's bark would be heard. Tsoula concentrated on the dog, she could feel the edges of it's mind. It let out a little whimper in it's sleep and then a growl. Tsoula backed off a little and then very carefully sent her mind back toward the dog again. This time, she was able to penetrate the mind of the sleeping canine and plant the image of silence and a picture and scent of Tsoula as a friend. She saw the dog's tail wag and then lay still.

She knew her mind magic was working. Grumpily she thought it would have been so much more enjoyable and faster to just kill the dog, but Pharzy was specific in not raising any alarms. She was safe enough now to explore the houses. She skulked around the first house and sniffed at all the windows. She did the same for the other four houses. Tsoula now had a mental map of where everybody was and how many young ones lay sleeping.

The first house had three young ones, one of them still suckling age. This one smelled very good to Tsoula, but in reality, he needed to be changed. The second and third houses had older kids and adults, too old for what Pharzy needed. The fourth house had two more young ones, and the last one only held geriatric adults.

This should be easy, she surmised.

She pulled a bag from around her neck where Pharzy had put it. This would allow her to transport the young ones without injury. Pharzy had bespelled the bag herself. Plus, if they cried once they were in the bag, they would not be heard.

She crept to the first window and sat up on her haunches, clearing the eaves of the small house. The windows had been left open due to the humidity of the jungle behind them. She poked her head down over the window sill and looked around. Tsoula could smell the young ones and was pleased to see that they were snuggled together on a straw mat and well worn blankets, but within reaching distance of her great head. The mother and father were across the room on their own mats, sleeping deeply.

Tsoula carefully grabbed the edge of the mat and began to pull it toward the window so she could more easily pick up the sleeping infants. She dropped the bespelled bag on the ground at her feet and stuck her head back through the window to grab the first infant. She carefully picked up the babe, blanket and all, in her gleaming teeth and, maneuvering gingerly, pulled the baby outside and placed it in the bag. The bag glowed for a moment, and the baby was gone. Tsoula went back in for the other baby but found a surprise waiting for her.

Another young one had awoke and curiously watched Tsoula. The child was sitting right next to the other baby and, to Tsoula's great annoyance, said, "Gou," which meant *Doggy*. It reached out a hand to Tsoula, and she made a decision. It was older than what Pharzy wanted, but not by much.

This one may be useful, she thought.

She was unsure of that, but she *was* sure that if this child woke the old ones or the adults, she would be discovered, and her hunt would end. Very carefully, she grabbed the girl by the little dress that she wore and lifted her through the window. The child let out a little squeal, but it was cut off abruptly as Tsoula dropped her into the bag, which once again glowed softly.

Tsoula carefully poked her head back down over the window edge and, seeing that the adults had not heard the child, she grabbed the last sleeping baby and dropped it into the bag. Tsoula could not hear anything coming from the bag and chuffed her doggy laugh silently at the ingenuity.

Having relieved the house of its precious contents, Tsoula grabbed her ill-gotten gain and made her way silently to the only other house that had young ones. She was easily able to empty that house of its young charges, and when she finished, she quietly moved away toward the last house in the village.

The door silently opened, and out stepped a young man. Tsoula was not good at judging the ages of humans, but she had found that some of the younger men smelled strongly of sex, something Pharzy had informed her was called *puberty*. This human smelled like that. She stepped back into the shadows for a moment and watched him, curious to see where he was going at such an early hour.

He ambled forward towards the only other little house in the village. It was very tiny and only had one small window near the top of the structure. It was haphazardly put together, as if it regularly got taken down and moved. Tsoula caught a whiff of the stench that emanated from the small hut as the human opened the door.

These humans stink, thought Tsoula. She wrinkled her large nose making her look fierce for a moment, but ruined the effect when she let her tongue loll out. Tsoula picked up her bag and, now that the human was inside the little hut, took off for the forest outside the little village. She had to get the young ones back to Pharzy.

I need to hunt in earnest.

Pharzy had promised that if she did this task, then she would be allowed to hunt however she chose, and her mouth began to water at the thought of the souls she would take tonight. Tsoula picked up her pace. The ground flew by under her massive paws. Hellhounds could cover a devastating amount of ground in a short time when they chose. She had already passed by several small villages and was making her way towards her destination.

She heard the cry before she saw the man. He was standing by one of the outlying buildings on the outskirts of the last village she would pass. She quickly blended in with the darkness surrounding her. She had stopped moving to see what the man intended. To her great surprise, he was moving toward her hiding spot.

Tsoula had only moments to think about how she was going to handle this latest development. Making up her mind, she took off at breakneck speed and was clear of the man before he could make it to her former hiding spot. She looked back, and her eyes glowed for a moment marking the man in her mind. She had a clear mental picture of him and had his scent in her nostrils. She would come back later when Pharzy released her.

That human, she thought, *will make excellent fun.*

Tsoula liked it when her prey had a bit of spirit. That human was willing to run after the large animal it saw in the woods rather than run towards the safety of its home.

Yes, this one will be fun.

She smiled her canine grin around the sack she was carrying. It wasn't long before she could see Pharzy and the others, including the new human, standing at the top of a small alcove nestled in the side of the volcano. Tsoula decided as she moved closer that this volcano was her new favorite spot on Earth. She had a few, but this one smelled of death, and she much preferred its scent to all others.

Taking a deep breath as she made her way towards the group. She heard a soft, "Well done, my love," from Pharzy.

Pharzy reached for the bag the moment Tsoula reached them, turning to gleefully address her sisters and the Russian. "See? I told you she wouldn't let me down." She lovingly stroked the side of the great hound's neck and turned, facing the others with the bag in hand. She held the bag out, and Lev took it from her.

He greedily set to examining its contents, then growled out, "The bag is empty, Pharzy. There are no children in here."

Pharzy laughed and clapped her hands together. Lev looked around and saw that the other two sisters were smiling at him as well. Then he heard the great chuffing laugh of the hellhound and knew he had made an error. Pharzy took the bag back from Lev.

"*Whatever* are you talking about, little man? Why, this bag is positively *loaded* with children—you just need to know where to look." She winked at Lev and threw the seemingly empty bag up in the air for effect. She caught it, opened it up, reached inside and, to Lev's astonishment, the bag glowed softly. From its depths, Pharzy produced a toddler with her little dress all askew. She looked at the people surrounding her and, not recognizing anyone she knew, began to wail.

Pharzy wrinkled her nose at the child and looked at Tsoula. "This is not an infant, Tsoula. Mommy specifically asked for infants."

Tsoula hung her head and spoke, mind to mind, with Pharzy.

"*I know mistress, but this one was laying with the infants and awoke. I took her before she could wake anyone else. She is not too much older than the others. She is still in clothes around her bottom.*"

Lev, shocked for only a moment, spoke up in defense of the great hound. "That is quite alright, Pharzy." He rubbed his hands together and continued. "I know that Olivier will have a use for her. She is a little young, but he likes that sort of thing."

Pharzy shrugged and placed the wailing child back into the bag, cutting off her tirade.

Lev took the bag once again and, with a grin and a look of longing at Lillith, who ignored him completely, he turned to go back into the open tunnel. "Follow me, if you want to know what these tests are about." He threw the statement over his shoulder in Lilith's direction. Lillith looked at her sisters and a sigh and a roll of her eyes followed Lev into the tunnel.

Ono laughed and said, "I think that our sister is bored. Hopefully, Mr. Avatov will give her something else to think about soon. If not, I fear that there will be many missing men from the surrounding villages." She laughed again and followed Lillith into the gloom of the tunnel.

Pharzy turned and looked at Tsoula. "You have done well, my pet. Were you seen?"

Tsoula once again hung her head, but when she looked back at her mistress her eyes were glowing.

"Yes, a man two villages from here saw something large run into the woods. He ran after me, but I was gone before he reached the spot he saw me. I have marked him and wish to return for him. May I go, Mistress?" As she was speaking her mouth started to water and she drooled as she pulled her lips back and bared her teeth. *"There is still time to hunt."*

Pharzy could tell that, if she did not allow her hellhound to hunt soon, Tsoula would go berserk, and she would lose control. Pharzy carefully stepped forward and laid a hand on Tsoula's head. The great hound looked at Pharzy, eye to eye.

"You may go, but stay to the farthest villages. Any prey you must take alone and quietly. There is no room for error, do you understand? We don't need to start a panic. Now is not our time. Soon though; soon you will have your fill. Now go, and come back before first light."

Before Pharzy could utter the last of her sentence, Tsoula was gone. Pharzy knew that Tsoula was trying to reign in her blood lust. In order for her to keep control, she must hunt. Pharzy threw one last look over her shoulder and went into the tunnel to join the others.

Chapter 11

Raguel loved midnight. The Master's creatures were either sleeping peacefully or foraging for food. The sounds of the surrounding jungle were a symphony to his ears. Each frog, insect, or nighttime animal contributed a different harmony to the music of the night, lulling the world to sleep. He sat and listened to the lullaby for a while, but he was restless. He was currently seeking information regarding a group of missing children. It would be more accurate to say they were infants, no more than three years of age. This would have been a normal occurrence a few years ago, but since China had lifted the ban on single children households, those numbers had dwindled until only those children with disabilities were the ones that ended up in the orphanages. Sometimes a couple who were extremely poor would give up a female child in favor of a male, but that practice had all but disappeared.

The great angel lifted his head, alert. The forest sounds had stopped. Not a sound could be heard. Raguel knew that meant there was a predator about.

What kind, though? One that walked on four legs or two?

He walked a minute more and came to a place that the locals avoided, at least the decent ones. This place was well-known for the more nefarious goings-on that happened there—drugs, smuggling, crimes of opportunity, even crimes of passion.

A bad place for bad people, he thought.

He knelt down to survey. His eyes saw perfectly well in the dark, so he had no problem making out the man who was moving around under the forest canopy.

Not a smuggler. He seems to be looking for something out in the woods.

He turned a moment later, and Raguel, who was well hidden, was able to get a good look at his face. It was a man called Jian from the local village.

What would bring him out at this time of night? He's a farmer.

Most of the local farmers were less than two hours from getting up around this time, and he felt sure that whatever called Jian to the woods was very important.

Well, more important than sleep, apparently, he thought.

Jian stooped down and inspected the ground at his feet. He held out his hand and spread his fingers out on top of whatever he had found. He stood suddenly and fled back towards his house.

He's scared, but of what?

The angel was curious as to what would cause such panic in the young man. He carefully walked to the spot where he saw Jian standing minutes before. He looked down to see a very large indentation in the earth. He held his hand out like he saw Jian do earlier.

A print—every bit as big as a man's splayed hand. No wonder Jian fled so quickly. If this beast is still hanging around, he would be in very serious trouble.

Rags decided to search for the beast himself. Something about all of this did not seem right, but it could explain where the missing children went. Although, if the beast had eaten them, there would be some sort of physical evidence. He searched the entire area looking for more prints. He found them. It looked to him as though the beast had been running and stopped at the point Jian had found the print. Maybe he had seen something in the distance and went to find out what it was. That could have been a deadly mistake for Jian. He was lucky he did not find the beast he had been searching for.

Since it looked like the beast had moved off in search of other prey, the angel decided that he would continue to watch for other monsters in the forest. The jungle around him was still quiet, and that concerned him a little. The animals were never bothered by Rags, so he did not think that it was him. He looked over his shoulder to watch Jian make his way back to his home. He was about halfway across his fields when, to his right, came an immense shadow.

The thing was traveling much faster than the small man and would be upon him momentarily. Raguel decided to intercept the great shadow. He took off at a fantastic rate of speed and was soon standing in front of an astonished Jian just as the great shadow reached him as well. Rags was astonished. Before him stood a great dog, with paws larger than a man's head, and a stench that was just as great. It was the eyes that let him know that this was no ordinary dog—they were a flaming red and trained directly on Jian. It walked slowly, menacingly, toward the small man who was retreating with a terrified look on his face. The damp ground beneath his feet squelched with each slow step.

Raguel stepped in front of the man so that the creature's vision was blocked. It growled slowly and the angel heard a voice in his head.

If you value your life you will get out of the way of my prey.

Rags took a step backward. This confirmed his suspicions.

A hellhound—here? To what end? He heard it growl again. *Why was it out here?* The Angel of Justice spoke. "I don't know what hole you dug out of, dog—" another growl came from the massive throat, "—but you'd better find your way back there, and fast."

Jian had now taken up residence behind Rags' back and was whimpering in fear.

You are blocking my way, human, and I will not tell you again to move. If you insist, I can start with you and have him as dessert. The great head swung in his direction, and Rags shook off the hands of the man cowering behind him. He turned to the frightened young farmer and smiled warmly, belying their situation.

"Jian, go home now. This pup and I have a little matter to settle."

Jian did not wait any longer and took off at a sprint for home.

Raguel did not look back at the retreating figure, choosing instead to focus squarely on the beast in front of him. In his mind, he willed the thing not to pursue its quarry.

"I don't know how you came to be here, beast, but I would suggest that you leave before you get hurt," Rags said in a low voice, maneuvering himself further into the field beyond the village causing the hound to follow him. The beast made a low chuffing sound, and Rags could swear that it was laughing at him. It spoke to his mind again, inaudibly threatening him.

Who do you think you are talking to, human? it asked as it slowly started to circle around Rags. He turned in conjunction, keeping the beast in his sight at all times, again taking the opportunity to place himself and the beast further from the sleeping folks in the village.

It doesn't know I'm one of the host. That's very good, he thought. *It probably also doesn't know that I know what it is, also very good. If I taunt it enough, it should go berserk.* From what he could remember of his training on hellhounds with Raphael, he knew that if you could send a hellhound into a blind rage, it would throw strategy to the wind, forego its natural cunning, and come at whatever was irking it, making it easier to control and take down. *Get this thing mad—now.*

"Well, now that *is* the question, isn't it? I assume from the look of you that someone's mangy mutt got loose, and judging by the smell of you, you just had to roll in the first pile of offal you came to, because you stink." Rags smiled winningly at the creature as it growled, getting angrier. "The fact that you can project your thoughts to me though, I have to admit, that is causing some confusion. I know!" He snapped his fingers as he continued to turn as the creature circled. "You are some kind of medical experiment gone awry and have escaped your evil master's clutches. Come, I will give you a bath and a biscuit." He smiled again tauntingly.

You mock, human, but you will not be laughing when your head is resting beside you and I feast on your still warm body. I do not take insults from one such as you, too stupid to recognize the greatness standing before you. It lunged forward slightly as if checking its adversary's reflexes.

Rags stepped easily out of reach, and the beast continued to circle around him.

"This has become tiresome, pup. Be a good doggy, and run home before I have to put you down." Rags had enough time to leap to the side and roll before coming to a stop and whirling around to meet the great red eyes of the beast.

Tsoula was enraged, both from the insults and the fact that twice now her prey had managed to escape her onslaught.

I am no mere dog of this plane. You mock what you do not understand, and tonight it will cost you your life. It sprang at him again, this time when Rags went to jump away from the claws and teeth, the beast changed direction almost as if by magic, and the claw caught him on the arm.

Rags hissed with pain and saw that a long jagged tear had opened on his arm, the edges blackened as if he had been burned. He turned to face the beast once again.

It sneered, knowing that its last blow had hit home, somewhat. *You are quick for a human, but I am faster and smarter. Have you made your peace with this earth, because you will not be on it much longer.* As the thoughts bombarded the angel's mind, Tsoula noticed the angry wound on the man's arm start to glow slightly and disappear. *No human could make that happen,* she thought.

The man looked up from his healing arm and smiled, wryly. "You have made a mistake yourself, pup." Rags waited for that to sink in a moment. "You see, you keep calling me a human, and yet," he looked down at his nearly-healed arm, still glowing, then looked back at Tsoula, "I am decidedly not human."

The beast stopped and cocked it's head to the side. Rags almost laughed at the purely canine expression. The beast shook its head and growled low.

What are *you?* she demanded. As the beast watched, her prey changed form, his tatty jeans with the holes in the knees and threadbare t-shirt were replaced by robes of blue and a breastplate and mail of the purest silver. The wound in Rags' arm glowed as it was covered in silver gauntlets ending in a magnificent silver sword surrounded by blue flame held loosely in his hand. From his back sprouted six wings donned with feathers of purest white, the tips of each ended in fine silver. A soft glow emanated from Rags as he faced the astonished beast.

You are an angel? the beast half-asked and half-stated.

"Nothing gets past you, mutt. Now let us finish your hunt." Raguel didn't wait for the beast to respond. He lunged at it with a righteous fury. "It's time to send you back to Hell, hound."

The hellhound jumped to the side just as the tip of Raguel's sword came down and planted itself in the dirt. Tsoula whirled around and thought that she had an opening. She pounced, but Raguel batted her away as if she were a toy. She came down and rounded back to face him again, completely overcome with bloodlust.

"Come! You must do better than that, dog. How is it that you escaped into the world? Where is your master? They must be insane or stupid to let loose a creature like you."

The creature let out a ferocious growl and ran at the angel. Raguel feinted to the left, but the creature changed direction. In a blink, both the angel and hellhound were battling across the open field, neither gaining or losing ground. Raguel grew weary of fending off the monster in front of him. He stumbled and went down on one knee. The hellhound took advantage of his perceived weakness and lunged. Just as the beast landed on Raguel putting ragged holes in his armored gauntlet, he thrust upward with the dagger he held in his other hand. The hound yelped in pain as it backed away from Raguel. It looked at the glowing wound in its side and knew that its time on earth was limited. Tsoula backed slowly away, suddenly mindful of how alone she was and how far away her mistress was.

This is not over, angel. My mistress will be back for you, as will I. Before Raguel could finish it off, the hound turned and, in a blink, it vanished into the surrounding forest. Raguel made to follow, but the small wounds that he had suffered battling the hellhound were aching him terribly.

Not mortal, but not comfortable, either, he thought, assessing his injuries. He would have to go and see Jophiel in order to heal properly. While he was there, he would talk with Michael about there being a hellhound in China. This was a new revelation and one that would not be welcome. If it was here on Earth that meant it's master, *no mistress, it had said,* would be here with it. *What are the demons up to?* Raguel turned and staggered back across the field toward the treeline he had emerged from. When he reached the treeline, a door appeared, and he stumbled through.

Tsoula made her way back to the mountain that housed her mistress. Her steps slowed as the wound in her side continued to leak her life essence. She had not been able to satisfy the hunger inside her. There was another reason she didn't want to return to her mistress, and the thought caused her no small amount of dread. *The angel lived.* Tsoula had never encountered one of the host, but she had always been instructed that, in that event, the angel *Must. Not. Live.* She knew that Pharzy would punish her for this lapse—if she lived long enough. She stopped by the door that led her inside the mountain and called weakly to her mistress. Within moments, Pharzy was with Tsoula outside the mountain entrance.

"My love, what happened to you?" she said in a soothing voice. "Who has done this to you?"

Tsoula was not a stupid dog, she knew that as soon as Pharzy knew about the angel she could be banished to the depths of hell. She would be lucky if her mistress banished her—she could leave her here to die. This type of death would not be a death she could recover from. This type was the permanent kind; she would never be able to run at top speed again, nor would she ever again know the feeling of tracking and sucking the soul out of her prey. Resigning herself to that fact, she began to relay the night's events to Pharzy.

"My mistress," Tsoula hung her head. *"I'm afraid that I have been bested, and I am sure that you will not like who it was that wounded*

me." Her strength waning, Tsoula laid on her side waiting for her final judgment. "*An angel intercepted me in my hunt. He has dealt a mortal blow. Please, if you don't send me back now, I will die.*"

Pharzy sucked in a breath as Tsoula gave her the facts. Pharzy was furious. Tsoula was made to be the best at everything, and to be bested by one angel was unacceptable.

"I am disappointed in you greatly, and the telling of your tale will determine your fate, my pet. Leave nothing out, and see that you do not displease me further. Tell me everything." Pharzy said it without a mite of concern for Tsoula's predicament.

"*My mistress, I went after my prey as instructed. I approached not the people or the houses, and he was alone. I was about to take him down in a field outside the village, but an angel intercepted me and demanded that I abort my hunt. I, in turn, challenged the angel with the intention of taking him down, but I did not know his true form…*" she took a deep, shuddering breath. *Not much longer now,* she thought. "*We battled for a while, neither gaining ground, until I made a mistake.*" Tsoula knew that taking this approach could spell her death, but she was banking on Pharzy not wanting to let her go. They had spent a long time together and Pharzy would be hard pressed to replace her loyalty. She continued, "*I underestimated the strength of the angel. He made me think he was weak and in my hungered state, I fell for his ploy. In the end, I was out my prey and mortally wounded. I was determined to return to you and tell you of my encounter so that you could protect yourself.*"

"Do not pretend altruism brought you back to me, my pet," Pharzy said, obviously still angry. "You returned to me so that I would send you back to heal; nothing more. You are trying to save your own worthless skin. Still," she said, softening, "you did not run away or flee the angel, my love. That shows loyalty. However," she raised her voice, anger overtaking her again, "failure in loyalty is still failure. Lilith will be furious."

Tsoula was miserable. She laid her head on her massive front paws and took a shuddering breath.

"*I am sorry, my mistress, that I have failed you.*"

Pharzy stood and walked away from Tsoula as if she were trying to determine the best course of action. From out of the shadows came Lev Avatov. He had followed Pharzy when she had excused herself from her sisters.

"Is there anything I can help with, Pharzy?"

She spun around at the sound of his voice. "Oh, Lev," she was clearly distracted. Tsoula hoped that was because she was trying to decide what to do. "No, I'm afraid there is no hope for this one. I was just trying to decide what to do with her."

Lev had moved closer to Tsoula and had knelt by her side. Tsoula growled, but it was a half-hearted attempt. With each breath that she took, the holy wound in her side was weakening her.

Not long now, she thought.

Lev laid a hand against her side, and Tsoula thought it was in an attempt to give her some comfort until she twisted her head to the side. It was then that she noticed that Lev was holding a vial against her shoulder. He was collecting her blood. Tsoula shifted suddenly, trying to get her jaws on the man, and Lev jumped backward. She thought to her mistress. *"He uses me, and you let him? Just let me die and be done with me. Maybe your next hellhound will be a better fighter."* Pharzy looked in the direction of Lev.

"You should think a bit more about anything else you want to take from me, human."

Lev jumped and turned to her in a panic. "I'm sorry, but I think that your hound is not long for this world."

Pharzy sighed, evidently making up her mind. "Yes, I know. Dammit." And with a wave of her hand a dark hole appeared under Tsoula. The great hellhound fell into the abyss and disappeared. Lev spun in a circle.

"Where did she go?" he asked in an awed voice.

"She has gone home. Come, Lev, let us go and see if we can improve my slave. Obviously, when she returns to me, it must be in an improved state." Without waiting for a response, she turned on her heel and re-entered the mountain.

Lev watched her go and, with a grin on his face, fingered the vial of blood taken from the hellhound and followed after Pharzy.

Raguel limped into the center of Eden. He was interrupted by a slight slip of a girl. She came upon him with a clipboard, a button down, sweater, skirt, and penny loafers. Raguel noticed the prominent shock of white hair in the otherwise raven tresses, and he smiled.

"How can I help you? I don't have you on my list, and I am not expecting anyone for a while. So, who are you?" She finished in one breath.

"I'm Raguel. Who are you?"

The girl stopped for a moment and said, "I'm June. I'm new here. Sorry, but should I know who Raguel is?" She stopped moving and waited for his answer.

This girl amused him, but he was sore, and it was urgent that he speak with his boss. "I'm an angel, June. More precisely, the Angel of Justice. I need to speak with Michael," he stated as if she should know.

June looked a bit sheepish. "I'm sorry, sir. Like I said, I'm new here, and I have not met everyone yet."

She looked so forlorn that Raguel immediately felt for her. "It's okay, June. There are many of us and only one of you. You are not expected to know everyone right away."

She smiled at him and said, "Thanks, Raguel."

"Please, call me Rags."

"Rags, Michael is not here right now, but I can show you to Uriel if that would do?" she asked, bouncing on the toes of her penny-loafers. Raguel noticed that her apparel and appearance, from her hairdo to the way her makeup was applied, seemed a bit dated. Having been active in the last couple of years all over the world, he took note of people's appearances, and he guessed that June was more in line with the late 1950s than the 21st century. He would have to ask her about that as time permitted. For now, Uriel needed to know what had transpired, and he had to get himself fixed up by Jo. He nodded politely at the girl. "Lead the way, June."

"Sure. Follow me." She took off at a swift pace. He decided that she was the type that liked to see a job done efficiently and effectively. Within no time at all, they were in the middle of a great clearing with a huge waterfall. Uriel was bent over a great map laid out on a table with a young man next to him. They appeared to be looking at a map of China and an area very near where Jonah's orphanage was located.

Maybe my news won't be a surprise, he thought, curiously.

June strode right up to Uriel and said, "Uri, I found Rags on the outskirts of Eden. He says he wants to speak to Michael, but I informed him that Michael isn't here at the moment, but I also told him that you might be able to help him." It seemed that her breath would never end. Then it did, and she stood in front of Eden's Guardian, expectantly. Raguel was impressed with June. She was very good at her job. He saw Uriel smile at her.

"Why, thanks, June. Once again I am very glad you are on our side. Of course I will see him."

June smiled at Uriel and, without looking in Raguel's direction, she left in the direction she had come from.

"She's something, huh?" Raguel smiled at his friend. "I'm not sure why you think you have to hide yourself away in the middle of Eden, but I cannot fault you for your choice of surroundings," Raguel told him in awe.

Uriel smiled and said, "I cannot take credit for this view, my friend. This is all Abe, here." He slapped the young man on the back. "He seems to have an affinity for the forest. It has been the topic of many discussions." Uriel's smile faltered when he saw Raguel stumble. He reached out and grabbed Raguel by the arm. Raguel hissed in pain and Uriel adjusted his grip. "What has happened to you? How have you come to be in such a state?" he asked with concern in his voice.

"I have just come from the village outside Haikou. There was a nasty surprise waiting for me there," he told Uriel.

"Sit," Uriel ordered, and a large chair big enough for the Angel of Justice appeared. He alit, gratefully, wincing a bit. "So, what awaited you there?" Ureil asked, interested.

"A hellhound, hunting in the village. A young farmer, Jian, was its next prey. Luckily, I happened to be looking for smugglers and came across Jian following prints in the jungle, or he would have been a late night snack," Raguel told him. "Unfortunately, I was only just up to taking on a hellhound. I'm afraid that I have practiced far too little recently for this type of skirmish." Raguel rose, walked a few paces from the chair and sat roughly on a log beside a large table in the middle of the clearing.

Abe had come up on the other side of him and was looking over the many wounds that he had suffered at the paws and teeth of the hellhound. Abe whistled appreciatively. "Man, I wish I could have seen that battle. I hope that thing looks worse than you do."

Raguel looked over at Abe, wincing again. "I struck a mortal wound to the hellhound. Unless it can reach its master in time, it is dead." Raguel smiled at Abe's nod of appreciation.

"Any idea who the master was?" Uriel asked.

Raguel scowled. "No, Uriel. I did get it talking, but I was a little busy protecting Jian. The thing escaped into the forest and..." he winced again "... I need Jo. Abe, will you get Jophiel for me?"

Abe looked over at Uriel who nodded, and he left the two alone to go find the healer.

"So what do you think this means, Uriel?"

Uriel turned away from him, clearly thinking of a response. "I think this means that we are on the right track, brother. I also think that after your visit with Jophiel, that you should warn your friend Jonah that things are about to get very interesting for him." Uriel was smiling. "For now, you must get healing and get some rest. And I," he snatched the map off of the table and hastily rolled it, "I must find Michael." Uriel spun away and left the clearing, leaving Raguel sitting on a log waiting for Jophiel and the promised relief.

Uriel is right about one thing, he thought. *If hellhounds are involved, then we are most definitely on the right track.*

Chapter 12

We at DeathAngel Airlines realize you have a choice when you fly, and we are grateful that you choose to fly with us. Please tip your flight attendant as you exit… also, your pilot really likes Guinness, for future reference…

The comical announcement came out of the cockpit as Sam brought the plane in for a smooth landing at the Haikou Meilon International Airport. As his plane taxied to a stop in front of a large hangar, he noticed a couple of guards. These guys didn't look like cops—more like military elite, armed with Tech 9s and what appeared to be flash-bangs. They were walking up to the plane as it stopped in front of the designated terminal.

Trouble, he thought. Sam looked over at Naomi and said, "Now the fun starts." He gave her a grin which she returned to him as he said, "Tell everyone to sit tight until I sort this out." He flicked a couple of switches and unbuckled his seatbelt.

Naomi followed suit, but the two split off as Sam made his way through the cargo hold to lower the doors. Naomi stopped in front of the others. She took off her uncle's old cap and shook out her brown curly hair, stretching and yawning. She was beat from the twenty-three hour ordeal, and it showed. She replaced the hat, smiled, and said, "Sam said to cool our jets until he sorts out the locals. Then I suppose it's on to whatever accommodations we have secured for the night." She slowly rocked back and forth as she spoke and looked towards Peter.

Wow, thought Paul, *She has got it bad, alright.* Unfortunately, the object of her affection had his head in his notebook and was talking to himself as he jotted. Paul took pity on her. "That sounds great;

right, Peter?" Peter didn't answer, engrossed in his scribbling. He tried again. "Personally, I, for one, am looking forward to a shower and something to eat. How about you guys?" He included both Peter and Maggie in his statement.

"Count me in. This girl does not like to be cooped up," Maggie said brightly. "Neither does *Peter.*" She said his name, simultaneously elbowing him.

"Are we here? I'm sorry guys, I had some ideas and wanted to get them down before I lost them." He smiled at Maggie and Paul sheepishly, and then looked at Naomi, who could clearly hear the gulp of the hard swallow Peter took when he saw her. She smiled, warmly, and he relaxed a bit. "Naomi and I were going to do a bit of sightseeing, if it's allowed, followed by dinner. I mean if she wants, that is… to… go… with me." Peter's countenance took on a worried look. It was obvious to Paul that they had not talked this over yet, and Peter was unsure what Naomi was going to say. She smiled and nodded, sparing him any more embarrassment. Peter let out a sigh of relief and gave her a grateful smile.

Paul turned to Maggie and said, "Well, that just leaves you and me. Wanna see some sights?" Maggie blushed prettily and smiled.

"I think that would be fun. But what about Sam?" Of course she didn't want Sam excluded. They weren't going on a date, after all. Or were they? She assessed the man across from her. She could definitely do worse. Max had been exceptional physically, there was no doubt about that, but Paul had a very serious sexy professor vibe going. *The long hair, the beard, the thin, tall frame,* Maggie pondered. She found herself comfortable. There was something oddly familiar about being with him. She also had had a couple of very insightful and entertaining conversations with him on their journey so far, and saw no reason to discontinue their getting to know each other. Sam tagging along may not be conducive to that process.

Peter came to the rescue. "He is going to meet up with an old friend of his, I think. We're supposed to meet up with him and our guide tomorrow after Sam works out the arrangements."

Peter grinned at Maggie and gave her arm a little nudge. "This is something, huh?"

Maggie smiled back, still thinking about the man sitting across from her.

Sam walked back into the plane as Peter said this and nodded in Naomi's direction. "The officials have given you guys the green light to leave the plane. There is a customs official waiting to verify your passports and take you to the hotel. I'll meet you there later."

Paul and Maggie left the plane, talking as they went. *That's nice to see*, thought Sam. He hated their tragic end and hoped that this may be the start of something new for both of them. Naomi and Peter were about to shuffle out as well when Sam said, "Peter."

"Yeah, Sam?" he said, turning in his direction.

"Don't do anything I wouldn't do," he said with a wink.

Naomi flushed and turned away from them with an, "*OMG, really?*"

Peter grabbed his stuff, looking embarrassed, but still smiling. "Man, I thought we were friends, Sam." Peter clapped him on the back and said, "I'll behave, I promise."

"Are you two finished?" The two turned at the sound of Naomi's voice. Peter lost the boyish grin when he noticed Naomi with her arms crossed over her chest, tapping her foot. She waited a beat or two before smiling at Peter. "I'm hungry, and I need a shower. Not in that order." She walked past the two, leaving Peter to catch up to her. Peter looked at Sam, shrugged his shoulders and followed Naomi, leaving a bemused Sam in his wake.

Sam lost his smile as the quartet left the plane. He turned and closed the door to the cargo hold. Strangely, he opened it again immediately, this time to a lush, green forest with a young girl waiting for him. As he walked through the door, all the Earthly trappings fell away revealing his pitch black robes and wings, his large sword hanging at his side, a reminder of the great task that waited for him. The young girl, June, was bouncing on her toes and looking at her watch. Sam smiled as he saw her. "June, how are you today?" he asked her.

"I'm fine, Sam. You're late," she said. She turned and started walking, and as expected, Sam fell in behind her.

"What's the latest?" he asked her as they walked.

"Well," she said, "Raguel showed up unexpectedly after fighting with a hellhound in China—it was all very exciting. Abe was there, too. Raguel came in hurt asking for Jophiel, and Uriel sent Abe and I to look for her…"

Sam looked over at her and then back to where they were traveling. "Is Rags okay?" he asked her.

"Oh, yes," she told him quickly. "Jo was not happy with him, but told him he would be fine. He's talking with Uri and Michael at the moment. Michael sent me to find you since you were *supposed* to meet with him twenty-two minutes ago." She finished her statement with a large breath and smiled at Sam, who returned her smile.

"So, lead on, mamacita." He bowed to let her pass, and she giggled at his playfulness. As they came to a couple of low hanging branches, Sam opted for black boots, cargo pants, a dark gray hoodie and cap with aviators, eschewing his angel guise for convenience.

"That's neat," June offered, impressed.

They stepped through a copse of brilliant jacaranda trees to a large clearing with an enormous waterfall at one end. Sam had not seen this place before. Eden was, after, all, different to each person. This iteration was compliments of his friend, Abe. Sam frowned at the memory of losing Abe after their fight with the Grunch, but he had been excited to learn that not only would he be able to work with him still, but that he would be working with Max, who was now Paul. *The Master works in crazy ways.* Uriel turned as the two walked through the trees into the open.

"Ah, great work, June." Sam saw June's face light up with pleasure at the compliment. She curtsied and quickly left the clearing.

Uriel smiled. "I'm sure she was, my friend. How are you, Sam?"

Uriel asked him, holding out his hand to shake. Sam grabbed it and pulled Uriel in for a bear hug.

"I'm fabulous, but I'm itching to start this new mission. Where is Mike? I thought he was with you?"

"They went off a few minutes ago to have a talk. They will be back in a moment."

Sam heard the new voice and spun around to see a lanky youth make his way through the trees. Sam smiled and said, "Abe?"

The young man nodded and walked up to Sam. "I didn't know if you would know me. I should have known better." He threw his arms around Sam and clapped him on the back a few times before releasing him. "So, are you keeping my boy Peter out of trouble?"

Sam grinned. "Not really. I always seem to be the one who gets him into trouble." The two friends laughed and Sam said, "Besides, he has Naomi to set him straight." Sam laughed again until he noticed Abe wasn't laughing.

"What do you mean, *he has Naomi*? Naomi and Peter? When did that happen?"

"Whoa, calm down there, chief. After you left them, they kinda gravitated toward each other. He helped her with everything after you died, and they're good for each other. He gives her someone she can depend on, and she gives him confidence in himself. It is really... very sweet." Sam folded his hands in front of him daintily, but Abe still looked apprehensive. "Besides, they're moving along at a snail's pace."

"Are they?" Abe seemed mollified.

"Yeah, in fact, they are having their first date as we speak."

Abe stood there for a moment and then nodded his head, apparently accepting what he was hearing. In life, Abe had been the only family his niece had, and he was just as protective now as he was when he was with her.

"At least I know that Peter will treat her right. You need to warn that fool if he hurts her I will haunt him for the rest of his life." He crossed his arms in front of him to show that he was serious.

Sam laughed. "Alright Abe—I'll let him know, but in all seriousness, you don't need to worry about it. He loves her, she loves him… they'll be great for each other, and you know what sort of man Peter is. He's gained my seal of approval. What more do you need?" Sam mimicked a rubber stamping motion, then clapped his hands together. "Now, where is Michael so we can get this over with?" Sam was impatient to be back with the others, especially after learning there was a hellhound on the loose.

"Ever the patient one, aren't you, Sam?" said Michael's voice coming from behind him.

He turned around and saw the archangel strolling in from the other side of the clearing with Raguel who was holding his shoulder and stretching out his muscles. His wings tipped with silver trailed behind him, and his sword strapped to his side almost touched the ground. Sam could see the signs of a battle on Raguel. His lips were pinched, and he grimaced every time he moved his arm. The two transitioned from angels to beach bums in a blink, and the atmosphere eased.

"Hey Rags. You've looked better, man. How's the arm?" Sam asked him.

"It's still a little sore, to be honest," Raguel said, wincing again.

"If he would learn not to play with stray dogs, he would be a lot better off," Jophiel said from behind the two angels, not unkindly. They stepped out of the way, and Jophiel walked through the hole they made for her, transitioning to flats, jeans, and a cute sweetheart neck tee in a whisper of pink as she went. "Hi, Sam," she said, a brilliant smile lighting up her face. "How have you been?"

"I'm doing well, Jo, but as you have already guessed, patience is not one of my virtues. So, tell me everything." Uriel laughed.

"Really, Sam. You could give June a run for her money. I've seen more stationary and patient hummingbirds." They all laughed and sat on the seats, which again had appeared out of nowhere.

Abe shrugged and said, "Thought you all could use some seats."

"I see you have wasted no time figuring out Eden, Abe," Sam said with a grin.

"Logistics, man. That's my thing."

Let's start, guys." Michael began pacing, while while Jophiel, Uriel, Abe, and Samael sat. "It seems that we have some unexpected company in China. Unfortunately, we did not get information as to who the dog belonged to, but we know that a hellhound is not normally left to wander alone, and never too far from it's master. So, that tells us that this particular dog was well trained. It would have been with its master for a long time. Does that ring any bells for anyone?"

The three members of the host looked at each other, but no one could come up with anything.

"I don't think there is a demon out there that is that attached to a hound. Aren't they all sort of reckless and stupid?" asked Uriel.

"The demons or the dogs?" Sam asked.

"I wouldn't say that, Uriel," called a new voice.

Another voice added itself to that one. "Did you decide to throw a party and not invite us?"

Two new angels had appeared in the clearing. The Healer and The Messenger, Raphael and Gabriel, came strolling up to the others.

"Never mind that," Michael said, waving away the accusation. "Who do you know that lets a hellhound loose without supervision, Raph? Or a better question would be, *why* do you know someone who has a hellhound?" Michael arched one perfect eyebrow in Raphael's direction.

"Well, since you asked so nicely," Raphael said in a sarcastic tone, "a few years back I had the pleasure of expelling a few Asmodean demons back to hell. It was the most enjoyable experience. The stench of sulfur and brimstone lingered in the air…"

Someone cleared their throat loudly, bringing Raph's attention back to the topic at hand.

"Yes, well, I worked with the host to clear a town of the infernals that had infested it, and there was a hellhound in the midst. As the host and I battled back the lesser demons, I noticed that the dog kept a watch on one of them—a sickly, oozing lump called Vaspar."

"Oh, I remember that one—disease demon, right? Nasty," Jo said, squirming a bit at the memory.

"Yeah, that's him." Raph went on, "Anyway, when the host would get close it would spring into action, protecting its master. *Only* its master. It was very odd."

"Yes, but who was it that controlled the hellhound?" Michael asked him.

"I was getting to that." Raphael held up a hand to forestall any other questions. "She was one of the Three Sisters."

"One of the what now?" Abe asked, trying to keep up.

"The Three Sisters. The Damnable Succubi, the Ba'al Enchantresses, the Fates, the Infernal Witches, the Moirai… they have many names, and have had many horrible things attributed to them throughout history, but the fact is," Michael expounded, "they are sisters; each one of them more beautiful and more twisted than the most perverse demon. They are Lillith, Onoskelis, and Pharzuph."

"Okay, I'm tracking now. Bad girls, right?" Abe waved Raph on to continue.

"You could say that."

"So, who owned the mutt?" asked Sam.

Raphael answered, "Pharzuph, the last of the Three, is the dog's master," he finished.

"I am familiar with her. Pharzy and I crossed paths a couple hundred years ago. She's… um… testy." Jo, again trying to be tasteful in her comments, said the word as if it tasted icky to her.

"Understatement of the year goes to…" Raph said, indicating Jo with his outstretched hand. "Pharzy is just as crazy as the rest of them, Jo."

"I wonder what the Three Sisters are doing with Lev Avatov, Raph?" Jophiel asked, still tending to Raguel. With the major healing done, she was in the process of tending to his minor cuts and scrapes.

"Knowing the Three, I'm betting they are about a very specific purpose, Jo. Or it could just be morbid curiosity. Or they want to torture him for some reason. Or seduce him for an even more esoteric reason." Jophiel wrinkled her nose at the prospect. "They are all over the map with their motivations, and they are all evil to the core."

"It could be that they just want to know what he is doing in that cave," Uriel said quietly. They could tell that he was thinking about something, but he did not enlighten them further.

"Well, if Avatov is messing with any of the Three, he'd better pray that he doesn't get on their bad side," Michael stated. "The Three Sisters are not known for their patience, or their charity, and they really don't like disappointment."

"What's the plan, brother?" asked Sam. "We have ARC out there looking for Lev. If the Sisters are with them, the danger to Peter and the others has just ramped up a few notches." Sam was getting himself worked up.

"Relax, Sam. We are going to add a few recruits to your arsenal. Gabe, Ariel, and Raph will be around to watch out for the hound while you guys work on your original purpose. If we're able to find Lev, we can shut him and his lab down for good," Michael said, hopefully. "Plus, I am gonna ask if we can borrow the dragon." Michael rubbed his hands together in anticipation.

"Whoa," Sam said. "You really want this to go our way. No one has seen that belligerent old lizard since the Yellow Emperor."

"Wow—Mike, are you sure about this? He's… unpredictable at the best of times." Jo was trying to be diplomatic in her description, but everyone assembled knew what she meant.

"He's nuts—is that what you're trying to say? He'd never help us," Uriel offered.

"Look, guys, I know all of this," Michael cut them off. "He was one of the originals, and therefore has been allowed to make his own path. That should work to our advantage. If I remember anything about the Yellow Emperor's reign, it was his incredible knowledge of all things obscure and ancient, and that he could not abide demons." The others still looked unsure, and, truthfully, Michael wasn't entirely sure of his plan himself. "Hey, it doesn't hurt to ask." He turned back to Sam.

"Go back to Peter and the others. I'll have Raguel and Jonah join you guys tomorrow in Haikou. You should not run into any red tape trying to get to the surrounding areas, so take Paul and see what you can find. Our intel tells us..." Michael paused, looking for Abe to take the ball.

"Oh, yeah. Thanks, Mike." Abe smiled at the archangel, then turned to address the group, finally able to contribute. "Intel says that Lev is working with the Triads in an underground facility, and it is definitely on..." a map materialized in front of them on the table, complete with Abe's notes, "...this island, here. Hainan. Beyond that, we are in the dark, so you have some searching to do, but we do have info rolling in from local operatives every few days. Check back; we may have more for you by tomorrow."

Michael looked around, apparently ready to adjourn the meeting. He rose, and the others followed suit.

"Well, that's that, then. Be ready—I will get everyone back here when we get more info. Until then, keep each other in the loop and, in the meantime..." he winked at the assembled host and Abe, "I'm going to go see a dragon about a man."

Chapter 13

The Buick GL8 lurched to an uneasy stop outside of the Peninsula Hotel, and Jonah stepped down from the driver's seat thankful to be on solid ground. Jonah didn't drive often, and due to the rental restrictions in Hong Kong, he had to be the one to pilot the van to the city where they were picking up the other ARC members. Being in the heavy traffic had rattled him, and he was thankful to be done driving for now. Rags hopped out of the passenger side and immediately began to tease his young friend. "Your driving is much improved, Jonah. I salute you on your creative application of the brake pedal combined with the windscreen wiper."

"Look, Rags, you know I don't drive often. That's why you drive the truck, remember? I much prefer to walk or use my bicycle, as you well know. But," he said, grabbing the keys and handing them to the valet, "we made it in one piece, did we not?" He took the ticket from the young porter and bid the angel, "Come on, let's go see what this is all about."

They stepped through the massive glass doors into the first five-star hotel Jonah had ever been in; a place that he could only describe as *obnoxiously palatial*. He had never been in a space as expansive as the lobby of this establishment, and it seemed incredibly wasteful to him. They walked, approaching the elevator bank that Raguel said would be used to transport the party down to meet them.

That's funny, Jonah thought, looking at the ashtrays placed prominently throughout the area, *I've seen this on television, but never thought I would see it in real life*. What he was referring to was the stamped sand in each ashtray, perfectly imprinted with the logo of the Peninsula Hotel. Jonah wondered if there were workers hiding away somewhere, just waiting to come and re-stamp after a careless smoker ruined the effect with the ashtray's original and intended purpose. The thought made him smile at the absurdity. *It's ludicrous what some people find important*, he thought, derisively.

"Here. We can wait here. They should be down any minute." Raguel directed his friend to a lush white and green sofa made of some unknown, but Jonah was certain, *very expensive* material. He sat patiently in the hotel lobby while an impatient Rags paced back and forth nearby. Jonah had asked Rags why he was always so agitated when he came to the city. Rag's answer had saddened Jonah.

Rags told him, "You asked because you care, and I admire that about you, Jonah. You always think of others before yourself, and that's rare. That you would be concerned for the well-being of a person—creature," Rags corrected himself, "that technically could not have anything wrong with them says a lot about you. Much in the same way that the Master cannot abide certain things, I cannot abide the perversions and injustices in society without it harming my spirit." As Raguel spoke, his face became taut.

That caused Jonah to ask, "Is it that much worse for you here than, say, back in the village?" Jonah imagined it was, simply because the population density made it more likely that Rags would come up against that which he detested much more often.

"Yes—but it may not be for the reason that you suspect," the angel said, knowingly. "What you must remember is that cities are not bad things—not in and of themselves, anyway." Rags looked like he was struggling for the right way to explain, but he continued. "It was always the Master's plan that man would build and dwell in cities, but not the way you currently experience them. See, the plan was for men to live in small groups first, and it would be there that they would discover how to help and look out for one another. It would be an ingrained behavior and a passed-on character trait to future dwellers that would ensure each community's success, and then, eventually, they would be ready to expand."

"So, what happened?" Jonah was genuinely curious about what went wrong.

"I'm afraid you also know the answer to that question, but it may not occur to you, because of its simplicity. The Fallen were the beginning of the end of everything the Master had intended, including this. When the Fallen took humans as mates, it was a selfish and lowly act, the likes of which had not existed before. That lustful act begat other selfish deeds and, from there—well, you know what the world is like now. I don't have to paint you a picture."

Raguel looked sad, but there was more to Jonah's answer, so he pushed on. "That wasn't the end of it, in actuality. Yes, the original plan of community and togetherness came undone, and in cities you can still see the fallout of that now. However," a flicker of hope danced in the angel's eyes, "we are seeing a return to a semblance of what was originally intended. Outside of the cities, in rural areas, where the population is sparse and neighbors must work together to make their lives prosperous, that's where we see it. Values such as family, faith, hard work, honesty, and simplicity, which you and your family display so well to others, are helping the community make a comeback.

"No," Rags said, sighing, "I don't see it in the big city. But," he looked at his young friend intently, "I do see it in *you*... and in Rachel. In Mai. Even in Rou, as young as she is. I see it in the way that you all come together for a baby's well-being. I see it in the farms and houses that surround you, and I see it across your countryside. I hate coming to the city, it's true—I hate seeing the women sell themselves, knowing it is just to feed an infant or an infirm parent at home. I hate seeing the stall merchants traffic in endangered, innocent creatures, knowing that it is just to keep food on their tables. I hate seeing the disgustingly rich victimize the poor and the ignorant and the desperate with drugs and crime.

"Yes," the angel said, gravely, "I hate the city. I long for the day when your work and the work of all of your villagers, everywhere, has finally come to fruition and people start to care about each other again, like they should. Does that answer your question?"

"Yes, and… thank you, Rags. I only hope that your faith in what we are capable of does not go unrealized." Jonah felt the burden that Raguel's expectations placed on him and his mother, as well as his kids and villagers.

Rags suddenly rose, smiling, and spoke exuberantly. "That's just it, Jonah. Don't ever assume that you have to do it alone. I mean, we don't, do we? We have ARC and people like you, and Peter, and others that have taken up our cause. It's the same with what you are trying to do. Just be yourself and that shining example—others will follow. Out of small endeavors grow… well, cities." The angel laughed and Jonah joined him. He felt better knowing that others would come alongside them and help build out the communities that would change the world for the better for his friend.

"Rags, why don't you tell me more about the large dog you saw the other night?" Jonah asked him in order to get his mind off his surroundings.

"It wasn't a dog, really. It was a hound—a *hellhound* to be exact. Are you familiar with the Three Sisters? No, why would you be. Anyway, hellhounds aren't dogs, exactly, but I like to taunt them with *dog* when I encounter them. I must admit though, it has been a dog's age since I last saw one." He elbowed Jonah in the side as he snickered and said, "Get it? A *dog's age*?"

Jonah laughed along with his friend, glad that he had made him feel better if only for a moment.

"I really don't understand why there is one in the forest near the village, though," said Jonah.

Rags sighed again, "I think that we will find your question answered today. The hound was hunting. They feed off souls, you know. They usually stalk their prey for days, making them afraid of their own shadow, before they finally kill them. The fear is supposed to make them more delicious to eat. Which is another odd thing." The Angel of Justice looked perplexed. "Jian was scared, but he was still functional, so I am not sure why this hellhound was after him. The only thing I can think of is that it was really weak. They have to hunt regularly, or they can get out of control. This one was in control, but only just."

The pair looked up as the elevator chimed and opened. Out of the elevator stepped two beautiful women and three men. They were all smiling, and the youngest man in the group was blushing furiously.

"Well, I *do* speak Chinese, but it's Mandarin. She was speaking Cantonese, and I didn't know that I was sitting in the wrong area. She just kept flapping her arms wildly. I thought it was some kind of dance," Peter said, defending himself. "I didn't know that she had just cleaned that area and was closing it for the night."

"If that man had not come and explained, you would probably still be watching her dance, Peter." Paul had found the whole thing rather humorous, especially since he could understand the girl perfectly. Odd, because Max didn't know Cantonese, but Paul did. *When they make you over, they are very thorough,* Paul thought. "She was trying to get out of there, and you were making her table dirty all over again. She had just spent the last forty-five minutes cleaning it."

"Don't be too hard on yourself, honey." Naomi looked sympathetic for Peter, and he brightened, "I definitely think the tip made up for it. It disappeared with a quickness," Naomi said with a grin and a giggle. She took the young man's arm and put it in hers, pulling him toward where the other two waited.

As they approached, Raguel grabbed Sam and said in a curt tone, "Let's get out of here now."

Sam lost the grin but nodded his assent. The others all stopped talking and looked first at Rags, then at Sam in turn, bewildered. Jonah took the opportunity to introduce himself while it was quiet.

"My name is Jonah, and this is Rags. Please excuse my friend's rude behavior. The city is not his favorite place to be. He is much more comfortable in the country at the orphanage. Please, follow me, and we'll get going."

Jonah was a soft spoken man and very patient, which is good when working with a hot-tempered angel. The others relaxed, and one by one introduced themselves to Jonah and Rags who merely nodded at each in turn. "Rags, what do you say to them?" Jonah asked him, like he would one of his children.

Rags rolled his eyes and said, "Sorry to be so curt. We are glad to have you here." His duty done, he turned to Jonah and said, "Can we go now?"

Jonah sighed and nodded. "Yes, we can go." He spoke to the assembled newcomers. "Follow me, please."

They followed along after Jonah and Rags, and Paul was able to study the big angel as they walked. He had been watching him ever since they had stepped off the elevator. He was bigger than Sam, and where Sam had a lighter complexion, Rags was dark with jet black hair. He strode with a purpose, and as Paul watched him, Rags opened and closed his fists in agitation. Jonah wasn't kidding when he said that Rags didn't like the city.

As they strode down the street, a child no older than five or six quickly reached the group and, sizing up Peter as a likely target, started to beg for money from him. He held up a little bowl and kept pushing it in his direction. Paul watched as Rags stopped moving, turned his head in the direction of the nearest alley, and peered intently. He just caught the head as it disappeared into the alleyway. Rags then turned and went back to the boy as Peter was getting ready to give him some money.

"Save your money, Peter. The child will not get to keep it." The Rags that only moments before looked ready to pounce on the world, knelt down in front of the child. He turned to run away but Rags grabbed a hold of his arm, gently. Jonah started to move toward Rags and the child when the angel held up his hand to stop him.

Paul was amazed to watch the interaction between the angel and the child. Paul listened intently as Rags asked the child about his family and what his favorite things were, in perfect Cantonese.

The conversation was not long, but in the span of a few moments, the two were fast friends.

Rags turned and held out a hand to the little boy. "Jonah, we have one more for dinner tonight."

"What about his master? Do you think he will protest us taking him?"

Paul watched Rags' head swivel towards the alley. The head had popped back out and was watching the party. Rags bent down to the child once again and asked him to wait with the group. He dropped his hand and walked to where the man was standing in the alley. A slight exchange between the two and then, as quick as a striking serpent, Rags' hand shot out and grabbed the man by the front of his shirt. A startled yelp left the man's throat. Paul could not hear what was being said, but he understood the intimidation and the threat that was in the offing. The color drained from the man's face as he clutched Rags' hands which were still anchored firmly on his shirt. He saw the man say something to Rags and the hands let him go. The man turned and disappeared from sight. Rags watched him walk away and turned back to the others.

He came back and held his hand out to the child and said, "Everyone ready?" Without waiting for a response, he and the child started walking, the two of them chatting as if they were long time friends. Sam stepped up next to Paul, shaking his head.

"He's an enigma. He can be the hardest angel one minute and then…" he gestured towards the child. "It's what makes him the best for his chosen role, but it is also the hardest on him in return."

Paul looked over at Sam. "He is not bitter about the cards life has dealt him?" Paul asked.

That angel may not be bitter, but I am, and I know it. Paul felt shame for what he knew to be miserable self-pity, and Sam looked sidelong at him, tsking and smiling at the same time. It was a wistful smile, one that had some sadness behind it, and Paul realized that Sam was feeling bad for his circumstances as one who had *been* there, not just someone who imagined what it was like to lose a love like he had lost in Maggie. Sam had lost his wife to his only son's treachery. He had been hurt at least as much as Max had. Sam picked up their conversation again after the two walked silently, in solidarity, for a minute.

"We have learned over time that our roles in this world are important. We may not always like them, but we are designed to complete what we have been chosen to do. Humans are lucky, comparatively."

"How so?' Paul wondered.

"You have free will, don't you? You get to choose which side to be on. You choose whether or not to take the moral high road, or to stoop into the pits of hell itself, or even do nothing.

If you choose not to decide, you still have made a choice. The old song lyric came back to Paul, and it seemed appropriate.

"Look, Paul, whatever it is that Lev Avatov is up to in that cave, it is not pleasant. He has chosen a path that will end in his destruction, and it's by his own making. He is messing with forces that he knows nothing about."

Paul looked over at Sam and said in a quiet voice, "I know exactly how Lev operates, he has no obligation to anyone but himself. As a matter of fact, I am sure that Lev thinks he has thought of a way to get what he wants and not be obligated to anyone in return. He is a master at deception and betrayal." Paul's face had taken on the look of granite, and his voice had turned to steel, just as Max's had always done in the past, but it was weird coming from the person that now talked to Sam. Paul looked up straight into the eyes of Maggie. Her expression had turned to worry, and as quickly as the anger had surfaced, it was gone with just one look from her.

Sam grinned, "That was a neat trick."

"What?" Paul said distractedly.

"The *Maggie-Melts-Stone,* thing" Sam said grinning wider. Sam could see the blush creeping over Paul and could not help laughing at his friend's expense.

Paul started to say something to Sam, but was interrupted by

Maggie, who said, "Are you guys okay back here?" The two men looked over at Maggie as she started walking with them a few paces behind the others.

"Ah, yes," Paul started. "We were discussing morals and obligations in society and the need to protect widows and orphans." Sam raised an eyebrow. Paul went on, "I was telling Sam that I think there are some people in society that, instead of trying to solve problems, they just try to find a way around them. Then they use that to their own advantage."

Maggie nodded thoughtfully. "I have seen a lot of that in history, although I feel that society has brought that on itself," she said.

"Oh? In what way?" Paul asked her, intrigued.

Maggie sighed. "Society thinks that everything has to be fair and just. Unfortunately, life is not fair or just, as Rags can probably attest. There is a balance to the Earth, and just like in the fairy tales, there are good and evil sides to society. The evil side is surreptitious. Insidiously, it leaks into our everyday, right under the noses of most people. They rarely look past their own personal space, so they can't see the evil that is around them."

Paul was impressed with the insight behind what Maggie was telling him and wanted to hear more about it, so he pressed her a little further. "I think I get what you are telling me, but can you give me an example?"

Maggie smiled. "Sure. Well, most recently... social media. This was a platform that was supposed to connect everyone, right? Keep you up to date on family or that friend you had in school, let you know of events in your area, stuff like that. If it was used for that purpose alone, it would be great. However, there's a darker side—people who use it for sale of illicit material, sex traffickers, pedophiles, scamming the public, political rhetoric, bullying—all kinds of bad stuff, and those were just some. We look over those things or hide them from our site in order to not have to deal with them ourselves. It doesn't mean they go away, they just don't exist in our personal bubbles. So you see, we humans can take a great thing and distort it into something nefarious without much effort. Most people don't know about a lot of those things, but I am certain that there have been more than a few that have experienced it first hand." Maggie sighed as if her statement weighed her down.

"I agree with you wholeheartedly, Maggie," Paul said.

Sam nodded and said with a grin, "That's why we need more Maggies in the world."

Jonah was standing by the rental, and he beckoned them all to get a move on. They all found their way into the van. Paul sat close enough to Rags and the boy that he could hear their conversation. It turns out that the boy's name was Neo, and he ended up with the man from the alley after his sister was taken. His parents had been killed and his sister was raising him. She had gone to the market one day and never returned. Neo wanted to find her and went into the city. The man from the alley tricked Neo and told him that he knew where his sister was. Neo had followed him, but the man told Neo that he would never see his sister again unless he did what he told him. Paul could see that the boy was close to tears and that Rags was about to blow his top. Paul reached out and tapped the boy, gently, to get his attention. Smiling, he asked the boy in perfect Cantonese, if he knew where the man was keeping his sister. The boy nodded that he knew, but that she would be moved in a couple of days. He had overheard the man making arrangements for a group of girls to be moved to the caves.

"What caves, Neo? Do you know? What else did the man say?" Paul asked gently. Neo shook his head. "Did he mention a city at all?" he tried again. Neo looked thoughtful for a moment, and then brightened a bit.

"Haikou," he said with excitement. Paul looked over at Rags who was watching him.

"At least we have a starting point." Paul shrugged his shoulders. To Neo, he said, "Xiè xiè nǐ."

The boy smiled and, very cheekily said, "You're welcome," in heavily accented English, making Paul laugh out loud.

"I think your name should mean *Scamp*, not *Gift*." Paul told him, wiping the mirth from his eyes.

Rags thumped the boy on the back. "Well done, my young friend. Paul and I will make a plan to get your sister back." Rags gave Paul a meaningful glance. "But for now, you will need to stay with Jonah until that can be arranged. Okay with you?"

Neo nodded and a few minutes later was sound asleep against Rags' side.

"You know I have to help him, right?" Rags said softly to Paul, trying hard not to disturb the sleeping youth.

"I know," came Paul's reply. "You know I have to help you, right?"

Rags nodded his understanding, and the two fell silent for the rest of the ride.

Chapter 14

The troupe finally pulled into the parking lot of the orphanage, and after filing out of the bus, Jonah showed them around and introduced them to the children. Neo was welcomed into the class with the other children and had already made a few friends.

Now that they had everything else settled, they made their way into the kitchen where they found Jonah's mom feeding an infant. She was talking to the baby as he was eating, and every few minutes he would wave his arms at her with happiness.

"How is he doing?" Jonah asked her as he bent over and kissed the top of her head.

"He is doing just fine. One thing is for sure, what he lacks in one area he makes up for in others. This baby can eat," she said, smiling at the burp that came from the infant at just that moment.

"Everyone, this is my mother, Rachel. Mom this is Peter, Maggie, Naomi, Paul, and Sam. They are here from the states, and Rags and I have been asked to help them out while they are here." He gave his mom a meaningful look.

She said, "Ah, yes. Well, the children and I will not be in the way then." She and the baby got up from the table, and as she was leaving the kitchen she said, "It was nice to meet you all. My son and Rags will take very good care of you while you are here. If they don't you just let me know, and I will box their ears." She smiled and, cooing to the infant, made her way out the door.

"Can she do that?" Peter asked the room.

"Do what, Peter?" Sam said.

"Box an angel's ears?" Peter questioned.

"Oh she can and has," Rags said as he pulled on his right ear.

"Wow, I travel all the way to China, and there is another Momma Rose waiting for me."

They all laughed at Peter and settled in around the table. Jonah went to the stove in the corner, and from a big pot he began to ladle rice into a waiting bowl. From another pot on the stove he spooned out mixed vegetables, and from the last pot he spooned out some kind of meat. The aromas were wonderful with a spicy scent that made Paul's mouth water.

Jonah brought all the food to the table along with some small bowls and tiny pitchers with sauces in them. He placed chopsticks on the table and asked if anyone needed a fork instead. Paul wasn't surprised when Peter raised his hand.

"I'll take a fork please. I never did learn to use chopsticks."

Jonah nodded and handed a fork to Peter. Once everything was settled, Jonah sat and said to his guests, "It is not much, but it should be filling." Jonah said a small blessing of thanks for the food and told everyone to help themselves.

Paul was amazed once again at the camaraderie that came with this group of people. Even Jonah, who they didn't really know, seemed to fit right in. The conversation came easily, and the laughter was plentiful.

Paul as Max Avatov had not grown up in a conventional family. After his mother disappeared, he had looked forward to the days Lev was out of town or out on business. Those were the days he was not subjected to cold stares or being ignored. He was expected to act a certain way, and he learned early on that the punishment for failure was brutal and swift. He had found it hard to relax even when Lev was gone, because Lev had people who reported on his every move. If he so much as sneezed wrong Lev knew about it. His only respite was when he was at school. Lev had sent Boris with him though, and much of what he did in college was reported back to Lev. It was more relaxed though, and that was where he met Leclerc.

Paul was shaken out of his memories by a question. "So what exactly are we looking for?" Peter had asked out loud.

"Well, we have it on good authority that Neo's sister is headed for Haikou. We can try to find out some information about that," Jonah supplied.

"Yes, that will be something to look into, but that is not the reason that we came all this way. We need to find out which cave Lev is hiding in," Sam said. "Our ultimate goal is to find him and stop whatever it is that he is trying to do. Now there is an added element."

They all looked at Sam expectantly, but it was Rags that continued the conversation. "A couple of days ago I found something that should not be here in China—or anywhere on this plane really."

That statement caught Peter's attention. He placed his fork on his plate and asked, "What was it, and why would it not be on this plane? Was it an alien or a monster?"

Sam put a hand on Peter's shoulder in order to make the rapid fire questions stop. "He will finish if you let him."

Peter grinned sheepishly, "Sorry, continue."

Rags took a breath and said, "I came across a hellhound out in the forest hunting a nearby villager."

Peter sucked in a breath, "Wicked," was all he said.

Rags nodded in agreement and continued, "Yes, pure evil."

"Oh, no. I meant that the hellhound was cool," Peter said by way of explanation.

"No he, actually I think it was female, anyway they are burning hot, not cool at all."

"Ah, never mind." Peter shrugged at Sam as Rags continued his story.

"I was able to save the villager from certain death and battled the hellhound for the village. We fought for a while before an opening arose. I was able to deal it a severe blow, but not without some injury myself. The dog disappeared with its tail between its legs."

Paul could see the artistic wheels turning in Peter's head. There would be a hellhound design in the future.

"If I was lucky, the dog did not make it back to where it's master awaited; however, we can't rely on that, so we will need to guard ourselves against attacks from a hellhound and possibly a demon or three," Rags finished nonchalantly.

"A demon—or three?" Maggie asked.

"We think that there may be more than one demon working with Lev."

Paul shivered at the thought. Lev was dangerous enough without adding three demons and a hellhound to the mix.

"Where did you last see the hellhound?" Paul asked.

Rags turned to him. "In the forest near here. Poachers like to use that route to smuggle animals into the Chinese black market. Many Chinese traditions and medical practices come from black market purchases."

"Which way did the creature go when it left you?" Paul was thinking that they could follow its trajectory and maybe find a cave or something in which Lev could hide.

"It went to the southwest. I was too banged up to follow."

"What is southwest from here?" Maggie chimed in following Paul's logic.

"Pretty much the coastline on both sides. There are some national parks located through the middle and a lot of trees and woodlands," Jonah told them.

"Enough cover for a wounded hellhound to make it back to its lair?" Peter asked.

"More than enough," Jonah answered him.

"How about any cave structures or mountains in the area?" Maggie suggested.

"That place is full of mountains. As far as caves are concerned, there are some old volcanic tunnels from the Haikou volcano in Hainan province. It is very touristy though. I can't see them making their camp there. Although they do not have the whole tunnel system mapped out. There could be some tunnels that are uncharted," Jonah told them.

"Okay, that is a starting point. We should go check that out tomorrow," Maggie said to the group.

"If you go, Mags, it's gonna have to be without me. I have to put in an appearance at the awards banquet," Peter told her.

"Yes, and I have to meet with the curator of the museum that we are negotiating with," Paul chimed in.

"Well, then I guess Sam, Naomi, and I will have to play the tourist without you," Maggie said sticking out her tongue at Peter. Paul felt a spurt of jealousy at the easy friendship the two shared.

"Okay, but don't go getting yourself into trouble. This is not the place for that," Peter told her.

"Yes, Dad," she said mockingly, and Naomi giggled. "Sam what do you say to a little tourism at the local parks?" Maggie asked him with a smirk.

Sam cleared his throat. "It sounds like so much fun, I can't wait."

"Awe, don't be like that Sam. Maybe we will find an adventure waiting for us," Maggie told him as he rolled his eyes at her. "Perhaps we will run into another hellhound," she told him without concern.

Sam's face turned serious. "Maggie, hellhounds are serious creatures. If given the opportunity they will kill you and suck out your soul. You had better hope that you never meet one. They do not give second chances, and they do not show mercy."

Maggie threw up her hands, "Okay, Sam—I get it, the dogs are bad news, which is why we need you to protect us." She smiled a smug little smile as he blew out an exasperated breath.

"You know, we have a lot of patience, but you are definitely trying mine." His actions tempered his words when he threw his arm around her shoulders and led her and Naomi from the room.

Peter and Paul watched the threesome leave the room. "I guess that leaves just the two of us," Peter said with a grin.

Paul frowned. "Do you think they will be okay? I mean, Maggie likes to get into trouble. Are you not worried that she will find some?"

It was Peter's turn to frown. "How do you know that Maggie gets into trouble? You don't even know her, really." Peter waited for Paul's answer.

"It is obvious from her past magazine articles about Lev Avatov that she goes looking for trouble, and we both know that Lev Avatov is trouble. He will not forgive or forget easily. No, I assume that he will be out for blood, and if they go looking in the wrong places they may find what they are not prepared to find."

Peter thought about this for a moment and then smiled. "You forgot one important thing, my friend."

"Oh, what is that, Peter?" Paul said with a smirk.

"You forgot that they have Sam with them. He won't let anything bad happen to them. It sometimes comes in handy that you hang around with the angel of Death."

"I wouldn't say that too loudly, Peter." Jonah had come to join the conversation. "The angels are well-known to some of us, but others should not be privy to this information."

Raguel joined in the conversation as well. "We are only known to some, Peter, our existence here depends on us keeping ourselves a secret."

"I still don't understand that though," Peter told Rags.

The big angel frowned and asked, "What don't you understand, Peter?"

"I understand about the angel war and the Watchers being cast out, but that was centuries ago. Why do you not show yourselves now? Surely the human race could use a little extra faith?"

Rags just shook his head. "The human race are imperfect beings who do not learn from past mistakes. They continue to make the same mistakes and conveniently forget the past. It is the reason wars happen; civilly and on a global scale. It is also the reason that slavery still exists in the world today. Man's moral compass is skewed. What was once wholly man was corrupted by evil, and after many generations later it has only gotten worse. Could you imagine what man would do with magic, alchemy, or knowledge of the heavens?"

He looked at Peter, and Peter could see the hurt in his eyes.

"I'm sorry, Rags. Sometimes my tiny human brain can't see the big picture, and my ever increasing foot ends up in my gigantic mouth," Peter said by way of apology.

Rags looked down at Peter's feet and said, "Your feet don't look any bigger than they had a moment ago. Sometimes I don't understand humans."

The three humans laughed.

"What?" Rags looked thoroughly confused. His confusion made the others laugh all the more.

Paul slapped him on the shoulder. "Do not worry about Peter my friend. His feet will remain on the ground for the time being, but we need to get to the city—me to the museum and Peter to his banquet."

Rags looked worried until Jonah said, "Don't worry—I'll take them. In the meantime, why don't you see if you can find any sign of that hellhound?"

Rags nodded and with a new purpose left without a backward glance.

"Bye, no really we'll be okay…" Peter said in a sarcastic tone, "What is his problem? One minute he's Chatty Kathy and the next he is, well, gone."

"Rags cannot stand going into the cities. You saw what happened earlier today." When Peter and Paul nodded Jonah continued. "When Rags goes into the cities he feels all the atrocities, he sees all the injustices, and he cannot stand them. As the Angel of Justice he has a hard time letting bad things happen. He is not allowed to interfere too much with the lives of humans, so he tries to stay out of situations where he feels compelled to interfere."

"Now this morning makes complete sense. When he came across Neo, I wondered why he took a particular interest in him. He knew what was happening to him and his sister and chose to get the boy out of that situation," Paul told Peter and Jonah.

"It's twofold, though," Peter added. "Neo said that his sister was missing too. I bet when they track her down they will find others like her or maybe even find Lev, since this is one of his deranged proclivities. If that is the case then I feel for whoever Maggie finds with those girls. She and Naomi would probably be the best ones to send into that situation; both of them have more experience with that than either one of us."

Paul couldn't help but agree, but it didn't mean he had to like it. He got up from the table, excusing himself, and went to find Sam outside.

"Hey, bud. How are you holding up?" Sam asked him, sympathetic.

"Better than expected, I guess. Keeping the old me at bay is a challenge, but I will manage."

Paul sat down on the bench where Sam had perched, and Sam turned to him. "So, I gotta ask—since when is Lev a scientist?"

Paul smirked and turned to the angel. "He is not. Like many other things in Lev's life, I suppose he required complete control over his experiments. He trusts no one, and I guess he must have learned over the years from the real scientists he worked with to do what he is doing now. Also," Paul cringed a bit, "the science is not so difficult when you are not following any sort of ethics or worrying about loss of life or harm. He is a monster who plays with his chemistry set; nothing more."

"Gotcha." Sam decided to change the subject. "You know, there's nothing saying that you and Maggie couldn't click now."

Paul just laughed bitterly. "Sam, I appreciate what you are trying to do, believe me, but I do not think that I could be with my Maggie as Paul. It would require dishonesty from me, and I am not willing to lie to the woman I love any more than I already am."

"You're looking at this all wrong, Max, and here's why. You are dealing with a past that, technically, no longer exists. Max Avatov is no longer your reality, or your identity. Anything you told Maggie going forward, provided it has to do with Paul, is the complete truth. You have his memories, his skills, his personality, etcetera, bro. You *are* him, and in that, you can't be false—so, go for it. She seems to dig you."

They were interrupted by Peter and Jonah and the slamming of the screen door. Paul just got up from the bench without looking at Sam.

Grabbing his stuff, he said gruffly, "Come—the sooner we go, the sooner we can return."

Peter nodded and the three men left to travel the distance to the city.

Chapter 15

Pharzy walked through the tunnel on a mission to find Lillith. Tsoula had told her some disturbing news before being banished back to the pit. If what Tsoula said was true, and Pharzy knew it was, then they needed to be exceedingly careful with their activities in the future. She rounded the next corner and bumped into something solid. She backed up a few paces in surprise, and when she saw that it was one of Lev's snake people, she struck out and grabbed it by its scaly throat.

"Tell me where your master and the others are now. I hope I don't look like a patient woman to you, because, trust me, I'm not," she told it, slightly tightening her death grip for emphasis.

The young Naga pawed frantically at the hand that gripped her, then stopped and nodded, fear emanating from it's young eyes.

Pharzy loosened her grip so the Naga could speak. It was a female, Pharzy discovered. *The clothes she's wearing are so ill-fitting that no one would be able to tell what she was... I must speak to Lev about dressing his minions better,* she thought.

"Massster isss down there. He isss ssshowing off hisss newessst accomplisssshment."

The exaggerated hiss in her tone told Pharzy that she spoke the truth. She shook the Naga and said, "You'd better not be lying to me, and in future you had better watch where you are going, or you may not run into someone as nice as I have been." She threw the young Naga to the side like a piece of trash and heard it's cry of pain. Pharzy smiled at the sound and continued down the tunnel in the direction indicated. She heard the raised voices before she saw anyone.

"So, this serum that I've concocted is, like any other, just blood plasma and some fibrinogens, but I believe this will prove to be the most potent yet, due in no small part to the donor of the materials. While it's true that we have tried different syntheses in the past, we have never tried working with a serum that is so…" Lev searched for the word, then smiled, "volatile."

"Yes, yes—get on with it." Ono was getting bored, and Lilith shot her a warning glance.

"Ignore her, darling. Please, continue—this is fascinating."

"Indeed. Thank you, Lilith." Lev continued, "It should give the subject the ability to regenerate cells at an accelerated rate, while at the same time providing stability and a certain level of resistance in the host. This increased viability allows for a more natural metamorphic contingent to materialize and ultimately a favorable prognosis of genetic symbiosis." Lev finished, seeming very pleased with himself.

Pharzy spoke as she polished her nails on the front of her jacket, "So many ten dollar words, little man. Can we get that in English, please?"

Lev looked at Lilith and smiled wryly. He bent slightly and looked Pharzy directly in her eyes, emphasizing the simplicity of what he was about to impart. "Pharzy, I am hoping that they will live longer and be stronger."

"Impressive," Lilith cooed at Lev. "When would this serum be ready?" she asked him.

"As soon as I am brought a subject robust enough to endure the testing, or maybe slightly after that." His earlier excitement had turned to frustration. "I am almost there, but there is something in the serum that is eluding me."

Pharzy watched as Lilith ran her hand down Lev's head in an affectionate stroke.

"I know, baby. It's very frustrating for you." Lilith's hand fell to Lev's shoulder and was joined by her other in a steady massage of the muscles in his neck. His head fell back, and he groaned with pleasure.

Pharzy wrinkled her lip at the display and chose that moment to interrupt. "Tsoula had some news." She said it without preamble.

"Oh, and what did the bitch have to say?" Ono said from her perch on the countertop. She smiled in Pharzy's direction. She knew it irritated Pharzy when she spoke about Tsoula that way. "Did she eat too much and get sick again?"

Pharzy marched over to Ono and smacked her across the face. The slap rang out across the room and gained the attention of everyone.

"You dare mock her when she brings you grave news? I have killed for less than this, you know." Pharzy's face had gotten really close to Ono's shocked one.

"You know I didn't mean anything by it, but if you insist on a challenge, sister, I'm game." Ono jumped off the counter while pushing Pharzy in the chest, causing her to lose her balance and fall to the cave floor. As Ono came forward and Pharzy was getting up off the floor to meet her, Lilith stepped smoothly between the fighting sisters, holding a hand out on either side of her body.

"Ladies, as much fun as it is to watch you two go at it, I am on a schedule, and whatever grudges you have will have to wait until we are finished here."

Lilith dropped her hands when she saw that the two had relaxed their stances. Pharzy was brushing off her skirt and Ono had resumed her position on the counter top. Lilith tapped her stiletto on the ground waiting for Pharzy to spill her secret. When she could take no more, she shouted, "For the love of Abbadon, Pharzy, will you tell us what is so important?"

Pharzy finished brushing a non-existent piece of lint from her skirt and said, "Tsoula battled an angel earlier tonight." She waited a moment for the explosion she knew would come, and she didn't have a long wait.

"*What*?!" Lilith and Ono said in unison.

"Where is she? Get her here right now, Pharzy. Does she know who it was?" Lilith had practically screamed the last question at her.

Pharzy shook her head.

"I can't. She was mortally wounded, and if I had not banished her back to the pit she would have died."

"At least tell me that she killed that angel?" Lilith asked. Her voice had gotten really cold and low.

"She dealt him a blow as well, but she didn't feel it would finish him. She thought to warn us about his presence before we were caught unaware." Pharzy knew that this would not placate Lilith, and she was glad for once that the hellhound was not around to feel Lilith's wrath.

"Well, did she tell you where she was when she encountered this angel?"

"In a little village just past the nature preserve. Not on the island. She did everything I asked, Lilith." Pharzy said, defensively. "She had marked the man she had seen earlier, and she was tracking him when the host found her. She told me she had the farmer cornered in a field without any fuss, and that's when the stupid angel chose to intervene."

Lilith did not look pleased. As a matter of fact, she looked murderous, and Pharzy began to worry for her pet. She spoke quickly, almost pleadingly, "She didn't know he was an angel, Lilith. He was dressed like a human and—"

"Seriously, Pharzy? That's no excuse. We know that the host disguise themselves—"

"Yeah, but she was fainting with hunger. She was focused solely on her prey."

Pharzy was hoping this was enough to stem the punishments that were sure to come Tsoula's way at a later date. Lilith started to pace, indicating to the sisters that she was thinking about what needed to be done next. The noise of her heels on stone was grating on Pharzy's nerves. With every *clack* her heels made, Pharzy would squeeze her fists. Lilith finally turned and looked straight at Pharzy.

"When will Tsoula be able to answer questions?"

Pharzy blinked at the turn of conversation. "She took a mortal wound, Lilith. I'm not sure she even made it back in time."

"Go find out, then let me know. We need to plan. In her wounded state, I'm sure the dog missed something. If she is holding anything back, Pharzy, she will be dealt with. Tell her from me that if I find out she messed this up or left anything out, I will personally end her."

As much as Pharzy wanted to tell Lillith to stuff herself, she knew that it would end in pain. She acquiesced. She bowed her head and said, "Yes, Lillith," in front of a stunned Lev.

Lillith snapped her fingers, and a portal, almost like a rip in existence, appeared before Pharzy. She stepped through without hesitation, eager to be back with her hound and away from her sister. As soon as she walked through the temporal gash, it snapped shut like her hound's hungry jaws.

"Bitch. I'm tired of her and her orders," she mumbled to herself, like a petulant child. She took a few steps into a quite different atmosphere and surrounding than the one she had left. Where the underground facility was rocky, quiet, mossy, and dirty, the place where the rift had brought her was bright, and loud, and multicolored.

Pharzy made her way down a long golden corridor. *This is more like it*, she thought. *Gold everywhere—so pretty and shiny.* As she walked, she ran her fingers lightly over the jewel encrusted walls. The way the facets caught the available light and made colors dance on the walls and the floors made her giddy. They sparkled as she walked past them, little motes of light danced off of her translucent chiffon robes.

The *click-clack* of her heels on the hall floor played in time with the *click* of her nails as they grazed over each jewel she found along her way. She stopped mumbling about the injustices most recently done to her and decided to focus on how she would make Tsoula pay for them instead. Maybe she would demote her to the bottom of the pack for a while.

Pharzy was so far into her own thoughts, she didn't notice a young human boy, dressed as an acolyte, who had appeared from a side corridor into her path. She stopped suddenly and angrily, poised and ready to strike.

She exclaimed, "Who are you and who are you working for?"

The young boy froze, terrified for an instant, before he smiled icily and spoke in a voice that Pharzy recognized instantly.

"Where are you off to in such a hurry?"

Pharzy smiled a pleasant smile and turned slightly to confront her questioner. "An altar boy, Abbadon? That's sick, even for you. Are you attending a wedding, a funeral, or have you converted?" She plastered the confident smile on her face as she took in the demon in front of her.

He circled her slowly, twirling the little satin pillow that once housed the rings for a wedding. The little cherub smiled. "Definitely not converting—the wine is unpalatable. Ring bearer, actually. At a recent wedding. The entertainment for the evening was me with the priest in the closet of the rectory. I do so love when the pious fall."

He smirked, and in a blink, where once stood a young blond boy of seven or eight, there stood a very formidable, very tall demon, replete with fine golden scaly skin, horns of black and gold, and great wings that surrounded his body like a shroud.

Pharzy smiled. Out of all the other demons in the pit, Abbadon was her favorite plotter. No one in the history of ever had been so successful in winning high-profile victims to the depths of hell. From Cain to Jeffrey Epstein, his victims throughout history were legends. The mighty and the powerful and the famous—that was where Abbadon did his best work, and Pharzy could remember his greatest achievement, some 2,000 years ago, when he convinced Judas to turn his teacher over for sacrifice. It was a giant coup for the Association, and it had cemented Abbadon in the annals of their dark records as the demon to beat.

"I'm sure that turned out favorably for us?" Pharzy asked with no hesitation. She knew the answer already.

"Oh, of course it did. The bride was sobbing and blubbering mascara all over her Carolina Herrera, the groomsmen—who are all sitting in jail—put the priest in the hospital with multiple broken bones, the lad has not said anything since the priest first put his foul hands on him, and the mother is positively inconsolable. She blames the father, and the two have had an enormous fight. It. Was. Glorious. Plus," he inhaled deeply as if still on a high from the destruction he caused earlier in the evening, "it rained. How is your night going?" Abbadon asked.

As if he didn't already know, thought Pharzy. Abbadon busied himself, picking at a loose jewel in the wall. As the bright sapphire fell from the wall into his clutch, another appeared in its place.

Pharzy heard him say "*Jackpot*," then stuff the jewel in his pocket.

"Well, nice chatting with you," she said, eager to get going. The massive demon whirled quickly, bracing one scaly arm on the opposite wall, effectively blocking Pharzy from advancing down the hallway.

Abbadon playfully twirled at the demoness' hair with the other hand, cooing, "Leaving so soon, Pharzuph? I'm *sooo* bored… couldn't you dally just a scoche?" At the question, his true form disappeared and he took on the appearance of a very well-sculpted, very well-endowed, very erect, and very naked man. Pharzy raised one eyebrow appreciatively.

"Do you get CNN on that thing?" Pharzy smirked, looking down.

'It *is* newsworthy, isn't it?" the demon said, proudly. Pharzy stepped back and waved annoyingly.

"Put it away. I need to speak to Tsoula."

Abbadon morphed quickly into Pharzy, doubling the sexy demoness from head to pointed toe. "Well, you could sit here and talk to yourself," she giggled, "or you could talk to me." He morphed again into the little boy. "So, spill. What's the problem?" It was clear that Abbadon had all the time in the world, and he indeed was bored.

"Cute. She picked a fight with an angel, and I need to ask her a few more questions."

That got Abbadon's attention.

"I thought you guys were hanging out with that human, Lev—the one who almost killed Olivier," he said. "Where did Tsoula find an angel?"

Pharzy was not alarmed by his questions. Yet. She was sure that there would be more, and those—maybe those would be worrisome. Abbadon was not without power or influence, and he cut an impressive swath through the things that displeased him. That included demons at times, and Pharzy quickly explained to Abbadon all she knew about Tsoula's encounter with the angel.

"I must go to her and find out what else she knows before it's too late."

"Oh, I agree Pharzy, we must find out what your hound knows about this angel before it is too late. I take it she is recuperating here?"

"Most likely she will be in her hole. I do hope that someone has brought her something to eat. Maybe I should take her a little something. That would help her remember better, I feel."

Abbadon morphed again, this time into Barbara Eden's Jeannie, complete with harem pants and blonde ponytail. He was having fun, and Pharzy let him. Everyone knew what a pop culture fan Abbadon was, so they just rolled with it. He crossed his arms in trademark Jeannie fashion, nodded, and two servants appeared. They were inferior succubi that often did Abbadon's bidding, and they always appeared buxom, nude, and overly made up.

There's no accounting for taste, that's for sure, Pharzy thought.

"Girls, there's a hungry, hungry hellhound down in the catacombs. Please take a couple of those frat boys that you have stashed away—don't bother to lie to me—and present them to her."

They looked surprised and disheartened at the same time. He clapped and shouted thunderously, "*Now!*" They disappeared immediately, off to do what he commanded.

Pharzy was grateful. "Thanks. That should perk her up." She continued to walk with Abbadon in step next to her, now in the guise of a cardinal, complete with black cassock, a scarlet fascia, and a scarlet ferraiolo tied at the neck in a bow.

"So, how is the human coming with his little mission?"

"Lillith is taking care of the human. He is a persistent one and thinks that his small human mind has impressed Lillith. She is growing bored and will have to have a few men brought in for her pleasures, or she will break Lev Avatov. Maybe she will use him, but I'm not sure he will survive that."

"I will send her some slaves to keep her mind focused. I am interested, shall we say, in the formula that the human is working on. Be a dear and get it."

"How?" Pharzy asked the question, voice wavering just a second. She did not have the sway over Lev that her sister did, and Lilith seemed to have her own agenda—an agenda that was completely unrelated to what Abbadon wished. *Lilith could not care less about what he wants, but I will suffer for it.* "What I mean is, should I seduce him like Lilith? Should I work with him to produce it faster?"

"I don't care if you yank out his guts and play Dueling Banjos with his entrails, Pharzy. Just get it. You know how I punish those who fail me." His expression never wavered, and for the first time since Pharzy had bumped into him, she felt real fear.

"Calm, yourself Abbadon," she said with false confidence. "We're fully aware of all the costs of this venture. It has been too long for us, all of us, to be trapped in this pit. You shall have your serum. We will have our revenge." The rapture in her voice stirred something in Abbadon.

"Let's find your hound, sweets. We can gather the information we need, then we can make a plan—" He was cut off by one of the succubi materializing, hand poised and mouth open to pose a question. Annoyed, Abbadon assumed his full form for a moment, just long enough to slice the demoness' head cleanly from her body and watch her disappear in a blaze of brimstone. "... in private... before your return."

Pharzy smiled, but she was terrified. The great demon had a

reputation for being mercurial and capricious, but he was positively unhinged.

He would destroy all of us on a whim, she thought, uncertain of what her future held. *Stop this, dammit. You are Pharzuph, one of the Three. You have power in your own right, cunning and beauty, and ruthlessness to spare. You should not fear this one*, she willed herself to believe it, and immediately felt more at ease. *Plus*, she reminded herself, *you have the favor of Alaric, which is something Abbadon does not possess. You'll be fine*, she reasoned.

Abbadon was the greatest schemer of all time, so maybe there was a way to get the formula for the Chairman and get back at Lillith for being such a bitch.

"I think that is a wonderful idea."

She laid her hand on his scaly golden arm, and the two set off down the hallway, Pharzy running her fingertips across the jewel encrusted walls as before, a big smile of satisfaction on her face.

Chapter 16

As the van rolled away from the country orphanage, Naomi became aware of the scenery. It occurred to her that she wasn't aware of many places on Earth where one could simultaneously view volcanic and snowy mountains, dense forests, jungles, and a desert. Naomi looked around at the unfamiliar terrain, awestruck. Her thoughts wandered as she settled her gaze closer to the ground and the treeline broken up by small villages and farms. They had been driving for about an hour and had seen many ramshackle houses and working family farms along the way. Some of the views were breathtaking, while others were heartbreaking. Naomi noticed that while some plots of land contained what looked like rice or lotus, there were the odd plots that had fruit-bearing trees. The majority were small plots of some type of grain.

"What are they planting, Sam? Do you know?" Naomi asked him.

"Mostly they are given the opportunity to pick what to plant on their plots, however, the government can induce sharecropping whenever they choose, and usually it's a poor yield for the farmers and their families. The system is corrupt and unstable, and has been for decades. Usually, they are given wide berth in choosing equally horrible options." Sam told them. "It's tragic, really." He shook his head. "The CCP are forever building up their industrial plants at the expense of the farmers; the people who grow their food. I just don't get it. Those in charge do whatever they can to undercut and strip bare the very farms that sustain them, all the while polluting the ground and water that the plants need. China has a real problem with heavy metals and other poisons in the food."

Naomi looked back out the window and sighed. "That is sad."

They passed another farm. And another. And another. The rural areas of China were starting to grow on Naomi, and the small fields ripe with lotus blossoms made a beautiful picture. The flowers gave off a soft pink glow in the bright daylight. As they went, she could piece together the processes that the workers followed to get the lotus crops to market. The lotus cupule, which resembled a shower head, would be plucked and the seed shell stripped. Then the seed embryo would be removed. It was all incredibly labor-intensive and time-consuming. Indeed, they had been passing farms for hours and, knowing that the plants would have to be harvested in a 7-day time period, she knew that these farms would be active until late at night, workers getting what they could from the plant and handing it off to others to take off and be processed for the market. It all looked so ordinary to Naomi, just like many other family farms she had seen in the southern United States. It was hard to believe that these people might have been told that this is what they would have to do with the rest of their lives. Sam's voice, and a jolt as they left the paved road, broke her from her thoughts.

"We are getting closer to the village that holds the caves, ladies. Any idea what questions you might want to ask?" Sam called back over his shoulder from the driver's seat. "The villagers are open to having people tour the caves, but even they will stop talking if you get too nosy," he warned.

Maggie noticed that his eyes were on hers in the rearview mirror.

"Sam, you act like this is my first rodeo," Maggie stated. "I am an old pro at getting information."

Sam laughed at her confidence. "We'll see, Miss Big-Shot Journalist."

They bumped along down the dirt road, throwing up dust in the hot sun, for a few more minutes. Eventually, Sam stopped their rented car outside Rongtang Village in Shishan town.

"Here we are, ladies. This may be the first stop of many for our adventures today. Don't forget to tip your driver."

The girls laughed at Sam's humor, and they exited the back seats.

All three travellers picked up packs that held water, some food, and Maggie's camera equipment. Then, after paying a nominal fee to the caretaker, they were allowed to explore Fairy Cave. Sam led the way and the girls followed along behind him.

"What do we know about this cave system, Sam?" Maggie asked. She had been in her share of subterranean environments, and she didn't see anything special about their current location—other than what it had to with their mission. It was dank and mossy-smelling, a bit cold, and came with all of the requisite sounds. Sam spoke, and his voice reverberated off of the stone.

"If I'm right, this cave is very old and connects to one of the original lava tubes from the volcano." As they walked, he pointed out an offshoot on the far side of the cavern they were in. He continued, leading the girls through a large opening into another tunnel. "I would have to ask, but there are a couple of legends about this cave. They say there were small creatures that lived here that purportedly turned an entire village to stone, all because they wouldn't let two orphans attend a festival." The group emerged from the tunnels into another cavern, this one bedecked by rock formations above and below. Sam walked them to a formation that was about the height of a human and spoke. "Another is about a goddess that lived in the cave, Kuan Yin. This stalagmite is said to resemble her; *be* her."

Maggie looked down at the base of the oddly human-looking structure, and noticed paper, a bottle, and a few small boxes.

Offerings, she thought. "So, is it?" Maggie asked Sam's back as he looked on.

"Is it what, Red?"

"Is it her? Is it Kuan Yin?" Maggie's ever inquisitive mind needed to be fed, but Sam wasn't going to oblige.

"What makes you think I would know that?" Sam smirked and cocked an eyebrow at Maggie.

"I have my suspicions, Sam. Is it her?" Maggie repeated, and Sam could almost picture her thrusting a microphone in his face and accusing him.

"No idea."

Maggie shook her head, disappointed.

"C'mon, it's through here." Sam said, pulling the two away from the goddess-stalagmite and into the next series of tunnels. As they appeared to be coming to a place that was hosting more natural light, Sam shook his head and said, "I have never known a fairy to be...well, fair. Most of them are wily and will take advantage of those that aren't clever."

Naomi stopped and said, "Wait, what? Are you trying to tell me that fairies are real? Little small winged creatures that bestow magical abilities on people?"

Maggie looked at Naomi. "Seriously? After what you have been through in the last couple of months you can ask that question?"

Naomi thought about it a moment. "I guess you're right."

They emerged in a comparatively bright chamber, lit from a series of ducts in the very high stone ceiling. There was a large pool at one end where water seeped, and then fell, from a series of rocks in a wall. The cave did have a glow, Naomi noticed. A pretty bluish-green hue that came from the light pushing its way through some ice at the top as well as the water all around made tiny sparks of light dance all around them on the walls.

"Ladies, excuse me. I need to—" Sam screwed up his face, searching for the description he was looking for, then gave up. "Eh, you'll see in a minute. Chill here." And he was off.

Maggie and Naomi shrugged at each other and pulled the packs off of their backs, set them on the cave's fairly clean floor, and sat on them.

Naomi picked up their earlier conversation. "I haven't really processed everything that's happened over the last few months very well, Maggie. When Uncle Abe died, I think I closed up a little on the inside. I guess I figured if I didn't have to deal with his death, then I didn't have to accept that there are things that go bump in the night. There's no denying the world has gotten exponentially weirder since I met you all. I had a janky old vampire try to kill me and everything, but I'll tell you—" she turned to Maggie, smiling, "—it really has been a great time."

Maggie smiled and gave Naomi a sideways hug. "It's okay, girl. It took me a while to accept as well. After Max died, for a while there I didn't want to go on. I was out of fight, but Peter was relentless. He hounded me until I talked with Dr. Jo. She told me that I had some decisions to make—about what my life would look like going forward and where I could do the most good, just like Max had done. I decided that I was going to find Lev Avatov and make him pay for his crimes against humanity; and against Max."

Naomi stood, stretched her hands above her head and yawned, shaking her head and shoulders. She smiled back at Maggie. "Do you know what we both have in common?" she asked. Maggie shrugged her shoulders. "We both have Peter. If he hadn't been there for me while I was dealing with my uncle's death, I don't know what I would have done. Probably curled up in a ball somewhere."

"I know. It's not a stretch to say that I'm back with everyone because of him." Maggie suddenly got serious, getting up to face Naomi. "Naomi, you do know that Peter thinks of you as more than a friend, right?" Maggie asked with an arched eyebrow.

"I know, Mags. I'm just not sure what to do about it," Naomi said truthfully. "I really like Peter. He is definitely not my normal type, but he gets me, you know?"

Maggie giggled. "Yeah, I know what you are talking about. Max was that for me." Maggie looked wistful for a moment, letting it all come flooding back to her. She never felt as safe or as loved as she had with Max. Her favorite place to be while he was with her was in his arms with her head buried in his chest. "Could you bury your head in his chest?" Maggie blurted.

"Huh? Who?"

"Peter," Maggie said. "Could you bury your head in his chest, like I could with Max? Does he make you feel loved and safe, Naomi? If he doesn't, it's no good, trust me." Maggie searched her friend's eyes. She saw the answer almost immediately, and she was overjoyed. "Oh, you could. I know you could. He loves you—you love him. Right on. Look, he isn't very good at relationships, but he will be good to you and will treat you right. You really couldn't ask for a better guy."

"I never thought I would love a dork, girl." Naomi shook her head, hugging herself with her arms, wishing that Peter was there with her. She suddenly missed him very much, and she made a mental note to make sure he knew it next time they were together.

"Peter doesn't really fall into the full-on dork category. I mean he is kinda a dork but he's cute. Also," Maggie said, returning to her pack to sit, "he's a genius. He's rich. He's got powerful friends—"

"Powerful, indeed." Sam stepped from the shadows, smiling. He had heard their conversation, and he was pleased with Naomi's confession. "Okay girls, if you have finished emasculating someone who isn't here to defend himself, I think we should get going," Sam said, wishing to register on Peter's behalf.

Maggie looked at Naomi who shrugged, "We didn't mean anything by it, Sam," Maggie said placing her hand on his arm. "I am truly thankful that Peter has you, Sam. You're a good friend to him, just like you were to Max."

"Peter is a good man. He is intelligent and loyal. He is also compassionate and caring. He can be goofy, but that is what makes him unique. He is unspoiled by the more immoral aspects of humanity. I like his innocence, and yet he surprises me with his toughness."

"I guess we know how Sam feels," said Maggie, bemused.

"Apparently, we also know how our lovestruck friend feels, too." Sam smiled kindly at Naomi. "Are you going to tell him, sis?"

Naomi looked from one friend to the other, thinking. "You know, my uncle died with things in his heart and on his head that he never mentioned, and I'm not going out like that. I'll tell him. I'll show him, whatever." She turned to Maggie, a single tear on her cheek, and grabbed both of her friend's hands. "I love him, Maggie. I love him, and it makes me sad. I hate that you lost Max—"

Maggie joined Naomi in a hug, both crying. Sam stepped over

to envelop the two in a massive hug. "We all lost Max, but he's not gone. Not really. The ones that love you never really leave you." He whispered into the air around them, and peace settled over the women. They all lingered under it for a few moments, feeling better and then disengaged from the tangle of arms.

"We'd better get to it," Sam stated walking toward the opposite end of the chamber. The girls scooped up their backpacks hurriedly and slung them, walking to catch up with the angel. Maggie's smile got bigger as she approached him.

"Do you think we will find anything in there?"

"I feel certain we will find *a* thing in there," Sam told them. "Fairies have a lot of power for such small beings. They're not especially helpful or happy, like in the human stories. They do what they want, when they want, and no amount of begging will help. The story about them turning an entire village to stone for slighting two orphans is probably true," Sam said in a grave voice. "Stick close to me, okay?"

The two women nodded, and Maggie employed the newest device in her arsenal. It was a small camera that could record in all conditions, even zero gravity and complete darkness, and was virtually undetectable. It was hidden in her earring and would record what she saw. Quickly, she put her hair into a neat bun at the back of her neck and followed the others into the cave. They followed the nicely worn trail through the brightly lit portion of the cave system. Maggie could hear the bats in the upper recesses of the ceiling. She couldn't see them, but she could hear them communicating with each other. She could also hear the water droplets that sounded against the tidy pools created by the water that leached through the walls. They sounded like the tinkling laugh of a fairy.

Sam came to a split in the path—one way was well-lit and the other looked desolate, dark, and most likely dangerous. In fact, there were ropes stretched across the tunnel mouth and yellow signs with gibberish writing on them.

"Any chance those signs say, *Come on in, we love visitors*, Sam?"

Sam ignored the ropes and set off down the darkened tunnel. Naomi broke a glow stick from her pack to illuminate the way, and she and Maggie followed Sam down the path. After walking for what seemed like forever to Maggie, they came to a larger cavernous area. Maggie had just walked in behind Naomi when she heard a startled yelp and saw Sam lunge after something. After a brief struggle Sam turned around to show the two girls a small elf-like creature.

"Calm down, you foul little thing. We need to talk," Sam said, clearly agitated by the squirming creature.

"Who are you calling foul, you big bird?"

The creature had stopped moving, and Maggie and Naomi got a clearer picture of just what Sam was holding in his hand. He was, by all appearances, a man, only in miniature. Dark brown hair, spiked in jags, rose up around his crown and ears. The little being had a beard and a golden earring in his ear. He was robed much like what they were used to with the rest of the host, including armor and a miniscule sword. Whereas Sam and the others typically sported metallic armor, this little man wore armor seemingly made from an insect carapace. The effect was primeval and wild. All of this in a creature no more than six or seven inches tall.

"Wow. Just… wow." Naomi couldn't believe her eyes, and the little man stopped his struggle and eyed her appreciatively.

"Like what you see, eh?" The little man raised an eyebrow and smirked, flexing for Naomi and Maggie. Sam turned back to the creature he held. "Knock it off, Caudel. We've got business."

"Samael, you great bull. Why now, and not one, two, three thousand years ago, do you show up? Business? What does the host want with me? I am wretched, forsaken. Sentenced to be away from everything, trapped in these caves. What more could you possibly do to me?"

The poor thing looked absolutely heartbroken at seeing the angel, and Maggie's heart went out to the little fairy.

Sam seemed to take pity on him. He set him down on a rock, seated himself adjacent, and began a conversation.

"I apologize for my heavy-handedness, brother Caudel. How has it been all these years?" Sam questioned. "I see that you have yourself a lovely subterranean dwelling. Have the local wildlife been kind to you?"

He was trying to be nice, but it was made awkward by something unspoken. Something desperate and tragic. The creature curled into a ball, collapsing and weeping openly onto the stone.

"Please tell me that you are here to release me. I can't take any more. I will choose. Tell Him, Samael. Tell him I have chosen. Am I to continue to slowly go mad in a pit of my own making?"

Naomi and Maggie looked at each other and back to Sam, who looked exasperated, helpless, and angry all at the same time. Maggie had no doubt there was an incredible and ancient story in the offing.

"What is he talking about, Sam?" Maggie asked, her journalistic mind already running through various scenarios.

Sam sighed and hung his head, saying, "Since Caudel has brought it up, and I know you will refuse to leave it alone, I will tell you. Caudel is an angel."

"Uh, what? Like you?" Naomi said, incredulous, surveying the tiny form.

"Exactly. Caudel is an angel from the first war." Sam turned to look directly at the little being, tears in his eyes. "He refused to pick a side and was sentenced to live his life like this." Sam gestured wildly to the creature on the rock and then swept his hands around the cave. "Some existence, huh?" Sam wept bitterly.

The girls could tell that he was truly heartbroken for the fairy's lot. He suddenly whirled back on Caudel, facing him and pointing an accusatory finger. "It was so simple, you fool. You little apathetic fool. All you had to do was choose." He turned to the women again, explaining. "All he had to do was choose a side and he could have lived completely differently." He turned back to the weeping ex-angel. "We could have been brothers for eternity, you and I. Caudel…" The angel of Death held out his hands to his friend, helplessly gesturing at his state, and the fairy flew at him, grabbing his hand, shaking.

"I am willing to choose now, great one, please help me. It has been so long since I have seen any of my brethren," Caudel wailed. "Is there no way to come back across the bridge?"

Sam wiped his eyes, refusing to look at the women. His attention was solely on his hurting friend.

"You say you're willing to choose now. When did this transpire?" Sam returned to the rock and set down the fairy gently.

"Almost immediately after the Canaan incident. I knew my fate was sealed then."

Sam grew angry and pointed a finger at Caudel again. "Oh, did the Master all of a sudden stop granting an audience to the host? Does He no longer listen to a repentant heart? Why haven't you sought Him out sooner?" Sam asked bewildered.

"I am not worthy, I had wasted so much time, costing us hours and lives, not really wanting to be one or the other. There was a group of us who felt the same, and we mourned. Oh, did we mourn. I could no more go back to Him than I could cut off my wings. Redemption was too far a street away for us, I know it."

Maggie piped up, listening to the story, "It may interest you to know that the angel you are talking to had to himself be redeemed. Why not you?"

The fairy screwed up his face, perplexed. "Samael, what does she speak? Redeemed how?"

Sam smiled warmly at his friend, recounting his tale.

"She's right, much as I hate to admit it. The tale is gruesome and long. Suffice it to say, I made mistakes, as you have, and was recently allowed back into the fold, which," Sam beamed, scooping up Caudel to look him in his eyes, "is why I'm here on business. The host needs your help."

"So, there is a way?" Caudel dried his eyes, looking pleadingly at the giant angel. "Please help me, great one."

Caudel looked so forlorn that Naomi chose to speak on his behalf.

"Sam, isn't there anything you can do? Think about how you were before Peter found you again?"

Sam looked to the sky, and after a moment's hesitation said, "Alright, Caudel. I can intercede for you, but you have to help us two-fold in return."

The fairy said without hesitation, "Anything I can help with, I will. I just want to serve the Master again."

Sam nodded and said, "If we help you, you must assist us on a bit of a scavenger hunt. Also, you must agree to lead a small army when the need arises."

Caudel looked at Sam and said, "I agree to the first. Whatever it is you search for should be no challenge for me, but I am intrigued by the second request. What kind of army do you wish me to lead?"

Sam looked skyward again and said, "Your kind—the Undecided. You will be allowed to torment people for an allotted amount of time, around five months." Sam raised an eyebrow at Caudel and his expression changed from cautious to intrigued.

"I am humbled, Samael. I would be honored to do as you ask."

"I have a feeling I am missing something. You?" Maggie asked Naomi.

Sam shook his head, kindly, saying, "Sorry, Red. There are things that you cannot be privy to, no matter how much I like you. When you get a chance, check out the book of Revelation—might give you some insight." Sam turned to Caudel, "So we have an understanding? Help us here and help *Us* later?"

Caudel nodded and said, "I will."

"Very well, then. Just know that you have sworn to do this and if you betray us there will be no second chance, I will take you myself."

"What's the mission, Samael?"

"First, tell me if you've heard about any missing people in the area, specifically children?"

"I have heard of children going missing. I take it you have an idea who is responsible?" Caudel asked intrigued.

"Lev Avatov is a monster! He steals the innocence from children and manipulates and murders to get whatever he wants." Maggie spat it out before Sam could answer.

Caudel raised a minute eyebrow in surprise at the venom in Maggie's voice. "Not a fan I take it?"

"Definitely not. Can you help us find the children? We're banking on the fact that, if we find the missing children, we will find him. Raguel said that the hellhound he tussled with came in this direction. We have word that Lev is working with the Triads, so my question to you is, is there a Triad compound that could house many children, a lab, a few dozen men and Naga, a large hellhound, and the Three? Did I leave anything out, ladies?" Sam asked them.

"No, I think that covers it. What we know of, at least," Naomi said.

Caudel whistled. "Maybe I should have asked questions first. A hellhound? I haven't seen one since the Asmodean War. And the Three?" Caudel had taken to pacing the length of the ledge while rubbing his hand across his chin in contemplation. "Lev Avatov must have a death wish to get involved with the Sisters. Abbadon is never far behind that lot. And Pharzuph is completely barking, a perfect mistress for the hounds." He turned to Maggie. "You are right about one thing, miss—only a monster works with demons."

"Do you know of someplace close by that would fit the description Sam just painted for you, Mr. Caudel?" Maggie asked him in her journalist voice.

"*Mr.* Caudel—I *like* her, Samael." Caudel winked at Maggie, and Naomi giggled.

Maggie rolled her eyes, and she started to tap her foot as she did when she got frustrated.

"I do happen to know where a place like that is, but before you go stomping in there and give yourself away—don't deny it—I can tell that is how you are, for I have lived a very long time," Caudel cut her off, holding up a diminutive hand, "let me go and investigate.

You guys can meet me back here tomorrow. I will have news then. I take it Raguel will be joining us?" Caudel asked Sam.

"I thought he should. We will also have three other humans and Raphael, Gabriel, and Ariel helping to find the wayward hellhound. If needs be, they can help too."

"Good, then let me go learn what I can, and I will report back here tomorrow with my news."

Sam nodded, and before Caudel flew away he said, "Caudel, if you know of any others, my offer will stand for them as well. They must choose, and once the choice is made there is no way to take it back. You will lead. They will follow."

Caudel nodded and launched himself from the ledge and was gone in an instant.

"That was so cool," Naomi squealed. "Peter is gonna flip his lid when he finds out."

Sam smiled and said, "True, he will be in that notebook wanting all the details. I think you two could have a good long talk about this later." Naomi blushed, and Maggie smiled at her friend.

"So, do you think we should look at any more places or go back and wait for the others?"

Sam answered with, "I think that we should go back. Caudel will be reliable in this. He has thrown in his lot with us and will keep his word."

"How do you know for sure?" Maggie asked.

"He will keep his end of this bargain, Maggie. He faces Death if he betrays us," Sam said in a grim voice.

Chapter 17

Lev watched as Lilith paced the length of his lab, yet again. She had kept up the pacing since creating the portal for Pharzy, sending her to the passages above the infernal catacombs where her familiar was convalescing She was a delicious enigma to him, as were her sisters. He was not positive what the three women were, but he knew that they were beautiful and had immense power.

I want her, he thought, lustily.

He considered her physical attributes as she padded around the lab. Lilith was not like the other women Lev had victimized in his life, and she had him enraptured. Slender and dark, she moved with a litheness and sensuality that Lev had never known in a human woman. He was not a fool, and he knew that she was not what she appeared. He didn't care.

He watched her take one more pass across his lab before saying, "You are going to need a new pair of heels if you keep pacing."

Lilith stopped pacing and looked at Lev with her frosty blue eyes. "My sister's mutt may have made it impossible for you to finish your work here, Lev. I will kill the dog personally if that is the case, but it will only be a small punishment compared to what the Association will do when they find out she had an encounter with an angel. Have you ever met the Chairman in person, Lev?"

Lev swallowed hard at the memory of his only meeting with the Chairman. It was right before the events that caused his carefully-ordered world to crumble. "I have. It is not something I care to repeat anytime soon."

"We had better hope that the mutt didn't give away our location, because I guarantee that whoever fails the Chairman will live in never-ending torture. He will send you to the brink of death, only to bring you back to health to repeat the process again and again."

"It's true," came the reply from Ono. "The only thing that scares Lilith at all is failing the Chairman."

"Well, we can't do anything about it at the moment, so let's get back to work. The experiments will be cared for by the Naga, and in the meantime you can lend your attention to another project I am involved with."

This statement got Lilith's attention. "What project?" She came up behind where he was sitting on a stool in front of a microscope. She ran her hand across the back of his shoulders, causing him to shiver in response.

"This is the slide of the blood, or whatever it is, that I took from the hellhound," Lev told her.

Lilith smiled, "I'm surprised you still have all your appendages."

"Yes, well, that animal had seen better days. She growled, but was too weak to do anything else."

"You had better hope that she doesn't remember you took her blood," said Ono. "I'm surprised Pharzy let you do it, but if Tsoula remembers, you can be assured she will want retribution. Not something you want, human."

If they aren't human, what are they?

He wasn't sure he wanted to know, mostly because of the complications it would cause. He did not fear bedding Lilith—he didn't care what she was, only that she existed and seemed to favor him. But he had to know.

He addressed Ono. "What are you, Onoskelis? Lilith?"

Lilith smiled a smile that oozed sex and danger all in one.

"Surely you have figured it out by now?"

She ran a finger across Lev's chest, but he stared at her intently. Blankly. She pulled her hand away, shaking her pretty head.

"I'm surprised at you, Lev. You know we aren't human—we've said as much. We have deep ties to the Association. We despise the host. Can you not put it together?"

"My assumption is that you are a demon of sorts, or a vampire."

Lilith smiled widely and suddenly transformed. Her head sprouted small and intricate cobalt-colored horns, beginning at either side of her forehead and following the contour of her scalp to where they ended just beyond and down behind her neck. Her hair was no longer neatly coiffed, but wild and black as coal. Her eyes glowed a bright blue. Her mouth contained sharp teeth that were not there before. Her body appeared clothed in nothing but icy blue and white, very finely-scaled, skin. She hovered above the ground and revolved slowly, allowing Lev to take in the other details of her appearance. Directly above the cleft of her rear, a delicate forked tail protruded and hung to her ankles.

If anything, she was more irresistible to Lev. His lust hit a fever pitch.

She enveloped the man, cooing, "We are the pleasures in the night, the fantasies come true, the downfall of men. We are succubi. I can reduce any mortal man to a simpering idiot. He will do whatever I wish, without hesitation, for just the promise of my gift. Does that frighten you?"

Lilith was running her hands all over Lev's chest and he had closed his eyes in rapture at her attention.

"I am not afraid of you, Lilith. I understand you. I want to know more."

Lilith smiled, "If you wish to know our secrets," she immediately transformed back to the form he knew so well, "and they are worth knowing, you have to give up a few of your own, starting with that one." Lilith pointed a blood red fingernail at the microscope in front of Lev. Lev looked to where she was pointing and smiled.

"It would be a pleasure to share this with you. I have found that the blood of the hound mixed with the common cold produces a virus the likes of which has never existed. I've tested it exhaustively, this latest time on a couple of the Triad guards." Lev reached for a tablet, flicked to a screen and read, "Let's see… *'High fevers, trouble breathing, deliriousness.'* I had to throw them into the lava tube to keep it from getting out. The watch command thinks they have food poisoning. Eventually, someone will notice that they are gone. Until then, I have time to perfect this new weapon."

Lilith smiled, "Well done. Show me—" She let the last of the sentence go unspoken and looked at Lev in anticipation. Lev grinned at her excitement and produced a vial with a small amount of what looked to be black goo in it. He unstoppered the vial and sunk a pipette into the unctuous mess, coming away with a small amount at the tip. He pulled a slide across the table and placed the slide on the microscope. He flipped a switch and the screen came to life. The screen was filled with the image of hundreds of blood cells.

Lev looked over at Lilith and said, "Now, these are ordinary erythrocytes from one of our new subjects before giving them the serum. I just wanted ordinary blood samples so we know what kinds of changes take place." Lilith nodded, showing him she understood, and he continued. "I took a cold," he told her, holding up another vial labeled *viral rhinitis*, "and I added just a drop of Tsoula's blood."

As he spoke, he replicated the action, poking the pipette into the little clear vial holding the virus. The contents of the vial hissed a little at the contact from the blood. Lev smiled at this and took the vial to the centrifuge. He let the vial spin for a few moments and pulled it back out. It now was as black as the substance in the hellhound vial.

"You may want to put on a mask, ladies. This stuff is contagious."

Lilith smiled, "How cute—he is worried for us." She laughed and said, "This cannot hurt us, Lev, but you go ahead and put on your protection."

Lev shrugged and put on his mask and gloves. Grabbing a clean pipette, he unstoppered the new concoction and used the pipette to get a sample. He turned back to the microscope and carefully added a drop of fluid to the sample on the slide. Almost instantaneously, the mutated black virus spread through the once healthy cells. They turned a sickly gray color and started to duplicate at an accelerated rate. Within seconds, all of the healthy cells were gone, leaving only the death cells. They were still multiplying until every space available held a death cell, leaving no trace of the tissue that had been normal only moments before.

"Ooh, that was fast. What kind of side effects does this concoction bring?" Lillith asked Lev.

He could tell from the excitement in her voice that she liked what she saw.

"Unfortunately, or fortunately, depending on your motives, it works so fast that by the time I start to note side effects the subject is already expired." Lev rubbed at his temples, clearly frustrated, but continued. "From what I can see, elevated body temperature is common. The subject develops a dry, unproductive cough that worsens until they start to cough up blood and tissue. Ultimately—and this is just a hypothesis—I think they die from either asphyxiation or shock. It is difficult to tell because it happens in the span of minutes." Lev was disappointed by the fact that the death throes of the subject didn't last a little longer. "I'm certain I could market this, but unless they want someone dead while they are still standing there giving it to them, I would have to try to lengthen the attack period of the virus. It's not fit to release into the general population at this point. It would be too easy to pinpoint the origin, and we don't need that kind of attention."

He started to pace as he thought about what he could do to make an incubation period for the virus that could contain it long enough for it to be hard to trace. Nothing that he had put the virus in so far could contain it.

"My current dilemma is that I cannot find anything that can hold the virus long enough to distribute it. It eats through everything."

At that precise moment the slide holding the virus shattered into pieces and Lev cursed as he rushed to clean up the mess. He berated himself for not paying closer attention. His cursing brought one of the many Naga into the lab. Before Lev could warn the creature away, it had already started picking up the pieces.

"Don't! You fool!" Lev yelled at the young Naga, swatting the pieces of glass from the creature's hands with his gloves, but it was too late.

Lilith smiled evilly knowing that the young Naga had become infected, and her smile widened when she witnessed Lev's callous treatment of the young, frightened Naga. He grabbed it by the arm and dragged it into the nearest cell. Lev threw the Naga inside and slammed the door. He started a timer that sat on a counter outside of the cell and grabbed a tablet. Lilith and her sister stood behind Lev as they watched the young snake-man. Panicked and confused, he started pounding on the door. Lev was entirely unaffected by the youngster's plight, Lilith was pleased to observe. He simply stared intently at the Naga, not wanting to miss any adverse effects.

A few seconds later the young Naga started weaving from side to side and stumbling around the small cell as if disoriented. In the next moment, the Naga started to vomit up blood. Less than a minute later, it was lying on the floor, unmoving.

Lev stopped the clock, it had taken only two and a half minutes from when the Naga touched the live virus until it's death. Lev shook his head. It was going to be difficult to explain this to Simon—not that he really cared about any of them, including Simon—but they were useful to him, and he did not want to upset the balance.

"Well, that was tragic. This will upset the Naga greatly. They might even entertain the idea of a revolt."

He went back over to collect the remaining pieces of the virus-infected glass and sent them down a specially designed hole. It extended down into the volcano itself, which allowed Lev to get rid of things that could potentially get out of hand.

Lev realized that the two women were completely silent. He turned to find that they had opened the door to the cell and were examining the young Naga's body.

"Don't do that. Come out before it is too late."

Lilith looked over at him and smiled.

"I told you, you silly man—this virus cannot harm us." Lilith bent down and grasped the great head of the creature laying on the floor, and ran her tongue along its bottom jaw to drive home her point. She licked her lips, looking at Lev and letting the head thump back down to the concrete floor. "But," she said, "I am very interested in how fast it works and how lethal it is. You say that it is contagious, too?"

"Very. A touch on bare skin or a cough near you will infect." Lev said this last from a good way back. "I am not sure how long it lasts after the host dies. I haven't sent anyone else in to see."

"Ooh, good idea—let's do that. Call another servant in here to tend to this poor, sick one." Lillith's eyes took on a frosty glint, and Lev could tell she was excited by the prospect of another death.

Lev went to the door and flagged down another Naga.

"One of your brethren has taken ill in the cell. Check on him while I continue my work."

Lev pointed to the cell that the girls had vacated before the new worker arrived. They stood to the side and watched as the Naga went into the cell to check on the young one. Ono shut the door to the cell just as the new Naga bent and touched its fallen comrade. Lev picked up the timer and once again started it. The three watched as the new creature looked from the fallen one to the three outside the door.

"What have you done, sssssir? Thissss issss not normal," the Naga said while looking out of the glass at Lev. It once again bent and touched the young male. "Thisss young one is burning. How have you done thissss?"

Five minutes passed and the new worker still looked fine. It had taken to begging for them to open the cell door and let it out. Eight minutes passed, and Lev was beginning to think that the virus had lost its viability, but then the captive started to rub its head with its hands. From that moment to the next, they watched as the Naga started to hiss and stumble, finally falling over the body of the other young one. It rolled and hissed as if it were very uncomfortable.

Almost as if it were on fire, Lev thought, excitedly.

At last, with one final toss of its body, the captive Naga lay still. Lev stopped the watch. Twenty minutes.

"Hmm, it seems that it remains potent even after the subject dies." Lev turned and made a note in his book and looked back at the two women. "You two suffered no ill effects, so, even though it does appear to affect non-humans, it doesn't affect demonkind. What we effectively have here, then," Lev was thinking out loud, "is a potent, deadly, untraceable—once we increase the incubation period by a few minutes, super-spreader, zero-loss contagion that could devastate not only humanity, but also pretty much any other entity that you might want to screw with."

Lillith smiled. "Alright Lev, you have earned a reward for your latest find." Lilith turned to her sister. "Leave us."

Ono smiled. "Don't break him, Lil. We need him. Have fun now," Ono called back over her shoulder through the closing door of the lab.

As soon as the door sealed shut, the demoness was on Lev, hands everywhere all at once, and she was moaning. Lev was ecstatic, never knowing where the next sensation would come from. She pulled back briefly, and he saw that she was entirely naked in her human form. Lev was surprised to realize that he was slightly disappointed that she wasn't in her true guise.

"Oh, you are a naughty boy. We are going to have a lot of fun together, you and I." She assumed her full demonic form and they went at each other again, more fervently this time. After a minute or two, she grabbed Lev lightly by the throat, saying, "Enough."

He smiled at her and said, "You are truly glorious."

"I know. You have seen and experienced enough for now." She transformed again, not only to human form but also fully clothed. She reached back and placed her raven hair in a neat bun, saying,

"Besides, you have to get back to work. This virus could come in quite useful in the near future, and I want you to create a way to deliver it to the masses. Something that they will never suspect. If I'm not mistaken, there is someone in particular who is in dire need of a demonstration of your formidability?" Lilith purred into his ear.

"I can think of a red-headed bitch who deserves something like this. I need to track her down. Yes," he said, something like obsession crossing his face. "I will get started on the delivery system right now."

Turning back to his computer, he never saw the fire light in Lilith's eyes or the evil smile she had on her face.

"Good," was all she said.

Chapter 18

The silver, rented Corolla cruised to a stop, and Maggie, Naomi, and Sam pulled up outside Jonah's orphanage. His mother was waiting for them as they walked up to the front door. She smiled warmly at the trio and invited them inside for some tea. Once they were all settled in the kitchen and Rachel had given them something to eat from the pot that was simmering once again on the stove, she asked what they had learned that day.

"We found an unlikely ally on our hunt today. I would prefer to wait until the others return before I go into anything further, though," Sam told her.

"Then wait no more, my friend, for we have arrived," Peter said grandly as he walked through the door; Jonah, Paul, and Rags trailing behind him.

Paul smiled at Peter's zest for life, and seeing that Maggie was watching him, smiled at her as well. Rachel got up to get refreshments for the newcomers, but Jonah waived her away and dished up some of the food from the pot on the stove. He grabbed a few glasses from the cupboard and placed them in front of Peter and Paul. Rags took the cup of tea but waived away the stew he was offered. After Jonah was seated and all were contentedly eating their food, Peter spoke up again.

"Paul and I were able to get our business concluded for a couple of days, but we will need to go back before we leave here to see to our flight plans, and the agreement with the Chinese government needs to be settled, right?"

He turned to Paul who, up to this point, was content to let Peter tell everything about their jaunt to the city. He was more eager to hear about what Sam and the girls found than the dusty old museum relics he would be bringing back to New Mexico.

"Yes, they are going to let us borrow a few pieces but the terms and the length of time has yet to be determined. They will contact our lawyers back in New Mexico and set all that up. I just need to know how many pieces will be returning so I can set up transport."

Paul looked over at Sam. "What about you three? Any lead on the girl, or on Lev and his henchmen?"

Sam opened his mouth to answer, but Maggie beat him to it.

"We found a fairy."

Paul said, "A what?"

At the same time Peter exclaimed, "For real? You have to tell me everything."

Naomi laid her hand on Peter's before the other could go racing out after his notebook.

"Easy, mister. There will be time enough later. For now, just listen."

Peter, who was in the midst of standing up, sat back in his seat. "Okay," he said huffily, but brightened when Sam started telling them about Caudel.

"We went to Fairy Cave, and there was a fairy in it."

Sam shrugged like it was the most normal thing ever to find a fairy in a fairy cave. Peter almost growled in frustration, causing Sam to smile and Maggie to take pity on him.

"His name is Caudel, and he is *really* tiny. Like, super-tiny. He is about six inches tall, with wings—and an attitude," Maggie told him. "Sam got him and his people to agree to help us look for the missing kids."

Rags bristled at the statement and growled at Sam. "Why would you make a bargain with the traitor? You of all people should know—" Rags asked him, clearly perplexed.

"It was *His* will." Sam stopped him, growling back.

The Angel of Justice said nothing more, just turned and punched the kitchen wall, making everyone jump.

"Rag-u-el, do not take your frustration out on my wall!" Rachel stood and glared.

"Apologies, Miss Rachel." Rags looked cowed and immediately touched the wall, healing the wood and plasterboard. Sam stood as well, laying a hand on the dark angel's shoulder.

"Careful brother. There is a purpose for everything." Paul watched Rags and Sam for a moment. It seemed as if the two were in silent communication, and something unspoken passed between them.

After only a moment, Rags blew out a deep breath and said, "I know, I know. I was here the whole time." Then he promptly turned and walked out of the room.

"What was that about?" asked Peter. "Man, is he ever happy about anything?"

Sam said, "Peter, give the guy a break. You are judging him unfairly. Think about what he has to deal with on a daily basis."

"Fair enough, but why did he have such a strong reaction to the fairy?" Peter asked him. Sam looked upward for a moment and then back at Peter.

"Do you remember us telling you about the war of the angels?" Sam asked him.

"Yeah, Michael said that there were angels that wanted to have human wives, and they created the nephilim children. Then they decided to stage a coup and the loyal angels fought the unloyal and misguided angels for the power of heaven. I don't see what this has to do with fairies, though?"

Sam sighed, "Angels and Fallen did do battle. It was awful, brother against brother. It is also true that there was a third side, a side that did not wish to battle at all, like Switzerland. They chose to remain neutral, going against everything that is ingrained in angelic beings." Sam held up a hand to forestall whatever Peter was about to say. "The neutral angels were not for heaven, but they weren't against it, either. The Master, in His wisdom, banished them to live on the Earth, a realm between two realms. The Master also shrunk their size and reduced their power so that while they still had some power to do good or evil, they were also protected from those things that were bigger than they were. Most of them were benevolent to this world, and continued to do good even though they were unbowed and unrepentant. There were also those that chose to harm the humans that they blamed for their circumstances. This is where humans get the myths of the Seelie and Unseelie."

Peter gawked, intrigued. "You know, if I wasn't the nerd that I am, you would need to explain, but as it stands, I follow you."

Sam smiled. "Good. Well, most of them started out in Albion—"

"Albion?" Naomi asked, screwing up her face.

"Sorry, modern day UK. Ireland and Scotland to be exact, but soon they moved on to other areas. The stories of the seelie and the unseelie are accurate, and apparently all of the tiny ex-angels had an agenda. Well, all except Caudel and his little band. They ended up alone in Fairy Cave, and more than likely all of the local myths of Fairy Cave are about them." Sam waited for the barrage of questions to come from Peter but found only a silent stare. "Hey—you okay?"

Peter slowly smiled and said, "That was about the coolest story I have ever heard." He punctuated his statement as he clapped his hands together and let out a whoop. "When do I get to meet Caudel?" he asked with excitement.

"Contain your excitement, bud. This is still serious business. We are supposed to go back and meet with him tomorrow. You guys are free to join us," Sam told Peter, Paul, and Jonah.

The three nodded in unison.

"Wait, why was Rags upset about your deal with Caudel?" Jonah asked Sam.

"He doesn't trust him, Jonah. He's not sure that Caudel has learned his lesson or repented. The two have had the opportunity to run into each other over the years, and although not outright evil, Caudel has a certain penchant for mischief and has been known to renege on his promises. That's why I threatened him before we left the cave." He said the last part to Naomi and Maggie. "He knows that I will follow through on my threat. I don't think we will have any trouble from him."

Peter shivered because he had a feeling he knew what the threat was.

"Do you think that Rags will be okay to meet with him tomorrow?" Paul asked.

"Yeah, the big guy will be okay in a bit. He just has to work through some stuff. At one point we were all very close." Sam suddenly looked like he was years away, reliving his past. "While not one of the Seven, Caudel was still our brother, and we all took it very hard when they withdrew from the ranks and hid."

"Well, I can't wait to meet him. What did you offer him to do this?" Peter asked.

"Come on, ese. How do you think I'm gonna answer that?" Sam asked him, crossing his arms in front of his chest. "You're gonna make me do this, huh? Well, okay then." He cleared his throat for effect, going rigid. Peter broke in, surprising the angel.

"You know I can't tell you everything, Peter, according to divine mandate and personal instruction from You Know Who. All will be revealed in its time." Peter did his best Sam impression. "I added the last part myself—it seemed more mystical," he said with a wink to Naomi who giggled in response. Sam smiled but nodded his head.

"I think the voice needs to be deeper, though." Sam turned to Jonah. "After we talk to Caudel, who hopefully will have some significant information for us, I am hoping to talk to some locals in that area to see if they have noticed anything. Is that a solid approach? If they know any other ways to reach our objective without being caught, I would like to employ their methods."

"As long as we aren't overly aggressive," Jonah considered, "they should respond favorably."

"That's a relief. You know, I believe you will really be able to help us here, my friend. The locals are more willing to talk to one of their own rather than an outsider."

"Forgive my asking, Sam, but couldn't you just compel them to tell us everything?"

Sam shook his head, "Free will, my man. Free. Will. They have to *want* to help us. That's where you come in. We need you to strike up some conversation with the locals while we play tourist."

"I guess I can do that. I know a few people in that area," Jonah said.

"Good. Hopefully, Caudel will be able to give us some insight as to where Lev and his ilk are holed up. Maybe you can see if there is a back door or anything we need to know about. I would like to know where we are headed and what we are headed into. Knowing Lev, it won't be a welcoming place," Sam said.

"Do you think that Caudel will find anything, Sam?" Maggie, who had been uncommonly quiet during this whole exchange, asked.

"He'll try his best. He has been around a long time and knows everything in the area. I wouldn't be surprised to find that he knew where they were all along and was only going to verify the information. Like I said, he *really* wants what I offered."

Caudel had a lot to think about. What Samael offered was a way out of his never-ending isolation. It had been a millennia since he had seen another of his cursed brethren. He was sure that they were around—just not around him and his cave. He zipped along the tunnels that connected many of the underground passage systems to his cave. The humans had only found a few of them, and there were many that were too small for them, but just right for a fairy to navigate.

He hummed a little at the thought of going home, and not really paying much attention, zipped around a corner and smacked right into the chest of a man.

No, not really a man, he realized, looking up. *A half man—Half man, half snake—person.* He couldn't really think of the name, but he had been told of them. He zipped around a bend quickly and watched to see if the snake-man had noticed him.

Evidently the snake-man did not see what he was exactly, because he heard a muffled, "*Bugsssss, I don't like bugssss.*"

Caudel watched as the snake-man turned and slithered on down the tunnel. He decided this was as good a direction as any to go, so he followed the snake-man at a distance. He fluttered along behind the creature until they both came to another divergence. Caudel could feel the heat in the tunnel rise significantly in the last few moments. He kept following the snake-man as he took the left fork of the tunnel. This went on for a few turns, until the snake-man stopped and went through an opening in the tunnel wall.

Caudel could hear the cries of infants from the hallway. He flew up toward the ceiling and into the room. He quickly found a niche in the rock above the door that afforded him a view of the entire room. He saw the snake-man take a clipboard from a table a short distance from a baby bed. Inside the crib was an infant that was clearly in distress. The child was a mottled red-purple color from crying for a prolonged period of time. The snake-man checked the baby's temperature and changed the soiled diaper, shaking its head at the smell.

The baby continued to wail, so the snake-man went to the small refrigerator and grabbed a bottle from it. The snake-man went to a wall and pulled something out of it. Steam issued from a hole that was opened and the snake-man shoved the bottle into the hole. It proceeded to make notes on the clipboard until it was sure enough time had passed. Then it collected the bottle from the wall, and after checking the temperature, gave it to the squalling infant. Caudel had seen enough of this and thought that he may be able to find out more information. Even if this was not one of the kids Sam was looking for, Caudel was sure that he would want to know. He left the room and proceeded a little further down the corridor, counting as he went.

One, two, three, four, five… six. He counted six additional rooms. Each one held an infant and a snake-thing. He was not sure whether or not there were any more rooms, but the further he went, the higher the chance went up of him being caught. When he came to a fork in the tunnel once again, he chose to go away from the crying and snake-people, and went down the darker, quieter side of the tunnel. Caudel could see as easily in the dark as he did in the light, so he had little concern about the lack of light in this tunnel.

Nothing… nothing… and, nothing.

Caudel flew on; getting frustrated. Just when he was about to turn back, he heard voices a little further up the darkened tunnel. He flew cautiously toward the voices, which sounded like a couple of people having a very loud discussion. Caudel slowed his flying and looked around for a place he could land and not be seen.

"What progress has been made, Lev?" The voice was deep and Caudel thought he heard some age and gravel in it

"Chairman, I assure you that we are very close to coming up with a solution for you. Our latest group of subjects are responding well to this newest iteration."

Caudel assumed the voice answering was this Lev, and the gravelly voice must be the Chairman.

"The problem that we seem to be having is the younger the subject, the more likely it is to adapt. A younger subject is also weaker, and usually does not make it more than a week before the body rejects the serum and the subject dies. We have obtained some older subjects and will be trying the serum on them. They are still young and healthy, but they are older than the current subjects so their bodies have more antibodies and are better able to adapt with the changes," Lev said with precision. "Trust me Chairman, we are so close."

"I haven't the least bit of interest in the methods or the science. I will give you four days. Your trials had better produce something. I have placated you for too long."

Caudel peered around but was unable to see the two men who were speaking. He decided to move a little closer. Caudel looked out across the room and spied another nook in the rough tunnel wall. He waited until the two men were speaking again, and flew up high in the shadows across the room to his new hiding place.

Just as he landed in the little hole, he heard Lev say, "You can count on me, Chairman, I will start the testing immediately on the older group. I will update you in two days' time."

Caudel could see the man, Lev, sitting at a metal table that held a large computer. The man on the screen did not look well. Caudel looked closer.

I would say that he is on death's doorstep—he looks bad. He appeared ancient and withered, with visible sores on his forehead. His hair was thin and missing in places, like a doll that had been the victim of a six year old's hair-pulling tantrum. His face was gaunt and drawn in where the jowls of an old man should be.

"No, you will have *results* for me in four days. I do not want to hear from you until you and your serum are before me, ready for my judgement."

The computer screen went blank as the Chairman cut off the connection. Lev cursed as he got up from the table. He ran his large hands through his hair and let out a pent-up breath. From the other side of the room, a woman strode over to Lev and struck him hard across the face. The man appeared shocked, his hand immediately jumping to the offended cheek.

The woman pushed her face very close to him, saying in a quiet yet deadly serious tone, "Do not appear weak in front of him again. He will not hesitate to find someone else to carry out his will."

She pushed back from the chair arms with her hands, smoothing her skirt and reaching to straighten the hair she held in a tight bun. Seemingly, her mood had changed almost immediately, and she became sympathetic.

"That did not go as planned, huh, love?" she purred.

Caudel thought she looked familiar, but he didn't remember her until she spoke.

That voice. I would know that voice anywhere, across aeons, he thought. *Lilith is here. The Three are here, and that meant that Pharzuph and Onoskelis would be close by.*

Caudel had a few run-ins with the Sisters over the years. Usually, it was them laughing at him as he flew quickly in the other direction, helpless to oppose them directly. He was not without power, but theirs was so much more than his.

"No," Lev spoke, still confused at the demoness' schizophrenia. He continued, wary, "I will have to cut into the new compliment of Olivier's girls in order to get a new subject group." Lev sneered, considering the fallout. "That will make the damnable vampire bat good and pissed. Normally, it would please me to no end to piss him off, but this time—" He let the sentence hang as if he expected her to know his thoughts.

"I will start the new subjects on the serum in seventeen hours. I will need that long to set up the testing rooms and assign workers. So little time—" He rolled his shoulders and continued, "Tonight is something else, entirely. Help take my mind off my worries, goddess."

He turned and grabbed Lillith around the waist. She smiled in answer, punching him in the gut. The man bowled over in pain, but then, surprisingly, he grabbed the demoness hard, pulling her to him, and devoured her body with passionate kisses. She responded in kind. Caudel decided that he could no longer chance being seen, and the current environment was making him nauseous. He must get his information to Samael and his two pretty allies. He was sure that this is what they wanted to know. There was no time to waste, literally. If Lev was going to ready the space and start testing this serum on a new batch of kids, Samael needed to know. Now.

He chose a moment the two were otherwise occupied, and flew out into the adjacent tunnel. He hummed to himself as he flew. This was going to get him in good with Samael, for sure. Preoccupied, he collided around the next bend with a human female.

Not human, he thought. *One of the Three.*

The Sister batted him and let out a little squeak. He heard her say, as he saw her shiver, "Ew. I hate bugs."

Smiling, he retraced his earlier path and flew off toward his own tunnels and cozy little cave.

Chapter 19

Pharzy was smiling to herself as she walked through the tunnels. She had learned so much in her short time back in the pit. She felt refreshed and *much* more relaxed about what had occurred between Tsoula, who was regaining her strength rapidly, and that accursed angel.

Abbadon was exceedingly charismatic, as always, and although she enjoyed her time with him, indeed her nethers still tingled, she was glad to be out from under his gaze. Abbadon was, himself, his only ally and friend. It was dangerous to try to use him, but his narcissistic tendencies played to her advantage. His ego and sense of self-importance knew no earthly bounds, and this time it was her awe at his seeming omniscience that allowed her to know exactly what Lilith had found in the human, Lev.

Lilith and Abbadon have a love/hate relationship. They love to hate each other.

Pharzy smiled and turned into a new section of the tunnels. She wasn't looking at the moment something careened at her out of the darkness, and she let out a little surprised squeak at the shock of it, swatting furiously with her hands at the empty air in front of her face. She turned in time to see the thing fly around the corner and said with a shiver, "*Ew. I hate bugs.*"

She listened for a moment and thought she heard humming. Pharzy narrowed her eyes and walked on toward Lev's lab. She heard voices low and thick with arousal, and not embarrassed or deterred as any human would be she walked into the room. Lev and Lilith were in the throes of physical passion, and for a moment she considered joining them but quickly dismissed the thought.

Not only would she probably kill the human from the sensual overload of a *pair* of succubi's undivided attention, she also knew that anyone other than Abbadon touching her right now would be a very big let down to her current mood. She cleared her throat, and she saw Lev's head whip up from between her sister's legs and around to look at her.

"Don't stop on my account, little man. You appear to be getting the hang of it," she told him with a giggle.

Ordinarily, Lev would have kept going, himself having many experiences with women and girls in the most crowded and unintimate of places, but Lilith pushed him away with a look of utter frustration. The loathing in her voice was not veiled. It was hurled in Pharzy's direction as her clothing rematerialized, and she resumed her human form. Lev, for his part, remained unashamedly naked in their presence.

"What did you learn, Pharzy?"

Pharzy looked appreciatively down at Lev's lower half, feeling a slight twinge in the places that Abbadon had so well tended just minutes before. She sighed, looking up at her sister.

"I learned that Tsoula will make a full recovery. In fact, she has almost regenerated enough to be at my side again."

Lilith made a dismissive gesture with her hand. "Spectacular. Pharzy, I don't give a shit about your stupid, slutty, mutt. Do you understand that there is an angel poking his nose into things here in China? What did she tell you about him, Pharzy?" Lilith asked impatiently.

"I was about to tell you, but you interrupted. Where is Ono?" Lilith lost her temper and literally hissed and spat venom at the demoness talking to her. Lev took a step back, not in revulsion, but in the eventuality that something of his might become injured in the exchange. He was still utterly infatuated with Lilith.

"Dammit, Pharzy. She ran off to play with some of the Triads. Tell me what your damn dog said."

Pharzy smiled, at least something around here was predictable.

"Tsoula is not a dog—"

"So help me, Cephas, Pharzy, I will end you if we debate over semantics—"

"Fine—she didn't have much else to say about the angel, except that the villager was not afraid of him. She said it was like he knew him or at least had seen him before. The villager had left and was out of sight by the time he went full angel on her. Tsoula seems to think that this particular member of the host has been in the area before. Many times."

Pharzy said the last glumly, knowing that their mission would be harder if the locals supported the beings they were attempting to oppose. Lilith was pacing as she normally did when she was thinking. Pharzy took this opportunity to ask Lev a question. He started to dress as she spoke.

"When did you acquire a fairy?"

Lev looked perplexed.

"A what?"

"A fairy. I just ran into one outside in the tunnel. Rude little thing. When did you recruit a fairy? Please ask it to be careful flying around corners in the future." She shivered, remembering. "They remind me of bugs, and I hate bugs."

Lilith had stopped pacing and looked at Lev.

"You haven't recruited a fairy, have you?" She waited, knowing what his response was going to be.

"I didn't know that fairies truly existed, actually." He brightened, quickly buttoning his shirt. "Is it still out there? Can we catch it? I would love to dissect it and see how we could exploit it." Lev was excited at the prospect of experimenting with yet another unknown, to him at least, life form and went to the door of the tunnel and peered out into the darkness hoping to get a glimpse of the fairy in question.

"It flew off down the tunnel, humming. That's what gave it away, you know? Insects typically just buzz. They don't hum sea shanties to themselves." She tsked and smiled as she hummed a few bars.

"Enough." Lilith's impatience had surfaced again, and she was reaching an untenable level. "I don't think that fairy was here to donate it's time, and I don't believe in coincidences. Lev, send your serpents out to see if they can spot the little interloper. We need to ascertain his intentions. Is he working for someone, or is he just curious? You can have him either way when we're done, love."

Lilith was exceedingly confident, and it turned Lev on anew. He gulped for air as he put on his jacket.

"Excellent idea. Naga can see in the dark as daylight. I am sure they can catch it." Lev poked his head out into the tunnel again and yelled, "*Simon!*" The women both looked at Lev askance and he shrugged. "What? They have incredible hearing as well as eyesight."

Within moments, Simon was poking his head into the lab. The Naga was one of the first Lev had appropriated and had been with him since the start.

"Yesssss massssster?"

"Simon, I have just learned of the existence of a tiny creature and the presence of said creature in my tunnels. It is no more than six inches tall. It has wings. It hums; it does not buzz. Take a few of your kin and hunt it down." He turned to the two women, inquiring, "Powers?"

"Oh, right. Watch out for its tail. And, they're tricky. Do not talk to it," Pharzy offered.

"You heard her. Take those precautions. Do not harm it. Bring it back to me," Lev commanded him.

"Yesssss massssster, it will be assssss you asssssk." Simon bowed as he left the lab.

"That isssss quite impressssive," Lilith said, mocking the slurred *s* that was the hallmark of the Naga's speech. Lev was too busy thinking of the possibilities a fairy may present to answer her. He was rubbing his hands together and pacing, deep in thought. Lilith frowned and pouted prettily.

"Love, you're ignoring me."

Lev stopped pacing for a moment and looked up at her.

"What? Oh, I apologize, darling. I have never seen a fairy. I must admit I am intrigued and deadly curious. I must get my hands on it." He resumed pacing, paying her no mind, even though she once again stood naked and magnificent in her true form before him. "I wonder where it came from?" he opined, seemingly unaffected at all. Pharzy was enjoying the fact that Lilith was seething because she had lost the attention of her newest plaything.

"I'd bet you never thought you would lose to a fairy?" Pharzy laughed in earnest at the look of malice Lilith threw in her direction.

"I have not lost him to a fairy. He is a human, and he is subject to distraction."

"Well, do something, then. I thought you were the Queen of the Distractors?"

"That I am, sister dear. Timing is everything. Let him work through this as he will, for now."

Pharzy clicked her tongue. "Whatever you say, dear." Pharzy laughed again. "By the way, Abbadon sends you his love." Lev stopped pacing.

"Who is Abbadon?" Lilith smiled at the emergence of Lev's jealousy.

"Not anyone you need to concern yourself with. He is an old, meaningless fling. You only need to concern yourself with the serum and the Chairman, remember?" Lilith pointed out to him.

"Yes, the Chairman and the serum. We need to get the older children from Olivier's stash in order to try this new serum. He is not going to be pleased," Lev told her.

"Leave Olivier to me. How many do you need?" Lilith asked him.

"Twenty to start. I can set them up in the rooms we already have available. Of course, we will have to dump the current specimens. They are of no consequence now, at any rate. I will have to have an older specimen for the Chairman anyway. He is going to have to transfer himself soon or his host body will disintegrate around him like in days past."

"They used to call that leprosy. It was wondrous to behold,"

Lilith spoke, longingly remembering the wasting disease from time immemorial.

"I'm surprised that they don't get more time with each jump, but with the amount of unwanted people in the world, I guess there aren't a shortage of hosts available." Lev was just thinking out loud at this point. He turned back to his microscope. "Well, I need to know what I'm working with. Can you see what Olivier has for us? Thanks, love."

Lilith was miffed that Lev did not look up from his microscope when he asked this favor of her, but Pharzy pulled on her arm.

"Let us do as he says, *love*." Her mockery earned her a jab with the sharp side of Lilith's elbow, causing Pharzy to snicker again as she rubbed her abused side. The two women walked out of the lab into the tunnel, one of them smiling and the other wearing a look of cold fury. As soon as they were out of earshot of Lev, Lilith rounded on Pharzy.

"What did that big boob, Abbadon, want?"

"Well, he really wanted to know what you are doing here, and what you are doing with the human." Pharzy told her.

Lilith suddenly looked concerned, yet furious at the same time. *How does she pull that off?* Pharzy wondered.

"You didn't tell him what is going on here, Pharzy?" It was a question posed as a threat. Pharzy bristled at the implication. She had told him everything, of course, to do otherwise would have been akin to suicide, but she wouldn't bother Lilith with that information. "Of course I didn't, Lil. He was interested in the angel, so I told him about it to distract him. He went with me to Tsoula, and we questioned her together. That's all."

Lilith looked mollified but only just.

"I really don't need Abbadon sticking his big nose where it doesn't belong. When he gets involved, all of Hell breaks loose, literally. I really can't afford that right now."

"Ahem," Pharzy said, pretending to clear her throat. "Don't you mean *we*?" she asked.

Lilith waved a dismissive hand.

"Of course. Don't be thick. You have to admit, Pharzy. Abbadon does like to create havoc. Everything he touches turns to chaos."

Pharzy was hard-pressed to disagree with her. "You're right."

"I know that he can be a lot of fun, Pharzy, but he is also a sneaky bastard that only serves himself," Lilith told her. "I don't need him ruining our chances here. This human Lev is as close to a serum as we've gotten. We need for this to work or Cephas will have our necks."

Pharzy paled at the name. "You didn't tell me Cephas was involved, Lilith. *Are you mad?*"

Her sister cut her off. "I'll handle Cephas, and Alaric, but we must make sure that we don't have an angel or fairy problem in the meantime. Let's go find Ono and do a little searching of our own. Agreed?"

Pharzy was marginally afraid of Abbadon, but Cephas chilled her already cold blood, stopping it in her veins. They could not, under any circumstances, fail.

"Agreed."

Chapter 20

Peter jumped out of the truck, not really waiting for it to stop. As a result he skidded on the gravel, almost landing embarrassingly in front of the others. They had arrived in the parking lot of Caudel's cave complex, and he couldn't contain himself. He bounced up and down on the balls of his feet, anticipating the encounter, until Naomi appeared beside him. She kissed him lightly on his cheek, taking his hand.

"Relax, sweetheart. You'll get a chance to talk with Caudel in a bit. I don't want you hurting yourself before that happens, okay?"

"Yeah, Pete. Let the rest of us get out of the vehicle before you go charging off into the unknown." Sam hitched a small pack onto his back while the others kept themselves free of gear. They had decided that since Sam did not tire, he should be in charge of the gear. Sam had shrugged good-naturedly and told Rags that he had to help.

"Angels don't tire, Rags. Who knew?" the angel of Death joked, then pointed to the remaining packs. "Grab some gear, hombre."

Rags complied, and the two angels split the remaining water and gear evenly between them. They weren't sure what Caudel would tell them or if they would have to leave suddenly or even follow Caudel further into the cave. They came prepared either way.

"Okay," Peter said impatiently. " We ready now?"

Maggie looked at Paul and smiled. The two of them linked arms with Peter and Naomi and started walking. They escorted Peter through the gates and onto the trail that would lead to the fairy cave with Rags, Sam, and Jonah following behind. The group made their way to the mouth of the cave and stopped. It was a bit of a hike, and the humans needed to catch their collective breath. Sam handed them flashlights.

"When we get inside and find Caudel, you gotta let me talk to him first. Understand, Peter? Fairies are a tricky lot, and if you don't lay down the law early, they can weasel their way out of a bargain," Sam told them.

"Okay, Sam, but then do I get to talk with him?" Peter asked.

"Sure, if he wants to. You guys can chat your fool heads off. Business first, though."

"Gotcha."

Sam could tell that Peter was already running through a list of questions for Caudel in his head. "This way, kids." Sam took the lead and led the crew through the cave. They retraced the way that Sam, Maggie, and Naomi went previously and before long found themselves in the cavern that held the statue of the fairy.

"Caudel, show yourself." Sam spoke with authority.

They heard a strange fluttering noise, and to his amazement Peter watched as a tiny man with six wings landed on the stone shelf beside the statue. He was amazed to find that the fairy's appearance mimicked, almost completely, the angelic beings he had encountered. Peter was fascinated, and he wondered if the tiny being wielded the same power as his larger brethren.

"He is so cool," exclaimed Peter who couldn't help himself. Sam glanced over, and Peter mumbled, "Sorry, Sam."

"Please, don't shush him, Samael. I like him. It's been a while since I have interacted with humans," Caudel told him.

"You know the rules, Caudel. Business first. What news do you have?" Sam asked him.

Caudel rubbed his tiny hands together and said, "I have some valuable information for you. I was able to find a lab with a bunch of tiny humans in it. They have snake-people watching them."

"Naga," Paul said it without thinking.

"That's it, Naga. I couldn't remember their name." Caudel slapped a tiny hand to his knee. "Thanks, kid."

Sam looked at Peter who mimicked locking his mouth with a key and nodded to Caudel.

"What else?" Sam asked.

"Well, it seems that the man who runs the lab is working with that she-devil, Lilith. I saw her and the man, Lev was his name I think, talking to an old wrinkled man they called the Chairman. This Chairman person didn't look particularly healthy to me... reminded me of the lepers back in the day. Same kind of sores. Anyhow, they were discussing some kind of serum. Lev mentioned how it was not working on the tiny humans, and they were going to have to start trials on older humans."

During his recitation Caudel was walking back and forth along the shelf. Peter was watching him with rapt attention. He had pulled out a miniature notebook and was making himself some notes.

"Did Lev say what kind of serum he was making or what the serum was for?" Paul spoke from the back.

Caudel looked at him closely for a moment, then at Sam. He nodded, and the fairy answered. "No, but the old Chairman was really interested in how long it would take for him to finish it. Seemed mighty anxious to have it as soon as possible." Caudel turned back to Sam. "The she-devil was interested in it too. I saw the wheels turning in her head as the two were talking. She was on the other side of the table from Lev, so the Chairman didn't know she was there."

"Then what happened?" Peter asked.

Sam rolled his eyes.

"The Chairman told Lev that he had four days to come up with the serum, or else." Caudel ran his finger along his throat to imitate the threat that was implied. "Then, the she-devil and Lev had a conversation about some older human children and a person called Olivier."

There was a gasp from the women in the group, and Caudel turned and said, "I take it you know him, too?"

"Vampire—and a nasty one, too. I'm sorry to hear that he got away and wasn't blown up like poor Max."

Peter could tell that Maggie was furious and shifted his pen and pad to one hand so he could put a comforting arm around her shoulders. No one noticed Paul shift in the back, clearly jealous of the fact that Peter was up with Maggie and not him.

"We'll get him this time." Peter told her, reassuringly.

Caudel whistled, "Boy, you guys sure know how to pick your enemies. These are very bad people. I didn't see the young girls you were asking about; only the tiny humans in glass boxes being tended to by the Naga."

"Can you tell us where they are located?" Sam asked him.

"Sure can. Turns out their lab is connected indirectly to my cave by tunnels. This was all created long ago by a volcano—the same volcano that they are using to heat their lab and dispose of the things or people they don't want others to find," Caudel told them.

"Is there a way we can get to them through the tunnels in your cave?" Sam asked him.

"Not unless you can shrink to my size," Caudel said, then laughed. "Oh, before I forget—I ran into another she-devil on my way back to my cave. I don't think she saw me for what I am though, she called me a bug. I beat it around the corner and made it back here without incident." Caudel seemed very proud of himself, and Peter smiled.

He saw something flash behind Caudel's back and shouted, "You have a tail!?"

"Where?" Caudel jumped and spun around, chasing said tail around in a circle. He laughed uproariously and slapped his knee again at Peter's look of chagrin. "Of course I have a tail, boy." He said it like it was a well-known fact that fairies have tails. "See?" Caudel turned slowly and modeled a roughly three inch tail that, oddly, resembled the tail of a scorpion. Everyone in the group was astounded except, of course, the angels.

Peter spoke first, "It's only that… See, none of the stories that I know of…. They never describe them with tails. Have you always had a tail?"

Caudel gave Sam a look that asked, *Is he for real?* When Sam shrugged, the fairy looked back at Peter and said, "Since I have been in this form, I have had a tail, yes. We don't usually let humans get this close to us, so they wouldn't have noticed."

"Back to business, kids." Sam was getting annoyed at the derailment. "Small creature, do you know if you were followed or if anyone else saw you?"

Caudel shook his head. "Only that she-devil saw me, and I'm pretty sure that I wasn't followed. Remember, I told you some of those passages are only big enough for me to fit through."

"Okay, so we need to know how we can get to the cave that has the children in it." It was Sam's turn to pace, the others watching him, like a slow motion tennis match.

"That's easy—they are near the volcano. There is a tourist site for the Haikou volcano up the road a little ways. Tourists are always talking about it. I can tell you in a few moments where it connects to the next cave, or even if we are in the right place." He said, puffing out his chest.

"How can you do that?" Peter asked.

Caudel looked over and touched his nose with his finger. "I can smell the difference. I have been living in these tunnels a long time, you recognize changes in the air," he told Peter, who was watching him in rapt attention. He turned and winked at Maggie. "There are also the snake thingies that have a sort of musky snake-odor about them. Stinks up the tunnel."

"That's not the only thing that stinks." The deep voice came from behind Paul, and he turned to see Raguel, who had been standing the furthest away, frowning.

Caudel looked over at the new voice, "Why don't you step out of the shadows, Raguel. I have known you were here from the start."

"I haven't been hiding Caudel, you have. Care to tell the others why?" Raguel asked him.

Caudel cleared his throat and said, "Yes, well, some things are better left unsaid, don't you agree?" Caudel looked at the faces, all interested in hearing his sordid tale. He sighed, "Fine, but I am telling you there isn't much to tell. I am hiding because, like all fairies, we seem to be prone to trouble. I choose to be mostly alone in order to keep myself from it. Unfortunately, because of the circumstances of our existence, we are constantly tested to see if redemption is possible. Many of my brethren have not learned the lesson that I have." He shifted his focus solely to Rags. "Is that not what the Master had in mind, Justice-bringer? Was this not *His* chastisement? Is forgiveness in light of redemption not the goal?"

Raguel thought for a moment, the stormy look never leaving his face. "Yes, forgiveness and redemption are the ultimate goals, but trust is something that has to be earned. We have not given that to you, Caudel. You must earn that, this…" he waved his arms to encompass Caudel's cave and everything around him, "is only a step, albeit in the right direction, with me. You have leagues to go."

Caudel looked at Raguel for a moment then nodded his assent. "Noted." His miniature tail swishing back and forth was the only thing that showed his irritation.

"Well, there is no time like the present to find your tiny humans. If Pharzuph did recognize me, the faster we get there, the better off we are." Caudel spoke to the group. "Now, I will need someone to take me with them," he said.

"Why's that?" Peter asked.

"You have seen the size of me, yes?" Caudel asked him. "There are any number of birds or cats or just about any other thing that would want to eat me out there," he said pointing to the way outside.

"Oh, right. Come with me, then. It will give us time to talk," Peter said enthusiastically.

Caudel wasn't sure this was a wise idea, and his face gave it away.

Raguel spoke from the back with a smile on his face. "Yes, Caudel, that *is* a good idea. Young Peter would be a great champion for you to get to know."

Caudel gave Raguel a withering look and flew to Peter's shoulder. "Come, young Peter, let me tell you of my adventures."

The two started back following Sam. Caudel was busy telling Peter of a pirate ship that he had stowed away on.

Paul waited until the others were out of earshot before asking Raguel. "Care to elaborate on why Caudel should not be trusted?"

Raguel looked at Paul and sighed. "He is atoning for his sins, but there is history between the two of us." Seeing that Paul was still waiting for a better answer, he continued, "During the battle of angels, Caudel and his band stood aside. They let the host die. I was almost one of them. I was engaged with three demons, and I called out to him in hopes that he would help me. He looked directly at me for what seemed like forever, then—" Rags shook his head, obviously still bewildered in the present day by what happened so many years ago, "—he just... looked the other way." He came back to himself and said, "If Michael had not come to my aid, I would have perished that day."

Paul laid a comforting hand on his shoulder. "I could not, even if I wanted to, sit in judgement of Caudel's action. I think in some ways, I was worse than Caudel."

"I don't see how that would be possible, Paul." The angel smiled grimly.

"Oh, but I was—at least, I feel like I was. Misguided by the man I called father. He had me believe that his way of life was the only way. He had me convinced that my mother had left me as a young child—left us. He told me that she did not want me, that I was nothing to her. Believing that he was all I had left in the world, I purposed myself to be the best brother and son that I could be, but in order to be those things I had to do the things that his favor required. Pretty soon, it seemed that there were two sides of me." Paul hung his head, remembering the duality of the life he had lived, and the shame that it brought him. "There was the side I let my father see—hard and cold to everyone, following orders and acting every part, the dutiful son to the dangerous crime boss. I hid, but treasured, the better side," Paul smiled, thinking, "the man who would help old ladies across the street and rescue kittens from trees. I was saved from that life by someone who believed that I could be more than what I was. I had only started actively working against the interests of the Bratva when I met Maggie. I was busy liberating slaves, waylaying stolen goods, weapons, and drugs, and trying to come up with a way to leave the family when I was killed."

Raguel looked confused.

"I was saved. There is no other way to put it. Saved from that life for a greater purpose. Michael and Maggie showed me that I was allowed to change my direction, change my values, even change what I fundamentally was—to be better. Maybe Caudel has learned from his past and has chosen to serve a greater purpose. Maybe all he needs is someone to believe in him." Paul smacked Raguel on the back, "After all, he *has* been given a new purpose. He has also lived up to his bargain so far. *'Trust the Master'*...that is what Uriel would tell me." Paul looked at him for a second more before starting his trek back to the surface. "Just something to think about, Angel of Justice."

Rags followed in his wake, pondering.

Chapter 21

It's not that much different than what you are used to, Abe. The divisions break down like this—"

"I understand the duties for the different specialists, Uri. I get that the seraphs are the scouts, the fighters, and the host troops, along with the cherubim. I also get that the cherubs do the intel and demo work. The thrones are the berserkers and shock troops. It goes off the rails for me after that… so, help." He threw his hands up in surrender, and Uriel laughed, continuing his tutelage.

"OK, so ARC exists to assist us, not only in the day-to-day missions, but also in our great battles. That's what we're talking about here. You run our strategy, along with Michael and Raphael. I handle the elites, the Hellbane and the Guard, along with Paul and some others. Peter works with Michael directly, but he also works in arms and armor, as is his talent. With me?"

Abe nodded, keeping up.

"Then, past the thrones, you have dominions and lordships, the next level in the hierarchy. This is where it gets interesting." Uriel's eyes took on a gleam, and Abe could tell that he was eager to have someone to teach. "Dragons, handlers, and our cavalry troops are at this level, along with first-level healers. Then, you have the strongholds and virtues—you won't deal with them much as they are our main healers, magi, and clerics."

Abe looked quizzical, so the angel explained. "Clerics lead prayer warriors and worshippers—very important when we fight the infernals. Don't ever forget that."

"Got it. What's next?" Abe was taking it all in.

"After them, you have the powers and authorities—our leaders;

generals and adepts. Finally, before us of course, you have the rulers and principalities. These elites fight Hell directly and have the best battle stories." Uriel winked, looking quite pleased. "I work with them— the Hellbane and the Guard. They get as close to the Under-realm as any, save for Samael and the Master. They are the only ones actually able to breach Hell. I know that's a lot to take in, but it'll all come in time. Just remember that you are an important part of our mission readiness, with a never-ending commission. Does that help?"

Uriel's conversation with Abe in the garden was interrupted by a call from elsewhere in the garden. Abe could hear it as clear as if it were right next to him, and he could tell it was Michael summoning Uriel.

"We'll come up with a solid support plan when I get finished with Michael. Thanks, Abe," Uriel said to him, and disappeared.

Abe nodded and walked off into the jungle.

"Michael, what did you find out?" Uriel asked him, jumping right into the business at hand.

"He said we can use the dragon but only if he chooses to help. Part of the condition of him staying in the garden was that he can't be compelled. Only he can choose if he wants to leave," Michael told him.

"He's an awful grouch," Uriel said unimpressed. "I only hope he is bored beyond belief and wants to get out and do something—that something being, fight a slew of hellhounds for fun."

Michael agreed. "He is the best defense against hellhounds, no doubt. I just want our people to have a fighting chance. Even the host will have a difficult time."

"Well, there is only one thing for it, then. You'll just have to go and ask him," Uriel said and clapped Michael on the shoulder. Michael raised a questioning eyebrow and Uriel corrected, "I mean, *we'll* go and ask him."

They had just started to walk, when a familiar figure popped up in front of them.

"Rags," Michael said by way of a greeting.

Uriel just inclined his head.

"Mike. Uri. What are you up to?"

"Dragon strategy. What'd you need, brother?"

"I'll get right to it. Did you know that Sam is working with Caudel? He has granted him a new purpose. How can he do that?" He started pacing in front of the two archangels.

Michael grinned. "Of course I knew. I think that it's a wonderful idea. Caudel was obviously ready." Michael stepped past Raguel and continued on into the surrounding foliage.

"How? How do you know? Do you not remember his treachery? The injustice of allowing the Watchers to fall?"

"I was there; of course I do. Rags, we are brothers, right? How could we be so opposed to each other on this?" Michael stopped walking, turning his full attention to the Angel of Justice. "When's it gonna be enough for you? How long does he have to suffer to fulfill your requirement of him? I know what he did, and I know he victimized you, betrayed you. Do you remember what happened with Sam and me? Penance paid is the ticket to entry. He has done that, Rags." Michael was again speaking of the fairy.

"Has he asked to be taken back among the fold? Has he been given a new directive, and has he been following it?" Uriel asked him.

"Yes to all, but…" Raguel started to say.

Uriel shook his head, "Then you should be happy for him. He has turned a corner and is back on our side. If you don't give him the opportunity to make a choice, his redemption cannot happen."

Raguel had stopped pacing and looked at Uriel. "Paul said pretty much the same thing. He told me that he has learned his lesson, and maybe all he needs is someone to believe in him."

Uriel smiled, "Paul is a very smart man—you should listen to him."

"It's just that… I'm not sure I can trust Caudel," Raguel admitted.

Uri placed a hand on Rag's shoulder and said, "You need to let it go, bro. Caudel has accepted his punishment and has requested forgiveness and redemption. Justice has been served. Don't make this personal. You'd better get back. Your charges are looking for you."

Uriel left Raguel to think on what he had said and followed Michael's path to the Dragon. Michael turned and waited for Uriel to catch up to him.

"Think he's gonna be okay?" Michael asked.

"I believe so. Raguel has a hard time letting go; always has. I am not sure he will be able to until Caudel seeks his forgiveness as well."

"However clouded his judgement, Caudel sinned mightily against our brothers. If I hadn't stepped in, he would have let Raguel die. It's not easy to trust someone who let you down so spectacularly."

"That would be a difficult thing, but not impossible. Come on, let's go find Ouryu. He should be around here somewhere."

The two angels walked around the garden for a few minutes looking for the ancient yellow dragon. They finally came to a field, and in the field there was a gigantic hill with a great old tree. Under the tree lay the golden dragon, its neck stretched out with eyes closed; a perfect picture of serenity. Michael hated to interrupt, but this was important. The two angels walked over to where the giant lay contentedly.

"Are you two gonna tell me what you want with me, or do I have to guess? Ordinarily, I would love a good game, but you are cutting into my nap time," said the great golden head. His words were punctuated with a yawn that showed rows of gleaming teeth and a long, serpentine tongue.

Michael held up a hand. "Peace, great one. We do not mean to interrupt your slumber, but we have a matter of some urgency, and have come to request a favor of you. Would you hear what we have to say?"

"I do not grant favors anymore, but I will listen to your urgent matter and make a decision." The great dragon flipped and slithered into an almost-sitting position, and crossed its front legs like a human would cross their arms. The movement made Michael smile.

"Thank you. I appreciate you taking time to hear us out. As you know, there has been a series of events in the human world that has triggered a response from the heavens. The nephilim have been actively recruiting and gathering forces all over the human world. We have our own forces who have been actively trying to stop them."

"Yes, as they have been for millennia, archangel. They are like a sickness—they always crop up, and you always beat them. You have not needed me for thousands of years, and I see nothing has changed, save maybe your confidence, Michael, so I will cheer you on: *Go on, you can do it!*" The dragon raised his clasped front claws up, first to one side of his great face, then the other, shaking them and smiling.

"Ouryu, that's just it. Things *have* changed, I'm afraid. The nephilim are still unable to keep a host very long, but they have new resources and are on the verge of creating a serum that will make it so they can tolerate a host longer—maybe even make one viable long-term. We are trying to stop this from happening."

The great dragon looked bored, and he was irritating Uriel.

"So what is it you wish for me to do? I haven't stepped a claw into the world of humans for a very long time, and your explanations don't really make me want—"

"The humans are fine. We need your help with the hounds."

That got the dragon's attention. It had been picking at a loose scale on one of its front claws, but stopped suddenly.

"Hellhounds, eh? I haven't seen one of those accursed things since some of the first battles of China. They were used to spread terror and create mayhem in the most well-ordered camp. When Emperor Fu Xi's forces were sleeping, I was guarding. It was this that allowed his forces victory time and again."

"Yes, well the infernal's dogs are back in China, this time in the company of the Three. One of the Seven picked a fight with it and, although he dealt it a major blow, we feel it survived. We are unsure if it has any friends, but usually where there is one there are more, as your great experience would tell you," Michael told the dragon.

The great dragon nodded its head and flipped back around so it stood on all ten legs. "That is usually the way. Demons feed off of fear, chaos, destruction, and all manner of other disastrous things.

They enjoy the catastrophes they create, and they ruin, utterly, everything." The dragon spit at the thought of it, melting a stone. The dragon shook it's great head as if trying to rid the picture of destruction from its mind. "You know, that is why I chose to fight alongside the humans. They were outmatched and outnumbered, and I despise a cheat. That's all the infernals know how to do. Anyway, I decided to level the field, as it were."

Michael, who was listening attentively, said quickly, "That is why you are needed again, friend. However talented and blessed, Shem's Line will be facing something that they will not be able to defeat without help. If three demons were able to breach the barrier, then what is stopping more from coming through?" Michael started to pace at the base of the hill. "Who knows what they intend? They may or may not bring the hounds of hell with them—"

"Who do you think you are working on, First?" The dragon came across annoyed. "I know, as do you, that your intelligence tells you much of what you will face, and demons are predictable. You know that in a battle such as this, there will be many, many dogs. Appealing to my fondness for the humans is a flawed tactic, as my friend Sun Tzu would tell you, for it is not constant. I don't always back the humans, as you well know, and your gambit has failed because I am not satisfied with what humans have become. The humans I assisted were courageous and bold, and yes, I'll say it," the dragon clicked its front claws in a snapping motion, "valorous. The humans today do not possess these qualities, you of all should know that, Michael. They live in greed and ignorance and perfidy. They are not worthy of my hand, nor yours. No, I have come to like the peace in this glade. I will stay here."

Michael let out a great breath and looked at Uriel. Uriel was watching the great dragon with speculation. Michael could see the wheels turning in his head. He glanced heavenward and within the span of a human heartbeat he heard her.

"Ouryu, you great lizard—I'll have a word with you, if you please." Ariel came storming out of the foliage into the grassy meadow.

Michael almost laughed at the expression on the great dragon's face. He actually squirmed a little to move away from the feisty little angel.

"Ariel, now listen—"

He started but was cut off by, "Don't you *Now listen* me. You have been talking and talking and talking about all of your grand adventures to me, but now that one is there in front of you, now when you are needed, you dismiss us out of hand. I didn't know dragons were such chickens."

The dragon roared to its feet, towering over the little angel who stood tapping her foot on the ground in front of him.

"I am *not* a coward!" he bellowed, with enough force to cause Michael and Uriel to take a step back as a small stream of fire issued from his mouth.

"Uh, Ariel?" Uriel said, "Maybe making him mad isn't the best play here."

But she wasn't listening. She was instead readying herself to square off against the dragon again. Ariel quickly grew to the height of the dragon, the teal tips of her wings were in direct contrast to the bright white. At her height she could—and did—look the dragon in the eye.

"We have been friends from the beginning, you and I. We have had many discussions about how you were integral to the Master and how you miss being in the world again. Why do you choose now to retreat to this lonely existence?"

The dragon sat on its haunches and looked at her, great bouts of steam issuing from its mouth, the only sign of anger from him.

"I do miss the world, but, honestly Ariel, they are living wrong. You know it as well as I." The dragon sat back, crossing his arms again.

"They always have—that is what makes them human, you know. We are not talking about *humans,* Ouryu. We are talking about the Chosen, Shem's Line, the fighters for humanity at ARC. You know their cause, their mission, and the consequences of failure. If you would not help them, then you disgrace yourself." She stepped back, taking a breath and steeling her gaze. "You disgrace the Master."

"They are worthy, Ouryu. Even if you don't see it, they are worthy," Uriel said quietly, taking a step toward the great beast.

"They… they cannot hope to win without you. This rests entirely on you, Great One, fairly or unfairly. You choose whether or not the Master's plan is realized." Michael somberly put things into perspective and walked away.

Uriel spoke again. "Remember, ultimately, who you would be doing this for, Ouryu. I know you will make the right choice." Then he, too, walked away, leaving Ariel and Ouryu alone in the glade.

Ariel shrunk down to her diminutive size again, and walked up the hill to join the golden dragon, sitting next to him.

"You know what it's like to fight for a race's survival and lose." She said it sadly, reaching out a hand to stroke the dragon's head.

"What if—what if I can't save them? What if it is another Snow Mountain?"

Ariel was surprised. "You don't think they're unworthy. You think you are. Look," she said, turning to the dragon's eyes to drive home her point, "there has only been one time in the history of ever that one being was able to save a race, and we both know how that went down. It was never up to you to save your brethren, and no one blames you for their fate. The only way you can fail is if you never try. The Master created us all for express purposes, and I think you know that this is yours. I won't pressure you, old friend." The Angel of Nature stood and turned back once more. "I want you to think about that, and when you have made your decision, come and find me. You know where I'll be."

"A dragon with performance anxiety?" Ariel had joined Michael and Uriel at a spot away from the glade, and she was recounting her talk with Ouryu.

Ariel spun around quickly and gave Uriel a sad look. "Anything that feels can have anxiety, Uriel." She sighed deeply. "Ouryu struggles with feeling like he is to blame for Snow Mountain. He feels like he could have single-handedly saved his people, and that in not doing so, he is somehow a failure. He wishes to not let us down, is all."

"That whole thing had nothing to do with him and everything to do with Cephas and Alaric," Michael said, remembering the horror of the massacre, and getting angry. "Why doesn't he use that to fuel his rage against the hellhounds that we are surely to be up against now?" Michael almost pled the case to Ariel, who had no control over the dragon's ultimate cooperation. "Doesn't he see? They won't make it without him."

Michael seemed a bit more concerned than usual, but Ariel spoke calmly. "Sometimes anger can be a great motivator. I think that Ouryu just needed a kick in the scales. Once he has made up his mind, he will see that I am right, or—" Ariel said, unflinchingly, her eyes blazing an almost black-purple, "—he will find himself expelled from Eden. Forever." Ariel turned and walked away from the other two angels, who just looked on.

"Remind me never to get on her bad side. She would be scarier than facing down ten hellhounds," Michael remarked, and Uriel nodded.

"I agree. If she can bring the dragon around, it will help Paul and Peter greatly. If not, well, Abe and I will come up with something. It would be nice to know exactly what we are dealing with, though."

Michael nodded in agreement. "If Ariel thinks this will work, I have faith it will. Let's go forward with our plans."

He turned and started walking, then stopped and turned back to Uriel. "Go ahead and make your contingencies, though. It's always good to have a back-up plan." He then turned back and continued into the trees and disappeared.

Chapter 22

Olivier marched through the tunnels on a mission. He was tired of that buffoon Lev taking everything from him. *We have an understanding, dammit,* he thought. *I stay out of his business, and he stays out of mine.* That was it, but now Lev had stolen Olivier's property, and he would pay dearly for it. He slammed through the door of the lab in which Lev was working.

"You have gone too far, Lev. How *dare* you steal what belongs to me?" Olivier had picked Lev up by the front of his lab coat and slammed him against the wall. His eyes had changed from their original brown to a fiery red color. Lev knew that Olivier would be pissed, but he was not afraid of him. At least, not usually.

"It was the Chairman. He needs answers before the end of the week. The girls are replaceable." Lev practically stammered the last part of the sentence.

"Olivier, put Lev down. You know that we can't afford for him to be hurt at this crucial time." Lilith had come out of the shadows at the back of the lab.

Pharzy and Ono, following behind her, chimed in. "Yes, Olivier. Put the nice human down."

Olivier snarled at all three of them, his sharp canine teeth glinting as they were exposed to the light in the lab. "You three had something to do with this? I should have known. You bitches can't keep your hands out of other people's business."

All three of them gasped. "That was uncalled for. We only want to make sure that Lev succeeds in finding a solution to an ongoing problem. You know how important this is to the Chairman and the others. I can't believe that you would only think of yourself at a time like this." Pharzy tsked at Olivier, and Ono stuck out her tongue at him in response to Lilith's words.

"You three think you are so clever. This human," he shook Lev, who was still trapped between the angry vampire and the wall, like he weighed less than nothing, "has taken everything from me repeatedly, and I am tired of it. He owes me his life at this point." The vampire looked dangerously at the man in his clutches. "I mean to collect."

Olivier went in for the kill, only to be yanked back by Lilith, who was far superior in strength. She picked him up and flung him across the passageway, demolishing a nearby metal cart in the process. He found himself sprawled on the ground, looking into the eyes of one very angry hellhound.

Tsoula had come back through the portal with the three Sisters, and she was not in an equitable mood. Olivier knew that to mess with her at this point would mean tremendous pain in the immediate future. He gathered himself and stood, brushing off pants and poking at a rip in his shirt.

"You have not heard the last of this, Lev. When these three trolls are done with you—and they will be done playing with you eventually—we will have some fun, you and I. In the meantime I will bide my time. Do not expect any other favors from me. I am all out."

He marched over to the portal in the shadows that the hound had just appeared from and walked through it without looking back. He was once again on a mission as he left the others in the lab. He ordinarily liked meandering through the corridors of the pit. He enjoyed the jeweled walls in their vivid colors, but today he could find no comfort in them. He was still seeing red and needed to find a way to vent his fury.

I should find Alaric. He will know how I can have my revenge.

His master was not happy with him after Lev caused the demise of the cabal. There were so many injustices that needed to be righted. Now because of this stupid human working for the Chairman, he is forced to give up his inventory. They didn't even allow him to keep ones he was going to feed on, they took them all. He kicked out and managed to dislodge a gem from the wall—the large emerald fell to the ground in front of him.

Well, this makes up for some of the girls, but not for all, he thought as he pocketed the five-carat emerald. At this weight and clarity, he could easily make $15,000. That would only replace one of the girls he had picked up recently. Lev took over twenty from him this time.

Olivier started walking again, this time running his long sharp nails over the gems covering the walls. He secretly hoped another of the superior gems would come loose from its anchor. Olivier had always thought of the pit as alive. The gems in the walls changed constantly because of the natural sloughing that occurred. Some of them were better than others, but all of them were exceptional. Olivier had walked these corridors for centuries and had only been on the receiving end a handful of times. Maybe his luck was about to change.

He rounded the last corner on his way to see Alaric and ran into Abbadon. He looked to be coming from Alaric's. He wrinkled his nose in distaste and said, "Abbadon," by way of greeting.

Abbadon ginned. "You look like you have yourself all wound up, vampire. What happened this time? Someone kick your puppy?"

Olivier snarled and said, "No, those sluts-in-heat of yours have caused me problems."

"Mine? I make no claims on them. They can create chaos all on their own. They need no help." Abbadon smiled. "Aw, but you look so down. Maybe I can help you. What exactly have they done this time?" he asked with a sympathetic grin and a pat on the shoulder.

"Everyone knows that you do not help without expecting something in return. What do you want, Abbadon?" Olivier asked him.

Abbadon put on a fake pout and said, "I'm hurt that you think I would not help you without expecting something."

Olivier sighed and started to push past Abbadon, who stopped him with a scaly hand. "You are smarter than Alaric said you were. You know he really isn't pleased with you at the moment, right?

Are you sure you want to visit him right now? He seems to be in a foul temper. Although, if you felt up to sharing, maybe we could work out a way for you to teach them a lesson."

As if to punctuate that last statement, Olivier heard voices coming from Alaric's lair.

"*I will not tolerate weakness!*" Olivier heard Alaric yelling... and an answering, "*Master, we were only expecting humans to be there, not the holy ones. They burned us with their holy fire. We only lost two, Master. I swear.*" This was followed by an unearthly bellow.

"I will not tolerate any more losses. First, Narcisse loses a whole cabal, now this? *I will not abide this any longer!*" This statement was followed by a scream and a loud crashing thud.

Olivier thought for the briefest of moments about which road he should choose.

"Why don't we go talk somewhere that is not this close to Alaric? He doesn't seem to be in the best humor."

Abbadon smiled and said, "This way."

Abbadon showed Olivier to a room off another corridor. He opened the door and ushered Olivier through it. Immediately, Olivier wished that he had not taken Abbadon up on his offer. The room into which Abbadon had shown him was all white. Lit as it was, it should have produced shadows on the furniture, but this room did not. He also noted that there were no corners in this room. All the walls were smooth and rounded to make one giant circular room. Directly in the middle of the room was a huge bed and as far as Olivier could see there was no shadow under the bed either. On one side of the bed was a fireplace and two high-backed chairs. Olivier had to wonder how the fire itself did not cast shadows anywhere.

Abbadon led Olivier over to the fireplace and motioned for him to sit in one of the chairs. He produced two milk-white glasses—one held a clear liquid, and the other showed the only color in the entire room, red. The second glass held blood.

Abbadon passed the glass to Olivier and said, "Freshly squeezed this morning." He sat down in the other chair and looked at Olivier for a moment before saying, "I understand that the human is close to finding a serum for the Chairman?" It was more of a question than a statement.

Olivier took a sip of the fresh blood and savored the taste before saying, "Yes, well... I don't know how close he really is, Abbadon. All I know is that he goes through children quicker than a vampire." He snickered at his own joke.

Abbadon smiled. "Cute." He toyed with the rim on his glass, looked down, and nonchalantly asked, "So, what is it that you do for them, exactly?"

"Well, up until today, I procured the children. That bitch Tsoula grabbed some as well, but that was only one time, because she got herself caught by that angel." Olivier smiled at the thought. "She deserved it, pompous flea bag."

"You'd better watch it. Now that Tsoula has recovered, she is not in a good mood—not that she ever was. She is really out for some angel blood now, and it won't matter who gets in her way." Abbadon told him and refilled the glass that Olivier had just drained. "I have a proposition for you." Olivier just looked at him over the rim of his freshly filled glass. "One that will allow you to have your revenge, and help me at the same time."

"I'm listening," was all he said.

"I need for the serum to be delayed," he said coyly.

"Delayed?" the vampire raised a furry brow, puzzled and suspicious.

"Just for a bit. You don't want Lev succeeding, do you? You want to hurt him, right? What better way than to make him fail at his new batch? At any rate, my reasons are my own. You want to hurt Lev the way he has hurt you, and I want him to fail to find that serum. It's a win-win."

Abbadon steepled his fingers in front of his face and waited for Olivier to answer.

The thoughts churned over and over in Olivier's head. He could practically taste the retribution that failure would bring to Lev, and the Three would go down with him.

"So, you want me to sabotage the work that Lev is doing right now? How would you suggest that I do that without them getting suspicious of me? I'm not exactly friendly with any of them," Olivier said with a sneer.

"There are many ways to accomplish our goal, just be creative. Why, you can poison the food and water to the subjects. Or," the demon said, standing, "there are local wildlife that could wander into the tunnels. It is truly amazing the amount of snakes that live in China—I'm sure that you can find one or two that can create havoc in the lab." Abbadon had obviously given this a fair bit of thought. "There are also all manner of creepy crawly creatures that can give false data and would then slither off into the darkness."

Olivier mulled over what Abbadon was telling him. He didn't really have to get his hands dirty—only provide the ammunition and let the inevitable happen. A few well placed accidents should help to cause Lev to really regret his recent choices.

"I see what you mean, Abbadon. I believe we can help each other in this endeavor." He rubbed his hands together, "Yes, I believe that this could be much more fun than dealing with Alaric." He stood, "I must be going. I have a lot of ammunition to collect."

Abbadon didn't bother to stand. "Have fun."

Olivier did not see the smile on Abbadon's face as he closed the door behind him. He had only gone a few steps before he had his *shopping list* created in his head. Time to go get his supplies and pay a visit to Lev's subjects. Maybe he could find a special one for Lev too—not to kill him, no that would bring too much attention—but maybe one that could make him sick. There were a few of those around too—a little venom from a more harmless snake or spider—just enough to make him sick for a couple of days. *It will seem like he's having a run of bad luck.* Just enough to throw him off course and off his timeline; then the Chairman would see to his punishment.

Olivier started to whistle a ditty as he practically skipped to the nearest portal from the pit. He couldn't wait to get started.

Chapter 23

The little band's rented bus bounced down the long Heinem-Haikou road, kicking up the ashy dust so it refracted the sun in the late afternoon sky. Peter had made good on his vow to question the resident fairy and was deep in conversation with him next to Sam.

"Does your tail have any special power, or is it only a tail?" Peter asked, sitting with his pen hovering over the little notebook he kept for his ideas.

Sam noticed that Caudel must really like Peter—he was answering all his questions with sincerity and a ton of patience.

Caudel laughed. "Well, now it does serve a purpose, make no mistake." He grabbed his tail and pulled it around in front of him.

"What's that?" Peter was literally on the edge of his seat.

Caudel laughed and said, "The tail is meant for defense, of course. You see this here?" Caudel lifted a small barb at the end of his tail. "This is what protects us from humans and other beings that wish to hurt us."

Peter scribbled in his notebook and asked without looking up, "What does it do?"

"Well, whatever we wish it to do, really," Caudel said. "For example, if I wanted to jab you with my tail and wished for you to see blue bunny rabbits attacking you from the air, that is what you would see, understand?"

Peter nodded wildly. "This is awesome. So your tail allows you to make someone see exactly what you wish them to see? Does it do anything else?" Peter asked him.

"Makes humans break out in great sores that cause them to go mad."

Peter stopped for a moment, taking in all that Caudel had just told him.

"That is *so* cool." Peter started furiously writing again.

Caudel and Sam exchanged glances, and Sam just shrugged and smiled at Caudel's bewilderment.

"Peter is in a league of his own, Caudel—the sooner you accept it, the better off you will be."

"Thanks, Sam," Peter said, grinning as he looked up from his notebook. Again, Caudel shared a look with Sam, who smiled at him in return.

The little bus carrying the intrepid adventurers tooled along the roadway. After a while, Jonah stopped the bus in the parking lot of the next tourist destination.

"We are here."

The Haikou Volcanic Park existed to allow tourists an up close adventure with a volcano system. Although the volcano had not erupted in thousands of years, it did not mean that it could not— only that it had not. Most people flirted with death on a daily basis. People who lived near the volcano knew that it could blow and wipe out an entire village or town, but they continued to live and work near them because the possibility of being killed by one, especially this one, was small.

Jonah turned off the bus and looked back at Sam who was sitting in the front seat. "What do you want to do?"

"I figure if you can talk to the locals, maybe you can get an idea of out-of-the-way tunnels that we can look into? In the meantime, we will take Caudel with us and poke around the grounds. If anyone can find us a way in, it would be him."

Jonah nodded and said, "I can do that. Can I take Rags with me? He usually has a calming effect on the villagers."

"Good idea, actually. The less he is around Caudel, the better," Sam told him. Sam turned to the rest of the bus occupants and said, "Okay, kids, who wants to go for a hike? Peter, you get Caudel. Maybe give him a break from the twenty questions for now, okay?"

"Caudel, if you were tired of my questions, you should have said something. Everybody else just tells me to be quiet," Peter said, by way of apology to Caudel, who had slipped into the hood on Peter's hoodie.

"It's okay, boy, only it has been a while since I have held a good conversation with anyone. Afraid I'm a bit rusty—and you're a bit exuberant. Just give me a breather, and we'll try again later."

Peter nodded his head forcing Caudel to duck down into the hoodie to keep from being clocked by the movement. They exited the bus and followed Sam down one of the many paths in the park.

"Okay, Caudel, use your sniffer and see if anything smells like home to you," Sam told him.

Caudel launched himself from the hoodie and zig-zagged along the path. Peter assumed he was sniffing as he went. Whenever other humans were close, he would either hide in the foliage or zip back to hide in the hoodie. They had walked for a little while, when Rags and Jonah caught up to them.

"Hey, we think there might be an entrance further down the hill. One of the guides mentioned that there was a tunnel that they found recently, but it is as yet unexplored," Jonah told them excitedly. "Let's walk down further and see if we can find the trail. We have to be careful because it is off-limits, and if we are caught there would be a lot of explaining to do."

The others nodded and pointed things out to each other while walking further along the path. Pretty soon they came to a place that shot off in two directions. The path was recently cut and had no entry markers placed in front of it.

"If they didn't want to draw attention to it, they failed," Peter said grinning.

"People in China always obey posted signs, Peter," explained Jonah. "To not do so could mean death."

Peter gulped and said, "This is not the first time on this journey that I am glad I live in the US."

Maggie, who had come up beside him, said, "Ditto. I did a

piece about totalitarian regimes a while back, China being one of them, and the human rights crimes associated. Just awful," she said, scowling. "The worst part is, these people almost have no fight left in them. After generations of families being brought up under the thumb of some dictator, it just becomes an accepted fact of life. Our people take so much for granted, like the fact that we can stand up to tyranny, and say what we like, and vote for our own interests."

Jonah thought, then spoke. "True, but some would say that it also gives too much freedom, and that it causes entitlement and corruption. And rebellion."

"Maybe, but it has been a while since we have had open rebellion on our soil. I only pray it stays that way," Maggie said earnestly.

Rags spoke up, joining them. "Me too, Maggie, although globally, the world has been uneasy for some time. Because of pride—and envy, and wrath—we have seen numerous small battles turn into larger skirmishes. Ultimately, it is the poorest among us who pay the price. Just look back over the last few months on a global scale, not just what we endured recently. Crime is at an all time high. Guns and other weapons, even bio weapons and weapons of mass destruction, are sold daily on the black market. People are bought and sold like possessions. Animals are hunted as trophies, and in some cases so are humans."

Paul said, "I have heard stories like these, and many others just like it. There is no justice in those things, and it is all controlled by the people who have all the money. They say money cannot buy you happiness, but if you have enough of it, it can buy you everything else."

"That's what my Uncle Abe said, too. He would have liked you, Paul," Naomi told him. "He also said the only way you can fight them is one battle at a time."

The rest of the friends nodded in agreement.

"Okay, our best course of action seems to be to send Caudel down the path to see what he can find." Sam pointed that direction. "This keeps us from drawing any attention, and nobody goes to jail.

Caudel, we will meet you back at the picnic area just up the hill. Please bring us back some good news, and we'll go from there."

With a wink to Naomi and Maggie, Caudel launched himself from the hoodie once more and was gone in a blink.

"He's right, you know," Peter said to no one in particular.

"About what?" Naomi asked, taking Peter's hand in hers as they turned back.

"You really can't see his tail, because he is so fast and little." Peter grinned while the rest of them groaned. "What? You can't. I tried."

Naomi tugged at him. "Come on, hun. Let's go see what Rachel packed in those bento boxes this morning."

"Oh, food? Great. I'm starved," Peter told her as he put his ever-present notebook back in his backpack. She wasn't sure when he retrieved it, but the fact he was putting it away meant he was quick on the draw. She giggled at her own pun. "What?" Peter asked her.

"Nothing. Just thought of something silly," Naomi said, practically pulling Peter after the others.

As the friends all settled down in the small picnic area to wait for Caudel, Naomi and Maggie unpacked the lunch that Rachel had packed for them from the constantly-used stew pot in the kitchen. When she asked about the pot, Maggie was told it was always simmering for those who find a way to the orphanage. Their door was always open to those in need, and it didn't hurt to have warm food and a bed available.

The friends shared the meal in the pristine gardens surrounding the park. They watched as a few groups of tourists meandered their way through, gushing about how lush the gardens were and how exciting it was to be in China on vacation. Peter heard more than one, "It's a once in a lifetime trip," from the passing people. Once they were through, they packed up the lunch and stored all the little bento boxes securely in a backpack worn by Rags, then the group loitered a little longer.

Maggie and Paul had walked back up the hill a bit, having a

lively discussion about Shaolin Wushu. Naomi and Peter passed the time propped against a tree, holding hands and speaking softly. Raguel, Sam, and Jonah kept an eye on the proceedings; having a discussion of their own.

"If my uncle were here, I wonder what he would say about this?" Naomi asked, holding their clasped hands up to the sunlight.

Peter considered, then pulled their hands to his mouth and kissed hers. "I think he would say that he wants you to be happy, and that if you are happy with me, you should go for it."

"I am. I really am."

"Me, too. Fell in love with you *while* you yelled at me," Peter said, smiling. Naomi, remembering, looked a bit embarrassed.

"I was so rude to you that day, sweetheart. You just caught me in a protective moment with Abe."

"Will you be that protective with me?" Peter asked her, curiously.

"Yeah, most likely, I will." She grinned, mischievously.

"How very Momma Rose of you," Peter said, grinning.

"I'll take that as a compliment, sir. She has managed to keep you alive and well-fed for a long time." She stopped smiling suddenly, turned to him and grabbed his face, pointing her eyes at his. "I love you, Peter."

"Back atcha, beautiful." He bent slightly to kiss her, when he heard a cough to his right. Peter and Naomi's tree was close to the bushes, and the cough came from the foliage.

"*Pssst.*"

Peter turned around and walked closer to the bush.

"Caudel?" Naomi asked.

"This is the right cave system. Go get Sam and the others, and I'll show you where you can enter the tunnels," Caudel told them.

Peter nodded, gave Naomi a quick kiss, and said, "We can pick this up later."

"Caudel has found our entrance. What do you want to do now?" Peter asked him.

"I think that you, Paul, and the girls should come with me and follow Caudel. I will send Rags and Jonah back to find a place for the bus. If we leave the bus in the parking lot, the guards will get suspicious. They can join us after dark."

Peter nodded once again and went to tell the others. Sam walked over to where Jonah and Rags were standing and told them about Caudel finding the right tunnel. He asked them to move the bus to a safer location and then come back after the park closed. Rags seemed reluctant to leave, but Sam reminded him that if Jonah was going to make it back in without being seen, he would need a little bit of help. The others watched as Rags and Jonah went off to stash the bus somewhere close by, then they made their way down the path once again to the roped off section.

With Sam keeping an eye out for the guards, they each slipped into the dense bushes where Caudel waited. It really was more of a deer trail than a path since they had not yet started to study the area. Caudel led them down the steep decline that the path followed and around a series of rocks and shrubs. They came to a small area that was covered with dense vegetation.

"Why are we stopping, Caudel?" Paul asked nervously.

"I've brought you to the opening."

Peter looked around, and then his face brightened. "Is it hidden by magic?"

Caudel laughed and flew over to the dense spot of growth. "No, Peter, just by weeds." He grabbed one of the stalks of vines and overgrowth nearest to him and pulled.

Peter could just make out the darkness on the other side. He stepped forward and took over parting the vegetation for Caudel who had already zipped inside. Sam went next, followed by the girls, and then Paul, with Peter bringing up the rear. The friends stood where they were for a moment, letting their eyes adjust to the darkness.

"I have some flashlights," Peter told them helpfully.

"No, homes. We can't afford to be seen," Sam said.

"I have another way," Caudel suggested.

He looked at Sam, who nodded and said, "Go ahead. Can't wait to see this," and chuckled.

Caudel went over to Peter and said, "This won't hurt at all." Before Peter could ask what wouldn't hurt, Caudel's tail had whipped out from behind him and sunk itself into Peter's cheek, just below his eyes.

"Ow. Hey, watch it."

He stopped talking for a moment as Caudel said, "No, *you* watch it, because now you can see it."

"What's happening? Whoa. *Whoa*!" Peter exclaimed, holding his hand out in front of him and waving it, which caused Caudel to fly off in a hurry.

"What is, Peter?" Naomi asked him before a small, "*Ouch,*" escaped her lips, followed by a gasp.

Maggie and Paul were next, and then the four friends stood, marvelling over the fact that they could see in the dark.

"How in the world were you able to make us see in the dark?" Peter asked Caudel, taking out his small notebook. "I can read perfectly as well. This is amazing."

"Remember, I told you that our tails can make you think whatever I want you to think? I wanted you to be able to see in the dark, and now you can," Caudel said matter of factly.

"I could have used this a few months ago." That came from Paul's direction.

"Oh, what were you doing a few months ago that you would have needed to be able to see at night?" Maggie asked him. "Were you robbing a tomb like those other daring treasure hunters?'

"Something like that," he told her with a smile.

"Well, when we are done here, Mr. Maxwell, we will have to sit down and have a long talk about your adventures," Maggie told him with a smile.

"It would be a pleasure, although I am afraid you would be bored," Paul told her.

"Okay guys, we will wait here until Jonah and Rags come back, then we will set out in search of Lev and his merry snake people," Caudel said.

"Naga," Peter replied helpfully. He sat on a rock formation with his head bent over his notebook, and he didn't notice the fairy's eyes roll heavenward.

While they had a few minutes—and Paul was otherwise engaged with Sam—Maggie took stock. It had been a little over eight months since Max's death, and this was the first time in a while that she could remember having fun. She wasn't entirely certain if it had mostly to do with their adventure or her company, but she did know one thing. When she was with Paul Maxwell, she didn't miss Max.

Chapter 24

Lev and the Naga were working furiously to set up the chambers for the new test group. He knew that he was running out of time. The Chairman had been adamant. If he didn't get results soon, he would probably not last the month. There was a change in the Chairman, almost a panic that Lev had never seen before.

Simon was working quietly on the other side of the room. Lev had noticed that the older Naga had been extremely quiet as of late and, in a rare act of kindness brought out by desperation for karmic favor, Lev asked him what was wrong.

"The young onessss are having an isssssue with replacing the old ssssssubjectssss."

"Didn't I warn you about them getting attached? They have to remain neutral, otherwise all sorts of problems could arise," Lev said in admonishment.

"Yessss Masssster, I know thissss, but the young onessssss are not happy with thissss place," he said. "The young onessss said this place isssss cursssssed. They have felt the awakening of the mountain, they say this is where the great lizard lives. They have heard thisssss from the local people when they venture out at night. They ssssay that there issss a great lizard that protectsssss the people from harm."

"Surely you have told them that there is nothing to be afraid of?" Lev inquired, suddenly uneasy that things could quickly go off the rails again.

"I have told them that, but there are truthssss to old ssssstories, I would not sssssscoff so."

Lev could tell that he had touched on a sore subject with Simon. His great tail was whipping back and forth with his ire.

"Oh, calm down, Simon, before you knock over everything. Why don't you go see if you can find out where the subject for this room is. Send in one of the others to finish. I have to go see to the other rooms."

Without a backward glance, Lev left the room to Simon. He did not like to admit it, but the Naga scared him sometimes. The only way to deal with that was to make himself scarier. He kept them on a tight leash, and his punishments were swift and severe. He was positive that they were afraid of him and his retribution. He was so distracted by his thoughts that he did not see the look that Simon gave him as he left the room.

Simon did, in fact, loathe Lev Avatov. He only tolerated the pompous little human because he knew the secrets of his people. He was sure that if Lev Avatov had not found them in Russia, they would be thriving, and not in the danger that they are in now. He, too, had heard the rumors of the great lizard. They were worrisome, and he was sure that there would be a reckoning before this was all over with. He wanted to make sure that they were well away from this pit before then.

Simon left the room after Lev, and found one of the young females to finish the room they had been working on. As he was leaving the room for the second time, he almost ran into the vampire, Olivier.

"I am looking for that snake, Lev—no offense," he said waving his hand in a dismissive way.

Simon just pointed in the direction that Lev went and moved on. He slithered slowly up the tunnel until he reached the room that the human females were being kept in. That is where he found his nephew. He was watching the young girls huddled in one of the corners, crying—all but one. That one girl stood apart from the others, staring down the two Naga, daring either one of them to come any closer. Simon stopped at his nephew's side.

"That one is feisssty."

Simon looked from the girl to his nephew and said, "You like thisssss one?"

The young Naga nodded his head in agreement and said, "Sssshe will not let ussss near the others. Sssshe is very brave. Can we let her go?" The plea was quiet and earnest.

Simon did a quick headcount. Twenty even. If even one escaped the human would be very angry—but if it died accidentally and had to be disposed of ... well ... these things happen.

"I think we can probably work ssssomething out, but firsssst we have to talk to her in order to help her. Doessss sssssshe know you sssspeak?" Since they were speaking Nagan and not English or Chinese, this was an obvious question to ask.

"No, we have not tried to communicate with her, only obsssserved her," his nephew told him.

"Are they still at the entrance?"

His nephew nodded the affirmative. "Yessss they are sssstill there, Ssssalina watches them."

Simon nodded his head and slithered toward the young girl only to stop about three feet from where she stood. He spoke very slowly first in his slurred English, then again in Chinese asking her name. The action caused the young girl to start and then answer slowly.

"I am Ming. I need to go home to my brother. He is all alone, and I need to find him," she told him.

"Ming, I am called Ssssssimon. We would like to help you, but you have to trusssst ussss." The other girls started to talk and wail all at once until Simon held up one of his long and scaly hands. "I am ssssorry, but I can only help one, but with courage sssssshe can help the ressssst. Are you willing to help the otherssss?" Simon asked her.

"How do I know that this isn't some kind of trap?" she asked, eyeing him suspiciously.

"You don't, but I will tell you that we, the Naga have been missssstreated too often by the human that holdssss you now, and have watched great sssssuffering. We will not watch it anymore, and we are relying on you to get ussss the help we need. Thessssse girlssss are relying on you assss well. Will you help ussss?"

Ming thought for a moment—biting her lip in worry—then nodded.

"Yes I will help, but I don't know what I will be able to do." Her tone was fearful but resolved.

"Aja will take you to a place where you can find help." He motioned to the young Naga who bowed to Ming. "He knowssss where help issss and issss willing to take the rissssk."

Ming nodded to Aja as she stared straight at his eyes. "I will go with you, but if you try anything I will die fighting you."

Aja smiled and said in his young lisping voice, "I will be a complete gentleman; you have my word." Ming smiled as his Chinese was not as good as the older Naga's.

"Alright, then. What do you need me to do?" Ming asked them. Simon made a deep guttural sound that sounded strangely like a purr.

"Aja will chasssse you through the tunnelssss, until you reach help."

"What? This is your brilliant plan?" Ming sounded dubious. She saw Simon's tail lash out and figured that she had made an error. "Forgive me, but I don't know how that plan will help."

Simon's tail wrapped around his lower body again as Aja answered her in his exuberant, boyish way.

"We will trick them. You will esssscape. I will chasssse you, and then I will kill you," he said with the same strange purr. Ming's face paled as she took a step backward.

"I thought you said you would be a gentleman. They do not go around killing girls."

All of the girls had suddenly cowered in the corner like before, and Ming took a fighting stance, ready to battle.

"What Aja means is that he will fake your death. He will come back and announccce that there was an accccident and that he had to dissssposssse of the body. That way they will not continue to ssssearch for you," Simon said, giving a side glance to Aja who had tucked his head at his error. Ming stepped forward again and gave Aja a small smile.

"So this is all pretend?"

Simon cocked his head to the side in confusion at the word.

"This is all an act. You will act like you are chasing me, and I will act like you mean to kill me?"

Simon straightened his head and said, "Yessss," with a small purr. Ming had come to recognize that the purr meant happiness, and the tail swishing meant annoyance or anger.

Ming held out a small hand to Simon and said, "Deal."

Simon gently reached out and took the proffered hand with a purr and a nod. "We will have to begin immediately, there issss not much time."

Chapter 25

Olivier made his way furtively down the hallway with one of the Naga, who was rolling a cart with food and drink for the girls. He had already laced a couple of the plates of food with slices of raw puffer-fish. Unfortunately for a couple of the girls, the chef that prepared the fugu was not the best at it. In fact, that was his first and last time preparing it. Olivier had made him taste the fish before leaving, and it was to die for. Olivier snickered at the joke which caused the Naga to look up at him and then away quickly.

They were just coming up to the door when it was thrown open, nearly bowling them over. A burst of energy shot through, past them. A few seconds later, another shot through the door in pursuit of the first yelling, "SSSStop."

Olivier regrouped and went through the door to find Simon standing in front of a scared group of girls. *His* girls. He could feel the anger rising, but he pushed it down.

"What has happened?" he asked.

"One of the young onessss hassss essssscaped. Aja hassss gone to collect her," Simon told him. Olivier seemed unperturbed at the fact that one of the girls had escaped.

"Yes, well I have no doubt that he will succeed. In the meantime, I ran into this one bringing food in the hallway. No doubt these girls are hungry. When were they last fed and watered?" he asked.

"They are fed three timessss a day and are given water more often. Why are you here?" Simon asked him.

"Well, until recently they were my property, and I wanted to make sure they were taken care of properly." He smiled, and Simon's eyes narrowed to slits.

Some of the younger girls were crying too hard to eat, but one or two of the older ones, obviously hungry, took to the proffered food, stuffing their mouths like they didn't know when their next meal would be. Olivier watched as they ate. He knew which of the plates were tainted, and as of yet none of the girls had eaten from them. He continued to watch until he noticed that Simon was watching him.

"I have also come to take four of them to their new chambers. They should be most comfortable. I will take them while your Aja is chasing the other," he told Simon, but before he could move to collect the four, Aja came slithering back through the door.

"Where issss sssshe, Aja?" Simon questioned.

"That one hassss had an acccccident in the hallssss."

"What kind of accccident, Aja?" Simon pressed him.

"Sssshe fell and her head hit the sssstoney wall. I heard a loud *crack,* and sssshe wassss sssstill."

"It issss not your fault, Aja. If sssshe had not run, then sssshe would sssstill be with ussss," Simon told him, laying a gentle hand on the younger Naga's shoulder.

There was a loud smack as the young Naga was wrenched from Simon's grasp. When Aja turned back to him, there were four long scratches covering his face. He held a hand to them as the blue-green blood seeped through his fingers.

Simon turned to face Olivier who's eyes had turned blood red with his anger. From the sides of Simon's head and neck came a hood like that of a cobra. His eyes had narrowed and his fangs extended fully. He looked fearsome, and the girls started to wail louder.

"You dare maim one of my brethren?" Simon asked him, venom dripping from his fangs.

"He has killed one of the subjects. He was careless and needed to be taught a lesson," Olivier spat, his own fangs growing to match the threat.

Aja and the other Naga had come up behind Simon, all of them had their hoods exposed and fangs bared. Aja's face had stopped bleeding, and the wounds he had suffered only moments before had closed over already, as if it had happened weeks ago, not merely moments before.

Olivier could see that he would carry scars and that quelled his anger somewhat. Before anything else could come of the argument though, one of the young girls screamed. One of the other girls was having a hard time breathing and seemed to be alternating between trying to breathe and vomiting. Simon became concerned and lowered his hood. He went to where the girl was, and noticed that another of the girls was doubled over, moaning, and clutching her stomach.

"Now what is the problem?" Olivier asked, seemingly annoyed. "They are sick. They need to be separated from the others so that they don't all catch it. I will take the four I came for earlier, that way there will be less contact with the sick ones," Olivier told them. He selected four of the girls and escorted them out of the room, throwing a parting remark over his shoulder. "I hope none of the others die on your watch, Simon. Your master wouldn't like it, would he?"

Simon looked over his shoulder and then looked at Aja. "I'm ssssorry that he hurt you, young one. Did Ming make it to the otherssss?" he asked.

"Yessss uncle, I watched until sssshe reached them ssssafely, then I came sssstraight back here. I ssssaw the evil one coming up the hallway and did not want you to be alone with him."

The girl on the floor had started to wheeze and her lips were turning blue. Simon looked around and spotted the plates on the floor. Most of them contained what they normally fed the girls, rice with pickled vegetables, ramen noodles with egg and tuna or salmon. Simon noticed that one of the plates contained a rice ball with a thin slice of white fish on top. Simon reached over, causing the remaining girls to retreat even further into the corner, and grabbed the offending plate. He sniffed the fish and wrinkled his nose. He knew what had caused this. Turning to the other girls, he asked, "Who elsssse ate thissss fissssh? Pleasssse, tell me." One of the girls in the front pointed to the girl who was clutching at her stomach. She had started to wheeze in the last few minutes.

"Anyone elsssse?" he asked fearfully. They all shook their heads in the negative. Simon gave a great sigh of relief.

Aja looked at him, "What was it Uncle?"

"Puffer fissssh," he told him. "Poorly prepared. I musssst go tell the massssster that he has losssst three of hissss ssssubjectssss to reccccent eventssss—and about Olivier. I think that the blood-sss-sucker had ssssomething to do with thissss. In the mean-time, thessssse two will have to go. Then I want you to go talk to the benevolent onessss, ssssee if there issss ssssome way to help them. Do not get caught."

He reached over and closed the eyes of the first girl, now dead. The other would follow her shortly. There was nothing that Simon could do for her. He stood and looked at the only other Naga in the room.

"Go keep an eye on Olivier assss he hassss taken four more with him. Find out what he issss up to, but do not get too clossssse. I will ssssee to the resssst."

Chapter 26

Peter was still making notes and adding pictures to his notebook, when he was clobbered hard from behind. He turned to see a young girl picking herself up off the ground a few feet from him. He got up quickly and made his way to her, calling out to Sam and Paul. The girl quickly backed up as Peter approached. He stopped, and so did she. They looked at each other for a moment until Sam and Paul showed up. Paul spoke quickly in fluent Chinese, and she answered him.

"Her name is Ming, and she is looking for the Benevolent Ones." He asked her some more questions, which were answered with alacrity. He turned back to the others and said. "The snake people sent her to the benevolent ones at the end of the tunnel. They are supposed to help her find her brother and get help for the girls in the tunnels. I believe that she is talking about us."

"Ask her if the snake people mean us harm?" Sam said. Paul turned back to the girl who was still fearful and crouching as if to escape. "Do the Naga wish the benevolent ones harm?"

"No, they are trying to escape themselves. They need help, and told me that my will to live would help them escape their master. They are very scary, but kind." She spoke quickly, and it took Paul only a moment to process what she had said.

Paul said to them, "She says that they want to escape their master, and they are willing to help us in return for our aid." He spoke quickly and confirmed what he had told the others.

"That's good. Pissed off Naga will help us immensely," Sam said. He paused for a moment, paced a few steps away and then returned. "Ask her, if we follow the tunnel she just came down if we will come upon her snake people?"

Paul turned back to Ming and asked her the question followed by another. He smiled brightly and shot off another rapid fire Chinese conversation with Ming responding by throwing herself at him and crying as he patted her back. He looked over at the others and said, "She is Neo's sister, the one we have been looking for. She says that the tunnel she came down will lead us back to the Naga and the other girls. She also said that the Naga she was talking to is called Aja. He was very nice, and his uncle is called Simon. They are the ones we need to seek out."

Paul gently stroked the girl's back as her tears subsided.

"What are we going to do with Ming while we are hunting her friends?" Peter asked the obvious question.

"We have someone in our party who, it turns out, knows how to handle children, and does in fact, have an orphanage. I don't think it will take much to convince Jonah to stay behind with her," Sam told them.

The man himself walked up with Rags a moment or two later.

"Night has fallen outside, and the park is empty. Who's this?" Rags said when they came up to the group.

"This is Ming, she is Neo's sister."

Rags' eyes got wider, and Sam continued. "We may have some unforeseen allies in the tunnels."

"Who?" Rags asked.

"It turns out that the Naga that are in the tunnels are less than thrilled with their boss and wish to defect to our side. We need to meet up with Simon and his nephew, Aja. They will lead us to where we need to go," Sam told him. "In the meantime," he turned to Jonah, "would you be willing to watch Ming here? She cannot go back into the tunnels again."

"Of course I will keep her safe. I will take her back to the village. I have an acquaintance there, and we will be sheltered." Jonah smiled with his kind eyes at Ming and told her that he had her brother at his orphanage, and if she would agree to follow him somewhere safe, he would reunite her with her brother.

Ming smiled and nodded.

"Good, it's settled then. We will go on ahead, and Jonah and Ming will go into the village. We will meet you in the village later," Sam said. The group said their goodbyes to Ming and Jonah and prepared to move off into the tunnels.

"Alright, Caudel. Lead the way," Sam told him.

The group made their way through the tunnels at a good pace since Caudel's gift was allowing them to see in the otherwise pitch-black tunnel. They had turned a few corners when they saw something in the distance. Paul reached into his pocket and pulled out his sigil. He nudged Peter to do the same and pushed a miffed Maggie behind him. As they got closer, they realized it was one of the Naga.

Sam stopped the group and said, "Are you Aja or Simon?"

"Aja," he said. "My uncle hassss ssssent me to lead you to him. Hassss Ming made it ssssafely out of the cavessss?" He sounded genuinely worried about her welfare, so Sam answered him right away.

"Yes, she is fine, thanks to you. Her brother will be very happy to see her again."

"That issss good. Sssshe was ssssspirited. I hated to think of what might happen to her. Come, I will sssshow you to my uncle Ssss-simon. He wissssshessss to ssssspeak with you."

Aja set off, slithering at a rapid pace. They followed along the corridors behind him. After every turn, there were doors to the sides. Peter realized quickly that the cave corridors were very similar to the underground complex of tunnels under the vampire cabal's lair. Some were closed to their prying eyes, but some of the doors were open rvealing a treasure trove of weapons or art. There was even a room that had some ancient looking animals that were squirming and wriggling to get out of the bags they had been trapped in. Paul had to grab Rags' arm on multiple occasions to keep him from diverting into those rooms.

His answer was always the same, "Now is not the time Raguel, but soon." Rags would look back at the room and Paul would have to pull him away. They continued on through the tunnels until Aja stopped them and motioned for them to hide. The troupe hid in the many shadows and crevices the tunnels held. They heard yelling and then saw two people enter the tunnel from a room near the end of the corridor.

"Of all the incompetent—I want him punished this time, Simon. No more babying him. He should know better than to let a subject escape, but to kill one in the process is unacceptable. Bring him to me this afternoon, and I will deal with him myself. I can't trust you to do anything anymore. Right now, I have to go hunt a vampire. Whatever it is he is trying to do will end now."

At the finish of the statement, one of the figures disappeared around the corner into one of the adjoining tunnels. It was Lev, presumably going to stop Olivier from his evil plans.

"Caudel," Sam called softly. Caudel flew up to Sam and hovered in front of him. "Can you follow Lev and find out what is going on and who we are dealing with?" Sam asked him.

"Yes, I can follow him. How will I find you later?"

"Don't worry," Sam said, grimly, "you will know where we are." Aja took Caudel and motioned for the others to stay put. The two approached the lone figure at the end of the tunnel. They watched as Caudel disappeared around the corner, and the other two figures came back to where they stood waiting.

Simon and Aja stopped about a foot from them, and they heard Simon say, "It issss not ssssafe here. Follow ussss pleasssse." Sam motioned for the others to follow behind Simon and Aja. They were close enough to see them, but far enough away that if someone came around one of the many corners, they could hide in the shadows. They followed the pair through another set of turns until they came to a larger chamber, This one looked like a small hall with tunnels that led in multiple directions like off-shoots. There was noise all around them. Groups of Naga were poised, watching them as they walked through the entrance.

"This is where you all live, right?" asked Peter from the back.

"You moved everyone from the tunnels in Russia to here?" Maggie asked him.

Simon turned and looked at Maggie. "I thought you looked familiar. Yessss, thissss issss where he moved ussss to. If we had had more time, we would not have come, but our tunnelssss were overrun by men poking into what Lev wassss doing in Russia. It wassss not ssssafe anymore."

"Why couldn't you have moved somewhere else? Why did you have to come with him?" Maggie asked.

"He offered ussss a way to essssscape before we were found. Ssssaint Petersssssburg issss not eassssy to get out of, essssspecially in the winter. We do not like the cold." He shivered a little as if remembering the cold. "They moved ussss the day the officialssss came to the tunnelssss." He continued, "He had hisss men blow the tunnelssss before we were all out. There were a few that were trapped under the rubble. Aja'sss mother wasss one of them."

Aja, who was listening to the story, let out a small keening noise. Maggie put her arm around him.

"I'm so sorry," she said quietly.

"The young girl, Ming, Sssshe reminded me of her. They had the ssssame sssspirit," Aja said softly.

"That was a very noble thing that you did, helping Ming like that. Now, thanks to you, she will be reunited with her little brother. They have no parents. All they have is each other," Paul told him.

"Yessss, now we musssst help the otherssss," Aja told them.

"What can you tell us about Lev's activities, his research?" Sam asked them.

"He issss looking for a way to prolong life," Simon told them. "He hassss tried many different thingssss, from growing hisss own subjectssss from eggssss, to taking otherssss and usssssing them to experiment on. He usssssed a few of ussss in the beginning, until I talked with him. Then he usssssed a ssssmall woman and her eggssss, claiming he had it. He had a lot of ssssuccessss with thosssse, but the filessss were losssst to him." He turned back to Maggie, "I ssssussssspect that you had ssssomething to do with that, you and the sssson."

Maggie smiled. "You are right. You only got back the files I wanted you to have. I gave Max…" She hesitated a moment on his name, "that file. I hid it under my clothes before you could take back the other files. It was about the small woman, his mother." Maggie told them. She heard hissing fill the air.

"We are ssssorry, sssshe was alwayssss nice to ussss, although sssshe probably doessssn't remember much about her time with ussss. He alwayssss had her drugged," Simon said.

Paul was reeling, not only did he find out more about what went on down in the tunnels, but hearing his old name thrown around like that and the pain in Maggie's voice made him angry. He wanted to punish Lev for the hurt he had caused. He felt a heavy hand land on his shoulder and looked back to see Rags with a grim expression.

"I know," was all he said.

"Lev hassss found a new ssssource to tesssst." Simon went on, "It issss the demonssss hound. Her blood hassss been used to create a new virussss. It issss deadly and workssss within minutessss. He tessssted it on ssssome of ussss. I had to torch the chamberssss ussssed in tessssting. Anytime anyone went inssssside they would catch the virussss and be dead in minutessss. Lev ssssaid he would ssssell it, but the demonssss want it."

"That's not good. Where does he keep this virus?" Sam asked.

"The room he came out of earlier issss hissss lab, but he issss never alone. He hassss the three demon women with him and the hound. They guard hissss information when he issss not in hissss lab," Simon said.

"Is there anything else? What does he need the girls for?" Peter interjected before Sam could ask another question.

"He usssses the girlssss assss hissss tessssst ssssubjectssss. He has taken ssssstem ccccellssss and modified them with the hound'ssss blood. If he is sssuccessssful, they will mutate into ssssomething unholy; sssomething that cannot be killed. He hopessss that thissss will make the ssssubjectssss sssstronger, make them a better hosssst," Simon said.

"A host for what?" Maggie asked him.

"For the Chairman," Aja said, and the hissing noises started again in earnest.

Chapter 27

ait, who's the Chairman?" asked Peter, turning to look at Sam, who looked skyward and nodded.

"He and his ilk are who ARC fights against. They are the creators of most of the bad things that happen in this world. They have had a hand in a lot of the world's problems. They fund wars, supply arms to hostile nations, control the media, control science, control the illegal drug trade, and many other illegal activities," Sam told him.

"Wait—I thought ARC fought against vila, and grunch, and vampires?" Peter said.

"Who do you think created those things? He's not really human at all." Sam looked very, very serious, and Peter was taken aback.

Raguel piped up, "He is one of the nephilim. He has been around as long as man has been around."

Peter said, "Their bodies were destroyed by the flood, but there was no place for their souls to go. They were not a part of the original plan."

"Remember, *Invasion of the Body Snatchers*," Sam told him.

Awareness crossed Peter's face. "Oh, yeah. So this Chairman is one of the snatchers?"

"Yes, until just this moment though, we did not think he survived. His host's bodies seem to disintegrate very quickly, and he must jump from host to host. It is very hard to keep up with what he looks like, because he is always different. He could be anyone," Rags said.

"So, let me get this straight. ARC is fighting the supernatural things like the grunch and vampires, but they are also fighting the nephilim?" Naomi said. "Man, I thought this was weird before. Okay, so this Chairman guy jumps from body to body, and if I'm following correctly, he is having Lev Avatov build him a better model?"

"Yessss, and he issss very clossse to ssssucccceeding," Simon told her. "We musssst desssstroy hissss work. He cannot be allowed to unleassssh them upon the Earth."

Sam looked at Simon. "I agree, this would not be a good thing. We have managed over the years to make the nephilim numbers dwindle until there are only a handful that have not experienced the final death."

"The final death?" Paul questioned.

"The final death is something that happens when an angel or one of the host army destroys any supernatural or unholy thing in this world. There is no heaven or hell for them, only non-existence. The same happens if an ARC member takes a holy weapon and kills one. This makes you a target as much as one of the nephilim. That is why you are given a choice," Rags told them.

"What are we looking at in opposition at the moment?" Sam asked Simon.

"There is the blood ssssucker, and the three demon Sisterssss. They have brought the houndssss with them, and the dragon mas-terssss triadssss watch over hissss and the Chairman'ssss interestssss," he told them.

"How many hounds are there at last count?" Sam asked in concern.

"The lasssst time I counted there were around fifty," Simon told him.

Sam started to pace. Peter could tell that Sam was thinking hard, or maybe he was talking to someone—he would stop every few seconds and stare at nothing then resume.

After only a few moments he said, "Okay, there will be some help coming. Simon, you will need to tell your people to be ready to go quickly, and they will need to take the girls with them when we find them. We will take care of the hounds and the rest. I think Caudel can help some, too."

There was some hissing between the amassed group of Naga.

This went on for a few moments before Simon turned back to Sam and Rags.

"We would like to help. The women will take the young onessss and the girlssss back to the entrance and wait. We will help you," he said, motioning to the group of males gathered around him. "We have our own meanssss of defensssse, and we know where everything is located. You will need our help," Simon told them.

"Thank you, Simon. I have to warn you, though, demon swords work like holy ones do. It is a final death," Sam told him.

"It might mean a final death for ssssome, but assss long assss one of us livessss our memoriessss will keep them alive," Simon said.

"Okay. We need to come up with a plan, and we don't have much time," Rags told them all.

"While you do that, I will see to the other side. Don't start without me." With a wink, Sam disappeared.

Eden was bustling with activity, the host had been alerted and the archangels had gathered in the war room. Abe was busily looking over sheets of papers and intelligence that had come pouring in during the last few moments.

"So, the Chairman is looking for a better body. That is interesting." He was rubbing the top of his head unconsciously and muttering to himself when Michael walked up to him.

"Abe, what are we thinking?" Michael asked.

"Man, Michael, I have never seen such a cluster f—, I mean, cluster since Nam. I don't like that the home team is stuck in a volcano with a pack of hellhounds, three demons, a vampire, and a bunch of twisted nutjob kung fu types. This is not good."

Abe started to rub his head again when, from behind him, Sam said, "You forgot the half snake-half men Naga. Good thing they are on our side."

"Indeed. The others sent me to get you." The two angels who were focused on Abe jumped and spun around to see a smiling June standing behind them. "Peter and the others will be expecting your help. Follow me." She turned and ran off without a backward glance.

The three followed at a more subdued pace until they reached the table that held a map of the world. This map was special. With a touch on any region, it would show whatever the angels wished to see. There was always an angel present to monitor the happenings of the world. That is how they were able to dispatch guardians and the host when needed.

Currently, there were three angels working on one side of the world map that included the western hemisphere, and on the other side were the archangels. They had pulled up the volcano in China where Peter and the others were waiting. Raphael and Gabriel were talking with Uriel and Jophiel. Ariel was not present, which worried Michael a little. He did not know what his stubborn friend was up to, but he hoped it involved a hesitant dragon.

When they reached the others, he saw that they were watching Raguel talking with Simon, Aja, Peter, Paul, and the girls about what they needed to do. Sam watched as Maggie pulled a couple of katanas from out of her bag. He wasn't sure when she got those, but he was glad she had something. Paul was showing Peter a couple of things with his medallion. They watched as his holy badge morphed from weapon to weapon in his hand. Peter was trying to imitate the actions and succeeded, but more slowly. Michael looked at Sam who was watching with a worried expression.

"I know you are concerned, Sam, but they are well on their way to a grand plan," Michael told them. "Raguel will not let them go before the appointed time."

"I don't want to see anyone get hurt, that's all," Sam said.

"Then it is a good thing that you are bringing reinforcements, bro," Michael told him and slapped him on the back. "Okay, I need you two," he said, pointing to Gabriel and Raphael, "to lead the host. Raph, you and Uri need to each take your berserkers and a Hellbane contingent, here," he pointed at one of the disused passageways leading to the central caldera, "and here. If it were me, this is where I would gather the hounds since there's more room to maneuver. Gabriel, you will report to the different sections to keep us all updated. Jo, you and Ariel will help the Naga with the girls. If you run across any little treasure troves, feel free to destroy them."

Jophiel nodded and said, "Where is Ariel, anyway?"

"I'm here," she said as she materialized from the surrounding forest. She looked over at Michael and shook her head.

Michael let out a sigh and said, "Right. Sam and Rags will keep an eye on our friends, keep the triads busy, and help us with the hounds when the time comes. Normally, the Three would be a priority here, but," Michael looked grave, yet hopeful, "we have never had an opportunity like this before. None of those hounds can survive. If we succeed here, we will never have to face them again."

"Michael that is suicide, there is no way that only two of you and a handful of host will be able to take on fifty hellhounds," Abe stated.

"He's right, Mike. We may have to rethink our position," Uriel told him. "Even as great as you are, you would not be able to take on that many."

"We may have no choice, pal." Michael said.

"I could come help you," Ariel offered. "Jo will be able to handle the girls, and the Naga will help her. When they are safely out of the way, she can come back and help, too. That will give you two more hands," she said tapping her foot lightly.

"That still leaves you outmatched twenty-five to one." Abe said. "I don't like it—you will be spread too thin."

"We will have to make do, because the dragon isn't coming. He has chosen to abstain." Michael looked at each of them in turn. "I can't tell you how important this battle is. We have come to a crossroads of sorts, and the outcome is too important. Abe, we are going to need some ARC reinforcements as well. Call all you can to action, and we will take them over. Let them know what is at stake, and give them the option to refuse."

Abe nodded and left to do what was asked.

"Alright everyone, it looks like they are getting ready to move out. Please check with Abe on who will join us and bring them along. May the Master protect us," Michael said.

Everyone was paying attention to the directions Michael was giving in preparation for the battle to come. Only Ariel saw June slip from the clearing. She smiled at the girl's tenacity. She had her own mission, and she was not going to fail. June knew where the dragon was and went in search of him. She found him in his favorite spot beside the cherry blossom tree in the meadow looking at the sky. She walked right up to him and started wagging her finger in under his snout.

"You are the most selfish dragon, do you know that?"

He opened one eye and looked at her.

"What would a little girl like you know about dragons?" he asked and snorted, causing her to take a step backward with the force.

"Plenty, although I must say, you aren't living up to the incredible picture that Ari painted of you. I thought that dragons were noble and liked to talk with intelligent people. They would help those in need and capture and hold the occasional beautiful maiden prisoner, but her love and friendship would make him want to let her go. Dragons walked the earth and roamed the skies with honor and fearlessness. Ariel told me that dragons were good, but—"

Ouryu raised his head and fire belched from his maw as he laughed at her romanticized thinking. He looked down and saw the hurt expression on her face, and his laughter stopped.

"What is your name, girl?"

"June," she said, wiping tears from her cheeks. "I guess my thinking on dragons really isn't correct. I'll go and leave you alone."

She turned to leave but found herself trapped by an enormous claw. She spun around and looked at the dragon.

"It has been a long time since I have heard anyone speak on behalf of dragons. Mostly they talk about how we like to eat people and steal gold." He looked at her. "Do you really think that dragons are noble creatures?"

"I think that any sentient creature can choose which path to follow.

Their choices determine who they will become, not descriptive words forced onto them by others," June told him, raising her head.

"I think I will keep you," he told her.

"Oh, no—you can't. I have to be there to help the others. They are counting on me. Please, let me go," she begged him.

"Where would you be going, and who would you be helping, little June?" the dragon asked her in concern.

"Michael and the others are off to take on three demons and about fifty hellhounds. They have asked for people to help, and I am determined to do my part. They were waiting on you to help them but, since you have decided to stay here, they are asking for volunteers to go and help. I volunteered, please let me go now," she said pushing against his enormous claw.

"You cannot go and fight hellhounds," he growled at her. "Don't be absurd. You would die a most horrible death."

"They need the help, and if this is the way that I can help them, then so be it. I'm bait. At least I'm doing something." She spit the words at him. "They will be leaving soon. Let me go. Now."

This time he moved his claw, and she ran into the brush at the edge of his glade. Ariel was waiting for her when she appeared.

"Well done, June. I think our dragon may come around after all."

June smiled, and the two women walked back to the others.

Chapter 28

Lev was fuming. *That damned vampire had caused one too many problems for him.* Between that Naga moron and Olivier, it would be a wonder if he would have any subjects left at all to work with. He knew how to handle those who caused too many problems. *They had accidents.* He wasn't sure how he was going to handle the vampire. He wasn't really frightened of him, but he was a realist and knew that he would need help to get rid of him. He went to the only other thing that he knew hated the vampire as much as he did.

"Tsoula—I would speak with you," he said into the darkness.

He was at the point in the tunnels where no light could touch. The small lantern that was lit in the tunnel could not penetrate the inky darkness in which she resided. After a moment, a horrendous smell greeted his nostrils. Tsoula poked her great head from the blackness.

"You have some scruff, human," came the thought, rolling across his mind. *"You stole from me, violated me. Tell me why I shouldn't kill you where you stand?"* She bared her eight-inch fangs. Mucus collected on her bottom jaw and tumbled over the side to splash on the floor.

Lev jumped back a step and said, "Because I will make you immortal," he told her. "You will be the foundation for a comeback the likes of which has never been seen. Even your mistress will be grateful to you."

"Go on," she said intrigued.

"Your blood will bring back the Chairman to a suitable host; one he will have no problem staying in. It will be glorious, and he will owe you his life. He will be forever grateful, and your kind will be elevated to their rightful status among the infernals. But before we can even begin, I need a little problem taken care of."

"What kind of problem can keep you from my glory?" she asked him, seeing the adoration of her mistress floating away.

"The vampire. He is conniving to stop me from creating the serum that will bring you glory. He is trying to destroy us—destroy your mistress. We cannot let that happen. I cannot defeat him myself because I am…"

"Weak," came the reply with another laugh.

"Mortal," he corrected her. "I do wish to see the serum created and your blood turn one lucky subject into a new host for the Chairman. Think about it, Tsoula—with that damned vampire out of the way, we can achieve your glory. He called you a dog."

That remark made her growl, "I am not a dog. I am the greatest of hellhounds. They all cower before me," she said.

"He said you were a failure, that you let a bird best you." Lev knew he was getting to her. "I want to make you immortal, and he is plotting to stop me. Will you help me get rid of him?"

Tsoula paced for a moment. The darkness of her body only revealed itself when she got next to the light. Otherwise, she was the darkness, and Lev was having a hard time following her.

"I will help you," she told him. "Let's go."

"Wait. I need to catch him in the act, otherwise there will be repercussions," Lev said, holding out a hand. He drew his hand back quickly when Tsoula snapped at it. He heard the huffing and knew she was laughing at him.

"I will call you when I need you, if that pleases you," Lev told her.

Tsoula walked slowly up to Lev and said, "Don't move."

Lev didn't know what she was doing, but when a hellhound commands you not to move, you don't move. Tsoula stretched out her giant nose and touched Lev on the forehead. Her fetid breath washed over Lev, and he was only just able to keep from wretching. When she pulled away Lev took a giant gulp of air.

"There," she said and gave her giant hairless tail a wag.

"What did you do?" Lev asked her.

"I gave you the ability to call me," Tsoula said. "Otherwise, I would have ignored you. Just know that if my mistress calls me too, I will go to her first."

Lev smiled. "Very good, I will call you when I need you."

Lev walked away from the hellhound. He looked back briefly before rounding the corner and in the darkness he saw two red eyes watching him. Lev hurried along the tunnels turning this way and that to try and get to the rooms they had set up for his new subjects. He came to the first room, and in the corner on the bed, he saw his fears realized. Coiled and perfectly still, a snake sat on the chest of one of the girls. As he moved closer, he could tell that she was dead. One of her legs was hanging off the edge of the bed along with her arm. The other arm was in front of where the snake lay coiled. Lev could see puncture wounds on her arm and knew she had been bitten by the serpent.

When he moved closer to the bed the snake stirred and raised its hooded head. The cobra stared at Lev intently. Lev turned and walked out of the room. He wasn't sure where the Naga were as he had not seen any in a few hours, but he knew they would be able to handle the snake. For all he knew there could be one snake in each room.

He hurriedly moved toward the next room, and when he walked in he found a young girl sitting in the corner on the floor. He walked to her and laid a hand on her shoulder, just as he made contact with her, something came out from under her hair, startling him into jumping backwards. It was a giant centipede, as long as his forearm. It had raised itself up so the front half of its body was in the air and the other half was still under the girl's hair. It was a deep russet red color, and its antennae were moving to and fro at a furious pace. Lev didn't have to see anything else, he knew that this one was dead, also.

Checking on the next room, he found another girl alive but only just, so he left her to her demise, anger pulsing at his temples as he went on to the final room. When he entered the room the girl looked up from where she sat at the end of the bed. The look on her face was pure fear.

Lev walked into the room, and the girl whimpered a little. He saw her mouth the words *help me* before looking at her feet. Lev stepped around the end of the bed and saw why she was so scared. Her feet were barely touching the ground and nestled right in between them lay another snake.

It was medium sized with a rather thin body—Lev figured it was probably a baby—its head and body were all black except for the numerous white rings going from its neck to its tail. This one was watching her, flicking its tongue in and out, testing the environment. Lev could see her shaking and knew it was only a matter of time before it launched itself at her. He couldn't afford to lose another one.

"I want you to listen to me, okay?" Lev told her.

She looked over at him and nodded. He picked up a broom from beside the door left by one of the Naga.

"When I tell you to move, pick your feet up quickly and place them on the bed. Do you understand?"

She nodded her understanding again and watched as he carefully walked across the room to the bed. The little snake turned and looked in his direction and slid a little to the side, partly under the girl's shoe. Lev cursed to himself, he would have to be quick.

"Now!"

Just as the girl started to lift her foot the little snake struck her before Lev could bat it away. He heard her suck in a breath at the immediate pain the bite induced. He cursed again and proceeded to take all his anger out on the little snake, striking it over and over again until it stopped moving at all. Breathing hard he threw the now ruined broom to the ground and turned to the girl, she was crying and asking for him to save her.

Disgusted he told her, "I can't help you now, stupid girl. I told you to move quickly."

Without another word, he left the room and the screaming girl behind. Lev was now in an extreme rage. He had had enough of that conniving bastard. He was more than glad to have Tsoula to help him get rid of the vampire forever. He was so caught up in his rage he nearly ran over Lilith in the tunnel. Her strong grip on his shoulder caused him to wince and snapped him out of his fog of rage.

"Love, what's the hurry?" she asked him in mock concern.

"That vampire is dead—I am going to kill him. He thought he was sneaky, but he's not as clever as he thinks he is." Lev's rage notched back up just thinking about killing Olivier.

"You are not strong enough or skilled enough to kill the vampire. You need to be concerned with the Chairman and the serum," Lilith admonished him. Lev ran his hands through his hair and growled in frustration.

"I can't move on with the serum while that vampire is out there killing the subjects I need to give it to," he practically shouted at her.

"You mean Olivier is killing the girls you need to test your serum?" Lilith asked, confused. "He was ordered to let you have those girls and find himself some others to play with."

Lev paced away from her and then back again.

"I know what he was ordered to do, but I think you underestimate how much he hates me. He would give anything to discredit me with the Chairman," Lev told her. "I need to be stronger, to have the power to defeat Olivier. I asked Tsoula to help me. Maybe she will do this for me now."

Lilith tsked. "I would have talked to Pharzy before going to Tsoula. She is very protective and very controlling over the hound. She would not appreciate you overstepping." Lilith crossed her arms in front of her ample chest and raised one hand to her chin as if in contemplation. Then with a discrete side glance she launched into her real motive. "Perhaps there is a way that I can help you?" she queried.

Lev stopped pacing for a moment. "How?"

"Well, it just so happens that I can grant you the power and skill needed to kill the vampire and get back on track with the serum," Lilith told him.

"Again, how—and what would you want in return?"

"The power would come from me, and in return, you would serve me." She punctuated this last part with a slide of her hand up his chest.

Lev thought about it for only a moment before saying, "I could think of worse people to serve, and I think this service would be mutually beneficial." He slipped his arm around her lithe body and squeezed for emphasis. "Where do I sign up?" he asked.

She cupped his face, both of their clothes dissolving as she gained her true form in the passageway. Her eyes glowed like blue fire.

"Right here."

She kissed him and mounted him, forcefully. With every thrust, he could feel the power flow into his body. Each nerve ending sung with the strength and vitality that flowed through it. No human woman had ever brought him to heights like this, and Lev was delirious with pleasure, reaching that apex over and over again. Thunder rang in his eardrums. His thoughts sharpened to pinpoint clarity, and he was filled with a new kind of knowledge. Forbidden knowledge. He craved it, just as he craved Lillith's lash. He wanted to suffer, and to wield whatever evil power she may be deign to bestow on him. Suffer he would, as along with all of this came a sharp pain in his chest, making him grunt in response. All too soon, it was over.

He smiled against her lips as he drank her in. "I am yours, Lilith. Yours forever."

She kissed him again, lightly, saying, "How do you feel now, slave?" She slid her hand down his face.

"I feel fantastic—like I can do anything in the world. Lift a car or break down a wall, or—"

"Kill a vampire?" Lilith said, finishing his sentence for him.

His clothes reappeared, and she returned to her buxom human form, clothed as well. The time for business was at hand.

"Yes, I'm going to do that right now, as a matter of fact." He spun to go and find Olivier when a sharp pain in his chest stopped him in his tracks.

"I think you should continue working on your serum, Lev," Lilith ordered him.

"I need to kill the vampire first." He struggled against the ache in his chest. "Why does this hurt?" He asked, opening his shirt.

There, on his once bare chest, was a brand—a circle burned into him. Inside was a bar with two crosses on the end supporting what looked like a lowercase *h*, with a cross at the top. Lev fingered the brand.

"What's this?" he asked her.

"That shows all others that you are mine. It will also let me know what you are doing and allow me to punish you if you don't do as I ask." She watched as his eyes got rounder with each statement. "You should feel honored. It has been centuries since I have allowed myself a thrall."

"That is not what I asked for, Lilith. Remove it at once."

Lilith raised one eyebrow and immediate pain filled his chest and dropped him to the floor of the tunnel He watched as the corners of her mouth turned up in an evil smile.

"You will not demand anything from me. You will address me as *Mistress*, and you will do what I ask, or you will regret it. That was just a taste of what could happen if you piss me off."

The pain in his chest disappeared, and his breathing became ragged as his loins became alive with pleasure. He looked at her.

"What...?"

"That is to remind you what you are in for when you please me. This you should do often."

"Yes... Mistress." He picked himself up off the floor. "And Olivier?" he asked as he brushed off his pants.

"I will take care of the vampire for you. In the meantime, go clean yourself up and wear something nice. I will come to you later for your next lesson in pleasing your mistress."

She patted his cheek, spun on one of her stiletto heels, and left him without another word.

Lev was humiliated but gritted his teeth and said, "Yes, mistress," to her retreating back.

Neither of them noticed the little winged creature that flew off back up the tunnel with a bunch of intel he needed to impart.

Chapter 29

The Naga had built themselves a home in the tunnel system and were well versed in its layout. The Triads had inhabited these tunnels for some time, but their knowledge was limited to what they could see. They were far too busy running their empire to have time to explore its depths.

Peter and Paul were extremely grateful for the help that the snake folk were providing them. Caudel had told them that they could have his cave after this was over since he would not be using it anymore, but Simon asked them if there was a way to move them all to Tibet.

"Why Tibet, Simon?" Paul asked him. "Is it because of the Buddhists there?"

"My father wassss from Tibet. That issss where he wassss captured many yearssss ago. I feel we sssshould go back there. I think there are otherssss like ussss there," Simon told him.

"Oh, I know that the Buddhists have Naga kings, and they created statues to them. They are believed to have magical powers that can help or hinder humans," Paul told the interested party.

"That might just be the perfect place for you guys, huh?" Peter said, slapping Simon on the back.

"Yessss, well, we don't hold magic, but we can defend ourselvessss if needs be and communicate with otherssss of our kind without being in the sssssame area. We don't go out into public unlessss it is needed, and then we go dressssed assss monkssss," he told Peter.

They kept walking down the hall, and when they came to the next turn of the tunnel two figures appeared before them. The group stopped, and both Paul and Peter stepped in front of Simon and Aja defensively, until they saw that it was Michael and Sam.

Peter smiled. "Good to see you two."

Caudel flew out of Peters hoodie, "Sam, listen—Lilith has claimed Lev."

"What? Caudel, what are you talking about? You didn't say anything to us about anybody claiming anyone else?" Peter accused.

"You wouldn't understand what I meant, Peter. No offense."

"When did this happen?" Sam said, gravely

"After I followed the poor girls and that vampire into the tunnels, I found that each of the girls was murdered by the bloodsucker. Not directly, though. He didn't suck their blood." Caudel was clearly vexed that Olivier had not just drained the girls himself. "He released something that would kill them directly into their cells. The last girl I was too late to save. I saw Lev kneeling over her, yelling at her because she wasn't quick enough, then he went out of the room."

Everyone in the group was saddened by the cruelty the girl faced in her last minutes.

"In the corner there was a dead krait. It was only a baby serpent, but in the other chambers I found a cobra, a centipede, and a spider that was as big as me. Needless to say, I didn't stay."

Peter watched as Caudel paced back and forth on air.

"What about Lev, Caudel? Where did he go?" Sam asked.

"Lev? Oh, I flew off after him and caught up to him as he almost ran down the she-devil, Lilith. He told her that he had asked Tsoula—Lilith said she was Pharzy's hound—to help him kill Olivier; I guess that is the bloodsucker, right?" Sam nodded and Caudel continued. "Lilith told Lev that he wasn't strong or skilled enough to kill the vampire, and that Pharzy would be mad if he used Tsoula without her permission. Lev asked her what he could do and she told him that she could help him if he became hers. She wasn't subtle in her message if you get my drift." Caudel acted all cuddly with Sam until the latter pushed him away.

"I get your meaning, Caudel. Continue." Sam made the hurry up gesture with his hands.

"Lev thought this was a win-win for him and practically threw himself at her. She kissed him—among other things."

"Other things?" Paul asked.

"That's right—never copulate with demons, kids," Sam said.

"Ugh!" Naomi and Maggie were clearly affected by the imagery, but Caudel continued.

"Sam, I saw the power flow into him. She branded him. He is lost," Caudel said somberly.

"That is—unexpected," Michael said contemplating the ramifications of this new information. "What was it he asked for again?" Michael asked Caudel.

"Uh, strength and skill, but he was not ready for the brand. When he tried to leave to extract his revenge on the bloodsucker, she sent him to his knees. She enjoyed doing it, too," Caudel told them.

"If I'm following this correctly, he sold himself to her in return for strength and skill needed to kill a vampire?" Paul asked.

"Seems like it, though it won't end well for him," Sam told them with a grim expression.

"Ah, he was a murderer and a thief," Peter reminded them. "I don't think it was going to end well for him, anyway."

"So was King David, not only was he redeemed, but he was used to redeem a nation. The big difference is the choice he made," Michael said softly. "Lev has made a choice that is not easy to come back from. It is not impossible, but it is definitely not easy."

"Oh," Peter said. "Well, where does that leave us at this moment?"

"You guys will have to be extra careful now. If she has given Lev power in this way, you will not be able to stop him alone. Luckily, the cavalry is on its way," Sam told them. "For now, we need to find Lev and that serum he is concocting. Let's go."

They started walking up the tunnels again when Peter turned to Michael and asked, "How did you find us in the tunnels, Michael? Have you been here before?"

"No, brother, but I am with you and know where you are always. You carry my sigil, and I have marked you," Michael told him.

"Wait, you can't cause me pain too, can you?"

Michael laughed and said, "Would I do that? Our marks are for your protection. It allows us to find you quickly if you are in trouble. The sigil, as you know, is further protection. What Lilith did to Lev is not natural. She has taken free will away from him, in essence making him her slave. He sold his soul to her for power that she gave him but will not let him use, unless it furthers her evil purposes."

"That's cruel. I almost feel sorry for him," Naomi told him.

"From what I know of Lev," Paul interrupted, "he will be pretty mad that he was duped into this bargain and will be trying to find a way out of it as we speak."

"That may be. As I said before, it is not impossible to come back from where Lev finds himself, but it is certainly difficult," Michael said. "For the sake of his soul, I hope he can pull himself back."

They resumed walking when Peter asked another question, "What about the Naga? What happens to them?"

"You are asking the hard questions, aren't you? Okay, Peter I will tell you. They go to a special place that's not in the heavens and not in the pit. It's nice," Michael told him and then raised his hand. "That is all I can tell you."

Peter sighed.

"Don't be upset, Peter," said Sam from behind him. "That is more than any human has gotten out of him in a long time."

"Yessss, it issss good to know of thissss sssspecial placccce. We do not have the education of our people and do not know what happenssss when we go under the ground," Simon told him.

"Thank you," Michael smiled, and nodded in acknowledgement.

"We are coming up on the lab. You need to be very quiet now," Aja told them. He slunk low and peered around the corner, but had to duck back quickly. The entrance to the lab was guarded by two hellhounds. They were laying in wait outside the door.

"Well, this is unexpected. Did you know they would be here?" Sam asked Simon.

"No. Lev hassss never had them guard the door before," Simon said.

"This must be another thing Lilith has done to keep Lev in the lab. We can't fight them in the tunnel, it is too restrictive. We are going to have to lead them to a more open space," Sam told Michael.

"Gabriel?" Michael said, and in a split second there was another angel with them.

"You rang?" he quipped.

"Look over there," Michael said and pointed.

Gabriel looked and saw the hellhounds. He whistled low.

"That's a problem. What can I do to help?" he asked, smiling.

"We need Raphael and Uriel, and the Hellbane. This is gonna take some maneuvering. Is the host in place?" Michael asked.

"Yes, they have all come through. By the way, we think that another came through who shouldn't be here. She may be planning a little revenge of her own," Gabriel told him.

"Another?" Michael asked.

Paul had a sudden thought, and knew it to be horribly true. He said it before he could stop himself. "Margueritte."

Maggie looked at him, shocked. Gabriel looked askance at him, but nodded.

"Yes. She is bent on revenge," Michael sighed. "Okay we will keep an eye out for her, too. Tell Raphael to hand over his side to Joshua. He did come, right?" When Gabriel nodded, he continued. "I suppose that the other girls are safe by now, right, Simon?"

"Yessss, they sssshould be to ssssafety by now," Simon answered.

"Good. Gabe, go get Naomi. Take Red to see Raph and then bring them here. I believe that Raph needs to see Maggie for a moment." Sam smiled, and Michael nodded in response.

"About time, too," Sam said.

"Time for what?" asked Peter and Paul at the same time.

"Need to know, gentlemen. You guys get ready," was his reply.

"This is going to get really ugly, really fast," Michael told him.

Chapter 29

*M*ar*gueritte. He had said it. I didn't imagine it, and I don't know where it came from.*

Paul was brand new to their group, and he should not have known what he knew. Granted, he wasn't new to ARC, so he may have heard of their adventures through the grapevine, but it didn't seem so based on their conversation. She had to know what he knew when this was over.

They made their way as she pondered, moving through the tunnels. Maggie and Naomi followed the female Naga and the young girls they had rescued out of the tunnels. Along the way, some of the young female Naga were seen slipping in and out of the group. Maggie thought they were probably looking for others of their kind, as the group had doubled from its original size. When they reached the entrance that would take them to safety, they found a young woman no older than eighteen standing at the entrance, tapping her saddle shoe on the ground.

"I had almost given up on you guys," she told them.

"Who are you?" Maggie asked her as she placed herself between the girls and this unknown person.

"It's okay. She's with us." The voice came from off to the right. When she looked, she saw Jophiel standing with another woman who was small with red hair with bright teal blue tips.

"Hi, Jo. Who's your friend?" she said, pointing at the young girl who was still tapping her saddle shoe on the ground.

Jophiel smiled, "This is June. She has come to lead the girls to Jonah. They will be okay from here—Jonah will make sure of it."

Maggie nodded at June. "Hello June, nice to meet you."

"

"Now that we have all met, can we get moving?" she said.

"June, patience is a virtue." Jo said, to which June rolled her eyes.

"I want to go, so I can get back in time to fight," she said as she threw up her fists in mock defense.

"I told you, little one, you will not fight this day." The voice came booming through the open cave.

All the women in the cave screamed at the same time. The noise was deafening.

"Quiet!" boomed the voice once again, and silence descended on the group.

"I told you once, you big lizard, I am too gonna fight," came the reply from June as she stamped her foot in annoyance.

"Not if we finish this before you get back, you won't." After this sentence, a long tongue darted out of the dragon's mouth. Maggie could swear that he was sticking his tongue out at June. She stamped her foot once again and turned to the two angels.

"Can we please go now?" she begged.

"Yes, June, you may go," The smaller angel told her and winked. Maggie saw June wink back at her as she rounded up the shell-shocked girls and left the cave.

"What about the Naga?" Maggie asked.

"Now that the humans are okay, they can help if they wish, or they can stay here," Jophiel told her. "When this is over, we will relocate them to another place where they don't have to fear man."

"Who is she?" Maggie whispered, pointing to the other angel.

"She is Ariel," Jophiel whispered back. Louder she said, "Ariel, this is Maggie and Naomi. Naomi is the receiver."

"Ah, it is nice to put a name with a face," Ariel said. She looked over at the great dragon. "It's nice of you to show up, Ouryu. I didn't think that you wanted to come."

"The little one said that she was going to come and be hellhound bait. I forbade it, but she decided to come anyway," he said.

"So naturally you had to make sure she would be okay," Ariel said with a smile.

"She has so much fire. I like it—it would be a shame if she had her flame extinguished," he told her.

"I guess we need to start heading back in there," Maggie said.

"Well, this is a surprise." Gabriel made them all start with his sudden appearance.

Naomi, with a hand over her racing heart said, "Friend of yours?"

Gabriel laughed. "I'm Gabriel. I have been sent to retrieve you and Maggie and take you to Michael, but Maggie needs to see Raphael first." He looked over at Ariel and Jophiel.

"Can you take Naomi in to Michael? We will be there in a minute. There are two hellhounds waiting at the door to the lab where the human Lev has the serum. They are planning something to get the hounds away from the door," Gabriel said with a smile.

Maggie guessed that he was looking forward to the fight.

"Go on, Gabriel. You take Maggie, and we will take as many as we can. You," Ariel said pointing at Ouryu, "stay here until I come back for you." The great dragon filled the empty space in the cave and would not have been able to fit into the tunnel.

Maggie went to stand with Gabriel. She called to Naomi, "You be careful, girl," then she and the angel disappeared from sight. When Maggie blinked, she was in another section of the tunnels, and before her stood a behemoth of a man. He was broad-shouldered and barrel-chested with a head of dark hair pulled up into a top knot. He grew an impressive beard of the same dark color. He arched one sooty eyebrow at the newcomers.

"Gabriel, what news?" he asked.

"Raph, I have been sent to bring you Maggie here, and also to tell you that Michael needs us to help fight some hellhounds. We only saw two, but we know there are more, most likely fifty or so."

"Ah, Magdalene, you and I need to have a talk before we go. I have something for you," Raphael told her with a smile. "Gabriel, make whatever changes that need to be made for me, will you? I will be over there talking with Maggie."

He lay one giant hand on Maggie's shoulder and led her over

to the side. Gabriel watched for a moment until he saw Maggie nod and the angel hand her something.

Gabriel smiled and said, "Okay, host, listen up. This is what you are going to do..."

Maggie couldn't believe what was happening. She was standing in a giant volcano with a group of angels, Naga, some demons, hellhounds, a vampire, and a mob-boss-slash-mad-scientist—not to mention half of the Triads in China. Now this brutish looking angel was handing her a sigil and telling her she had been chosen by him to help rid the world of these things.

He told her that it was her choice, but he had been watching her, and he liked the way she thought problems through; that she was a warrior.

Maggie thought about this statement. She had been through many tough situations since she had become an investigative journalist. She had had numerous close calls. One had almost killed her, but all of them involved her risking her life to rid the world of evil and corruption. Now she had been gifted with the same type of weapon that was gifted to Peter and Paul. She held the round disc in her hand and looked at the depiction in the middle. It was plain and looked a lot like a hook or an upside down inverted *J*. She flipped it around and looked at it from the other direction then flipped it back. She looked up at Raphael, who smiled and turned the object in her hand, flipping it to the way she had it originally.

"That is my sigil, and from this day forth you will be under my protection—and I, yours," he told her. "Say my name, and think of something that you can protect yourself with," he prodded her.

Luckily, she had seen both Peter and Paul wield the same power previously, and now that it was her turn she was already a fairly deft hand. With confidence but quietly, she spoke.

"Raphael." Before the sound completely left her mouth, the disc disappeared and in her hands she held a pair of katanas, just her size and bright red. "My weapons of choice," she told him.

He nodded his understanding and said, "You do the same to

put it away. It can change depending on the situation, so it may not always manifest itself as these, but if that is what you are used to, they will appear most often."

"Cool. Why doesn't Naomi have one?" Maggie asked, confused.

"Most women do not have the gift that you were given. They usually have a power, an ability like hearing thoughts, being empaths, or even projecting images to others. Your friend, Naomi, is a receiver, meaning she has the ability to receive images or projected thoughts over a long distance. You were gifted in another way, that's all. This allows me to present you with this gift instead."

"Nice! I accept this gift and will do my best to help when I am able," she told him solemnly.

He laughed and said, "I thank you," bowing from the waist. "When this is all over, I would like to spar with you, I think."

"I accept," she said and smiled. "Now, how about we go kick some hellhound tail?"

"I like the way you think," he told her, and the two walked back to where Gabriel was waiting. As she slipped the medallion into her pocket, there was a searing pain in her hip. She hissed and pulled the medallion back out of her pocket. When she put her hand inside her pocket she felt a hole in the pocket itself and when she investigated further she found a burn on her hip from the medallion.

"Your sigil just bit me," she accused him.

"Oh, I forgot." He reached over and laid a gentle hand on her hip. The pain receded and he said, "There is a mark that goes along with the medallion. It will also protect you. I apologize for not warning you earlier that it would appear."

"Oh, well at least it is on the hip, but I can't say it will do much for my bikini line," she said, still miffed about the oversight.

Gabriel came bounding over. He was everything light to Raphael's dark. He had almost a glowing aura about him, with an angelic face, light golden hair, and blue eyes. He was what all her friends would call a hottie, although she much preferred her men with dark hair and eyes.

"Are we ready?" Gabriel asked in his enthusiastic way.

Maggie smiled and said, "Definitely," at the same time that Raphael said, "Let's go."

"Great, this will be fun," Gabriel told them, and they winked out of the small cave they were in.

Chapter 30

The hellhounds are still at the door. What's the plan, Mike?" asked Peter.

"Caudel, how fast do you fly?" Michael asked him.

"I am the fastest flyer I know," he said with a cheeky grin.

"Good, I'm counting on it, because you will have to be faster than a hellhound," Michael told him.

Caudel's face lost all expression as the meaning of his words sank in. "You mean, I'm the bait. You're throwing me to the literal wolves?" he asked, practically flying backward.

Peter held up a hand, which Caudel ran into instead of his face.

"Well, hounds, but yes, that is the plan. We need to lead those hellhounds away from the lab so Peter and the others have access to Lev. Who better to lead them away than the leader of a fairy army."

Caudel made an audible gulp, straightened his shoulders and nodded. "Alright, I'll do it."

"Good, now—"

Michael was interrupted by the arrival of Raphael, Gabriel, and Maggie.

"Michael, guess what?" Gabriel asked.

"Uh, what?" Michael waited for the answer.

"The great lizard came," Gabriel said. "He's here. He came, thanks to June and Ariel."

"There's a dragon!" Peter nearly shouted in his excitement.

Gabriel smiled broadly and nodded, and Michael placed a calming hand on each of their shoulders.

"That is excellent news. I think I would like to hear more about our little June later, though." Michael told them.

Peter turned to Gabriel and whispered, "This is awesome."

Gabriel, who was just as enthusiastic, nodded.

"Okay, so Caudel will be gathering hellhounds and taking them to the cavern to meet a dragon it would seem. See Caudel, you only have to be fast," Michael said.

"Easy for you to say. What will you be doing?" Caudel asked him.

"Sam, Gabriel, Raphael, Jophiel, Ariel, and I will be killing the hellhounds you bring us with the help of our lovely dragon, Ouryu. Would you rather do that?" Michael asked him.

"Uh no, I can be as fast as the wind," Caudel said sheepishly.

"Paul, Peter—when Caudel leads them past here, I want you to take Maggie to the lab with you. Raguel, you go with them just in case. Lev, even with extra strength, shouldn't be a match for the four of you. When you are done, you can meet us in the cavern. We need everything in that lab destroyed. The Naga say there are disposal tubes that run down to the lava field below us, dispose of the serum in there. Naomi, you go with Jophiel and help her and Ariel. Simon, you and Aja take your Naga and help with the Triads. They are used to you and will not expect you to try anything. Get rid of as much as you can in the same way. Anything that will blow up should be moved to the entrance where a team will be waiting to get rid of it safely."

They all nodded their understanding of the plan and moved to their designated locations. Gabriel would stay with them, until Caudel made his move, then he would go back to Michael and the others to warn them.

"Good luck, Caudel. I know you can do this."

Caudel nodded to Peter and flitted into the shadows at the top of the tunnel. They watched as he made his way down the hallway to the door of the lab.

"Who let the dogs out?" came the loud cry from down the tunnel. "It smells like they haven't had a bath in years."

Caudel's taunting was working. The first hound lifted its ugly snout and growled. The other just watched with its great head on its paws.

"Boy, you guys—or is it girls—are ugly. I'm not sure you haven't already died, and the humans have forgotten to bury you," he quipped, then laughed uproariously at his own joke.

The hellhound who had growled now stood and advanced on Caudel. The other was growling now, too.

"Oh, you think you could catch me? I'm pretty sure I could outdistance an ugly dog like you."

That was the final straw. One hound leapt up and tried to catch Caudel, and the other was swiftly following the first. They made a couple of clumsy tries at him, and then Caudel yelled, "Catch me if you can, you great mutts." He took off down the tunnel. The two enraged hellhounds followed in his wake.

They passed by where Peter and the others were hiding and they heard Gabriel say, "That's my cue," before he disappeared.

Paul looked down the tunnel to where the lab door was located. He didn't see any more hellhounds and motioned for the others to follow him. When they reached the door, Rags motioned that he would go first. He opened the door, and they all quickly filed in and stopped cold.

There in front of them was a petite woman dressed all in black. Her hair was braided in a long French braid down her back. She was holding a 9mm handgun pointed right at Lev who was holding a vial in his hand. It looked to Paul like a Mexican standoff.

"Margueritte?" This came from Maggie.

Paul sucked in a breath as he recognized the woman when she turned her head to glance briefly at Maggie.

"What are you doing here?" Maggie asked, concerned.

Margueritte did not turn to look at her, but instead stared straight at the man she was about to kill.

"I am here for revenge, mon amie. This monster has taken everything from me—my daughter doesn't know that I live, and my son is dead. He stole years of my life. He stole parts of me, too."

She suddenly broke, crying desperately, but she kept the gun in her hand rock steady, aimed directly at Lev Avatov's head.

Paul's heart was wrenched in two. He knew who he was, and he wanted to shout out the truth to her.

"He took Rene too. Everything I have ever loved."

No. This is where it gets tough, but you can do this. The thought came to Paul, and thankfully, Raguel stepped forward.

"Margueritte, this is not the way," Rags said quietly. "This will not stop your pain, this will only add to it. I know that you are a just woman, and I know that if your son were with you right now, he would tell you that this man is not worth your soul. He is not worth the remorse or guilt or anything else that you would heap onto yourself if you killed him. Why are you letting him waste any more of you?"

While Rags was talking to Margueritte, Maggie nudged Peter and pointed out a shadow moving slowly and silently in Margueritte's direction. They watched as it closed in on her before shouting a warning. Peter had his sword up in a moment and was running towards the shadow, he saw Maggie with a red katana running with him. The gun went off as the warning startled an already tense Margueritte. Paul was by her side in a moment and took the gun from her. Rags went to where Lev was standing, a small stain of red was spreading across his shoulder. Lev ran at Rags and tackled him to the ground. Rags grabbed for the vial that was in Lev's hand, but was only able to grab his wrist. The strength that was given to him by Lilith was formidable.

Margueritte got up and would have joined in the fray after losing her gun, but Paul grabbed her around the waist and said, "If you want to hurt him, destroy his work. His master won't like that at all."

She nodded, and he let her go. Paul unstoppered the closest refuse tube, and Margueritte threw whatever she could reach into the volcano.

They heard Lev yell "*No!*" in the background, and the two of them smiled.

Maggie and Peter were circling the hellhound that was in the room with them, each of them held a blade out in front of them. The hellhound was waiting for the perfect moment to strike.

"She doesn't like you, you know." The strange voice invaded Peter's mind. *"She only tolerates you because you were friends with her uncle. You will never be more than friends."* Peter shook his head and tried to clear the thoughts from his mind. *"And this one, blames you for not dying instead of her love. She would rather he be here than you."*

"Stop it," Peter shouted.

Maggie looked over at him. "Are you okay, Peter?"

"There's a voice in my head," Peter told her.

"Don't listen to the voice, Peter. It lies," Rags yelled. "Hellhounds will try to make you believe you are unworthy, and torture you until you do something drastic."

The hound howled its outrage, finding Peter's mind closed off from its machinations, and Peter found a new confidence. Rags flipped Lev over and finally got him to release the vial in his hand. It rolled away from the fighters, and Lev redoubled his efforts to get to the vial first.

"Margueritte! The vial!" yelled Rags. Margueritte ran over and grabbed for the little vial where it had rolled under a table. Lev grabbed her ankle after he punched the angel in the face. She shrieked when he pulled her back roughly until Rags knocked his head onto the hard floor. He released her and continued his struggle with the angel.

Paul was using an axe that he had conjured to destroy anything that was too big to fit in the disposal hole. He stopped for a moment when he heard Margueritte shriek, but continued when he saw she was okay. He was at the servers, swinging furiously, when Olivier entered the fray. He heard Margueritte yell, and turned to see Olivier holding her up by the neck.

"I'll take that," he said as he grabbed the vial from her hand. He tossed her away like a ragdoll.

Peter was still in the grips of the hellhound, so Maggie could only think to do one thing. She threw her katana, which had become a dagger, right into the side of the hellhound. There was a loud shriek, and it disappeared.

Maggie ran to Margueritte as Paul confronted Olivier with his big war axe. Rags was still holding on to Lev, and Peter was holding his own against another hound.

"Margueritte, are you okay?" she asked the older woman.

Margueritte moaned in response and was silent again.

Olivier was faster than Paul's big war axe, so mid-swing he changed to a scimitar. When he missed again, he tried a different tactic. He switched it to a shield and ran into the vampire which pushed him into the tunnel through the open door. Olivier picked himself up and in a flash he was gone.

Paul went back into the room and heard Lev yell, "Tsoula!"

Before another second had passed, another hellhound barreled through the door, this one much larger and darker than any they had fought so far. It roared in, knocking Rags to the floor. Lev got up and stood behind the hellhound.

"So we meet again, dog." Rags said, getting up off the floor.

"I told you, if we ever met again, I would kill you," Tsoula said to him. *"I will also take your friends with you. Oh, they will make a lovely meal for me and my pack."*

She backed Lev toward the open door. Paul made a grab for Lev, but was swatted away to hit the wall, hard.

Down little human. I will get to you in a moment. Lev, tell my mistress I will be a moment, Tsoula said before kicking him out the door.

"Come on, dog. Let's finish this." Rags changed into the angel, Raguel, his human clothes fell away to be replaced with armor of purest silver. His long sword rang as he pulled it from its sheath. The silver blade lit with a blue fire, his wings were folded carefully behind him.

Tsoula wasted no more time. She pounced at Raguel, who spun away just in time to knock the hound into the nearest table, sending the few remaining items on them to the ground.

Maggie and Peter picked up Margueritte and Paul and moved them out of the way. Paul came to just as they set him down. He shook his head and looked over to watch the drama unfold.

Tsoula was stepping over the bits of mangled metal that were the lab table, and was trying to gauge Raguel's next move. Raguel was standing still in the middle of the room, watching the hellhound closely. He had already fought this battle once, and it did not go quite as he planned. Tsoula gathered herself for another pounce. This time, she ran straight up to it and bounded off the wall and over Raguel's head. As he brought his silver sword up to meet her, she twisted away, and he heard her chuff in her doggy laugh as she bounded out the door. She was gone in a flash.

"What was that about?" Peter asked. "Why didn't she stay and fight?"

"She was only interested in distracting us long enough for Lev to get away," Raguel said.

Paul was angry at himself for being caught unaware, he picked up his medallion from the floor and was swinging the war axe at the servers with a vengeance.

Raguel spoke softly. "That is enough, Paul. We still have work to do. Our vengeance is not complete."

Chapter 31

Lev flew down the tunnel at breakneck speed, looking for wherever Olivier went with that vial. That bastard has caused him problems for the last time. Before he could get much further, he was joined by Tsoula.

Where are you going, Lev? came her voice in his mind.

"I'm going to catch that bastard, Olivier. He got away with my virus—I mean our virus. It was the one that was going to make you famous. He stole it and ran away with it like a child. I need to find him and get it back. Want to help?" he asked her.

Your mistress will not be pleased with you. Why don't you let me deal with Olivier, and you go find Lilith? Tsoula said.

Lev contemplated what she had said. It was better he go find Lilith now than have her come looking for him, or worse, cause him pain again.

"Okay, Tsoula," he said, slowing down his frantic pace. "I will go find Lilith. Please, come and find me when you have that virus."

She nodded her great head and bounded off down the tunnel in search of Olivier. Lev watched her with a pang. At least he still held the Chairman's serum. He pulled the syringe from his pocket. He regretted not getting to try it out on any of the subjects. He wasn't sure it would work. There was still time if they could get out of here now.

He went down an adjoining tunnel where he knew they would be waiting. The light from the first tunnel only cast a paltry beam into the darkest dark he had ever seen.

"Lilith?" he called into the heart of the dark. He waited a beat or two then tried again. "Lilith?"

"I'm coming, Lev," she said as she oozed from out of the darkness.

"Have you finished the serum?" she asked, running her hands all over his chest.

"Yes," he told her, pulling the syringe out of his pocket. "But I haven't been able to test it yet."

"Well, let's go get one of your subjects and test it out," she said, practically purring with excitement.

"We can't. There are infiltrators in the tunnels."

"What do you mean? Rebels?" Lilith asked laughing.

"No. That bitch Margueritte has brought friends with her to get revenge on me."

She laughed again. "I gave you great strength, Lev. What do you think your ex-wife will do to you?"

"She had help. The man I wrestled with was bigger and stronger than me. Tsoula knew him."

"Tsoula? What was she doing there?" Lilith asked. "I sent a hellhound to watch you. Why did you need another?"

"Tsoula came because I called her. Olivier showed up and took the vial with the virus in it. I needed it back, but she kicked me out of the room when she saw the man I was fighting. She said they had seen each other before."

Lilith turned away from him and called into the darkness, "*Ono. Pharzy.*"

The two demonesses came out of the darkness to join their sister.

"Yes, Lilith?" Ono said, brushing her red hair back with a sweep of her hand.

"We may have company. Pharzy, are they ready?" Lilith asked her.

"Yes, they are ready. I only released a handful, but with the current state of the world, we should be set."

Lilith waited only a beat before saying, "Let them loose."

Pharzy stuck her head back into the darkness. A shrill whistle could be heard on both sides of the curtain of darkness. It only took a moment before the first hellhounds came through the curtain. There were a significant number of them waiting for instructions when Tsoula came bounding up.

"The angel I did battle with before is here, mistress. He has brought human friends with him. I am not sure how many, though. I only saw four," she reported.

Pharzy looked at hounds before her, they were crowding the hall now, still waiting for orders.

"Tsoula, share with the others."

Tsoula took a second and projected the image of the Angel of Justice to the rest of the pack.

"Anyone that is with this being is a target. They can have as much fun as they like with them, but they will need to destroy them in the end." She paused and looked at the great hound. "Please do not take all night. Ono and I have a hot date." She winked in Ono's direction and received a smile from her.

"Pharzy, let them go. They are stinking up the hallway and I will have to shower again before we leave," she whined.

Pharzy blew out a sigh and said, "Fine."

She addressed the assembled pack, waited a beat, then shouted *"Go!"*

The hounds that had collected around them took off without a look back. Tsoula had given them the picture of their enemies, and they were off to hunt their prey. The beasts howled with their excitement.

Pharzy smiled. "I love it when they do that."

Lev grabbed Lilith by the arm and felt immediate pain in his chest. It wasn't enough to bring him to his knees. This was the only warning he would get.

"But, I need the virus."

"You said that Olivier had it. It is safe. I saw him just a moment before you called me. He is on the other side. We can deal with him later. For now, I want to watch the fun," Lilith told him. "Come on girls, Lev is going to take us to where we can watch the show." Lilith took Lev's hand from her arm, and wrapped her arm around his. "Lead the way. And, get that serum ready to test, love. We may not have much time once this has begun."

Lev ducked quickly into his lab and grabbed a needle and syringe, clumsily drawing the liquid as the she-demon practically dragged him to their vantage point. After loading the liquid, he discarded the vial and shoved the syringe in his pocket, relishing the idea of his triumph for the Chairman that everyone would soon see.

The foursome stopped at the fork in the tunnel. They watched as four humans, two of them brandishing holy weapons and the third carrying the fourth, passed them in the tunnel. They were followed by a large angel brandishing a silver sword, clearing a path from one side of the tunnel to the other. The hounds were following, each one trying to get a clear path to the humans. Just like wolves, they enjoyed the weakest prey first, but they were denied by the great sword that could destroy them with one great swipe.

Pharzy hissed as they all passed. "That is not fair, Lilith." She stamped one of her dainty feet. "My hounds have waited a millennia to have fun again, and this angel is going to deny them."

Lilith smiled, "Patience, Pharzy. They are headed for the great cavern. There is plenty of room for the hounds to surround them there." Lilith stopped, as a thought occurred to her. "Wait a minute, didn't you leave others here to guard? Where are they?"

"They must be with the others," Pharzy replied.

"Then how did they," she pointed in the direction of the angel and humans, "get into the lab?"

"Do you think there are others with them?" Ono asked. "Maybe they lured the hounds Pharzy left to the angel, and he killed them."

Pharzy hissed again, "I will kill him myself."

"It won't matter when they reach the great cavern. The hounds will be able to use the shadows and circle around behind them. Let's go watch," Lilith said. "I love when they go in for the kill."

They followed the hounds down the tunnel, laughing about what they would do to them when they had them surrounded. Each new horrific detail made Lev smile. He was used to violence. He enjoyed causing others pain. It was one of the reasons he loved Lilith so much.

Peter and Maggie watched as Raguel took another great swing at the advancing hellhound army.

"Where did they all come from?" Peter wondered aloud.

"They came from the pits, called into action by their master," Raguel said. "Keep a look out for the Sisters. They have to be around here somewhere."

"We are almost there, Raguel," Paul called from out in front. He was carrying the limp form of Margueritte who had yet to regain consciousness.

They slowly backed their way down the tunnel, keeping the hounds in their sights at all times. Every few feet, one of them would try to breach the one-angel barrier that Raguel made. He would swing his great sword, and the creature would either jump backward out of his reach, or it would disappear when Raguel's great sword made contact. When the latter happened, the whole pack would howl as if in collective pain at the loss of a member.

Paul finally reached the opening to the great cavern. It was, of course, dark inside. Paul could see through the darkness thanks to Caudel's timely gift. He saw what waited on the other side and smiled. They each passed through the opening to the great cavern, and as Raguel passed through he made a great leap backward putting some space between him and the pack. This exposed the humans for a moment, but in their fury the pack took advantage of this error. They launched themselves howling in their excitement.

Peter and Maggie watched in horror as hellhound after hellhound entered the cavern. They saw them launch their attack. Peter stood at the ready and set his jaw. The first hound pounced, jumping high with the intent of landing on Peter. He braced himself for the impact and raised his sword in defense. But the hound never made it to him. Out of the darkness, a giant claw extended and knocked the first wave of hounds away from the humans.

Paul shouted to Peter and Maggie, "This way! Hurry!"

He ran towards the back of the cavern. When Peter and Maggie turned around, they saw the creature the giant claw belonged to.

Maggie had to pull Peter's arm as he stood transfixed by the great golden dragon before him.

"Come on, unless you want to be hound chow." That remark got Peter's attention. It was then that he noticed Michael and the others standing beside the dragon.

They had been waiting for this moment. The cavern was lit from the inside by the glow of the many angels that had come to help. The light filled every crevice in the cavern until it was as bright as daylight. The many hounds that were trying to circle the dragon stopped and looked back at Tsoula who stood motionless on a large outcropping by the entrance.

So we meet again, dragon.

She projected her thoughts into the minds of everyone around her. She looked over at Raguel who stood with sword drawn, every inch a warrior in gleaming silver armor. His wings folded gently behind him when he landed.

You have some powerful friends, bird. I don't think that it will be enough. I, too, have powerful friends.

As she finished this statement, Lev walked in accompanied by Lilith, Pharzy, and Onos. Lilith's eyes widened for a moment, and then focused on one person in particular—Michael.

He walked forward slowly and stood in front of the others. "You should leave, Lilith, you are outnumbered, even with your hound army," Michael told her.

"Oh, but I like a challenge," she purred, then smiled. "Besides, I don't have anything on the books today. I'm bored, and this looks like fun."

"You three always were trouble. Okay, have it your way."

Michael shrugged as if this was just another day at the office. He looked to those on his right and then to those on his left. Each of them nodded their readiness.

"Now," he said quietly.

The dragon was the first to strike. He let out a great bellow and blew flame across the cavern as Tsoula jumped out of the way just in time. Raphael and Uriel led the host, the Hellbane operatives, and ARC members on the right side of the cavern. The left side was led by Gabriel and Ariel. Sam, Raguel, and Michael were to the front, and the dragon protected the rear.

Upon the first blast of dragon's breath, the hounds scattered and regrouped in smaller packs. The demonesses took a stance in the middle facing the three angels. Lev was standing behind them. With Lilith's gifts, he would be able to hold his own. Lilith took a piece of obsidian from her pocket and crafted a long black sword for Lev. She handed the sword to Lev, who smiled and swung it a few times to get a feel for it.

Pharzy and Ono moved to the right and left of Lilith, and the three sisters created fire from their fingertips. Pharzy's flame was gold, Ono held red, and Lilith's was ice blue. The hounds gave a great bay, each side moving in tandem. They advanced on the waiting host.

Paul placed Margueritte in Jophiel's capable hands and rushed to protect Raguel and Uriel. As the hounds advanced on them, Paul called his weapon forth. This time it was the clutch of throwing knives, which he proceeded to throw at the advancing hounds.

Fire spewed over top of them onto the back flank of the hounds. Those that were too slow to jump out of the way were consumed, and the others attacked in earnest. Raguel blocked the first of the attackers, while Paul crouched and threw three dirks in succession. The first two missed, but the last found its mark. He conjured a shield just in time to block a burst of gold fire from Pharzy. She grinned and sent another volley in his direction. Paul blocked this one too and sent a long spear in her direction, which she deflected with ease.

"Paul, that is not one that you want to mess with. Why don't you go help Peter. It looks like he could use your skills," Uriel said, nodding in the direction of Peter, who was trying to hold off two hounds at once. Uriel sent his own golden spear off in Pharzy's direction, pulling her attention away from Paul.

Paul took that moment to run to Peter's aid.

"Peter, choose the right weapon for the best outcome," Paul yelled to him, throwing a dagger in the direction of the closest hound. He hit it in the rump sending it sprawling onto its side.

Peter called a spear and stabbed it into the scrabbling hound.

"Good job," Paul said.

The ground shook as the dragon swung its great tail into an advancing group of hellhounds. Only two were able to jump out of the way, the others lay stunned by the hit, and the host were there to finish them off. Paul glanced back to where Michael, Sam, and Raguel stood. Michael was fighting Lilith, Sam had Ono, Uriel was still battling Pharzy, and Raguel was taking on Tsoula. Their battle was taking them all over. Raguel would fly up to escape the reaches of the advancing hounds, and Tsoula would leap off outcroppings and bound off walls to reach him. At one point, Raguel flew close to the dragon, Tsoula followed and leapt off an outcropping, only to be swatted away from Raguel by a massive claw. The dragon was about to pounce on Tsoula when one of the other hounds bit it on the tail. Ouryu let out a great roar and grabbed the hellhound in its teeth, shaking until it disappeared.

"Paul, watch out!" yelled Maggie, when he was bowled over by a hellhound.

Paul could smell the foul breath of the beast as he struggled to keep it from his throat. He called forth a small dagger and, gathering his strength, he put his feet under the hound and pushed as he swung the blade into its side. The hound made a yelp and disappeared.

Maggie bent over Paul. "Are you okay?" she asked.

"Fine. Thanks for caring," he said, winking.

Maggie helped him up and was unceremoniously shoved to the side. She heard a clang and looked back to see Paul locking swords with Lev Avatov. Paul must have shoved her aside to save her from Lev's black sword. She watched as they matched swords, Paul effortlessly swatting away the clumsy sword play by Lev. She could tell that Paul had had some kind of training in weaponry, of course with his background in historical archeology that would not be surprising. Still, there was something familiar in the stance, the style, that set her on edge. She felt like there was something there she should remember. *Maybe they had met before? Met fighting?* The thought was ridiculous.

Maggie saw it happen in slow motion. One of the host threw a hellhound which collided with Paul, knocking him to the ground. Lev took the opportunity and was going to run him through. Without thinking things through, Maggie ran and jumped on Lev's back, knocking the obsidian sword from his grasp. When she threw her legs around his waist she felt a poke in the back of her thigh. She immediately felt light headed and her grasp on Lev lessened letting him fling her from his back.

"You have caused problems for the last time, *you redheaded bitch!*" Lev screamed, grabbing the obsidian sword from the ground. He was so close to his retribution, he could taste it. Maggie was still trying to clear her head. Before Lev could use the sword on her, Paul was back and tackling him from the side.

"Careful, Paul. He has... something in... his pocket. It jabbed me... in the leg," Maggie called weakly. Paul nodded, but Lev's face grew white. He shoved Paul off of him, enough to pull from his pocket the syringe with the serum for the Chairman.

"*Noooo!*" he screamed. He turned back to Maggie, his rage doubling his strength. He effortlessly knocked Paul back again, yelling at a still dazed Maggie. "*My serum. This time you will die!*"

Chapter 32

Simon and the others had succeeded in gathering all the Triads together, and with a concentrated effort, had managed to herd them toward the great cavern. They had just entered when he heard Lev yell. What he saw was a demented person with a large black sword scrambling and running after a redheaded girl. Without another thought, he slithered forward to help.

He feared he wouldn't make it in time, when the dragon knocked a hellhound into the demented man's path, making him stumble. Simon watched as Lev tripped with his sword at its lowest point and fell. He saw Lev's body falling on the point of his own sword. Then he lay still.

He heard a yelp and watched as the hellhound that caused the fall was consumed with bright blue flame. One of the demon Sisters was cursing the *dog* that had caused her sweet Lev to die. The golden dragon swished its great tail and hit the outlying wall. Simon heard the crack and saw the water running out of the rock. He altered his previous course as the human Paul was helping the one they call Maggie up off the floor. The hellhounds were just about defeated and the great angels were battling back against the demon Sisters.

He heard a new voice enter the fray. "Now, I don't think this is a fair fight at all. First, I would have thought you of all people would conduct an equitable battle."

The newcomer was dressed in an immaculately cut purple suit. He wore a ring on each finger and had a crown on his head.

"Abbadon." Michael turned to Uriel. "They'll let anyone in here, Uri. It's getting so you can't even get a decent Asmodean at a battle anymore." Turning back to the demons, "I didn't realize you were invited to this," Michael told him, deflecting the blue fire Lilith threw at him.

"He's not. He just likes to stick his nose where it doesn't belong," Lilith said. "I don't need his help to kill you, puny angel."

"She called you puny, bro. Are you gonna let her get away with that?" Sam laughed and deflected the red fire thrown his way.

Raguel and Tsoula came into view, each of them trying their best to gain the upper hand. Michael watched as Raguel landed a blow to Tsoula's side. The beast slid sideways into her mistress who picked the hellhound up and threw her back into the fray.

"You will not fail me again, Tsoula!" she yelled. "*Kill him!*"

Tsoula, obviously wounded, took off after the angel once more. *I will kill you this time, angel.*

"Come on, dog—let's end this," Raguel said. Ouryu was busy in the back fighting off the last of the hellhounds. The host was picking them off as the dragon knocked them away. The dragon was swinging his tail around wildly, and Simon was afraid of the water behind that wall.

"I have a new toy, Michael," Abbadon said.

Michael continued to fight with Lilith while Abbadon casually stood in the corner. Ariel had come over to join in the fight so that Michael could split his attention between Lilith and Abbadon.

"Oh? I recall I don't care for your type of toys," Michael told him.

Abbadon walked over to where Lev had fallen, and nudged his body over with his shoe. "Our dead friend here was creating an interesting new virus. One that is highly contagious and kills with apparent swiftness. It is a shame that he is dead, he had such a brilliant, devious mind," Abbadon lamented.

"Whatever Lev was working on belongs to me, Abbadon. You will keep your nose out of my business," Lilith yelled, sending a volley of fire in his direction. Abbadon swatted the fire away as if it were an annoying gnat.

"While you have been playing with the birds and lizards, I have acquired the virus that Lev was working on."

He held up a small tube of dark oozing liquid. It almost looked as if it were alive in the way that it moved. Tsoula's head whipped around to look at the vial in Abbadon's hand. She diverted her path from Raguel, her new aim was to get the vial from Abbadon. She bounded off one of the stalagmites straight at Abbadon, but a great claw swiped her from her path.

"Why don't you stay and play? It seems that I have run out of your playmates," Ouryu told her with a belt of steam.

You don't want to mess with me, lizard. As I remember it, I bested you the last time. I will do it again, Tsoula taunted.

"You dare to bring that up, dog? Fine, let's finish what we started all those years ago."

With a great swing of his tail, the dragon tried to knock Tsoula down again. She jumped up to land on his tail as it passed and sank her jaws into it. The dragon roared and swung his tail upward with all his might in order to smash Tsoula into the rock above.

"Ooh, now this is entertainment." Abbadon snickered. His smile turned to a pout when he said, "I was telling you about *my* new virus."

He emphasized the "my" for Lilith, who angrily turned and threw more blue flame in his direction. This time he had to duck in order to escape.

"You bastard! You are really beginning to piss me off, Abbadon!" Lilith said, her eyes raging.

"Well, it is your fault I have it, Lilith. If you had listened to your friend, Olivier, you wouldn't be in this mess," he said mockingly.

"Olivier—where is that bloodsucker? I will kill him myself. I kept Lev from sending Tsoula after him," Lilith said, looking about as if she could find Olivier in all the fighting. Tsoula landed in front of Lilith.

You kept the human Lev from letting me deal with the bloodsucker, and now my blood is in the hands of Abbadon? Lilith could hear the incredulity in Tsoula's thought. Before she could answer, the dragon swung his massive tail down between them, causing Lilith to jump one way and Tsoula the other to avoid being crushed. When his tail landed, it caused a crack to appear in the floor. It was really a very small crack but, by the look of the glow that emanated from it, Simon knew that it had reached the magma below. He looked over to where the water still flowed freely from the wall. As the demons were still fighting amongst themselves, Simon took the opportunity to find the nearest holy one. It was a female, and she was tending to the one Lev had kept prisoner before.

"Missssstressss, I need a moment of your time," he told her.

Jophiel looked over to see the Naga, Simon, standing before her.

She smiled and asked, "What can I do for you, Simon?"

He tilted his head as if he liked the sound of his name coming from her. He noticed a strange peace come over him, and knew it must have come from her. He was humbled that she would wish him peace with so much going on around her.

"Missssstressss…" he started, but she cut him off.

"Please, call me Jo."

"Jo, we have a dangeroussss ssssituation unfolding."

"Abbadon has not come to fight, only to gloat. So, I don't think it is something Michael cannot handle, Simon. Thank you for your concern." She turned back to Margueritte who was still a little woozy from her earlier encounter with Olivier.

"No, Jo, you don't undersssstand. It issss this place we are in danger from," he told her, pointing to the wall behind the dragon and then pointing to the newly formed crack in the floor. She looked at both things, and it suddenly clicked with her.

"Gabriel" she called, and in a blink, he was in front of her. "Gabe, we need to get everyone out of here, now. Please let Michael know we are all inside a ticking bomb."

He nodded once and was gone. She saw him reappear at Michael's side. Michael looked in her direction and she pointed to the wall, and then the floor just as Simon had. He nodded and talked again with Gabriel, who disappeared to spread the message.

"Thank you, Simon. Please take your people and the ARC

members to safety. We will bring whoever is left with us, but we must clean up this mess first," Jophiel told him.

He nodded to her and bent down to help Margueritte stand. She recoiled from his touch, and Jophiel, knowing there was not any time to lose, laid a hand on her shoulder and whispered, "*Sleep*." Margueritte slumped against the stone, and Jophiel picked her up as if she weighed nothing and passed her to Simon.

"Quickly, Simon."

Simon, carrying a limp Margueritte with him, passed Paul and Maggie. He said, "Follow quickly, we musssst go."

They dodged a swing of the dragon's tail as he still fought to catch Tsoula, who had succeeded in causing a number of gashes on the dragon's golden hide. They found Peter and Naomi hiding behind an outcropping to escape the swishing tail and pouncing hellhound, and to stay out of the reach of the demonesses that were still flinging fireballs in every direction.

"Peter, Naomi, come on. We need to get out of here."

"Why? The battle yet rages," Caudel hollered as he poked his head out of Peter's hoodie. He felt compelled to hide when Pharzy saw him flit past her and flung a ball of gold flame in his direction.

Paul pointed to the water, which was slowly making its way closer to the crack in the floor.

"Because when that water reaches that crack, there will be no more cavern," Paul said.

"What are we waiting for, kid? Let's go," Caudel told Peter.

They collected the rest of the Naga and were just about to slip past Abbadon, when he looked in their direction.

"Where do you think you are going? Things are just about to get explosive. You don't want to miss the fun." Abbadon flicked his fingers and the rock above the door collapsed, creating a barrier of rock and debris.

"Abbadon, you have sealed your fate." Michael immediately went full angel.

Peter saw the anger and retribution on the archangel's face, and remembered how frightening it was when you first see them in this fashion. He heard Naomi cry out and felt her face against his back. He turned and pulled her into his arms.

"It's okay, Naomi, it's Michael. He won't hurt you, ever." He pulled her hands from her face and told her, "We need to shift this rock. Can you focus on that?"

She nodded, and without looking in Michael's direction, started to shift the loose rock from in front of the door.

Peter noticed that one by one the angels all went into full angel mode. When it was Sam's turn, Peter looked away. That was one angel he did not want to see turn. Michael stood in front of Abbadon. His six wings fanned out behind him. In one hand, he held a great golden sword and in the other, a shield as tall as him. His golden armor glowed, and a helmet now covered his head. Next to him stood Uriel, his wings the color of the setting sun with a beautiful, flaming sword of amber, followed by Raphael who was in red and gold. His wings were white with golden tips and he held a flaming scimitar. Gabriel, who was all in white, had a short sword and a dagger. Then the small Ariel in teal, with teal tips to her wings. Jophiel was in pink with the lightest pink at the tips of her wings. Raguel in dark blue with his silver sword and wing tips, and finally Sam in black with his black wings and black long sword.

Peter looked back long enough to see Abbadon and the Sisters change into their true forms as well. He shivered at their leathery, scaly skin and membranous wings. It was something that would haunt his dreams. He turned back to the rocks in front of the door. It seemed the Naga were incredibly adept at using their tails, and were able to shift enough rock to allow an escape. It was not going to be easy as the hole was not big enough to allow but maybe two at a time to go through.

"You guys go first. Paul and I will keep watch until everyone is out," Peter told Maggie and Naomi.

"I'm a guardian, Peter. I'm going to stay and help," Maggie said.

Peter turned and looked pleadingly at Maggie.

"If you want to help, please do not make the woman I love go alone. For me."

"Please, girl, don't make me go by myself," Naomi pleaded. "I will already be worried about them. Don't make me worry about you as well."

Maggie did not look pleased, but nodded. Truth was, she didn't really feel that well. Whatever was in Lev's pocket that stabbed her was not good. She had grabbed the syringe off his body when he fell, and after breaking off the needle, stuck the rest in her pocket. She would look at it later. They put Margueritte on Simon's back and he slithered through the hole, holding Margueritte with one hand and using his other hand and tail to push himself forward. Next was Naomi, Caudel, and Maggie, followed by the Naga.

Paul looked back to the water as it drew perilously close to the crack in the floor.

"Come on, Peter! We gotta go now!" Paul shouted as the last of the Naga went through.

Peter watched Paul climb through the hole and hesitated, looking back at the angels who were now battling the demons. It seemed as if it should be an unfair fight, but the demons seemed to be holding their own.

"*Peter! Come on!*" he heard Paul yell.

He looked over at the dragon in time to see Tsoula pounce on his neck from a ledge she had jumped to. The dragon howled in pain. Peter took his weapon, and calling on Michael, changed it into a crossbow. He took aim at Tsoula and let the arrow fly. It hit its mark a little low, but was enough to knock the hellhound from the dragon. The hound fell before the dragon who took the opportunity presented, and with one bite the hound was gone.

The dragon looked at Peter and nodded. Peter nodded back but felt the ground shake. He looked over at the crack. Water was flowing into the crack now. Steam issued from the vent, causing a plume of magnesium chloride to be created.

The dragon yelled to Peter, "Thank you, but go now."

Peter jumped into the hole as he felt another rumble. He was afraid that the hole was going to swallow him. He planted his feet against one of the rocks and leapt forward just as the hole gave way. Paul pulled him from the other side, and they landed a few feet from the hole.

"Man, Peter, I thought you were not going to make it. We need to get out of here," Paul told him.

They started running, and, every few minutes they felt a tremor go through the volcano. They caught up with the others just as they were making their way into the cave that led to the outside. They heard the explosion at the entrance to the volcano. They turned around to look at the tunnel entrance and were entranced by the light that was swiftly travelling up the tunnel.

Paul's eyes widened. He grabbed Peter and pulled him just as the shock wave hit the entrance. The two men were blown from the entrance and found themselves some distance from where the opening used to be. Now there was nothing but rock.

"No!" Peter yelled. "What about Michael and the rest?"

"Pete, calm down. We're fine," came Michael's voice from behind.

Peter nearly jumped out of his skin. "What happened? Where is the dragon? Did the demons get away?" Peter asked the questions in succession.

"Slow down. Take a breath, ese," Sam said, shaking his head. "The dragon is back where he belongs, and the demons opened a portal and fled when the dragon punched a big hole in the wall letting in the seawater. Along with the buildup of gas and steam, the seawater reacted violently with the magma in the crack the dragon made. Boom," he said using his hands to demonstrate a violent explosion.

"Let's go get the others and get out of here. This place will be crawling with police soon," Rags said, slapping Paul on the back and leading him in the direction of his friends.

"At least no one was hurt," Peter said to Michael.

Michael shook his head sadly. "Violence of any kind has a price. Someone always gets hurt."

Epilogue

In other news, scientists have discovered that an underwater explosion off the coast of China was the cause of the massive tsunami that hit the Philippines last night. The death toll is presumed to be in the thousands. A massive effort to search for survivors is underway.

Maggie clicked off the television in her hotel room. This was the first opportunity the friends had to clean up after last night's events. As she stood with a towel in her hand, she stared down at the red welt on her thigh. Her shorts barely covered it as it had grown to double its original size. Her light head was gone, but she worried about what was in that vial. She pulled the broken syringe from the pocket of her ruined jeans. There wasn't a lot left in the syringe, and she was afraid that it would dry up before she could get it analyzed. She threw her ruined jeans into the trash can and heard a clang. Reaching back into her pocket she pulled out the little red disc that Raphael had given her the night before.

"Raphael," she whispered, and the red katanas appeared in her hand. She said it again, and it was gone.

"Neat trick, huh?" Raphael was sitting at the little writing desk in the hotel room watching her flipping the disc over in her hand.

"Woah, you guys really know how to make an entrance, don't you?" she said, as she bobbled the disc, almost dropping it.

"Are you going to tell anyone?" Raphael asked.

Maggie looked at him questioningly. "Tell anyone what?"

"Are you going to tell any of your friends that you were jabbed with Lev's serum?" Raphael asked her.

"What? How did you know?" Maggie asked him.

"Maggie, you and I are connected now. I will always know when you are hurt and where you are—it is how we protect those who help us. Now I think that your friends have proven themselves worthy of your trust." Raphael picked up the pen that was on the pad next to the phone and started to doodle on the pad. "As far as what is in that serum—well, we have some scientists in ARC that should be able to find out for you. I can tell you that it is changing you in a way. Changing you, but not harming you."

"Well, that is a relief. I don't like the change part, though. I really want to know what is happening inside me right now. When will I be able to meet up with your ARC doctors?" she asked him pacing.

Raphael lay the pen back down on the pad and rose to meet her. He dwarfed her in size and sheer girth. He put his hand on her shoulder and made her look him in the eye, which meant tilting her head skyward.

"I want you to go to ARC headquarters for a while," Raphael said. "You need to have those tests done, and I want to see what you can do with that katana of yours."

"You are leaving something out, Raph. What aren't you telling me?"

He turned away from her and then back again. "They think that the serum you were injected with was meant for the Chairman. If that is the case, and they know that you were injected with it, since Lev yelled it to the heavens, well, that puts you in serious danger, Maggie. The demons will not stop looking for you. They want your blood since it holds the serum the Chairman needs to survive."

Maggie sat down on the edge of the bed. "Let me get this straight. That monster Lev was creating some kind of Dr. Frankenstein serum for this Chairman, who will now send his hoards of monsters to look for me and steal my blood? Is that about right?"

Raphael ran his hands through his hair. "That about sums it up, yes."

"You want me to go hide out at ARC headquarters to keep me away from them, right?"

"Yes, but Maggie, we are talking about a wide arsenal of monsters that the Chairman has access to. So far, you have only experienced a few of them. The vampires, grunch, vila—those are just the tip of the iceberg. The history of your world is full of myths and legends that aren't myths and legends. There are worse monsters out there, believe me. Please, for your sake as well as that of your friends, please consider coming to ARC where I will be able to train you against those monsters."

Maggie thought of her friends. She was very glad that they had all made it out safely, including Paul, who had shown himself to be very useful.

"What about the others? Are they being trained, too?"

"Peter learns from Michael and Sam, Paul is taught by Uriel, and I believe that your friend Naomi will be training with Ariel. Does that make you feel better?"

"Yes, thank you. How long would I have to be gone?"

"It depends on what we find out about the serum, but I would guess about one of your Earth months."

"That's a long time. What about my job? I'm not sure that Mikey would let me off that long."

"I think that he would be okay with it, but I can ask for you," Raphael said, smiling widely. *Maggie wants to know if she can have some time off. What do you think?* Raphael said to the room.

"Sure, she can have as much time as she needs," Michael said from behind her.

"OMG, will you stop doing that? Now I understand what Peter says about you guys just popping in. And what do you mean I can have as much time off as I want? You're not my boss."

"Aren't I?" Michael said, morphing into the visage of Mikey, her editor at LACE Magazine.

Maggie was thunderstruck. "All this time and you have been my boss. Why?"

Michael laid his hand on her shoulder. "We have always kept track of you, Maggie. You proved yourself over and over as someone who helps others. You sacrificed your time to find sex traffickers and drug lords and put them behind bars. We just helped you along the way."

She looked up at him as tears streamed down her face. "What about all the bad things that have happened in my life? What about Max?"

Michael looked grave. "Maggie there is a reason for everything that happens in life. You and your friend Susannah were kidnapped. You escaped, and Susannah was rescued later. You chose to use that experience to reshape your life. You went on to help hundreds directly and thousands indirectly by putting that organization out of business. You did the same with Lev Avatov and the vampire, Olivier. Your trials in life have made you into the person that you are. Without those experiences, good and bad, you would not have made the choices that led you here." Michael sent a wave of peace through Maggie. "Maggie, you have a choice in all of this, of course, but we are asking you to trust us once again and go to ARC for a little while."

Raphael started to say something, but Michael held up a hand. Maggie took her time thinking through the many things she had been told. The angels waited patiently as she mulled over the pros and cons. Finally, she looked at Raphael and Michael in turn, their eyes showed their worry over her answer.

"I'll do it. I'll go to ARC. I think I want to learn more about this Chairman, and to do that I need to start at the beginning and learn quickly. When do we start?"

"Right now," Michael said.

And in a blink of an eye, they were gone..

About the Author

Michelle A. Sullivan was born and raised in Fort Myers, Florida, and is a voracious reader with a three-book-a-week habit turned author. She brings a lifetime of dwelling in the fantasy worlds she so loves, together with a vivid and clear vision of a world where ARC is humanity's only hope.

She is bound by a passion for the subjects that the ARC series addresses, and her characters are relatable, fun, and flawed—just like their creator. Unlike her characters, Michelle is deathly afraid of spiders and being bored.

She and her spider-killer/editor husband share their home with various adult children and three equally-scared pooches.

A Black Horse is the second volume in *The ARC Series*.

Visit Michelle online at:

arcauthor.squarespace.com